HIDEOUS NIGHT

Martyn Rhys Vaughan

Published by
Llyfrau Cambria Books, Wales, United Kingdom.
*Cambria Books is a division of
Cambria Publishing.*
Discover our other books at: www.cambriabooks.co.uk

To my muse with the soft, brown hair

Reviews

"The work of a highly creative mind, and also a perceptive mind. Using fiction to reflect the dark side of human nature e.g. the risk to humanity's future is not artificial intelligence but natural stupidity."
John Gabb-Cousins (from Facebook).

"Martyn Vaughan writes extremely well with a style harking back to the likes of Ray Bradbury and Isaac Asimov and the stories are finely crafted and well plotted."
Rob Southall – Domains of Darkness.

"A mind-bending mix of physics and environmentalism. Vaughan tells an exciting story and manages to weave important aspects of quantum theory into it. He also has an important message about what we are doing to damage the world's environment, in the bleak picture he paints of a planet which has gone past the tipping points and is sliding towards cataclysm. All in all, thoroughly recommended."
Penny Brown. Amazon. Quantum Exile.

"I read your latest book. Very good - I couldn't put it down!"
B J Howard - personal e-mail. The Cave of Shadows.

"Thoroughly good read! So much imagination and informative too while being a very good fantasy novel."
BH Reads. Amazon. The Cave of Shadows

"Hard science fiction with concepts going back to the ancient Greeks. The story pulls you along quite well, even if the baddies could have put up a bit more of a fight at the end."
Chris G. Amazon. The Cave of Shadows

"Martyn Rhys Vaughan's book is shot through with big ideas and big questions and in that sense it's a bold and brave undertaking.
The book picks up pace throughout and is never less than entertaining, but the fact that the speculation is set squarely within the realms of possibility means that a book which at first seems like science fiction melding with fantasy might actually be a guidebook, a guidebook to chaotic times ahead."
Jon Gower. Nation.Cymru. The Cave of Shadows

"A gripping story with lots of twists.
This is a remarkable novel which starts off as a fantasy story in a series of mysterious lands where two characters confront a series of deadly perils. But there is something different about these lands which disturbs the two central characters who appear to be living in two completely separate universes.
Then everything changes and their different experiences are united in a completely unexpected but satisfying twist."
Penny Brown. Amazon. The Cave of Darkness.

HIDEOUS NIGHT

"… and see the brave day sunk in hideous night…"

Shakespeare: Sonnet 12

CONTENTS

PART ONE: THE NEAR ONES

One

"The Earth is a farm. We are someone else's property."

Doctor Céline Dubois stared at the e-mail that she had just opened. The words appeared to be a quote of some kind but clearly on a topic with which she was not familiar. She had opened the e-mail because the name of the author had stirred a vague memory but now she was wondering if CERN's powerful spam and virus filters had let something untoward slip through.

She leaned backwards in her chair and ran the fingers of both hands through her thick, chestnut hair. Her reflection in the computer screen mimicked her motions and, involuntarily, she leaned forward to inspect the image more closely.

Was that a white hair or two, slightly above her right temple? If so, it, or they, hadn't been there yesterday.

She frowned at her quizzical expression and leaned back again.

This was ridiculous – how could a woman of her standing, at the forefront of unlocking the mysteries of the cosmos, be worried about a few white hairs?

And who exactly was this idiot who was sending her ridiculous messages about farms?

Her eyes flashed to the top of the message.

Yes – a "Marius Larsen": she had not misread the name. She knew little about him except that he had been working on particle physics somewhere in the Norwegian Arctic, but she had not heard any news of him for several years and had assumed he was dead. She ran a quick on-line check on him, absorbing all the relevant facts in seconds. He certainly hadn't made any significant discoveries in the eldritch realm of quantum particles or she would have heard of them. She was a kind of human magnet, she thought in brief self-congratulation, sucking in data, theories, conjectures on the mind-bending world where quantum theory and relativity met. Those two intellectual masterworks had met but had not made a fruitful union: despite all the years that had passed since their first encounter, they remained suspicious of each other, warily circling, trying to find a weakness in the other's formulation so that one would emerge triumphant as THE explanation of reality; of what lay behind the phenomena of the everyday world. And if anybody were to be there at that climax, to be the one to lift the victor's arm, it would be she – Céline Dubois!

For a moment she sat there feeling the warm glow of her expected triumph flood through her veins like a warming drug. Behind closed eyes she saw the conferences, the speeches, the moment when she would be called in from the side of the stage to receive the first of many awards. The warmth continued to flow and involuntarily she pressed her thighs closer together to extend and enhance the tingling pleasure that the visions afforded her.

Then it passed and her mind snapped back into its usual cold efficiency.

She had been enjoying the visions of her future for so long that her computer had gone into sleep mode. She pressed the spacebar and the peculiar e-mail reappeared. She glanced down its sentences noticing, not for the first time, that the letters on the screen seemed slightly blurred (overwork of course, what else could it be?) and a small frown line appeared on her previously unblemished forehead. This man was seriously ill – not to say deranged! She stopped reading about halfway down and the e-mail was swiftly consigned to the Bin, never to reappear.

She stood up abruptly: tall, well-built rather than slim, exuding an air of confidence and competence. She pressed her hands into the small of her back to alleviate the stiffness that had developed from too long in front of the computer and then raised her arms so that her strong hands with their well-manicured nails pointed directly at the ceiling. Then she relaxed.

3

Her office was high up and, crossing to the large picture window, she looked out over the tame but pleasant landscape of this little finger of Switzerland where CERN was sited. From where she stood she could see the Route de Meyrin and the scurrying ant-like forms that thronged it. How little most of them knew! she mused. How little of reality they understood or *could* understand! They thought they knew what existence was about, what the real world was, but all they knew was simply a painted veil over the true reality; a shadow play of insubstantial figures behind which lay the true universe – the universe of immaterial fields and forces, of warped space combining with the elasticities of time; of ghostly particles which could pass unhindered through light-years of lead and were at that very moment pouring through their bodies like the demons and devils of ignorant imaginations! She pitied them. She hated ignorance.

She returned to her desk and called up the latest diagnostic data from the ATLAS and CMS detectors and saw a small outlier in the ATLAS data. She was leaning forward to examine it more closely when an LED on her console winked into life. Responding immediately, she depressed a small button.

'Yes?' she said.

'Madame,' came a soft female voice marinaded in a gentle German accent, 'You asked me to remind you when there was half an hour before the meeting of the Heads of Department.'

Ah yes – Emilia. A most attractive young lady. I must make sure she joins my permanent staff, Dubois thought but all she said was 'Thank you, Emilia. What would I do without you watching over me?'

'You are too kind, madame,' was the reply, with the slightest hint of pleased laughter, and the line went silent.

She stood in silence for a moment or two, running the agenda items through her mind and briefly contemplating the line she would be taking at the meeting. All thought of the e-mail and its deranged author had been obliterated, with the intention that they would never rise again. She spent some time looking at the Departmental reports, absorbing their statements and

4

implications without effort.

The conference room was large and circular with concentric rows of seats. As she leisurely entered, Dubois saw at once that the other Department Heads were already seated, obviously trying to curry favour with the Director-General. The usual three Translators were visible behind a glass panel set into the front wall of their own room, which was in an elevated position behind the Director's seat. Although the official language for these meetings was English, some of the Heads, particularly the Francophone ones, insisted on using their native tongues. Many of those Heads were male but fewer than had been the case in previous years, Dubois noted to herself. There was definite progress.

The Director-General was Francophone and immediately unleashed a rapid-fire stream of French at the Department Heads; so rapid-fire that the Translators had difficulty keeping up.

Dubois gazed down unconcernedly at her organiser pad on which the agenda was displayed; being trilingual she had no need of the translators. In any case, real-time machine translation was so good these days that human translators were an endangered species. She noted the Director's slightly barbed comment on the fact that she had been the last to arrive but ignored it: she had had four seconds to spare before the designated start time and, being a woman used to dealing with nano- and picosecond intervals, that was more than enough.

The meeting had a lot to discuss: The Large Hadron Collider was unquestionably beginning to show its age now and attempts to accelerate particles to higher and higher energies was being bedevilled by energy loss into the unwanted generation of copious amounts of synchrotron light.

Due to the failure to produce the expected Supersymmetric particles, the Standard Model remained obstinately firm and the early promise of new physics had not been delivered. More and more it looked like humanity would have to venture into the far tera electron-volt domain if nature was to be forced to give up her secrets.

Dubois frowned slightly at this point in the Director's speech. Why must everything that was regarded as obstinate and secretive be described as female? It was yet another example of unconscious bias. The fact that the Director was using French with its two types of grammatical gender was no excuse: he did exactly the same thing when speaking English.

He had now moved into a lachrymose delivery: it looked more and more likely that the venerable LHC would not be the device that ventured into the unknown tera electron-volt region. The LHC had achieved much, not least the identification of the Higgs Boson. But that discovery had merely filled in the last blank in the Standard Model and its discovery had been satisfying but not revolutionary.

Gregson, Dubois's neighbour on her right, swore audibly as he tried to adjust his headphones, which had slipped somewhat. A gangling, resolutely monolingual American with a tangle of mousey-brown hair which hung down nearly to his eyes, he was having more trouble than the Translators in keeping up with the Director's machine-gun delivery.

The Director stopped in full flow and fixing Gregson in a gimlet stare, commented acidly in English: 'I share your disappointment and frustration Dr Gregson, but please moderate your language. After all, there are ladies present!'

There was a ripple of laughter in the circle of Department Heads, but Dubois did not join in. Her lips twitched politely but there was no smile.

The Director resumed his torrent of French and returned to the topic of the difficulty in reaching higher energies. Reluctantly it must be accepted that the torch must now pass to another organisation, he explained.

'The ILC,' Gregson muttered, 'why is he taking so freaking long to get to the point?'

A severe look from the Director indicated that he had heard

that comment as well, but he ploughed on, forcing silence on the assembled Heads by the sheer force of his delivery.

'The International Linear Collider,' he announced in a tone which suggested that he had just produced a large white rabbit from a small top hat, 'the ILC, situated in the Kitikami highlands of Japan. The next generation, which will take mankind into new and undreamt-of lands where new discoveries will assuredly be made!'

There was a bubble of excited comments from the attendees but the Director imperiously waved them into silence.

'Obviously, the ILC will be attracting experienced scientists from all over the civilised world. We must ensure that CERN is not under-represented at this magnificent facility. You will not be surprised to hear that I have been in regular communication with the esteemed Director of the ILC and he is most anxious that CERN personnel play a part in the new discoveries which await. I have therefore drawn up a short-list of the most suitable candidates from the members assembled here and will shortly be announcing the names of those who I will send on a short-term loan to the ILC. It may be that permanent appointments follow, of course.'

Now the Heads broke out into loud chattering which the Director did not attempt to quell. Instead, he sat down, with an expression which showed self-satisfaction and tolerant amusement.

He indicated that he would accept questions and the next twenty minutes were spent in a question-and-answer session in which he was asked a great many questions but which he answered in a way which left the questioners not much more informed than before they had asked.

Finally, the meeting returned to the more workaday issues which confronted the Heads of Department. The refrain was usually the same from each member: power losses; excess synchrotron photons; the difficulty in getting good staff; the quality of wine on offer in the dining area.

Dubois did not make any complaints: she merely said: 'There are no problems in my Department, Monsieur Director.' Which was not entirely true but it would need to be a big problem indeed before she would admit that she needed help.

Finally the Director turned to Gregson and with the air of a headmaster addressing a somewhat slow student, asked: 'And your area Dr Gregson? You too do not have enough electron-volts?'

Gregson shook his head. 'There are power problems of course but no worse than those of my colleagues.'

'Then you have no problems? Good. Therefore I...'

'No,' Gregson interjected, 'There are problems. Staff problems.'

'Staff problems? The usual difficulty with obtaining sufficiently qualified assistants?'

Gregson shook his head. The others turned to look at him. Disciplinary problems were unusual at CERN where everyone shared the same work ethos.

'My staff are concerned; worried.'

The Director laughed theatrically and looked around at the others.

'Worried? Concerned? What - they think I am working everyone too hard?'

Gregson looked sharply at the Director and for a moment their gazes locked together.

'No. They are frightened of ghosts.'

Two

An astounded silence fell over the conference room as if an intangible, muffling blanket had been thrown on top of the men and women it contained. Several people looked at each other as if seeking confirmation that they had indeed heard what they believed they had just heard. There was at least one half-choked guffaw.

The Director-General stared long and hard at Gregson. Finally he spoke, placing unusual gaps between his English words.

'Dr Gregson. May I ask if you are attempting to be amusing?'

Gregson met his gaze without any apparent embarrassment.

'I am reporting what I have been told, Director. I believe that it is important in management to listen to the concerns of one's staff. That's all I am doing.'

The Director sat down hard and spent a few seconds looking at his hands. After what seemed some considerable time he lifted his head and resumed his study of Gregson.

'I am an exceedingly busy man, doctor. I am busier than you can possibly imagine. I have no time to listen to what appears to me to be an exceedingly ill-timed attempt at humour. But still, under the infinitesimal possibility that you are neither a failed stand-up comedian nor a lunatic I will ask you to explain your worries outside of this meeting. I will choose someone senior to yourself to have the honour of listening to your tale.' And with that, his hard gaze flicked abruptly to Dubois and his speech switched seamlessly to flawless French. 'Dr Dubois, as the most senior officer here, I'd like you to listen to Dr Gregson's tale of the supernatural and if there are any creatures which have escaped from a Hollywood B-Movie prowling the august

9

corridors of CERN you will get rid of them immediately. Is that clear?'

Dubois nodded, whilst performing the Herculean task of keeping her features emotionless. 'Of course, Director.'

The Director switched his gaze back to Gregson with a look that appeared to contain the grim message: *You will not be on the shortlist of the scientists who will be seconded to the ILC.* But he simply said: 'The meeting is concluded. Thank you.'

A short time later Gregson and Dubois were facing each other in the latter's office.

They remained silent while Emilia brought in a tray with a coffee pot, two cups and a small dish of Viennese pastries.

Dubois gave a broad smile; an expression which somewhat startled Gregson as he had never seen Dubois smile before. It altered her features quite remarkably, he concluded.

However, as soon as the office door shut Dubois's face snapped back into an inscrutable visage which could have been carved from granite, so little animation did it display.

They stared at each other for a short while, during which Gregson thought that this must be what an experimental animal feels as the hypodermic approaches.

'Well?' Dubois finally said. She leaned back in her chair, entering a shaft of sunlight as she did so. Gregson noticed how her polished nails caught the light in a momentary flash.

Not a bad-looking woman he thought but her stare rapidly extinguished such considerations.

There was a pause which lengthened into a silence.

Dubois's immaculate eyebrows rose into elegant curves.

'Well? Ghosts? Where are they? What are they doing?'

Gregson had begun to regret not raising the concerns of his staff in an informal way. Why had he spoken up in front of the Director in such a reckless manner and immediately relegated himself to the bottom of the food chain? He became uncomfortably aware that Dubois was staring at him, waiting for him to speak and that until he said something, silence would reign.

'Well, uhh, I, I,' he said hesitantly, 'I haven't actually seen anything myself.'

Dubois's stare continued to bore into him like the thrust of a terrible needle. 'What has been seen?'

'My people talk of figures they have glimpsed. Grey, insubstantial figures.'

'And what do these figures do? Do they steal souls or replace babies with changelings?'

Gregson became conscious that he was shifting his position back and forth in the chair in a manner which could be interpreted as squirming. He forced himself to become stationary.

'I can see that you are mocking me Dr Dubois, which is not a fitting way to deal with a friend and colleague.'

She gave a transitory smile. 'Oh, we are friends, are we? I hadn't realised that.'

Gregson tried to meet her stare with his own. 'That's all I know. I'm sorry that the concerns of my staff have annoyed you, doctor. I think I had better leave. No doubt you are much busier than I.'

Dubois was unabashed. 'Not so simple as that, doctor. The Director has instructed me to find out what lies at the bottom of your people's concerns. If they are worried about something then they will not be operating at peak efficiency and neither I nor the Director would want that.'

Gregson nodded and made to rise from his chair but Dubois raised a hand to forestall him.

'Doctor Gregson, you have not finished your pastry. Please consume it before you leave. I hate waste.'

***

Dubois stood by the side of the great cylinder and ran a hand admiringly over it. Inside she knew there was a sea of liquid

11

helium in which positronium atoms were coming into existence and self-annihilating in mere nanoseconds.

What was it like to be positronium, she idly wondered. Did a few nanoseconds seem like a lifetime, an eternity? What if entire molecules could be constructed on such ephemeral foundations so that life, consciousness itself, could emerge?

Was positronic matter the scientific equivalent of a ghost?

She became aware that the technicians were staring at her, confused by her silence and so she turned to them. She tried to smile at the little throng of Gregson's staff members but smiling did not come easy to her in such situations and so she abandoned the effort rather quickly.

She reached behind and patted the massive cylinder which loomed above her.

'You are doing some quite valuable work here,' she said in English, in what she fondly believed was her best friendly manner, 'X-Ray lasers will be extremely useful to humanity once they are perfected. The penetrative power will be invaluable in studying the internal structure of matter.'

'We were rather hoping for medical applications,' a small blond woman at the front said in a rather sharp tone.

'Yes, of course,' Dubois answered whilst giving the woman a quick head-to-toe examination. 'I keep forgetting that there are other disciplines than physics.'

A few of the people interpreted this as an attempt at a joke and there were a couple of extremely half-hearted stage laughs.

Dubois tried again and, turning briefly to the great cylinder, she said: 'And to think when all the protons are decayed there will be nothing in the universe except positronium and stray photons.'

Nothing.

Blank faces.

Dubois's lips twisted briefly. Typical. What were these otherwise intelligent people lacking that they could not see that physics was the only true philosophy and everything else was that

12

discipline's faint shadow or pale reflection?

She gave up and returned to her usual brisk manner, addressing them as if they were students on the first day of their first term. 'Ghosts. Tell me about them.'

Some of the assembled throng turned and looked at each other. Others looked at the floor. Nobody spoke.

'Come on!' Dubois rapped, her short temper flaring, 'I have been sent here under instructions from the Director himself. I strongly suspect that you are wasting my time, and more importantly, his time. Convince me otherwise!'

She pulled a chair from under a nearby table and sat on it with the air of a bored audience member waiting for the performance to begin.

One of the nearby men shuffled forward, adjusting his spectacles as he did so.

'It's hard to explain…'

'Try.'

'Well,' the man continued, after throwing a quick glance behind him to see if he had the approval of his peers, 'it's like a grey mist which appears sometimes.'

'A grey mist. Only a mist.'

'Yes.'

'Do you clean your spectacles thoroughly may I ask?'

Another man pushed his way forward.

'That's not fair, Dr Dubois. You can't just sit there and mock us. I've seen it too – and I don't wear glasses!'

Dubois showed no sign of being affected by the rebuke. Without any expression other than bored resignation she asked: 'And you saw the same - a featureless grey mist. Are we perhaps dealing with an air conditioning problem here, do you think?'

The second man scowled. He clearly was not familiar with Dubois's manner.

'No – not exactly. I've seen it on three occasions but on the last time it appeared to have a – have a structure.'

'Explain.'

13

'It seemed to coalesce, to take on a form. It looked like I was looking into a big pipe. A kind of cylinder.'

Dubois threw a sharp glance at Gregson who was standing beside her.

'There's a lot of "appeared" and "seemed" here, doctor. This is not the kind of observations I would expect from people with scientific training.'

Gregson looked like a man trying to control his temper. 'Please show some respect to my staff, doctor. I believe they are reporting some phenomenon under difficult circumstances.'

Dubois shrugged and returned her gaze to the assembled technicians.

A slim, mousey-haired girl forced herself to the front, pushing between the two men who had spoken.

'Dr Dubois,' she said in a quiet but firm voice, 'may I ask something.'

Dubois's expression softened somewhat as she looked at the young woman.

'Of course, my dear.'

The woman looked directly at her interlocutor and said in a slightly bitter voice: 'Do you think we could sit down?'

'What? Why, yes, of course,' Dubois replied, suddenly realising that she was sitting while everybody else was standing.

She waited until the noise of chairs being dragged out had ended and, attempting a smile, she said, 'Now my dear, can you tell me what you saw?'

The woman continued to look directly at Dubois.

'My name is Bruna Agnelli, doctor. And I am responsible for calculating the production and annihilation of the positronium quasi-atoms. I use differential equations to adjust the flows. I am very good at my job. And I too have seen these things.'

Dubois's smile, feeble even at its peak, vanished completely.

'Ghosts. You saw ghosts. Did you use differential equations to monitor their production and destruction?'

There was a sudden eruption of angry expostulations from the technicians and Dubois realised that she might be pushing them too far. After all, she had a report to make to the Director. It would not do to alienate these people to the point where they refused to co-operate. Still she waited to see if she had crossed the point of no return.

She had not. Bruna said, in a voice which had tension crackling beneath it: 'I did not use that foolish word, doctor. But neither am I the country bumpkin which you take me for. There are phenomena occurring here which we do not understand.'

Dubois did not reply immediately. Instead, she was thinking rapidly. She had tried to mock them into admitting that they had been mistaken and they had not made that admission.

Therefore there was something unusual happening here. Not supernatural of course, for there was no such thing. But there could be a mundane explanation.

She resumed her usual authoritative manner.

'What exactly did you see, Ms Agnelli?'

'I saw the tunnel which Piotr spoke of. It was not fully clear – what is the word – it was *hazy*. Like something you see on a hot day when warm air is rising from a road. And there was something else which it seems that only I observed.'

'Please stop these theatrical pauses. What was this other thing you observed?'

'I thought I saw people. People at the other end of the grey tunnel.'

Dubois reached a conclusion. There was possible danger here. Was an unfriendly nation using some form of beamed surveillance which had gone wrong and had revealed their existence?

Now in full forensic mode, she rapped: 'Was there anything happening at the time of these appearances – these "apparitions"?'

Bruna looked at the two men who had spoken earlier.

'We considered that, doctor Dubois. And we noted that just

15

before each appearance there had been a particularly energetic sequence of positronium annihilations.'

Dubois's mind slipped effortlessly into the rules of scientific inference. *Look for a Phenomenon A which always precedes Phenomenon B. Then A is correlated with B and may be in a causal relationship.*

She had done all she could for the time being.

She stood up suddenly, thrusting her chair back under the table from which it had come. She turned from the assembled technicians, erasing them from her mind. They could tell her no more.

She wanted numbers, quantitative data.

She turned her gaze onto Gregson who had stood up at the same time as her and now waited on developments, like a sacrificial lamb.

'Dr Gregson,' she said, 'I want this helium tank tested for any fissures that might be allowing positronium into the atmosphere. Also consider quantum tunnelling. I want the air in this lab monitored 24/7 and any deviations from STP and gas composition recorded. This will begin now and be reported to me by 19:00 every day. The testing stops when I say it stops.'

Gregson seemed to be biting his lip but he merely nodded and said: 'Of course, doctor.'

And with that, she was gone.

Three

Hilda Krause sat somewhat nervously at the table in the dining area; unconsciously stirring her coffee over and over again. She was a dark-haired woman with thin features which seemed permanently frozen into a display of nervousness. Deep down she knew why she felt nervous, but she would not let the reason rise to the surface. She would let events take their course.

She heard someone draw back the chair on the other side of the table and looked up. It was Céline Dubois: of course – who else would it be?

'Hilda!' the other said in a warm, throaty voice, 'So good to see you again! It seems like ages!'

Krause met Dubois's excited gaze with a dull, flat expression.

'I know you speak perfect German, Céline but do you mind if we converse in English? I really need the practice.'

Dubois slid smoothly onto the chair and pulled it closer. 'Of course, darling. Your wish is my command!'

The other continued to stir her coffee, silently.

After a few minutes of soundless study Dubois finally said: 'What's wrong Hilda? You seem very down today. Is it something I said? – I'm sorry if it is. I know I'm perhaps a little too blunt sometimes; a little too abrupt. It's just me – you know I don't mean anything by it.'

'No, it's not you; it really isn't. I had some bad news today. Otto's been diagnosed with Lou Gehrig's disease.'

Dubois's face went solicitous and she said, 'My dear, how terrible for you. I know you're friends with him. Friends for a long time in fact.'

Krause nodded. 'We were students together in Berlin. We had great times together. We had no problems; the whole world

17

lay before us. Really great times.'

Dubois leaned forward with a slightly mischievous expression. 'Not too great I hope!'

Krause drew back slightly. 'Céline, please! This isn't about you, you know.'

Dubois accepted the admonition. 'Sorry again. That's all I seem to be saying these days. I am sorry to hear about this and I really feel for you.'

'And what about Otto?'

'Yes, him as well, of course. Poor man.'

Dubois slid her fingers across the table so that the two women's fingertips touched.

'Now can we talk about us? How have *you* been? How is the work going?'

Krause pushed her cold coffee away and straightened her shoulders, pulling her hand away as she did so. 'Badly. No-one except me seems to know what to do. These new technicians! I have to spoon-feed them everything; nursemaid them along. They know nothing but they think they know everything!

'When I point out the poor quality of their work they just shrug and try to blame me! And the Director's noticed. I feel he's looking over my shoulder all the time!'

Dubois nodded. 'Yes, he's a difficult man. He's even tried to browbeat me! I singed his wings a bit and that was that.'

'But everyone's saying the same thing, Céline. Everyone's complaining about their staff. Don't you have these problems?'

Dubois didn't answer immediately. In fact, she hadn't had any problems with her staff, possibly, she mused, because she always demanded the highest quality of people and the Director had ensured she got them. And Gregson's technicians seemed sharp enough. The way they had responded to her barbs was proof enough of that.

And yet Krause's words were not a total surprise to her: she had heard complaints from others that the quality of the new intake was noticeably poorer than previous years.

'I don't know what to do,' Krause was saying, 'I can't get them to do the basics. Is it me? Am I too easy-going, too gentle?'

Dubois smiled. 'Too gentle? Never. That's the way I like you.'

Krause did not seem to realise that she had been complimented and continued, 'Well I can understand why you don't have these problems.'

She realised that perhaps it was time to enquire about her companion. 'And how is your work going? Very well, I suppose - seeing as you don't have any problems.'

Dubois felt a tinge of irritation the way this meeting was going. It wasn't the light-hearted, playful banter which she was used to with Krause. She resumed her polished, efficient manner – it was up to Krause now to conjure up the softer side of her companion.

'My main activities are fine.

'I'm ahead of schedule and steadily climbing up the electron-volt ladder. What lies at the top I'm not sure but whatever it is I'll get there. But the Director has loaded another job on me.'

'How so?'

Dubois spread her arms wide. 'He's got me chasing ghosts.'

'Ghosts? Céline, be serious please.'

Dubois explained the situation as she saw it and gave a little chuckle at the growing incredulity on Krause's face.

'And have you caught any ghosts?' the latter finally said.

'Not a one – not even a playful little – what's the English for "poltergeist"?'

'Poltergeist,' Krause said, feeling very slightly triumphant as she imparted the information.

'Yes, of course. Two weeks now and not the slightest sign of anything coming from Beyond The Veil.' She dropped the pitch of her voice as she uttered those final three words in an effort to convey capital letters. 'I will call off the hunt any time now and hope that he doesn't send me off on a quest to bring back a unicorn or two. You know, sometimes I wonder if it's time he stepped down.'

Dubois's expression suddenly softened, and she slid her hand back across the table.

'But enough of all that nonsense. That's not the kind of thing we usually talk about. I want to talk about us. Why haven't you come to see me recently? I miss you.'

Krause did not allow the hands to touch and remained sitting straight-backed on her chair.

'I don't know. Everything seems such an effort these days. I – I'm so damned tired.'

It was Dubois's turn to sit up straight.

'Tired? You haven't come to see me because you're *tired*?'

Krause wilted slightly under the other's stare.

'It's worse than that. A terrible dragging lethargy. Lassitude – is that a word? It's pulling me down. I ...'

She suddenly leaned forward and rested her face on her arms. There were muffled sobs.

'I just wish - I wish...'

Dubois, finally accepting that her friend was in genuine distress, leaned forward to stroke her hair.

'What do you wish, my love?'

Krause lifted her face, revealing eyes glistening with tears which had not yet fallen.

'I wish the world was a better place. I wish I were eighteen again.'

Then to Dubois's astonishment, Krause brought a clenched fist smashing down onto the table.

'I want to feel alive again!'

* * *

Dubois saw no more of Krause that day. Or the day after. Or the day after.

An invitation to share a bottle of wine at Chez Dubois was not answered.

And so it was, that an ordinary day at Gregson's station was turned into Hell as one particular lady descended like an avenging Fury on the helpless inhabitants.

'Where are these fucking ghosts!' Dubois thundered as she burst in on them. 'Where are they, you useless band of cretins! Show them to me now or I'm reporting every one of you to the Director!'

Gregson tried to stem the tsunami of anger and was brushed aside, treated as one of his own technicians.

She forced them all to stand in front of her, Gregson included, and marched back and forth in front of them. They had only ever seen firing squads on old videos but each one felt that he or she was now facing one.

'How many apparitions, appearances, manifestations have occurred since you first reported them to me, Gregson?' she snarled at the astounded scientist, 'How many?'

'Well…,' he began.

'How many!' she shrieked, 'How many? Don't use transfinite numbers – positive integers will suffice!'

He squared up to her, face almost against face.

'None.'

'None,' she echoed in a dangerously quiet voice, 'I wonder why. Could it be…' She looked around theatrically and then snapped her stare back at Gregson and thundered 'because there aren't any! Not one. Not one fucking one!'

'Dr Dubois, this kind of bullying conduct …'

'Is all no-hopers like you deserve. The monitoring is over. You can go back to playing cards or looking out of the window or whatever you actually do down here because by God there doesn't seem to be much else going on!'

With that she turned on her heel and was gone, leaving a shaken group of scientists and technicians behind her; people who felt lucky to have survived their encounter with a human tiger.

* * *

The Director pushed a glass of brandy towards Dubois; who ignored it.

'Gregson has made a formal complaint against you, of course,' the Director said in what was, for him, a kindly voice.

Dubois was unmoved. 'On what grounds?'

'What grounds do you think, Céline? Bullying. You humiliated him in front of his staff, whom you then proceeded to terrorise.'

Dubois shrugged. 'He deserved to be humiliated. He's a non-entity.'

The Director raised a finger and waved it back and forth in a pastiche of the annoyed schoolmaster.

'Not fair, Céline. He's no supernova but he burns steadily and reliably.'

Dubois finally picked up her glass and took a sip.

'Henri come on. When did we start tolerating the mediocre, the just-getting-along? Fifteen years ago, ten years ago he wouldn't have got a job here. Or if you'd taken pity on him he'd have been fetching you another bottle of brandy. And it's not only him – everybody tells me the same story. And the world outside – the rise of populist non-entities who give the people exactly what they want: simple so-called solutions to complex problems. Simple answers for simpletons.'

The Director raised the thick eyebrows that clung to his face like a pair of fluffy, white caterpillars.

'Céline you are famous for your sharp wits and equally infamous for your sharp tongue. I respect your intellect, which is truly remarkable, but I have this entire place to manage. We are in the process of losing our pre-eminence in particle research to the USA and Japan. We were nearly there but it looks like others will claim the prize. You know as well as I what we are reaching for – the final answer to what lies behind the phenomena – what Kant called "the thing-in-itself". And you, as blindingly bright as you are, cannot do it alone. I need the whole site working as one. I cannot allow dissension and resentment to grow and sap our

22

energies.'

Dubois shrugged. 'Your faith in them is touching but I don't want anything to do with them. I see no reason why I should co-operate.'

But Dubois was not the only possessor of a short temper.

The Director gave a guttural snort and forcibly threw his glass against the nearest wall of his office. Dubois started at his sudden explosion of anger and the noise of shattering glass.

'You, Dubois, will damn well do as I tell you. Just remember who you are talking to. I'm not one of your green as grass college boys. I was studying fundamental forces while you were sucking your mother's tits. So I am now giving you a verbal warning. The next time you disappoint me it will be a written warning and I will refer your case to the TREF. And the time after that, it will be you fetching me a bottle of brandy and polishing the tables! Do I make myself understood?'

Dubois was not used to bending the knee but she realised that this time it was politic to accept the rebuke and so she said in as neutral a tone as she could manage: 'Yes Director.'

'You may now leave, Dr Dubois,' the Director replied, in an equally neutral tone. 'Let us not have this type of conversation again.'

He watched Dubois leave and as the door shut he pressed a button on his desk and said: 'Marie, get someone in here to clean up. There's broken glass on the floor.'

Immediately outside the door, Dubois stood in a rare state of indecision.

Should she march back in and tell the old goat to stick his commands into where the sun does not shine?

Eventually she shook her head; a referral to the Tripartite Employment Conditions Forum would not sit well on her record and she moved away from his door, just as a young man was approaching with a brush and dust pan.

She shook her head then ran strong fingers over her forehead. They were glistening with sweat as she looked down

23

on them.

I am losing control she thought. *I must get a hold of myself, find out what is wrong with Hilda. I need someone to listen to my problems for a change.*

The pager on her lapel suddenly buzzed.

'Dr Dubois, you are needed in the main synchrotron control room. We are about to commence.'

Her face twisted in self-disgust. Of course, it was about to fire up in the next half an hour! She had forgotten all about it. Typical of the Director to schedule a meeting at such an inconvenient time – he probably didn't even know there was a firing taking place!

She hurried to the control room and stood imperiously among her own technicians.

These people at least could be relied on – she had hand-picked them all.

'Potentials OK?' she asked of her deputy.

'On the button doctor,' was the smooth reply.

She smiled at him, feeling the pleasure of being able to smile at someone - and also failing to notice his surprised expression.

'Let's do it,' she ordered in the familiar crisp tone that they were used to. Her people turned to the serried banks of equipment which they could adjust like expert organists sending one of Bach's masterworks echoing to the fanned ceiling of a great cathedral.

She looked at the glowing, multicoloured screens, feeling the pleasure of control, of ownership of what was about to happen. Perhaps this was what mothers felt when they sat in the audience looking up at the stage as their daughters graduated. Before her, multiplied across many monitors, was a picture of the great muon spectrometer, in all its thirty metre-diameter splendour. Its massive circular shape seemed to Dubois to represent a great disc-like door which barred the way to a vast cavern. And in that cavern, she knew, were uncountable treasures, not of cheap trinkets like gold or diamonds, but secrets

24

– secrets of how the universe was constructed. For decades now humanity had been diving deeper and deeper into the dark oceanic depths of reality, searching for the ultimate bedrock of existence. Each time the divers had believed that they had reached the bottom of the abyss some new discovery would reveal that there were still darker, more mysterious depths below them.

One day, soon, thought Dubois, the scientist-divers would reach the abyssal floor and finally, completely, know what the true foundations of reality were. And the long quest that had begun with Leucippus and Democritus would be at an end. And, she – Dubois – intended to be one of those scientists!

And now, deep in the labyrinthine coils of the great machine, anti-protons were being generated, soon to be sent flashing soundlessly down the circular track at a significant fraction of light speed. Normally anti-proton would be sent smashing against anti-proton, she reflected in some exasperation, but this was one of the Director-General's pet projects.

Before the speeding particles had gone halfway, they would meet normal matter protons hurtling in the opposite direction. And then there would be minute flashes of radiation as annihilation occurred. The instruments would be watching, waiting for anomalous behaviour; particles or quanta not expected; not understood.

This had happened at the dawn of the universe, she mused, glad to be thinking of abstractions again. But why had the mutual destruction not been total? Why had matter survived? Why was there something rather than nothing?

'Everything nominal,' her deputy announced, his face a multicoloured patchwork as he bent close to the monitors. 'She's behaving beautifully.'

She smiled briefly. Normally she would have admonished him for his use of offensive gender-specific terms but this time she let it pass. She had had enough confrontation for one day.

The experiment came to what seemed to be a satisfactory

end and everyone looked happy, she thought. Of course, the traces would have to be closely studied but that would take a day or two. Only then would they know how successful the run had been.

She decided to call it a day and have a drink in her office.

'Well done everyone,' she said, 'We'll go through the traces tomorrow at the usual time.'

A few technicians looked up from their screens in mild surprise. Gratitude was not something they were accustomed to.

She left, not looking back, and began the walk back to her office.

Her feet seemed to drag in a way which surprised her. She did not think she had become so tired.

She approached the elevator doors.

And stopped.

There it was. She could see it.

Before her was a vague, insubstantial, diaphanous grey mist. She could see the wall beyond it.

The mist seemed to be swirling, slowly rotating. And gradually thickening. The distant wall became obscured,

It appeared to be forming into a solid-looking three-dimensional object with a circular edge.

A big pipe?

No – a tunnel!

Hitherto frozen into stunned immobility she lunged towards it.

She would solve this mystery!

But as she got within two metres it winked out of existence, leaving no indication that it had ever been there.

She was alone.

Four

Dubois sat in her office; mind whirling.

In front of her sat her drink – not the usual mineral water she had been expecting to pour but a large glass of cognac.

What had happened? What had she seen?

She directed all her analytical powers at the memory of the event.

Could it have been the result of some internal state – a function of unusual electrical activity in the brain? She was not a migraine sufferer but she knew that visual disturbances were sometimes present in a migraine attack.

Was it something worse, a form of hallucination?

Was the pressure of her job finally getting to her?

No. The thing that had happened – it was too real. It had been out there in true three-dimensional reality. In any case, the idea that her job was too much for her was simply laughable. She could do this job in her sleep – unlike most of her *soi-disant* peers.

She drank the remaining spirit in a single movement and with eyes focussed on infinity she thought deeply.

What Gregson had said was true.

How could she admit that without having to apologise to him? The idea of having to act out that scenario was deeply distasteful to her.

Never mind. There were things happening here that were vastly more important than egos and pride.

There was a phenomenon occurring on an apparently regular basis which had no place in the laws of physics.

And Dubois knew her laws of physics.

But how could it be studied, analysed, understood, if its appearance could not be predicted?

That was not how science worked. If something was

27

random it was almost impossible to study. How could a control variable be established? How to alter the input and measure the output?

Dubois stared at her empty brandy glass.

She had to have data; lots of them.

And then she realised that there was a way to confirm what she had seen without involving Gregson; a way to proceed without admitting fallibility. The buildings had Close Circuit Television cameras. Like everywhere else in the world security could not be taken for granted; there would always be someone trying to infiltrate, if not to steal hardware then to steal ideas. It was not unheard of, even in the supposed selfless world of science.

She smiled a quiet smile to herself.

She would track every appearance of this thing: compare them; note every aspect of their generation; their existence; their dissolution.

How typical that no-one else had thought to do one simple action; instead they had merely gazed at the phenomenon with dull, sheep-like eyes.

She raised her empty glass at some imagined foe.

'What are you?' she said quietly, still smiling, 'well, I'll find out. You can be sure of that.'

And with that implied warning, she shut her systems down and left her office.

The woman at the security desk acknowledged her pass and wished her a goodnight.

She was not at all surprised when Dubois did not return the greeting, for the latter had never done so in the five years that she had been passing the desk.

Dubois passed out into the Genevan night, seeing nobody, thinking of nobody —the only images her mind could create were of a mysterious mist that had tried and failed to form some kind of a tunnel, some kind of a conduit.

But a conduit to where?

* * *

Dubois was not used to requesting favours. Normally if she wanted something, she would simply ask for it and accept it without a second's thought.

She would ask for something: an object, a task, a report, a print-out, a coffee.

She would ask and it would be delivered. Was there anything else to say or do?

But now she was having to request that someone did a favour for her, having to ask without the certainty that the favour would be delivered.

It was a most unusual, not to say irritating, situation.

'Why do you need to see the recordings, Dr Dubois?' the technician asked again, looking up at her as he lounged insolently in his chair, hands behind his head.

Normally Dubois would have given a hard stare and said very slowly and carefully: 'Because I do.' Now she had to think of a reason why she would need to see the recordings which obviously had nothing to do with her actual job.

In an instant she had it.

'I believe that there have been leaks from the feeder pipe for the main synchrotron,' she said, whilst feeling a note of surprise. Why, lying was so easy! She must do it more often!

'No-one's told me,' the technician replied.

'That's odd,' Dubois said smoothly, 'I thought I just had.'

'I mean via the usual channels.'

Dubois was finding deception steadily easier with each passing second.

'I am here under orders from the Director himself. This is a matter of extreme urgency.'

'What sort of leaks are we talking about?'

Dubois's voice exploded in genuine anger, at both her actual situation and how she would feel if her play-acting were real. 'Dangerous leaks! Gamma rays, alpha particles! God knows what else. Shall I go back and tell the Director that people have died because you wasted time in cross-examining me! We're talking about a custodial sentence here for reckless incompetence!'

That was enough. The technician sat up straight and with tightly compressed lips turned to his control panel.

'When and where?'

She gave him where and when she had seen the manifestation.

She leaned forward eagerly, pushing him slightly out of the way, without realising that she had done so.

The monitor was showing an empty corridor and then she saw herself come into the frame.

Dubois was shocked to see how dispirited she looked on the screen, seemingly dragging one foot behind the other as if wearing an invisible ball and chain.

Her image stopped abruptly.

This is it! Dubois thought.

She watched herself stand completely still, apparently staring at something.

But where was it?

Her image lunged at one of the walls and then stopped, looking blankly around.

There was nothing there.

The real Dubois stood up, fists clenching and unclenching, in wide-eyed disbelief.

'Saw something bad?' the technician asked, noting her discomfiture. 'I didn't see anything.'

'There may have been an ionisation flash,' she said, trying to get her spinning feelings under control.

She gave him the other times and locations that she had got from Gregson.

And with a growing sense of disbelief and a concern verging on fear she saw the same silent-movie pantomimes played out before her as people gesticulated and pointed at innocent emptiness.

There was no more to see. Without a word she turned and

left the technician who for some moments stared in wonder after her.

'Scientists!' he eventually grunted and then turned back to his magazine.

* * *

Dubois stared sourly at the Director. As usual, he was spinning things out, enjoying being the centre of attention up there are on the podium in front of the microphone; no doubt imagining himself as some rock star in front of an adoring audience.

Even the nearness of Hilda Krause did not lift Dubois's spirits. They had spoken before the Director had come in and Dubois was relieved to find that Krause was still talking to her after their unsatisfying encounter a few days earlier. But there was still something wrong with her, that was obvious. A spark had gone out of the woman; her face seemed to sag and her eyes no longer twinkled with vivaciousness.

'I don't know what's wrong, Céline,' she had said, 'the doctor is running some blood tests and will let me know soon.'

Dubois had run a soothing hand over her shoulders and said, 'Don't worry, everything will be alright. You've been working too hard again. What have I told you? The Director won't even notice. Just think about yourself for once. Think about us.'

Krause had nodded but had taken a seat some distance away from Dubois.

Dubois looked around at the people in the crowded Conference Room. All the great and good were here, she noted. When the Director finally reached the end of his interminable ramblings they might actually discover why they were all here.

Her gaze rested for a second on Gregson's face who appeared to have been staring at her for some time. She observed the open hostility on the man's face and turned away quickly.

Perhaps she had been too dismissive of her colleagues' concerns. Maybe she needed allies in her quest to understand the weirdness which was stalking the institution.

How to make amends? She didn't really know. She had done her best to convince the Director that the ghost stories were simply overwork.

Her subconscious suddenly alerted her to something the Director had just said.

Kitikami Highlands? Japan? He was talking about the International Linear Collider!

'And so,' the Director was saying, in a tone which suggested that he was about to unveil some wonderful discovery, 'I am pleased to announce the first tranche of colleagues who will be seconded to the ILC. For twelve months initially, but obviously with the possibility of an extension if things go well.'

She sat up straight, all thoughts of mysterious phenomena, of the bruised egos of co-workers, even of Krause's depressed state banished from her mind.

'I'd like the following colleagues to join me on the stage,' the director was saying as he picked up a print-out from the table next to him.

Dubois felt her heartbeat suddenly accelerate. Surely it was impossible that her name would not be among those selected for this honour!

And indeed, it was impossible. Her name was the second to be read out from the alphabetically ordered list and in her excitement she failed to hear that Krause and Gregson were also among those called to greatness.

In a slight daze she made her way to the stage and stood looking down on the throng below, watched its size shrink as more and more people joined her. Finally, the Director reached the end of his list with some Polish name beginning with "Z" and the vanguard was complete.

'I'm sure you'll want to join me in congratulating your co-workers who have earned their place through diligence and hard

32

work,' the Director said to the remaining members of the audience. There was a short round of desultory clapping from the remaining scientists which soon petered out.

Yes, thought Dubois *It looks like they want to congratulate us! Poor devils!*

She had sudden memories of the little girl she had once been, growing up in Villeneuve-les-Avignon.

How far have I come! she thought, *And how far will I go!*

She suddenly realised that in her excitement she had failed to notice that Krause was standing next to her. She turned and looked directly into her face, ignoring the lack of matching excitement in her tired features.

'What did I tell you?' Dubois breathed girlishly, 'Everything will be fine from now on. This is the start of our new life!'

Krause nodded slowly without enthusiasm. 'Yes, a new life. But "new" doesn't always mean "better", does it, Céline?'

Dubois stared at her silently for a moment, while inside her mind a little voice said *No it doesn't.*

Finally she said: 'Trust me. I will look after you whatever happens.'

Krause nodded again and then turned away, leaving Dubois alone and silent in the middle of the chattering group of excited scientists.

Five

Dubois was in high spirits as she returned to her office that day, all remembrance of grey mists and spectral visitors ejected from her bubbling mind. Her career was back on track. Soon she would find herself back in the forefront of particle research, and the controllers of the ILC would rapidly find that they had a mover and shaker in their midst whom they would quickly find invaluable.

She threw a beaming smile at Emilia and was about to brush past into her office when her secretary said: 'You have a visitor, madame.'

'A visitor?' Dubois replied, 'there is no appointment in my calendar.' She tried throwing another smile at Emilia. 'I'm sure I haven't forgotten – I'm not senile yet!'

'No madame. The visitor said that he was given approval by the Director.'

Could it be a delegate from the ILC already? Dubois thought excitedly. 'His name please, Emilia.'

Marius Larsen? She pondered. The name seemed familiar but she didn't recognise it from her researches into the structure of the ILC.

Then it hit her.

Marius Larsen – the author of that ridiculous e-mail.

'He'd better have a good reason for coming here,' she hissed to the suddenly alarmed Emilia and stormed into her office.

As she did so her uninvited guest rose to meet her and Dubois found herself looking up into an impossibly distant face, for her visitor was an exceedingly large man. He was also a somewhat strange looking man for he seemed to be utterly, totally hairless – not even eyebrows or eyelashes. A colossal hand totally enveloped hers and she found herself involuntarily shaking hands with the massive stranger.

'Céline,' a basso profundo voice said, 'it's wonderful to meet you at last.'

She extricated herself from that over-familiar grasp and took her normal seat, glad to have the barrier of a desk between them.

'Marius Larsen,' she finally said, 'I looked you up but you seem – I mean, you don't quite look like your pictures.'

The huge man grinned. 'Yes, I had a little accident a while ago that robbed me of all my body hair. Quite a blow – I was very proud of my beard. Made me look a bit like one of the old-time pirates, I thought. Still the ladies seem to like me as I am now – they say they love my soft, smooth skin.'

Dubois stared at him with growing puzzlement. This didn't sound like the dry, scientific conversations she was used to in the august laboratories of CERN. But the man's voice and gaze were oddly hypnotic.

Finally, she gave her head a little shake to clear it and said: 'I am very busy, Larsen. Why are you here? What do you want?'

Larsen leaned forward and said in a slightly quieter voice: 'What do you know of my research?'

Dubois's mind flicked back to the search she had done on him. Her excellent memory served up all the relevant details on the man and what he had been doing.

'You were working on something involving an exciplex laser in Norway.'

'Correct Céline.'

'An approach which I have always regarded as a complete dead end. And I don't recall giving you permission to use my given name. Kindly use my title when addressing me.'

Larsen bowed his great head. 'Of course, Dr Dubois. And you will afford me the same courtesy I hope.'

'Naturally, Dr Larsen. But I repeat I am very busy. How did you get into this complex in the first place? – I certainly didn't invite you.'

Larsen grinned again. 'Your Director and I are drinking

35

buddies. He took me under his wing during his time in Oslo. God, that man can put it away!'

'I am ecstatic to hear these Boys' Club stories. Now get to the point.'

Larsen leaned back and took his gaze off Dubois, seemingly focusing on something far, far away.

'There was an accident with the laser. It became vastly overloaded. I was partly responsible for that due to my exuberant approach to staff-management. Before it broke down it produced something I had never seen before – a sphere of ball lightning.'

Dubois snorted. 'As you know there is no physical theory which allows ball lightning. It belongs in a compendium of folk tales, along with crystal energy and dowsing.'

'Nevertheless, I created it – accidentally. And more importantly, my colleague and I came in contact with it. It burned all my hair away but, more importantly, it gave me a new faculty.'

'You can run faster than a speeding locomotive?'

Larsen ignored the barb. It appeared he was inured to sarcasm.

'Doctor, have you ever wondered why there is so much suffering in the world?'

Dubois looked startled. 'What? – have we started a new conversation?'

'No, this is relevant. I'm not talking about doomed love-affairs or even war. I'm talking about disease – in particular, the degenerative diseases.'

'Doctor Larsen, you appear to have misread my title. I know nothing of biology or medicine.'

'Neither did I but I have learned much since that fateful day. Surely you must have watched wildlife documentaries and seen animals suffering under a heavy load of parasites. Trypanosomes, amoebae, flukes.'

'I prefer to relax with a pleasant bottle of Chablis or Chateau Neuf.'

36

'Stay with me, doctor. Why are humans prone to diseases in which their own bodies turn against them? You surely must realise what I am talking about.'

'Cancer, MS, Parkinson's. The list is extensive I am aware. Scientists are no more immune than the humblest peasant.'

Larsen's voice became quieter so that Dubois was forced to lean slightly towards him.

'I have discovered, doctor, that they are caused by human parasites.'

Dubois shrugged. 'That is not unlikely but why have you come here rather than one of the medical research institutions?'

'Because these parasites are not biological. They are entities from outside this universe.'

Dubois felt a little electric shock of alarm as she realised that she was sharing a room with a lunatic. How long would it take security staff to get here?

She moved her hand surreptitiously nearer to her intercom button. Larsen noticed the movement and gave a bitter smile.

'No need for over-reaction, doctor. I am not violent. You are in no danger from me. But listen, you enjoy testing hypotheses – stay with me on this one and analyse my reasoning.'

Dubois relaxed slightly – but not completely. She would not call for help at this stage but would stay alert.

'Not from this universe. Well, that's original at least. Makes a change from Mars or alpha Centauri. Where do they come from?'

'They told me that they come from between the quanta of spacetime.'

Dubois threw up her hands. 'Doctor Larsen, I know that your qualifications are mediocre but what you have uttered is a mathematically meaningless noise! Even if spacetime is quantised, to talk of things between them is just a sad example of pushing an analogy too far!'

Larsen was unmoved. 'They may have lied. They enjoy playing with human emotions. Did you recognise the quotation in my e-mail?'

'No.'

'It was by a man called Charles Fort. Or possibly by another man who was commenting on Charles Fort.'

'I have not heard of Charles Fort. And the fact that I do not know the man is sufficient proof he is not worth knowing.'

'Nevertheless, his statement happens to be true. We *are* property.'

Dubois set her lips in a thin line. Mental inferiors she was used to but outright madmen were something new.

'Look, let's cut this short. Where are these parasites, irrespective of where they originate? Why has no-one else seen them? How is it that you can see them? What do I call them?'

Larsen seemed withdrawn now, as if he had just lost a last hope. 'It was a side-effect of my contact with the ball lightning. I could see things that humans could not normally see.'

'What – your retina could detect ultraviolet radiation? I'm told that's quite dangerous. Or you could detect things by echolocation, like the Greater Horseshoe Bat?'

Larsen shook his great pink head. 'No, I think that we can all see them but there is a filter in our brains which prevents the images from being registered. The accident removed that filter somehow. As to what they are called – they call themselves "hran".'

'An odd combination of consonants, clearly not Indo-European. You are to be congratulated on coming up with a suitably unusual word.'

'Thank you for your praise but unfortunately, I did not invent the word. It is what they call themselves. As to what they look like, they have no fixed shape in this world. But they have eyes – that at least is a constant feature. Their eyes take the shape of a perfect equilateral triangle of glowing red dots.'

'So the hran are geometers. I like them already. But Dr Larsen – you have uncovered them, revealed their hiding place. And yet you live – why is that?'

'They killed Einar, my friend and colleague, whose only crime was to be able to see them. Like me he had come into contact with the ball lightning. But they have different plans for me – with me, they simply like to torment. I currently have two forms of cancer and I recently had open heart surgery for stenotic valves.'

'And how old are you doctor?'

'Fifty-two.'

'Your conditions are not unknown for a man of your age.'

Larsen shrugged in a gesture that indicated resigned acceptance.

'They also torment me by raising false hopes and then dashing them. Such as this conversation we're having now. I had thought that you, one of the sharpest minds of our generation, might be intrigued by my story, sufficiently intrigued to look further into it. But I was wrong.'

'I won't dismiss you just yet, Doctor Larsen. So, you're saying that these creatures cause us to have these dreadful diseases. So, remove them – and we live forever – right?'

'No, I have never claimed that. There would still be infectious diseases; they're nothing to do with the hran. And cancer can have multiple causes – ionising radiation, for instance. But the average human lifespan would be significantly greater. We would simply wear out, gradually, gently – like carpet slippers.'

'A nice metaphor. And animals – are they parasitized by these creatures as well?'

'Yes – but only by the lower grade hran. They prefer creatures with advanced nervous systems. They feed on the electrical impulses given off by complex brains.'

Dubois smiled a tolerant smile, the smile a teacher gives to a child struggling with its multiplication tables. 'And I, doctor, I like to think that I possess a complex brain. Is there an invisible hran on my back as I speak?'

'No. But there is one over there in that corner. In the

shadow.'

Dubois felt a pang of nervousness again. Once again she felt uneasy in this man's presence.

'In the shadow? Why in the shadow?'

'They don't like light. I don't know if the world they come from is one of total darkness or simply low illuminance. They can't tolerate electromagnetic radiation above the yellow-green part of the spectrum. I killed one once with a burst of far ultraviolet.' He paused. 'At least, I think I did.'

Dubois had had enough. 'Alright, Larsen – that's it. I hope you can find the treatment you so obviously need but you've wasted enough of my time. Get out and take that hran in the corner with you!'

Larsen studied Dubois for a moment. 'My, you're a cold one, doctor. There must be a reason you're the Ice Maiden. Have you had a good fuck recently?'

Dubois was speechless for a moment and then she stood up and pointed to the door.

'If you're referring to my choice of partners, I can tell you now that I am immune to your no doubt immense charms. I can think of nothing worse than having a man use a piece of meat to inject some kind of white slime into me! Now get out!'

Larsen also rose but remained motionless, staring at Dubois for a few seconds.

Finally, he said: ' "You can think of nothing worse." Well, Dr Dubois, you have obviously led a very quiet life.'

And the dialogue was over.

Six

Dubois passed the glass of Chateau Neuf du Pape to Krause, smiling as she did so.

'Here you are, Hilda, you've earned it,' she said.

Krause accepted the glass and took a tentative sip. She did not smile.

Dubois leaned back into the softness of her armchair and used one foot to remove the last remaining shoe from the other foot. Schoenberg's "Verklärte Nacht" was playing softly from hidden speakers. Low illumination made the room look like some hidden cave, with deep shadows occupying the corners; deep shadows to which Dubois gave not the slightest consideration.

A cave where we can hide from the pressures of a world that is slowly going mad, Dubois thought approvingly to herself.

She stretched her legs out in front of her, digging toes into the yielding pile of the carpet, feeling her calf muscles stretch as she straightened her legs and then relax as she pulled them back. Looking at the ceiling, she gave a deep sigh and smiled broadly.

This was perfect. Everything was perfect.

She took another sip of the wine and then, looking up, noticed that Krause's glass was almost untouched and was resting on the small table next to the sofa.

'What's the matter, Hilda?' she asked, 'this is your favourite. Is there something wrong with it?'

Krause's lips jerked into an unconvincing smile. 'The wine? No, there's nothing wrong with it.'

Dubois put her wine down and, crossing to the sofa, sat next to the other woman, placing a protective arm around her.

'Then why are you so down tonight? If there's nothing wrong with the wine then what is it?'

Krause gave another unconvincing smile and turned moist eyes to her companion.

'Me, Céline. There's something wrong with me.'

Dubois immediately went into protective mode.

'He's demanding too much of you again, I knew it!'

Her eyes blazed like those of a tigress seeing her cub threatened.

'That man! He's not going to get away with treating us like workhorses with his endless demands! I can take it; he doesn't worry me but others...you...'

Her words trailed off as she remembered how she had burst into the Director's room with bellowed complaints about letting Larsen into the building to harass her and, unforgivably, to waste her valuable time. She smiled as she remembered how he had spluttered some unconvincing justification before she had stormed out.

But Krause was speaking again. 'No, Céline, it's not the Director. In fact, he's been very kind to me. The thing that's not right – is me.'

Dubois's attention snapped back to the present and her companion's obviously distressed state.

'Something wrong with you – what? What is it?'

Krause made little wringing motions with her hands as she looked up at Dubois.

'I've had the results from the blood test. There's something wrong with my thyroid. It's not producing enough of the hormone. That's why I'm always tired and depressed.'

Dubois's mind whirled. Problem with the thyroid? What did the thyroid do? How serious was this? Was there a cure?

Then, suddenly, it didn't matter.

'Hilda, whatever this means we'll face it together, you and I.'

Krause reached for a hand and held it tightly.

'Céline, I always feel safe when I'm with you.'

A strange light seemed to enter Dubois's eyes.

42

'I told you I wouldn't let anything harm you and I meant it. I'd rip this universe to pieces with my bare hands before I'd let anything happen to you!'

Krause smiled a normal smile and then they kissed.

* * *

Dubois did not think of herself as a claustrophobe and she felt not even a slight twinge of nervousness as she stood in the ATLAS service tunnel which ran one hundred metres below the Swiss countryside. Lost in a little reverie of pleasant self-satisfaction, she was standing next to the great cylinder which held the beams of charged particles. She reached out, almost touching it, marvelling to think that before long invisible beams of relativistic protons would be flashing through its gently curving twenty-seven kilometres on their way to a fiery doom. After that doom a shower of particles would spray out, some to be detected by the titanic seven thousand tonne ATLAS detector.

From time to time she liked to leave the computer screens behind and admire the great machines themselves which produced those torrents of data that scrolled, seemingly endlessly, on her screens. This was one of those times.

How far humanity had come, she marvelled, from muddled beliefs about earth, fire, water and air as the primary building blocks of the world to the modern understanding of what those foundations actually were. Yet still, there were mysteries. How was it possible that baryonic matter was such a small component of the universe, as if it had been an afterthought of some absent-minded demiurge?

It was her job to pursue those last mysteries, to capture them and force them into the light of scientific examination to finally yield the last answers.

It was then she heard a babble of voices coming closer along the tunnel. She stood still trying to interpret what the voices were

43

saying before realising they were not in one of the three languages in which she was fluent. Before long a gaggle of yellow hard hats came into view and Dubois saw that a group of people were being guided around by the Director-General himself.

As the group approached Dubois could see that their faces were oriental and then she recognised the language – Japanese.

The Director noticed Dubois and brought the group to a halt and turning to his guests he gave out a rapid stream of their native language in which Dubois recognised her own name and having completed that he turned to Dubois and, in French, said: 'Céline! What an unexpected pleasure to see you down here! Naturally, I believed that you'd have been staring at a computer screen as usual. I didn't realise you were down here with the rest of the moles.'

I bet you didn't, Dubois thought sourly, *Otherwise you would have needed to inform me that you had important visitors. What are you up to, you old fox?*

The Japanese group had a translator with them for the rest of the Director's talk was in French.

'This is Dr Céline Dubois, one of the most talented young ladies we have here.'

Dubois bristled inwardly at that phrase but said nothing.

The Japanese bowed in unison to her in response to the Director's introduction.

'We are all pleased to meet such an esteemed lady,' the Japanese translator said in unaccented French, 'we are hoping that you will be among those joining the international team when the ILC comes on stream in the not too distant future.'

Dubois smiled and said 'Yes. I believe I am.', throwing a quick glance at the Director as she spoke.

'Ahh … Céline, I am showing our guests the Chateau de Voltaire in a few hours' time. Perhaps you'd care to join us,' that worthy said.

'Delighted,' Dubois replied, with her best smile. *I'm not going to be left in the dark about anything to do with the ILC, whatever your plans for me, Dear Director.*

The group went on their way leaving Dubois to ascend the hundred metres to the surface alone.

She stood in the bright sunlight, gazing at, but not seeing, the mural on the wall of the control building.

Things were clearly starting to move fast, she mused to herself. She would have to be on her best behaviour from now on so that no possible impediment could be found to prevent her from fulfilling her destiny on the other side of the world.

There were discoveries to be made, great discoveries, discoveries which would rank highly when the histories of science in the twenty-first century were written.

And the name "Dubois" would be there on the most important pages.

* * *

Dubois lifted the wine to her lips, listening intently to every word coming from Mr Takahashi.

'We have great hopes for the ILC, Dr Dubois,' he was saying in English.

'Oh, please call me Céline,' she replied. She didn't really know how to gush but was giving it her best shot. 'I know it will be a great leap forward from what we have here. And I hope to be there right at the centre of things!'

She felt Takahashi's gaze flick up from her court shoes to her décolletage but decided to ignore it. There were bigger particles to smash at the moment than worrying about trivialities.

'I'm sure I can find a place for you, Céline,' he replied, with a slightly lop-sided smile.

Dubois decided that perhaps she had been a bit too successful at gushing and steered the conversation back into safer areas.

'What do you think the peak energies will be, Dr Takahashi?' (He had told her his given name but she had decided not to use

45

it for the time being.)

Takahashi took the hint and became slightly more business-like. 'Oh, I think we will be easily able to reach the upper tera electron-volt region. If we don't see signs of supersymmetry then I'm afraid we will all have to go back to the drawing board.'

Dubois took another sip of her wine. The Director had really pushed the boat out for this one! she thought, enjoying the *pétillant* kick it was giving her.

'Do you think we will be facing a crisis in physics then?'

Takahashi nodded gravely. 'I think we will. And not only in physics: fewer and fewer people are coming into the discipline. It seems physics is too hard for them. They all want instant answers and if they don't like the answers then they just say it isn't true.'

Dubois nodded gravely. 'I have seen the same thing. The turning away from hard facts merely because one doesn't like them. The quality of the recent intakes have been – well – let's not be cruel. Just not what they used to be.'

Takahashi gave his lop-sided smile again. 'Well, there can be no doubt about your standards, Céline.'

She said nothing and he returned to the original topic.

'My own son is one of those we have been speaking of. He has got in with a crowd of people who believe that the future can be foretold from observing astronomical patterns. He seems to believe that there are invisible entities controlling our lives and apparently we can contact them by various ridiculous procedures, which I won't attempt to describe. I looked over his shoulder once when he was scanning some of those laughable websites. I can still remember what he was typing.'

Dubois raised a tailored eyebrow. 'And that was?'

'He had typed "Ours is a pseudo-existence, and all appearances in it partake of its essential fictitiousness."'

Dubois smiled tolerantly, being careful not to show the outright contempt that she was actually feeling: this was a man she would need in her precipitous climb to the top.

46

'That does seem a rather odd thing to believe,' was all she said.

Takahashi shrugged, resignedly. 'And it's not even original. Apparently, he was quoting from the works of some American called Charles Fort. I don't suppose you've even heard of him.'

Dubois's grip upon her wineglass tightened involuntarily.

That was odd. The obscure charlatan's name had come up twice now in a short space of time.

'No, I don't believe I do. He's clearly not a particle physicist or I would be very familiar with his work. No doubt he's running some commune in South America as we speak!'

She tried to laugh but for some reason it came out as a kind of grunt. Despite her superficial dismissal there was something disturbing in the conjunction of these two references. She shrugged it off and was searching for a new conversational topic when the Director rescued her.

'Hiromoto!' he said jovially, 'you really must stop monopolising Céline! There are other geniuses on my staff, you know. And there's still some smoked salmon!'

Takahashi gave a quick bow to Dubois and allowed himself to be whisked away into the chattering throng. Dubois watched him go, thinking that she had made a valuable contact. She would have to be careful about keeping him at arms' length, of course, but she was quite familiar with the necessary procedures. He would be a very useful rung on her ladder to greatness.

She drained the last of her wine and looked around at her so-called peers with a satisfied smile. Then just as she put her glass down on a nearby table a phrase rose unbidden into her mind:

Earth is a farm. We are property.

Seven

Dubois studied the reports about Larsen and his academic record. With slightly narrowed eyes, she read the documentation about the incident that had occurred earlier in the man's career.

There had been a research station near Alta in Norway and, as Larsen had said, there had been an accident during the preparation for the firing of an excimer laser. There had been an overload that had caused electrical discharges which had struck two men, Larsen himself and his assistant, a man called Einar Olsen. There was no report of ball lightning.

Both men had apparently recovered from the discharge with only superficial burns, although an odd aspect of the event was the total loss of all hair from their bodies. However, Olsen had died shortly afterwards but without any explanation for his demise being discovered in the autopsy.

Larsen had then been dismissed from his post of head scientist for breaching Health and Safety regulations and for inappropriate behaviour towards women.

Since then he had had no permanent position but had spent the intervening years going from job to job, each one being of lower status than the previous. True to his word, he had known the Director-General during the latter's time in Oslo, but despite being well-connected he had not been able to restore his position as one of Europe's foremost researchers.

Quite a sad story Dubois thought but then she closed the site down and leaned back in her chair.

The man was obviously an attention-seeker. He had been held in reasonably high regard in the fairly small world of particle research and then had thrown it all away through a moment's carelessness. And because of that, a man had died. Since then, it appeared, he had tried to deflect the blame by coming up with weird stories about invisible parasites. The very fact that he had chosen such a jaw-droppingly ridiculous story showed that he was well on the way to some kind of breakdown.

She shook her head, trying to imagine what it must have been like to have lost a high position and, more importantly, the respect and admiration of those who had been his peers.

Well, nothing like that was ever going to happen to her, she vowed. Nothing. Ever.

Her reflection in the computer screen stared impassively back at her as she leaned forward to put the machine into standby.

That was that. Never again would she waste any time considering the life and times of Marius Larsen. There were limits to compassion and he was well past those.

Her intercom gave a gentle buzz.

'Dr Dubois,' came Emilia's voice, 'Dr Krause is here to see you.'

Dubois rose as Krause came in and, holding her hands, guided her to a nearby chair.

'Hilda, good to see you,' she said softly, 'how are you now?'

Krause smiled up at her companion. 'I'm feeling fine now, Céline. Well, perhaps not fine exactly, but a lot better. And I've only been on the thyroxine for a short time.'

'Good to hear.'

Krause smiled again. 'I think everything is going to be alright now. I feel more energetic, more alive. It's like a big black cloud has lifted. I can see the world as it really is, a wonderful place, full of light!'

Dubois sat down next to her, reaching for her hands again. 'Wonderful, Hilda. The world is what we make it, never mind what the misery-mongers tell us!'

Krause gave her a coy little glance with a mischievous sparkle in her eyes.

'And Céline – perhaps it's time for one of our special nights again!'

Dubois smiled, a very broad, satisfied smile.

* * *

Dubois looked up at the medical doctor with a mixture of puzzlement, irritation and a touch of worry.

'What, are you sure? I don't have any other symptoms.'

The clinician gave a kindly smile which sent his eyebrows slightly above the rims of his spectacles.

'No doubt, I'm afraid Dr Dubois. You are definitely in a pre-diabetic state.'

Dubois thought rapidly, trying to find some benign explanation, some way out of this ridiculous news.

'But slightly blurred vision — surely that's just eye-strain? I do work long hours you know, and I spend a lot of time staring at those damned computer screens.'

Another kindly smile. 'Yes. I'm sure that's part of it. Look, I'm not saying you are a diabetic, I'm simply saying you are in the peri-diabetic state.'

'Explain.'

The clinician moved closer and for an unpleasant moment Dubois thought he was going to touch her but he merely sat down on the nearest chair.

'Blurred vision is certainly an indicator of diabetes. But obviously, blood tests are required to make a diagnosis. Your glucose levels are elevated at 150 milligrams per decilitre.'

'Meaning?'

'Dr Dubois - the reading is high but not outrageously so. You are at risk of diabetes, and you need to take some precautions. But there's no reason why you can't halt this trend. I see a lot of it in people who are basically sedentary; it's by no means uncommon.'

Sedentary.

The word seemed almost insulting as if she was some kind of bookworm instead of a high official. Of course, she spent a lot of time at the desk. What was she supposed to do – push the particles around by herself?

'Do you play any sports, doctor?' he asked.

Dubois looked back on her earlier life. She had been a keen tennis player in her younger days but as she had avidly sucked in more and more responsibilities, like a human black hole, her interest had dwindled and died.

'No, not really,' she finally said.

'Well, that's probably it,' he said, 'I'm not going to write you out a prescription at this stage, it's far too early to be thinking about metformin. Just try and get out of that chair more often and stretch those legs.' He smiled again. 'That's all, Doctor.'

Dubois left his consulting room with her thoughts swirling. *Pre-diabetic. Prescriptions. Get out of that chair.* Those were things that were said to *old* people, whose careers were winding down, not to thrusting, vital people like herself.

She felt a sudden pang at the realisation that there were other things in life than advancement and the collection of the glittering prizes of life; drab, drear things that surely only other people needed to worry about.

Not her.

She passed several people on the way back to her office. They acknowledged her but she did not reply, lost in her thoughts.

Back in her office she woke her computer from its sleep and stared at the text that was displayed. Were the letters a bit blurred?

She stared for some time and then was forced to admit it.

They *were* slightly fuzzy.

She put it back to sleep and drummed her strong fingers on the desk.

Pre-diabetes. Ghosts. Grey mists that were both there and not there.

Why was she faced with these issues that were not part of her normal responsibilities? In her usual work she had no doubts, no worries. She could out-think every one of these second-division types which this place seemed to be stuffed with. But this was different.

How could one out-think diabetes?

Then she felt ashamed, thinking of how she was becoming self-absorbed. Had not Hilda faced a similar problem and had she, Dubois, not been the strong one then, assuring her friend that everything would be alright?

Yet somehow it was easier to deal with other people's problems than one's own.

Unconsciously, she straightened herself in the chair and thought: *This is ridiculous. Get a grip, woman; there are far worse things than this that people have had to deal with.*

She strove to banish visions of disease and decay from her mind and pulled a folder towards her. It was the documentation about her forthcoming secondment to the ILC in Japan and eagerly she began going over the details. Not long now!

The second page gave a list of those who had been selected to spend some time there and she smiled at the sight of her own name and that of Hilda Krause. The smile faded somewhat as she studied the other names, which included, *inter alia*, Dwight Gregson.

There were a few other names which identified people she had had little to do with, giving a grand total of fifteen people – most of them run-of-the-mill seat warmers, in her humble opinion.

The rest of the documentation showed technical data about the ILC which she absorbed avidly. The last few pages were of glorious full-colour pictures of the gleaming machinery that comprised this great leap forward in the tools that humanity would use to unlock the last secrets of the universe. Each photograph had below it a little block of text describing the functions of the apparatus shown.

Dubois frowned – the text was unnecessarily small. Surely it was not time to adopt reading glasses?

She pushed the folder away, annoyed that her study of it had ended on a slightly sour note.

She sat for a while lost in her thoughts again, not all of which were pleasant, and then she pressed a button and said: 'Emilia, get me another bottle of my usual mineral water, please.'

* * *

The Director-General and Takahashi looked down from the dais at the assembled chosen few. The audio-visual presentation had just finished and now came the usual round of questions and answers.

Dubois made sure that she was the first to ask a question and, having received an answer, immediately went on to ask a question about the answer. Finally, satisfied that she had made her impression, she allowed the others present to ask their questions, secure in the knowledge that most of the significant statements had already been given to her.

The meeting broke up in a buzz of excited comments. Dubois watched them go, smiling at their evident excitement, almost as if they were teenagers going on their first holiday without their parents, she thought tolerantly.

She took her time about gathering her papers together, wondering if Takahashi would come down and speak to her.

And indeed he did.

'Good to see you again, Dr Dubois.'

'Céline.'

He smiled. 'Yes, of course, forgive me. I can see that you are very interested in our project.'

'More than interested, Dr Takahashi!'

'Hiromoto.'

She gave what she hoped was a girlish smile of gratitude. 'Thank you – Hiromoto.'

Takahashi gave a small bow to indicate his pleasure at the exchange of small intimacies.

There was an awkward silence and then he said: 'Are you a lover of good food, Céline?'

She nodded. 'Yes - I like all parts of classic French cuisine – Provençal as well, of course. I come from good peasant stock; you see!'

Takahashi nodded again but Dubois could see he didn't understand the intricacies of French regional identities.

'And Japanese cuisine?'

'I'm afraid I know very little about it, except what I've seen on documentaries.'

Almost imperceptibly, he had moved closer. 'Perhaps I could introduce you to some of our regional delicacies then, Céline.'

Dubois thought quickly: it was far too soon to offend this man; he would almost certainly be useful to her when she was in Japan. Far too soon...

'Yes,' she finally said, 'that sounds like a pleasant idea. As long as I can find time after all my new work, of course!' Almost imperceptibly, she reinstated the original distance between them.

'That will not be a problem for one as brilliant as you. The Director thinks very highly of you, you know.'

'That's – nice,' she replied. 'But I really must get back ...'

Takahashi held a hand. 'One moment, please. He was telling me of a special project you have been working on.'

Her mind whirled. *Special Project? What did the old bluffer mean by those words?*

Takahashi continued smoothly: 'In Shinto we have tales of demons, of spirits that descend from the elements to plague mankind. In Kitakami there is a museum of demons and the locals perform dances to propitiate them. I hear that you have been battling demons here too.'

She groaned inwardly. She did not want to be viewed as some kind of crazy ghost-hunter.

Damn the man for mentioning it!

'No, no,' she said, smiling as broadly as she could, 'it's

54

nothing. Nothing at all. Just some people can't handle the pressure of work and had some kind of nervous reaction. They saw things that weren't there, you know, or rather, misinterpreted what they had seen. It's all sorted now. All over.'

'So I don't have to worry about demons snatching me away while I'm here then, Céline?'

Dubois tried to generate an even broader smile. (*God, this was hard on the mouth muscles!*)

'No Hiromoto, no demons here; you have nothing to worry about. Nothing to worry about at all!'

Eight

Dubois stood, hand in hand with Krause and watched the lanterns drifting down the Kitakami River. It was a magical sight: lantern followed lantern after lantern, in a seemingly endless flotilla. The throng was so great that by looking up the river the women could see the lanterns merging into one seamless mass of softly glowing light. It was the last day of the Michinoku Performing Arts Festival which she and Krause had watched in open-mouthed wonder. Earlier they had witnessed the Onikenabai Dance, entranced by the performers in their colourful costumes, but somewhat alarmed by the hideous demon masks that the performers wore.

'They look so real!' Krause had said, unconsciously gripping Dubois's arm in her nervousness, 'Thank God, they are only masks!'

Dubois had been about to say something reassuring when one of the dancers had stopped directly in front of her and for a few moments she had found herself looking into a terrifying, scarlet face with staring eyes and bared fangs. Her heart had jumped as she found herself thinking: *What if you were real? What if you were real!*

But the dancer had moved on to complete his performance in the Demon Sword Dance, and the fear had evaporated.

And now she was by the banks of the river watching the lanterns drift by, and everything was warm and secure. There was nothing to fear; it was a world in which fear simply could not exist.

As she turned to Krause, her partner's face was suddenly lit up by a blaze of multicoloured light and a second or so later there was a loud crackling noise, coming from the sky.

They both looked up in time to see a vast explosion of

56

dancing sparks bloom in the dark sky like a gigantic, incandescent chrysanthemum.

'A fireworks display,' breathed Krause, 'Oh Céline, this is simply too wonderful!'

Indeed it was, thought Dubois. They had only been in Japan a few days and still felt like they were tourists at the beginning of a beautiful holiday.

The flight had been long but thankfully uneventful, with only one stop-over, in Qatar. *God, that had been hot!* And now here they were in the mystic land of the Rising Sun! Dubois found herself experiencing an unusual emotion: gratitude to the Director; gratitude for putting her name on the list of those to be seconded to the ILC.

The women stood there for some time, motionless with wonder at the celestial display which seemed never-ending. Just when they were certain that it had indeed finally ended, the whole sky seemed to erupt into a scintillating cascade of every colour the human eye could visualise, forming flowers and streamers of swirling beauty.

After a moment of awestruck silence, Dubois turned to Krause and said, 'Hilda, this is simply too good to be true. I can't think of what I've done to deserve it.'

Krause gave her a quick hug. 'Just by being you, Céline. Just by being you!'

And with that they left the site to return to their hotel.

* * *

The first few days at the International Linear Collider were like a dream come true for Dubois. In a state of near-permanent excitement she was shown around the workings of the tremendous complex; marvelling at the colossal pipes which would soon contain the speeding protons, gazing enraptured at the huge disc of steel which fronted the muon detector. Sometimes she had the feeling that she was wandering lost through the steel intestines of a great metal giant; a giant which was now slumbering but soon would wake to active consciousness.

And when the giant awoke what things would he discover! Now, finally Nature would have to admit that she had met her match in the massed intellects of Homo sapiens at its finest, and slowly, reluctantly at first but with ever increasing alacrity, would reveal what lay beyond the veil of ignorance and bring all the hitherto hidden mysteries into the searchlight of human reason. Mysteries no more!

As Dubois stared at the vast cliffs of steel which surrounded and dwarfed her, she wondered what the world would be like when there were no more mysteries, no more secrets, when humanity finally had the answers to the things that had troubled it since the first anthropoid had lifted its dull eyes to the stars. What would people like her do then?

She smiled a secret smile to herself: that would be their problem; she had no intention of holding back her probing. Come what may, that veil would be lifted and what lay beyond brought into the light - she vowed it!

The people who had been seconded from CERN formed a little tightly bound group at first in those early days. Gradually they would drift apart, they all knew, as they took up differing posts in the normal running of the ILC.

Dubois found herself being friendly, talkative even, with her fellow secondees. They were like students from the same year who had been brought together on some shared training course. At present no rivalry had developed; but it assuredly would.

Those who knew Dubois were pleasantly surprised by her unexpected openness and even tried to laugh at her laboured jokes. Those who did not know her well, simply took her as a slightly awkward but essentially good-natured co-worker.

And so the days wore on.

She and Krause spent much time together, exploring the neighbourhood. Both liked the verdant exuberance of Tenshochi

Park and hoped that they would still be working at the ILC come the springtime so they could wonder at its cherry blossoms. However, they did not stay long at the Demon Museum for Krause found the representations of the creatures strangely disturbing.

Gradually the great complex prepared itself for the first firing of the accelerator, like a titanic beast of prey tensing its muscles to spring upon its quarry. Tension hung in the air like the rising electrical potential before a thunderstorm and Dubois's CERN colleagues noticed that her newfound light-heartedness seemed to be deserting her, as her conversation became ever terser and more detached.

Then the day before the first firing, Dubois and Krause were sitting in the huge communal dining area, enjoying their lunch, when Dubois suddenly stiffened and, putting her fork down, said: 'I don't believe it! What is he doing here!'

Krause followed her gaze and, seeing no-one she recognised, meekly said: 'Who, Céline?'

'That madman Larsen, that's who. Oh, Good God – he's coming over!'

Krause stared in something approaching wonder as a huge, utterly hairless man came to their table and smiled down at them.

'Céline! Marvellous to see you again! And who is this charming young lady?'

Dubois was infuriated to see Krause flash Larsen a radiant smile and was about to snap a rebuff when Krause said: 'I'm Hilda, Hilda Krause. And you must be - Marius Larsen, I believe. Céline has told me about you.'

Larsen sat, without waiting for an invitation, the chair creaking alarmingly as it fought to support his not inconsiderable weight.

'Oh, no,' he said, grinning, 'I'd better be on my way then if Céline has told you about me!'

'Oh no, mister Larsen, Dr Larsen', Krause continued with what could only be described as a girlish giggle, 'you couldn't possibly be as bad as … I mean, you can't be…'

She spluttered into silence.

Larsen threw his head back and laughed a throaty laugh which was like a distant thunderclap. 'Oh, but I am. I'm completely mad.' He rolled his eyes theatrically and spun a forefinger around his temple. 'But I'm not dangerous. I'm just a pussy cat.'

And to Dubois's horrified indignation he reached over and gave Krause's thigh a friendly pat.

Dubois could stand no more. 'What the hell are you doing here, Larsen?' she hissed.

'Céline…' Krause began to say but she was waved into silence.

'Just looking around,' he replied, 'I'm very impressed.'

'You've no right to be here,' Dubois continued stonily, 'you're not a research scientist now, if you ever were, that is. How did you get here?'

Larsen seemed to have an inexhaustible supply of grins and he produced another, seemingly unmoved by his frosty reception.

'Oh, I know Hiromoto. We go a long way back.'

'Don't tell me,' Dubois groaned, 'you and he were drinking buddies in Tokyo.'

'You're not far off – Osaka actually. And I'm here by his personal invitation.'

'What as? Some kind of mascot?'

Larsen smiled, a strange, tired smile. 'Céline, Céline, don't you get tired of all this gall, this bitterness? You have this terrible drive to be superior to everyone else. You are so very sure of yourself, of your position, of your future. But there is much you have not experienced. You have not yet realised that all of us, every single one of us, are walking on a thin layer of ice over a deep lake of pain.'

'I don't need fortune cookie philosophy from you, Larsen, thank you. I can afford to wait until Chinese New Year and then

60

I can get all the homespun homilies I could possibly need.'

Larsen looked at her directly, in a gaze which Dubois found she could not break.

'Are you an admirer of Shakespeare, Céline?'

'No, I found his paper on muon decay somewhat simplistic.'

'A facile jibe, Céline, and not worthy of you. I recommend that you study his *Hamlet* and meditate upon the famous comment of the eponymous hero to Horatio. And with that, ladies, I bid you a good day.'

When Larsen's immense bulk had passed safely out of earshot Krause turned to Dubois and said, 'Céline! Why were you so horrible to him! I found him quite charming.'

Dubois shrugged, feeling an odd sense of guilt. 'The man is deranged. He says he's not dangerous but with his build I don't trust him. He's too weird, too outré.'

'In what way? He is a physicist, I believe.'

Dubois hesitated. She had not mentioned Larsen's incredible beliefs to anyone else, least of all Krause, and she saw no reason to share his delusions now.

She leaned over and touched her companion's hand. 'You'll just have to trust me, Hilda. He said things to me which prove beyond doubt that he is a lunatic. He had some kind of breakdown in Norway a few years ago in which a man died because of his carelessness and I think the memory of that terrible event has driven him more than a little mad. Let's leave it at that, shall we, dear?'

Krause looked doubtful. 'Alright, Céline,' she finally said, 'if you say so then, of course, I will accept what you say.' She looked across the sunlit dining area where Larsen's bulk was still visible in the distance. 'But he did seem such a nice man.'

* * *

The great day of the firing had finally arrived. The assembled physicists had been as young children on Christmas Eve, waiting

61

for the magic to occur, willing the time away. But deep below the surface of the massive complex, tremendous energies had awoken and gargantuan magnetic fields had snapped into existence; fields so powerful that no biological entity could be anywhere near their unshielded might.

A beam of protons was generated, and each proton instantly obeyed the urgent demands of the magnetic force and began their mad flight along the confining torus.

More and more energy was pumped into them and gradually their speed increased; gradually, inexorably, ineluctably. Faster and faster they flew; their velocity coming nearer and nearer to the impenetrable barrier of c, the speed of light itself.

And then they met another torrent of subatomic particles coming towards them at the identical speed!

Most of the protons from both populations passed each other by, harmlessly.

But a few, a miniscule fraction of the total, met each other in a point to point collision. And in that collision both were utterly destroyed, flashing into quanta of hard radiation and a torrent of energetic, ultramicroscopic debris, spiralling in all directions into the waiting detectors.

Of the survivors, their reprieve was only temporary: they would circle again and again until either they collided head-on with their brethren, or the controllers would decide they had learned enough and they would be discarded.

Dubois stood there in the control room watching the data scrolling upwards, disappearing at the top of the monitor to be replaced by later information surfacing at the bottom. The quality of her vision did not seem to have deteriorated and she found she was able to compensate by standing a little closer to the screens than the others. None of them dared to challenge that privilege: she had already begun to make her mark. As they stood like acolytes around a shrine the monitors cast ever-changing patterns of coloured light and shade over the earnest faces of the scientists.

'There,' she said, tapping the screen with an expertly manicured fingernail.

'Where?' said Williamson, an obese, sweaty Englishman she had already learned to detest, 'I don't see anything.' He looked again at the monitor that was displaying the wildly curving tracks of the particles which had been caught in the act of fleeing from the nanoscale collisions.

She suppressed an annoyed sigh. 'Look, Peter,' she said as patiently as she could, 'there's a very faint track there.'

The others crowded in, and finally one of them said, 'Yes! I see it! What the hell can that be?'

She turned to face them. 'It's why we're here. It looks like a new one to me. One with a very high mass.'

Williamson said, breathily: 'A Majorana fermion?'

'Don't be ridiculous!' she snapped, 'how could it be with that energy? If Majorana particles exist they're almost certainly neutrinos!'

She felt a flush of satisfaction flood her veins. There would have to be weeks of study, of course. The experiment would be run again and again to make sure the results were repeatable - the gold standard of the scientific method. Only after much checking to eliminate the possibility of wishful thinking would any announcement be made.

But she had seen it first! She had been the one to notice the anomaly in the wild medley of particle tracks.

She!

'I don't know about you,' she said, giving them a view of her best smile – a look which they would come to learn would not be granted to them very often, 'but I think we deserve a drink!'

As she stood in the bar a few minutes later, she sipped her Chablis and thought: *Everything is going the way I envisaged it. God bless the Director for sending me here; I forgive him everything!*

It was then she saw Larsen standing at the other end of the room and as she caught his eye, he lifted his glass to her in an insolent greeting.

She scowled.

Damn the man! Why did he have to be here!

Nine

Dubois sat at her private desk poring over the particle track printouts, occasionally switching her gaze to the dense columns of real numbers which accompanied them.

The answer was here! She knew it was.

All she had to do was...

Her red-rimmed eyes flashed as she heard the knock at the door.

Why couldn't Takahashi hurry up and get her a secretary – having to answer to people banging on the door was simply too much!

'Go away!' she yelled, 'I'm busy!'

'Oh, I'm sorry Céline, I didn't mean to ...'

Dubois jumped up and went to the door.

'Hilda! I'm sorry, I didn't know it was you,' she said hurriedly as she yanked the door open and ushered the worried-looking Krause in.

'I know you're busy, Céline,' the latter said in a dispirited voice, 'but you're always busy these days. We haven't been anywhere or done anything for ages.'

'I didn't mean to sound so unpleasant,' Dubois said, taking both of Krause's hands in hers, 'here, sit down a moment and talk to me.'

Krause obeyed but having taken a good look at her companion she said, 'Goodness, Céline, you look awful.'

Dubois felt a momentary flicker of irritation but fought it back down. *No, no tantrums with Hilda, not with her!*

'Well thanks,' was all she said, softening it with a weak smile. 'I love you too.'

'No, no, sorry Céline, I didn't mean ... it's just your eyes – they're so tired-looking.'

65

Dubois shrugged. 'I'm afraid there's something a little bit wrong with my vision. I'm getting a bit short-sighted, so I have to press my nose up against the printouts. It's only old age. Comes to us all!'

Krause removed her hands from Dubois's grip and gave Dubois's fingers a small kiss.

'You must slow down, Céline. It's like your trying to do the whole research all by yourself.'

That's because that is exactly what I am doing, thought Dubois – but she could not admit it.

'Alright, you win' she finally said, 'let's go into town tonight and have a few drinks. Just like old times.'

'Just like old times,' Krause repeated, 'I didn't think we'd got that far out of touch.'

Dubois tried to smile again, but in her tiredness she found it oddly difficult.

'We haven't, Hilda, you'll see.'

* * *

The bar was crowded with about an equal number of Occidentals and Japanese, plus a scattering of Chinese and Koreans. Dubois found the din extremely wearing.

Krause had foolishly ordered some sake and found she didn't like it while Dubois was sipping umeshu, having decided that the Japanese wines were not up to her exacting standards.

She made a decision and leaned forward so that Krause could hear her above the chatter and said, 'I'm sorry, Hilda, but I don't think I want to stay much longer. It's too noisy here. for me.'

Krause looked disappointed. 'Oh, Céline, I was just starting to enjoy myself. Could we go back to my place then?'

Dubois was torn. She had never turned down an invitation from Krause before. Surely she couldn't?

She essayed another smile. 'I'm very sorry, Hilda, but I'm

really exhausted. Some other time, perhaps?'

Krause gave a little moue of disappointment and was about to say something when they were both aware that another had joined them. Dubois turned to find Williamson had sat down next to her. She could smell the sweat and alcohol on him from where she sat.

'Evening ladies,' he slurred, slapping an overfull glass on the table 'you were looking lonely, so I decided to join you.'

'What do you want, Williamson,' she snapped, 'we were just leaving!'

'No, no, don't be silly, the night is young. Hilda, another drink, sake is it?'

Krause put her hand over her glass. 'No, no thanks, Peter. I don't really like it.'

Williamson seemed incapable of taking hints and simply nodded, running his hands through his thinning sandy hair as he did so.

'Well, how are you girls finding it here? Made any discoveries today?' He leaned forward. 'I made a discovery – there's a bar a few streets away where the drinks are half the price of this place!'

Dubois said nothing and made a little motion of her head in Krause's direction to indicate that it was time to go. But Krause did not notice and apparently thought it was her duty to be polite to the man.

'Oh, well Peter, I'm not really a drinker. To be perfectly honest I'm happy with a fruit juice.'

Williamson seemed to find that hilarious and rocked back in his chair so far that he seemed in imminent danger of toppling backwards.

'Yeah, right – a German who doesn't drink! Now I've heard it all!' He steadied the chair, belched, and then leaned forward. Dubois's face wrinkled as alcohol-laden breath washed over her. 'Hey, do you know Velasquez has gone missing?' he continued.

'Who is Velasquez and why should I care about him?'

Dubois said and began to stand. To her horror, Williamson held her arm and prevented her from rising.

'You know, Luis Velasquez. Looks like a Mexican drug baron. Slicked back hair, thin moustache like a shoelace stuck to his face!'

Dubois admitted that she had seen him in the crowd but that was all.

'He's gone missing. So what? Maybe he discovered you need more than high school algebra in this place and scurried back to Madrid, or wherever he comes from.'

Williamson reached for his drink, failed to grasp it properly and knocked it over. Ignoring the spreading patch of spirit on the table he continued: 'No, he's really gone, vanished, disappeared. His room has all his stuff in it. No-one saw him leave. The police have no record of him. It's like – like – I don't know - he just evaporated!'

'He's probably in some brothel somewhere,' Dubois snapped, and this time succeeded in standing up, 'who cares?'

'Brothel? There's a brothel in this dump? Hey, can you take me there, girls!' Williamson said, and finding the idea hilarious, broke into loud guffaws that were audible even over the general hubbub.

But Dubois was already walking away with Krause in tow.

But as they reached the exit, Dubois heard him yell: 'Disappeared! Bloody disappeared! Just like you two bitches!'

* * *

Dubois became aware that someone had come into her room almost silently and was now standing behind her. She turned to find Hiromoto Takahashi standing behind her with an oddly nervous smile distorting his features.

'Oh, Hiromoto,' she said with a slight sense of relief, 'I didn't realise you were there.'

He bowed. 'Humble apologies, Céline. I did not intend to

alarm you. I just wanted to know how things are progressing.'

She relaxed and indicated that he should take a look at the charts on her desk.

'It's early days, Hiromoto,' she said, 'but there is definitely something beginning to appear in the data. No-one in the world has ever probed these energy levels before so we are true pioneers. And the ILC is capable of so much more. Soon we will be reaching unheard of energy levels, and then Mother Nature will have to accept that we've finally beaten her!'

Takahashi leaned over the printouts but Dubois was puzzled to see that he was not studying them in any great detail and was shifting from one printout to the next without comment. Finally, he swept them all together and assembled them into a single stack. Turning back to her he said: 'You are doing wonderful work here, Céline. The Director-General did not exaggerate when he described you as one of the sharpest minds of this generation of physicists.'

Although she accepted that judgement merely as a plain statement of fact, she tried to look pleased and grateful.

Takahashi seemed to be struggling with his words but eventually he said: 'Céline, it is a custom of mine to try to get to know my esteemed colleagues on a more personal basis. That way I find we can all work together more harmoniously. Would you do me the honour of having dinner with me tonight?'

Dubois's thoughts tumbled over each other in a confused jumble for a moment. The invitation had been wholly unexpected and for an instant, she did not know how to react.

'Tonight? Well, Hiromoto, that's very kind but I really… I really…' She turned around and picked up one of the printouts at random. 'I really must do a significance test on these data.'

But Takahashi was unabashed. Having come so far, it did not seem that he was prepared to retreat.

'Some time later in the week, then? Come, Céline, I make this offer to all my first rank staff.'

Dubois decided that further prevarication would not be in

her long-term interest. In all probability, the invitation was just what Takahashi said it was.

She did her best to summon up a smile and said: 'Of course, Hiromoto. I'd be delighted.'

The next morning, the day of the dinner appointment, Dubois and the other secondees from CERN were standing in the central control room watching the energy levels being traced out as a rapidly rising green curve on the monitor screens.

'Keep going, my beauty,' she said to herself. But it appeared that she had spoken more loudly than she had believed for Gregson turned to her and said, 'Well, well, so you do have emotions after all, Céline. I was beginning to wonder why the Ice Maiden wasn't melting in all the heat coming off this equipment.'

Annoyed at having been overheard, she did not bother to turn to look at him but merely said in a studiously neutral tone, 'Gregson, don't you have some little plastic soldiers you could be playing with?'

He found no reply to that and she smiled a satisfied smile.

That smile vanished almost immediately as she saw the green curve suddenly stop its hitherto relentless rise, shudder momentarily, and then plunge downwards.

'Merde!' she snapped as a howl of disappointment rose from her colleagues.

'What happened?' Krause asked plaintively.

'Bleeding energy into synchrotron radiation, obviously,' Dubois snapped again, 'Shit! Shit! And we were nearly there!'

She had a quick word with some of the technicians and came back stony-faced.

'They've had to shut it down while they find the leak,' she told the assembled physicists, 'We won't be doing anymore today.'

Another groan rose from the crowd except for Williamson who looked around and said, 'Well, that's that! I'm going to the bar. Who's coming with me?'

The control room emptied rapidly and Dubois found herself

alone with Krause, who gave a weak smile and said timidly, 'I'm sorry about that, Céline. I know you had a lot riding on this one.'

'No-one's fault, Hilda. Except perhaps those useless technicians.'

She was wondering whether she should launch a search for culprits when she realised that Krause was speaking again.

'So what shall we do tonight then, Céline?'

With a start she realised that Krause had not been told of the dinner appointment and, somewhat sheepishly, she turned to her companion and said: 'Well, nothing, I'm afraid Hilda. I'm having dinner with Hiromoto this evening.'

'Hiromoto? Dr Takahashi? I hadn't realised you were on familiar terms with him.'

Dubois held Krause's shoulders and looked her full in the face.

'It's just a routine thing, Hilda. He does it with all the top staff.'

Krause did not look at all mollified.

'He hasn't asked me.'

* * *

Dubois was relieved to see that the cutlery was European as she sat down at the table. The dishes which the servant brought in were almost entirely unfamiliar to her but Takahashi took her through what was being deposited on the table. There was a preponderance of rice, of course, coupled with bowls of miso soup. There was a fish broth called "oden", he explained, and there was plenty of seafood and vegetables deep-fried in a light batter.

Dubois's sophisticated palate found little that she did not approve of and gave a secret smile at the vision of someone like Gregson sitting at this table and lamenting the lack of hamburgers.

Takahashi was speaking.

71

'I am glad that you like our cuisine, Céline. Many Westerners know nothing of our food except mass-produced sushi.'

She took a sip of her wine, which she was pleased to find was French.

'I always do my best to fit in with foreign cultures, Hiromoto. I find that is the only respectful way to behave.'

He gave a nod of appreciation.

'Thank you, Céline. I realised as soon as I met you that you are a sophisticated lady. Tell me, when did you realise that you wanted a career in physics?'

She thought for a moment. Her thirst for knowledge was such an integral part of her being that she had never really wondered why she had that need.

'I'm not sure. I was always very good at mathematics but I think from an early age I knew that I didn't want to be a mathematician. Creating all those abstract worlds held no appeal to me. I wanted to use my talent to find out what this world is made of; what lies at the bottom of reality; what its foundations are.'

Takahashi nodded. 'I feel exactly the same way. I believe we have a lot in common, Céline.'

Dubois took another spoonful of oden and gave a polite nod.

'Tell me, Céline, do you find that your work gives you much time for personal matters?'

She tensed slightly. 'I don't give that side of things much consideration, Hiromoto.'

Takahashi spoke again, in a wistful, tired voice. 'I used to think like that, Céline. But when my wife died, my view of what is important changed profoundly.'

She desperately wondered how she could pull this conversation back into neutral waters.

'I'm sorry to hear of your loss,' she finally said.

'It was pancreatic cancer,' he said, looking down at his plate. 'Very sudden. Very sudden.'

'Once again, I'm sorry to hear that.'

He looked up abruptly. 'Do you not think perhaps there is more to life than equations and graphs and electron-volt measurements?'

She decided that she had made a mistake in accepting this invitation and she could not persist in a deception which could only end in hurting this man.

'Hiromoto,' she said, very softly, 'I am spoken for.'

He became motionless for a brief instant and then he said: 'I am sorry. I did not know that. I did not intend to embarrass you.'

She gave a quick, and completely genuine, smile.

'That's fine, Hiromoto. And you are right – there are things just as important as physics.'

He looked relieved at her tone and the conversation slowly drifted back into the work-related issues.

The servant removed most of the items from the table and bowed when Dubois turned down the offer of another bottle of wine.

Feeling much more relaxed, Dubois said, 'That was a truly wonderful meal, Hiromoto. You must find little time to do this kind of thing with all your responsibilities.'

He nodded. 'That is true. But my problems are not all to do with synchrotron radiation bleeds.'

'And what other problems do you have?'

'Staffing problems.'

'Oh, what kind?'

He fixed her attention with a worried, piercing gaze.

'People are disappearing.'

Ten

An odd chill seemed to have fallen over the dining room. For some reason which she could not fathom, Dubois felt the hairs on her neck rise slightly as if an unseen peril had just entered and was silently circling them.

'Disappeared?' was all she could say, 'I don't quite follow, Hiromoto. You mean they haven't been seen for a while? Surely that's not unusual with these highly-strung scientists. Quite a few of them are more than a little odd if you ask me.'

Takahashi gave a small frown to indicate that he had not approved of Dubois's comments, which she had instantly regretted. 'No, Céline, I do not mean that they have simply neglected their duties. Two people have not been seen for some weeks and are nowhere to be found on the ILC Complex. Their quarters show no signs of any preparation for departure, and in both cases their personal belongings are untouched. Items which anyone simply leaving would have taken with them are still there; family pictures, for instance.'

'And who are these people? – Just in case I can help.'

'Luis Velasquez and Jan Nieuwpoort.'

Her brow furrowed. Velasquez she knew about but now there was another one.

She wanted to help and almost desperately tried to think of something useful she could say. But after a minute or two of searching, she shook her head and said: 'I'm sorry Hiromoto but I don't know anything about them or their personal circumstances.'

'No, of course not. I shouldn't have mentioned it. I shouldn't have troubled you. Let's talk of other things.'

And both parties tried to talk of other things: of physics; cosmology; the limits of human understanding.

But their talk seemed pointless; too ethereal; too abstract, and when the end of the evening came Dubois was glad of it.

* * *

The leak took longer to fix than Dubois had expected and for many days she had nothing to do but go over the reports that had been drawn up on the data which had been received immediately prior to the breakdown.

She cursed several times as she went over them. There had unquestionably been signs of something new in the spray of particles that had exploded from the proton-proton collisions. There was something there just beyond reach. Only a few more data points and she would have caught that new particle in the net cast by her powerful mind. She would have dragged it up from the depths of ignorance and mystery and held its struggling form up into the light.

So carried away was she with the vision she had conjured up that she triumphantly whispered, 'Got you!' as she held up her empty hands.

Then her desk intercom buzzed, shattering the delicious dream.

'Yes?' she snapped; in English for her new Japanese secretary spoke no French.

'Dr Dubois. There is someone to see you.'

'What an unexpected pleasure!' she snapped, 'Just send the visitor in, Watanabe.'

'Dr Dubois…' There was a note of tension in Watanabe's electronic voice.

'What now?'

'Dr Dubois – it's the police.'

The police? What could they possibly want?

She shrugged. She had nothing to fear.

'Just send them in,' she repeated.

The door opened and a very short, balding man came in and

75

introduced himself as Inspector Nakamura.

'I am honoured to meet you, Dr Dubois,' he said in heavily accented English.

She waved at the chair in front of her desk and sat down herself.

'I am a very busy woman, Inspector. Shall we just get to the point.'

He nodded. 'Of course; I am also very busy. The Director has asked me to investigate some events on this complex.'

'Specifically?'

'Missing persons.'

Dubois frowned but all she said was 'Oh. I had heard a rumour that a few people had gone home.'

'We don't think they've gone home, Ms Dubois.'

'Dr Dubois.'

He nodded. 'Of course. No, their disappearance seems more disturbing than that, doctor.'

'In what way?'

'No-one in any of the cases saw them go. No-one said good-bye to them. There was no indication from any of them that they were unhappy or that some incident in their home countries had required them to leave. Their rooms still contain most of their clothes and all of their private possessions.'

'I see. Strange I agree. But why are you talking to me about it? Velasquez and that Nieuwpoort person. I honestly don't know them.'

Nakamura nodded as if in approval of the statement, but he went on: 'No doubt that is true, doctor. But I am not talking about those revered gentlemen although they form part of my study. I am investigating a more recent disappearance - that of Dr Marius Larsen.'

Dubois gave a slight start at that unexpected name but then she relaxed and smiled.

'That's easy to explain, Inspector. Larsen had no official role here. I believe it was purely a personal visit at the invitation of

76

the Director. He must have tired of watching other people working, discovering things, while he stood around like a shopfront mannequin. It must have been very disheartening for someone who once had a career of his own.'

'No, doctor. I regret you are missing the point. If he had left in any normal way there would be a record of his method of departure – unless you are suggesting he swam back to Norway.'

Dubois flushed angrily. She was not used to being patronised.

'I repeat: why are you talking to me?'

'I accept that you did not know the honourable gentlemen you referred to earlier. But you did know Dr. Larsen.'

'Hardly. I knew something of his work – such as it was. He came to see me in Switzerland. Then he joined my friend and me at the lunch table – completely uninvited, I might add. And then he left.'

'Yet it was observed that you had been arguing with him. That you were somewhat – how shall I say in English – somewhat aggressive to him.'

'Aggressive? Who said that?'

Nakamura remained silently impassive.

It suddenly occurred to Dubois that she might be under some kind of investigation. She threw up her hands and tried to laugh. 'Aggressive? *Moi?* Have you seen the man? He's like a walking mountain!'

'His physique is not the issue. It remains true that you were one of the last people to have any kind of social contact with him, and that contact was not friendly.'

Now she was outraged. She leaned forward.

'What? Are you suggesting that I murdered him? Bludgeoned him to death with a computer printout? Forced him to swallow positronium?'

'If you look back over my words, doctor, you will note that I have made no accusation against you. It might have been the case that he was telling you that he intended to leave Japan and

77

you, in an upset state, were remonstrating with him.'

She leaned back again. 'No. I have no detailed memory of that very brief meeting but as I recall he was his usual boorish self. And he was showing my friend some unwanted familiarity. I am not concerned about people not showing me the respect that goes with my position but bad manners to my friend – that I will not tolerate.'

Nakamura remained silent for a while and then said slowly. 'Very well. It appears that you are unable to – what do you say – throw some light on this problem. Which is a pity.'

'It is a pity, but I regret that I cannot help you. I have nothing more to say on the matter.'

He bowed his head briefly and stood up. Even when he was fully standing their eyes were almost on a level and he asked quietly: 'Dr Dubois, I take it that you have no plans to leave Japan?'

Her eyes returned his gaze steadily, unwaveringly. 'None whatsoever. I have much to do here and I will not return to Europe until I am ready to take the results of my studies with me.'

He bowed fully and left.

Dubois gazed at the door he had just shut and thought deeply.

Something was wrong here.

She had tried to ignore these fleeting concerns, but she now had the feeling that, behind some kind of veil, powerful, unknown forces were gathering their full strength, their full potency.

Some kind of climax was being foreshadowed, as when high cirrus clouds warn of the approach of the thunder.

For some reason that she could never explain, she turned her head and looked searchingly into the shadows that lay heavy in the corner of her room.

'Whatever it is you're planning, no more delays,' she said softly, 'let's see what you can do.'

There was no reply from the shadows.

Eleven

Dubois was in high spirits. The day of the restarting of the great accelerator was surely approaching fast. It could be seen in the smiling faces of the scientists, both the native Japanese and the visitors from elsewhere.

There was an excited buzz of conversation in the air as if a new term at University had begun and people who had not seen each other for months were re-establishing old friendships.

And there was no greater friendship to be re-established than that between the scientists and the gigantic collider which they both commanded and served.

Not that it had been entirely silent in the past two months, of course. It had been run at progressively higher energies to see if the haemorrhaging of its energies into synchrotron radiation would reappear.

Gradually, gradually, as the weeks had passed the energies had approached the level at which serious discoveries could begin again.

Soon the Director, she had willed, would issue the command and the protons would obey the invisible urging of the magnetic pulses and flash down the tunnels at speeds closer and closer to that of light!

And now, finally, the Director had assembled them all in the Conference Hall and confirmed that tomorrow was the day.

Anticipation seemed to crackle in the air.

'I would now like you to split into your Work Groups and prepare your plans for full operation. As usual, we will give priority to Work Group A.'

There was a very faint groan at that announcement which, faint though it was, Dubois heard and gave a small, secret smile.

Work Group A was hers, of course.

The briefing ended and the group broke up into individuals, all seeking their Work Group colleagues.

Dubois had been so enthralled by the prospect of resuming her searches that it was not until that moment that she realised that she had not seen her companion at all during the morning. She looked around the rapidly emptying Conference Hall, expecting to see Krause's slender form revealed as the crowd thinned.

But Krause was not so revealed and when there were only a few people left in the room, Dubois was forced to accept that she was not present.

How odd.

Krause usually shared Dubois's excitement at the challenges of discovery.

She had not missed an important announcement like this before.

How odd.

Then with a sudden stab of worry, she thought: *She must be ill!*

She hurried down the seemingly endless corridors to Krause's office and, brushing past Krause's secretary, burst into her room.

It was empty and looked like nothing had been touched all day. Her computer screen was black and silent. There were no coffee stained cups anywhere.

She burst back out and, almost accusingly, demanded: 'Where is Dr Krause?'

The secretary looked up at her and said, 'Dr Krause has not reported in today, Dr Dubois.'

An icy lance of fear stabbed into Dubois's heart.

* * *

They were all sat in a small interview room. Dubois, Takahashi, Nakamura and two men Dubois had never seen

81

before. Two days had passed since Dubois had last seen Krause. A thorough search of the complex had not discovered her.

There was no sign of her at any of the transport stations serving the area.

A CCTV search in Kitakami City had not shown her.

Dubois stood up, unconsciously wringing her hands together.

'She must be somewhere,' she said in a broken voice, 'she can't have just vanished. That's not physically possible!'

'We have searched thoroughly,' Takahashi said quietly, 'I assure you, doctor, we have searched every square centimetre.'

'That's simply stupid hyperbole!' Dubois snapped, 'and you know it! She must be somewhere on this site. If we can't find her it must because someone is hiding her; someone is holding her captive. There can't be many places where that could be done.'

'I assure you we have looked,' Takahashi said stolidly. 'And we will continue to look until we find her.'

Nakamura looked up from studying his fingernails. 'Dr Dubois, did Dr Krause have any enemies here?'

'Any enemies!' Dubois cried, 'Of course not! She was completely without malice. No-one could have disliked her. She was... she was...'

Dubois slumped back on her chair and put her head on a hand. 'She was my love.'

Nakamura nodded. 'I did not think the lady could have any enemies. But it was necessary that I ask in order to remove the possibility of – what do you say? – foul play.'

There was silence. All those present stared at nothing for some time and then Nakamura said quietly: 'We have a possible sighting.'

Dubois and Takahashi turned to look at him.

'What? Where?' Dubois asked.

Nakamura turned to the two hitherto silent men. 'Tell us your story.'

'Wait,' said Dubois, 'who are these two? I don't recognise

82

them.'

The nearest, a gaunt man, who was tall for a Japanese, said, 'I am Akihito Okada and this is my brother, Haruchika. We are technicians working on the confinement fields on the lowest level of the collider.'

'And you saw, Hilda – Dr Krause?' Dubois said, leaning forward eagerly.

'We did. Dr Krause had asked us to check whether there was a physical tear in the metal of Pipe Blue 45. We took her down to that level and she spent some time examining the cylinder. After some time we had a call asking us to go to another task. And so we called out to Dr Krause and began to run away.'

'You began to run away? That's a strange way of putting it,' Dubois commented.

'Forgive. English is not our first language. To say again, we were walking away when we felt something in the air.'

'What?'

The speaker looked at his brother and said: 'You say it.'

Haruchika took up the story. 'We felt a disturbance. Our hair stood up like a frightened cat. It was as if we were in a powerful electrical field. Everything seemed to be happening slowly.'

'Dr Krause? Dr Krause?' Dubois urged.

'We looked back down the corridor to where we had left her. We could not see her.'

'You couldn't see her? The corridor was empty in such a short time?'

'We could not see the esteemed doctor. But we could see something else.'

'And that was?'

Haruchika looked at his brother as if seeking permission to continue, then he turned back to the others.

'We could see that the corridor was filled with a mist. A strange grey mist.'

Dubois felt as if she had been punched in the stomach. She

83

cried out and almost crashed from her chair. Takahashi rushed to her to prevent her toppling to the floor.

She looked around, seeing nothing, hearing nothing except a roar of blood in her head.

For the first time in her life she felt real, gut-wrenching, existential fear.

She had succeeded in confining her own inexplicable experience to her subconscious and had not thought about it for months.

Now it had coming roaring back, screaming: *You did not imagine me! I am real, real, real!*

'Dr Dubois, are you alright?' Takahashi gasped, cradling her head so it did not fall onto her chest.

She did not answer but turned wide, staring eyes to him; the eyes of a frightened, hunted animal.

'I'll get her some water,' Nakamura said, leaping to his feet. He came back a few minutes later and Dubois gratefully sipped the water, tepid though it was.

'What is it, Céline?' Takahashi whispered, shaken by what he could see in her eyes.

With a mighty effort she calmed her screaming thoughts and stood up.

'There is something wrong here; terribly, horribly wrong. Some danger that I don't understand is lose in this complex.'

'Lose?' Takahashi said, his brow furrowed, 'I don't understand. Some animal? There is nothing dangerous in Japan.'

She began to walk back and forth in front of her puzzled audience.

'The grey mist. It has been seen before.'

Nakamura looked down as his tablet, ready to start typing. 'By whom?' he said.

'By me. I saw it at CERN. When people were disappearing there.'

Nakamura typed furiously and then, looking up, he said, 'Are you suggesting that the kidnappers are using some kind of

84

smoke screen, a form of camouflage, to hide?'

Dubois nodded. 'It must be something like that.'

'But, doctor,' Nakamura continued, 'your idea doesn't explain how the kidnappers can get away unseen. No grey mists have been seen on the surface. The mystery remains.'

Dubois sat back down and gulped the water.

There was more to this than she wanted to accept. Nakamura was right. What she had seen could not be the whole answer.

He was speaking again.

'It seems to me that there is a common feature to these happenings, which none of you, despite your brilliance, have observed.'

Stung by his words, Dubois snapped: 'And what is that?'

'The common feature is the operation of powerful particle accelerators. You know your scientific method, honourable doctors. If something is common to all the appearances of the phenomenon then it is at least a part of the cause of the phenomenon.'

Dubois reluctantly nodded; she had, after all, reached the same conclusion herself, although she had not permitted that thought to intrude on her waking mind.

Nakamura continued: 'Therefore I have a recommendation to make.'

'Which is ?' Takahashi asked.

'It is surely obvious. The accelerators, wherever they are, must be shut down and never operated again.'

The room burst into uproar.

'That is ridiculous!' Takahashi shouted, 'Absolutely ridiculous! You have no idea of the money and expertise sunk into this project! Billions and billions of dollars! Decades of planning! And you want us to turn it off, throw the key into the sea and go away and just do something else!'

Nakamura smiled. 'Yes. That is exactly what I advise you to do.'

Dubois stared at him, wondering if he could clarify the opaque chaos of her thoughts. 'Explain.'

Nakamura stood up, still shorter than the two sitting technicians. 'I am not a scientist. But I am trained to look for patterns. And I believe that there is some part of what you have done which has upset, shall we say, a kind of balance in the natural order of things. You have opened a door - and something has come through.

'And it is collecting people.'

Twelve

Dubois and Takahashi were unanimous: the collider would not be shut down: *could* not be shut down. Too much was at stake to justify the end of an international project solely on the theory of one man. In any case, the decision could only be taken by the vote of the entire Directorate, and who would be prepared to stand in front of them and talk about grey mists and invisible kidnappers?

It was too ridiculous even to contemplate.

As the time lengthened since the meeting with Nakamura, Dubois had once again convinced herself that there could be no absurd paranormal explanations for what had happened. She reminded herself of Sagan's dictum: *Extraordinary claims require extraordinary evidence.*

And what was the evidence? A grey mist that some had seen at approximately the last sighting of the victim?

Was that enough?

Dubois knew that stage magicians could perform seemingly impossible feats with – what was the phrase? – smoke and mirrors. That there were sinister forces behind the disappearances, she did not doubt. But the perpetrators, once unmasked, would prove to be solidly human.

But a small voice inside her asked: why had nothing happened after the disappearances? Where were the ransom demands?

She leaned forward and cradled her head in trembling hands.

This was all too much. She was fully equipped for solving enigmas in science; she lived for the unmasking of such mysteries. But *this*. This was beyond her.

She leaned back and stared at the ceiling of her office.

'Hilda,' she whispered, 'where are you?'

The intercom buzzed. She answered it with a dull, flat 'Yes?'

'This is Technician Simms. I'm sorry, doctor, but we have another bleed.'

Oh no! she thought, *Another one! What is the point of carrying on with this whole farcical business? It is all going to be for nothing. My whole career is going to end in failure. I will just be a footnote in the annals of science.*

'And what do you want me to do about it? Stick my finger in a hole?'

'The Director says he'd like you to take a look at it.'

'Me? I'm not a technician. I'm not known for dirty fingernails.'

There was a pause, then 'He's standing right next to me. Do you want to speak to him?'

Dubois thought rapidly. Relations between her and Takahashi had cooled somewhat since the abortive dinner date. It would do her prospects no good to be awkward, and it was still not absolutely certain that the project was going to end in abject failure.

'Tell him I'll go down,' she said, 'but I want another physicist with me. I don't see why I should accept all the responsibility.'

There was another pause, and then Simms said, 'He says that is fine. If you go to level Orange 12 a colleague will meet you there. You are to meet him or her in fifteen minutes.'

'Tell him I am eternally grateful for this career opportunity,' Dubois said and switched the intercom off with an angry gesture.

She didn't care anymore.

* * *

Dubois arrived at the requisite level; portable magnetometer slung over her shoulder.

A man was already there, peering at the great cylinder which should have been holding the speeding protons. He turned.

She groaned audibly: it was Williamson.

'Céline!' he cried, 'wonderful to see you!'

She looked at him quizzically. Although it was warmer down here, he was a little underdressed, wearing only a T-Shirt and shorts.

'Hello, Williamson. Let's get on with it, shall we? I've got a hundred and one better things that I should be doing.'

He gave an odd grin. 'Yeah. Me too!'

She stood next to him, conscious of the smell of acrid sweat rising from him.

'So the Director thinks it's here, does he?' she said.

'Yeah. The Technicians have some kind of industrial dispute going on, which is why we've been lumbered with this job.'

'It's not really my field,' Dubois muttered, 'I must have annoyed him somehow.'

She switched her machine on and stared down at the flickering display; reading without effort the data displayed there.

As she did so, she became aware that Williamson was now standing so close that their hips were touching.

She moved a little to the right and carried on reading the figures.

He moved an equivalent amount, so their bodies touched again.

She turned. 'Whatever you think you're doing, stop it right now. I am in no mood for games I assure you.'

He gave that grin again. 'You know, Céline, I don't think you're quite the little Frozen Knickers that you like to pretend.'

She looked him straight in the eye and said, carefully and slowly, 'Please stop this inappropriate behaviour. I do not want this kind of attention and I must warn you...'

Her words were cut off as Williamson made a sudden lunge and flung his arms around her. The magnetometer crashed to the floor.

He pressed his mouth to hers while holding her in a crushing embrace. He was so tight up against her that she could feel his erection through the thin fabric of his shorts.

89

'Come on, come on,' he said in a rasping voice, 'there's no-one here!'

With a terrific effort Dubois straightened her arms, pushing him violently away.

'You bastard!' she snapped, 'I ...'

And then it happened.

Abruptly there was a feeling of electrical potential in the air. Dubois felt her hair begin to lift from her scalp.

The air seemed suddenly heavy and viscous as if they had been plunged into a transparent liquid, and the corners of metal objects shone with the colours of the spectrum. Williamson's red features blurred before her.

There was a throbbing which was not heard but felt in her internal organs. Waves of compression and rarefaction pulsed visibly in the heavy air above her.

And then, just where the corridor curved away, a thin grey mist formed and began to advance towards them.

She heard Williamson give an incomprehensible cry and saw him turn to flee. But, just as in a nightmare, he could not move.

She made no effort to run. If this thing had taken Hilda, then she would join her in whatever lay beyond.

And she saw the mist open up so it revealed a kind of tunnel.

And were there figures at the far end?

Light flashed into actinic brilliance and then almost total darkness as the mouth of the tunnel approached.

And in the instant that the light vanished, Dubois thought she could see three spots of glowing redness, forming a perfect equilateral triangle, and it seemed that those spots were staring at her.

And then the mouth of the tunnel reached her and all was darkness.

PART TWO: THE FAR ONES

One

There had been darkness.

Now there was nothing; a nothing that was less than darkness.

Now there was oblivion.

Dubois was alone in nothingness, bereft of any external stimuli, any sensation, any indication of life.

Never had a human creature been so utterly sundered from every aspect of existence; of any sign that there was an external reality.

And yet she could scream, and so she did.

She screamed with the deep, visceral knowledge that all was lost; that this was death and all she had known and fought for was nothing; every action, every thought, every volition – all had been in vain.

Her reward for her struggles was this – a void worse than any imagining; a measureless emptiness in which even the blackness of the deepest night would have been a comfort.

And yet there was something.

There was still a mind, an ego that had known it had been Céline Dubois.

An entity that could scream, for she knew somehow that she was screaming even though she could not hear it or feel it.

There was something.

She forced herself to remember who she had been and what she had done.

She forced herself to remember that there had been life, and in that life there had been love.

And then she knew that she was no longer screaming even though she did not understand how she knew. She just knew.

So this was death, the untethered ego thought, as a great stillness and calm flooded through that orphaned mind.

She had always thought that the reward for life would be nothingness but now in what felt like death, there was something amiss with that interpretation, for there was something in the void and that something was still called Céline Dubois.

She began to think, remembering the meditations of an ancient countryman of hers, who had long ago envisaged a situation like this.

Her mind somehow fought its way out of the clinging pit of horror and despair, and the mind that was still the mind of Céline Dubois began to think.

It is a logical impossibility for nothingness to be experienced, her reason told her, therefore this is not nothingness – it was a *something* that she did not yet understand.

And as that thought came to her she realised that she was no longer in nothingness but appeared to be at the centre of a titanic sphere of featureless grey obscurity.

And to know that there was a greyness encircling her entailed that there was, after all, an external stimulus.

She seized on that possibility and thought *I will believe that I am not nothing; I will believe that I am something and there is a world independent of my thoughts.*

The grey uniformity that now enveloped her stirred a memory and that memory was of a mist that had formed a tunnel and had swept her up like a helpless fish in a net.

And she thought: *The grey mist. The tunnel of mist. I am not dead. Somehow I am in that tunnel.*

Then she realised that something else had changed. She could see the outline of her body as a vague series of transparent lines, looking like a stick drawing of a human that a child could have drawn, if a child could inscribe drawings on the air itself.

The more I believe in my reality, the more I conjure that reality into being! she decided and forced her tumbling mental processes into a firmer, tighter, calmer order.

Believe! She commanded herself.

And slowly, slowly, the insubstantial series of lines became a set of interconnected curves that more and more resembled a human body. Her body!

Legs were now definitely visible; she could even see the court shoes that she knew she had been wearing when she had been captured.

Was it possible to walk? Was there a surface to walk upon?

She tried to move, to move this insubstantial ghost of a body.

And the legs did move but she had the feeling that she was walking not on a proper solid but something that moved and buckled like a huge trampoline. It caused her to sway back and forth in an alarming fashion.

As she walked over that strange surface, holding her arms out horizontally to steady herself, her body slowly continued to become more substantial, more realistically physical. Looking down she could see the swell of her breasts mounding the top she knew she had been wearing on that fateful day.

But although she appeared to be walking – to where was she walking?

She stopped and stood there waiting.

Things were changing, had changed immeasurably since that dreadful awakening. Perhaps all she had to do was wait and maybe normality would return.

And, as if in answer to that idea, she began to see shapes in the greyness, vague, undefined suggestions of structures, of objects, delineated only by subtle gradations in the grey hue of that unknown surface.

Slowly, agonisingly slowly, those things took on a more recognisable structure. It was like watching an image developing on old-fashioned photographic film in some ancient darkroom. She thought she could see the beginnings of a landscape, a horizon perhaps.

The real world!

She decided that all she had to do was wait and normality would be restored.

But instantly on that thought, there was a soundless, blinding flash of intolerable light which felt like it had started within her skull and exploded outwards.

She fell forwards and discovered that the surface was no longer yielding but hard and rugged.

She felt a tremendous wave of heat press down on her.

And then oblivion again.

* * *

She awoke to heat and to pain in her face. She lifted her head and could taste the metallic taint of blood. There were small specks of gravel on her lips and in her mouth.

She realised she was lying on hard, rocky ground and, until a moment earlier, had been lying with her face pressed into it.

She spat the gravel out and rubbed her face and lips. Her hand came away streaked with blood. She had obviously fallen face-first and hit the ground with some force.

Slowly she straightened her arms to push herself into a crouching position.

And suddenly the blood and pain didn't matter anymore.

It was the real world! She was back! She had escaped from that grey Hell!

Dubois carefully stood up, brushing the sand and gravel from her chest and arms, and looked around.

The initial joy faded a little as she did that.

In all directions stretched a yellow and brown scrubland with no vegetation more than a couple of metres high. There were a few things that looked like withered Joshua trees. She had never seen Joshua trees but believed she recognised them from travelogue programmes. Everywhere she looked there were huge, grey, splintered rocks. And all lay rippling under a shimmering curtain of heat haze.

The heat! Now she felt it! It was like being trapped inside an oven with a sadist controlling the thermostat!

She found a flat-topped rock and sat heavily down on it.

This was preferable to that nightmare of nothingness, but only marginally so.

It meant that she would now have a normal death, instead of the weird fate she had been expecting.

Then, once again, determination seeped back into her.

This was the normal world. It was not some crazy science-fiction "other dimension". This must be the planet Earth, though obviously not Switzerland or Japan. Somehow that tunnel-thing had transplanted her to another part of the normal world. And if so, somewhere, not too far away, there would be a town, some type of habitation, or at the very least some wandering tribe.

She had not died in the realm of nothingness and she would not die here,

She would find help and would eventually find her way back to civilisation.

And what a tale she would have to tell!

Dubois gave a little wry smile. Would anybody believe her?

She looked up, directing her gaze to near where the sun blazed in a cruelly bright sky, but being very careful not to catch even a glimpse of it.

She had her directions now. She looked around, hoping to see the smudge of a distant township on the horizon but there was nothing. The desert – for that was indeed the terrain she had been thrown into – looked the same in all directions.

There being no reason to prefer one direction to any other, she chose one at random and began her trek into this new unknown.

Soon she realised that she was desperately thirsty. She had had no drink since her meagre cup of morning black coffee – and she had no idea when that morning had been. Already her life in the ILC had started to seem unreal.

The ground over which she was walking was desperately

stony and uneven. Dubois stopped and broke the heels off her shoes but soon discovered that was very little help. She was no steadier in the pared down footwear; just unsteady in a different way.

She walked on in the killing heat and glare. Huge wet patches appeared under her arms and chin. Her pantyhose was soon ripped and laddered beyond any practical use and she removed it and threw it away. It felt cooler for a few seconds and then exactly as uncomfortable as it had been earlier.

This land was nothing but dust and sand or sand and gravel or gravel and stones. It was the same in any direction; a bleak, inhospitable killing field. And one where the temperature created false hopes of water as the rippling waves of burning air produced illusions of distant pools.

Dubois's fortitude began to waver. It was beginning to look as if this wasteland was uninhabited and this was indeed the place where her bones would lie and whiten under a pitiless sun.

Then she heard a faint buzzing noise just on the threshold of audibility and, scanning the air, she saw a distant black dot moving slowly against the brilliant cloudless sky.

It must be some type of aircraft, she thought with a sudden burst of hope. This land could not be uninhabited after all! There were people here!

'Aidez moi!' she yelled, and then, realising that where she was didn't look like any Francophone area that she knew, 'Help me! Please help me!'

The black dot continued its journey across the sky and Dubois finally realised that it was getting smaller. Whatever it was, it was not coming in her direction.

The effort of shouting and the sudden collapse of hope had left her exhausted. Her head dropped and she sat down on the hot sand, no longer looking at anything.

After a minute or so she looked around and then crawled into the shade of a huge boulder. She knew it would not be long before she succumbed to this deadly place.

She shook her head at the irony of her escape from one death trap straight into the clutches of another.

No food. No water. No hope.

She sat there in the shadow and watched it lengthen. Behind her she knew the fierce sun was setting. In front of her, the Belt of Venus had thrown an indigo band over the eastern horizon.

Already the desert air was starting to feel noticeably cooler.

Would the morning sun find her still alive, she wondered, and realised that she was beginning not to care.

Her chin dipped and before she knew it, she was asleep.

* * *

She woke to bright sunlight that bored its way through her eyelids as if they were not there. She felt cold and stiff even though she knew the temperature was rising rapidly. The night had been as cold as she had feared and she was still wearing the light clothing she had dressed herself in on that last normal morning; now so very, very long ago.

With some difficulty she forced her stiff joints to work and slowly stood up, resting a hand on the boulder to steady herself. Looking around, she could see that no magical transformation had occurred in the night: she was still lost in this wilderness of sand and rock.

Was there any point in struggling on, she wondered, there was no hope now. No-one was going to save her. Whatever force had done this to her had clearly possessed no concern for her well-being. Something had thrown her into this nightmare and she would never know what it had been.

For some minutes she stood there, irresolute. And then, without really knowing why, she resumed her hopeless trek.

The heat grew steadily, remorselessly, beating around her in great waves of shimmering torment. She saw a ridge of gravel and shingle ahead of her and thought to herself: *One last climb.* She would reach the top of this dune and then stretch out and die. All she could do now was hope that it would soon be over.

She climbed slowly up, losing her footing several times as the loose stuff moved under her, once sending her almost back to where she had started. But eventually she did reach the top and, as she had promised herself, stretched out on the hot stones and waited for death.

It was then she heard voices, distant human voices.

Two

Dubois returned to consciousness, not knowing how long she had been out.

She was in shade, inside a type of hut. She struggled to sit up, throwing off the thin blanket that been placed over her.

She blinked in the unaccustomed gloom and ran her tongue over her cracked and blistered lips. There was movement in the gloom: she was not alone.

'Who's there?' she said in English, 'who are you?'

A figure detached itself from the gloom and came nearer. Dubois was relieved to see that it was a woman. A woman of indeterminate age and wearing what could only be described as rags.

'Hey, you rest yourself, lady,' the figure said in a strong American accent, 'you're gonna be just fine. We're looking after you now.'

Dubois managed to get herself sitting upright. Her head was swimming and her mouth was as dry as the desert outside.

'Water. Do you have any water?' she managed to say, in a croaking voice that she did not recognise as her own.

'Sure honey,' the woman said and a few minutes later brought back a tumbler that seemed to have been carved from a type of gourd. The water was warm and stung like mild acid, but Dubois concluded the pain was her fissured lips reacting to the liquid and finished it with her second gulp.

Now that her eyes had adjusted to her dim surroundings, she could see her companion better.

The woman looked neither old nor young; simply grubby and weary. Her hair was so greasy it had formed itself into separate strands that clung to her scalp. Her leathery skin was criss-crossed with a network of fine lines, marring what would otherwise have been a reasonably young-looking face.

And on one side of her neck was a lump of flesh that terminated in an open lesion.

Feeling invigorated by the water, Dubois looked around and then back to her companion. 'Where am I?' she demanded.

'This is Arizony' the other replied, 'where do you reckon it'd be?'

'Arizony?' Dubois replied, 'I don't know of such a place.'

The other woman grinned, showing a mixture of blackened teeth and gaps where teeth had once been. 'My, don't you talk diff'rnt, lady. Where you from?'

'France,' Dubois replied, 'You must have heard of France.'

'No, I sure ain't,' the woman replied, 'must be long way from this here place.'

Dubois was puzzled. She did not expect everyone to share her educational status – but not having heard of France?

'Could I have some more water? 'she asked, giving up on the conundrum, 'I have pre-diabetes. I need water.'

The other shook her head. 'No, you just done had your share, lady. Frank'll be awful mad if you gets some more.'

'Frank? Who's Frank?'

'Well, he kinda runs things round here, lady. Say – what's your name?'

'Dubois. Céline Dubois.'

'That's a right fancy name, Céline. I ain't never heard no "Céline" afore.'

'Well, that's my name. What's yours?'

'Mary-Lou. That's what my momma called me.'

Dubois was about to compliment her new companion on her name when a shaft of light fell over the two of them. Turning, she saw that a cloth had been drawn back from a doorway and two other women had entered the hut. For a moment they were simply silhouettes against the backdrop of sand and stones and then as they came nearer Dubois could see that they were about the same age and condition as Mary-Lou.

The nearer of the two ignored Dubois at first, and speaking to Mary-Lou said, 'Frank'll be here soon. You done his vittles?'

'He'll be awful mad if it ain't ready,' the second newcomer said.

'I ain't stupid,' Mary-Lou said, 'they're in the pot right there.'

The first newcomer turned to Dubois and, while staring at her, addressed Mary-Lou, 'Who's this here tramp?'

'I done found her lying on the ground right there, Inez,' Mary-Lou said, pointing vaguely out of the hut, 'didn't seem right to just leave her there.'

Inez looked Dubois up and down. 'How'd she get here? She's too fuckin' fat for you to carry.'

'She could walk some even though she was half asleep,' Mary-Lou said, in a strangely nervous voice.

Inez continued her examination of their new guest. 'She looks alright. If she does her turns Frank'll likely keep her.'

'Turns?' Dubois said but the woman had finished with her and, turning away, said: 'I sure hope Frank gets here soon. I'm right starving myself to death stood here.'

'Yeah, me too,' the second said.

Dubois tried again. 'Look,' she said, in the voice she used at meetings to stamp her authority, 'Can someone tell me what...'

Inez spun on her heel and gave Dubois a stinging back-handed slap.

'Shut your face, bitch. We speak when we're spoken to round here. That's the way Frank likes it. You'd better learn real quick or you'll be buzzard meat.'

Dubois had crashed to the floor of the hut, not with the force of the blow, but in sheer astonishment at the woman's actions. She had never suffered physical violence before; not from her parents; not from her acquaintances.

It was a new, utterly astounding experience!

She ran a hand over her cracked lips and, once again, saw blood on it.

'Why did you hit me?' she said plaintively, 'what had I done?'

102

Inez ignored her, but talking to Mary-Lou she said, 'This one ain't gonna last long, after all. Seems like she's dumber than a jackrabbit.'

The third woman approached Dubois and, grinning wolfishly, looked down and said: 'That right, little lady? You dumber than a jackrabbit?'

Mary-Lou came between them. 'Justina, you leave her be! She ain't done nothing! If Frank takes a liking to her, maybe he'll leave us alone for a spell!'

Dubois lay still on the ground, not daring to move in case it earned her another blow.

But while she lay there she was able to get a better look at her new companions and she observed that each one of them had some type of physical deformity: Mary-Lou had the large excrescence on her neck; Inez a bulging thyroid and Justina a twisted jaw and one eye much smaller than the other.

'Can I get up now?' Dubois finally ventured to ask.

'Yeah, sure,' Justina said, 'just make sure you don't say no more dumb things.'

She and Inez laughed at that.

Dubois rose unsteadily and looked at the two newer women. 'Cochons,' she said in a voice loud enough to be heard.

Inez struck her again. 'You talk so's we understand you or you won't be talking agin!'

Dubois rocked on her heels but this time did not fall.

She weighed up her options: none of the women looked particularly strong. They were all scrawny and somehow withered looking. Could she ...

But she did not have to make a decision, for the flap over the entrance was flung to one side and a man came in.

She whirled to meet him and was shocked to find she was facing a large, fierce-looking individual. He was not as big as Marius Larsen but was still an imposing slab of a man. His eyes were large and bloodshot and the flesh around the jaws had decayed somehow, permanently exposing the underlying flesh and the jagged and blackened teeth. He reminded Dubois unpleasantly of a hungry predator, or an angry ape displaying its canines. She noticed as he came in that one leg was withered and was dragging behind him. And behind him walked a gigantic mastiff, the size of a small pony, also showing permanently bared teeth, from which drool was hanging.

She was so shocked by their sudden arrival that she stood silent and motionless as the man strode up to her.

'Well, what we got here?' came a booming voice, 'who's this fine little lady?'

Dubois found that she could not speak and remained staring up at that ghastly face.

Finally Mary-Lou said, 'She says her name's "Céline".'

'Well, ain't that a pretty name. Where you from, little lady?'

'France,' Dubois said, finally getting her vocal cords to move.

'Ain't never heard of none such place,' the man, whom Dubois guessed must be "Frank", said and, seemingly losing interest in her, turned to Mary-Lou and said, 'You got them vittles, woman?'

'Sure thing, Frank,' she said and, crossing to a large pot, began to scoop mounds of steaming slop into a crudely fashioned bowl.

The man sat down on the small log which served as the only chair in the hut and began eating noisily. On finishing, he belched loudly, wiped his hand over his exposed gums and held out the bowl again. Mary-Lou dutifully filled it.

'Where's Carlo's chow?' he said, on finishing the second bowl.

'Right here, Frank,' Mary-Lou said and threw the dog a large bone which had a small amount of meat hanging from it. The dog rose on its hind legs and caught it in mid-air. Dubois heard the crunching noise as the powerful jaws snapped down on the bone. Carlo turned and went outside with the bone.

Frank looked at the three women and nodded. 'OK, girls.

104

All yours.'

The women immediately went to the pot and, taking three much smaller bowls, ladled themselves the remains of whatever it was that Frank had been eating.

Dubois watched them and then said: 'Do I get any?'

Inez looked over her shoulder. 'Why, listen to that fine, high-bred lady over there. You done much to get some chow, lady?'

'I just got here,' Dubois pointed out.

That seemed to enrage Inez, who crossed over to her and raised her hand. 'I'm just about sick of your lip, bitch!' she snapped and made as to hit her. But a large hand grasped her wrist and stopped its motion.

'I decide who gets hit around here, Inez.' Frank looked at Inez, then Dubois and then back to Inez. 'Give her some of your'n.' He then sat back on his log, running his finger around the rim of his bowl and then licking it.

Inez crossed to Dubois with a small bowl that held a pitiful amount of some glutinous substance at the bottom and handed her a crudely carved wooden spoon. As she did so, she leaned in close and whispered in Dubois's ear, 'Watch out bitch. I ain't done with you. You and I got some business to sort out.'

Dubois ignored her and rapidly finished the meagre meal; the first she had had since – since when?

She had no idea.

After copying Frank and licking up every molecule of the bitter-tasting broth, she felt marginally better. A brief memory of the meals she had enjoyed at the ILC flickered across her mind but was quickly gone. Such memories were of no value here.

She tried once again to gain some knowledge that might be useful.

'I still don't know where I am. Who are you people?'

Frank stared at her. 'You don't know? This is Arizony, little lady. And I'm Frank and these are my girls. And now you're one of my girls.'

Dubois caught a glance between Mary-Lou and Justina which looked like an expression of relief. Inez remained stony-faced.

Then the dread meaning of what Frank had said sank in.

'One of your girls? No, no, I'm not anybody's girl, Frank.'

To her surprise he roared with laughter and then said, 'Lady, you got the wrong idea of what things are like here. I don't know about this "France" place but here I'm king. And I sure as Hell got the power of life and death over you.'

Dubois heard Inez chuckling and then she said, 'All I ask is that you take me to some town where I can find out what's happening to me. I'm no use to you – I don't know what to do around here.'

Frank stood over her and pulled one of her hands towards him and made it describe a circular motion against his groin.

'You got the wrong idea about yourself, lady. You're plenty use to me.'

Three

Dubois spent a restless night in the hut along with the three other women, who all slept like those awaiting the last trump.

Once she went as far as the doorway but could not escape through it because of the chain that Frank had attached to her right ankle. She stood there, gazing out over the dark land, wondering, not for the first time, what could have happened to her. How had she got to this strange place? It seemed like the USA, but something was subtly different. She pondered the meagre amount of information that she had been given. Take the name they had given to this Godforsaken wilderness: "Arizony." That could be a corruption of "Arizona" she supposed. She had not been to that part of the USA, but her surroundings fitted in with what she had seen in documentaries about the American South-West. But where were the people? There appeared to be no-one in this area apart from Frank and his women.

And yet as she reached that impasse, something happened to give her new hope. Out over the dark horizon, there had moved a small black object, an object that seemed to be carrying red and green lights. And twice as she had watched, a brilliant shaft of light had flashed down from it; a powerful searchlight, seemingly searching for something.

Searching. Could it be searching for her? But if it was, would they be any better than this dangerous quartet that she stumbled onto? She no longer had a blind expectation that things would turn out for the best.

But if it was searching for her, it did not find her because she saw the red and green lights fade slowly into the black emptiness.

And it came no more.

The morning came with a surge of harsh sunlight and a blast

of heat. To her surprise, Dubois found she had slept, despite her certainty that she would not.

Frank came in with his dog padding heavily close behind him. He had his own hut of course, which was twice as large as the one that held his three, now four, women.

He seemed in a good mood and, despite his ominous action the day before, he made no move on Dubois.

'Up we get, girls!' he said, 'You've had all the sleep you're gonna get this side of supper!'

The original three women made complaining noises, but all threw off the light blankets that had covered them and slowly got to their feet.

Breakfast was not part of their routine apparently for they all immediately threw on the greasy rags that passed for their clothing and, after making use of the urinal bucket, headed out after Frank and Carlo. Dubois noticed that Frank had a kind of holster, which she had not seen before, strapped to the thigh of his weak leg.

But Inez stopped at the doorway and looked back into the hut and called to the others to stop.

'Well, lookee here!' she sneered, 'Our Royal Highness here wants some more shut-eye. What's the matter, your majesty, honest work beneath you?'

Frank stuck his head back through the doorway and glared at Dubois.

'Out,' he said, without raising his voice 'Now.'

Despite his calm manner Dubois knew that defiance would be extremely unwise. She hurriedly used the urinal bucket and made to leave, only to find Inez barring the way.

'Bucket,' Inez said, 'last one out empties it. Get your ass in gear or I'll make you drink it all.'

Dubois went back for the bucket and poured the dark yellow liquid out on the sand immediately outside the hut, without meeting Inez's gaze. As she straightened up she received another stinging slap across the face.

108

'You dumb bitch!' Inez snarled, her bulging eyes seeming ready to jump from her skull, 'Not near the fucking hut!'

Dubois half-raised the bucket, wondering if it was finally the time to return Inez's violence but once again Frank intervened. 'Stop it, you two!' he bellowed, 'How many times I gotta tell you – I hand out the licks around here!'

Dubois returned Inez's look of hatred and then the two joined the other three as they set off on their journey into the wilderness. Carlo moved behind them as if he were ready to cut off any escape attempt.

Dubois managed to get herself near to Mary-Lou, who so far had shown no animosity towards her.

'Where are we going?' she whispered.

Mary-Lou gave a half-smile at her companion's naivety.

'Why, lookin' for food, Céline. It don't come lookin' for us!'

Dubois looked around, at the arid, tawny desolation through which they were walking.

'What's there to eat around here?'

'Lizards, mainly. Some time we get lucky and catch a rabbit. Once we even found a dead bighorn. That damn thing lasted weeks!'

Dubois considered Mary-Lou's words. This didn't sound like a normal lifestyle for the inhabitants of a modern American state. How could things have become so bad that these people were apparently living on the edge of starvation?

They trudged on. Dubois was glad that the other three had no inclination to come near and chide her. The exception was Carlo, for several times she turned around to find him sniffing at her heels. However, one thing was rapidly becoming apparent: she did not possess the stamina that these people had. But with a tense feeling in her stomach, she knew that any request for a respite would be met with scorn from Inez and, possibly, violence.

She looked at the lesion on Mary-Lou's neck and could now see that the rent in the flesh went deep.

'Does that hurt much?' she asked, indicating the wound.

Mary-Lou gave a fleeting smile. 'Sure does. But I can't do nothin' about it. Just grin and bear it, I guess.'

Dubois gave what she hoped was a sympathetic smile in return and looked at the other three, who were now some distance ahead. She saw that despite Frank's deformed leg he was leading the crowd of women. It was evident that no one stopped until Frank stopped.

And then, miraculously, he did stop - just as Dubois was about to risk it and ask for a rest.

They had come to a halt in the shadow of a vast, sloping boulder. Dubois did not like the angle at which it was leaning and had visions of all of them being flattened as it came crashing down. None of the others was worried and they all found smaller boulders to sit on. Dubois noticed that the other women were carrying gourds and small baskets.

Dubois went up to Frank, feeling like a little girl again asking for a favour from a short-tempered parent.

'Could I have some more water, please Frank,' she said, 'I have pre-diabetes you see.'

Frank stared at her. 'Pree-doabetes? I ain't heard of that belief. We're all good Christians here. You'll get more water when I say you will. Don't you bother me none, no more, if you know what's good for you.'

Dubois returned to her patch of shade, knowing that Inez was glaring at her but pretended not to notice.

After a few more minutes Frank rose to her feet, his three original companions following almost instantly.

'Like the little lady over there said,' he announced, 'we need more water. Let's find some.'

They resumed their seemingly endless trek. The heat grew and grew. Every time Dubois thought it could not possibly get any hotter she was almost immediately proved wrong. Rivulets of sweat rolled down her forehead into her eyes, blurring her vision still further. She was losing moisture that she could ill afford to lose; she knew. She wondered briefly if she should make a break for it and, being the last in the line, she stopped and looked around.

But she had forgotten that she was not precisely the last in the line for as soon as she stopped she felt a muzzle push against her ankle and hear a deep growl. Carlo was his master's eyes and ears – she had forgotten that.

They crested a low ridge and Dubois was surprised to see a huge channel stretched out below them on a wide plain, flanked by low, greyish bushes.

'OK, girls,' Frank said, 'first one to find water gets a kiss. The last one gets a kick.'

Dubois was not sure if that was meant seriously or not but had a feeling that humour was not Frank's strong suit.

Justina came up to her and pushed a gourd into her hands. 'Here you are, I've been carrying this long enough.' She suddenly noticed something about Dubois's hands and grabbed them roughly, holding them up into the sunlight.

'Hey, take a look at this, girls!' she cried. Dubois had no idea what had caught Justina's attention but remained there with her hands imprisoned by the other woman, desperately trying not to drop the gourd. The other women joined Justina who pointed to Dubois's fingernails. Dubois saw that there was still some polish on them, although now cracked and peeling.

'Well, ain't that pretty,' Mary-Lou breathed, 'Where'd you get that done?'

'A long way from here,' Dubois replied, knowing that it was pointless to try to speak the truth.

'You won't be keeping that long,' Inez said, 'looks like it's quite a spell since you done some work.'

Dubois shrugged. There seemed no point in replying.

They all turned back to Frank who was gesticulating to them to join him.

'This ain't no rest period,' he said, showing distinct signs of irritation, 'don't you hang back no more, hear me?'

They nodded their agreement and began the descent to the plain.

As Dubois approached the huge channel she could not stop herself from asking questions; after a lifetime of seeking knowledge the habit was hard to break.

'What is this place?' she said to Mary-Lou.

'This is where we'll find water. Old folks say this is where there used to be so much water it kinda rolled along the ground. Called it the "Colorady", I think.'

The Colorado! Dubois knew roughly where she was now. This meant that "Arizony" was indeed the state of Arizona and this was where the Colorado River had flowed. But where was it? What had happened?

There was no more time for wondering, let alone asking questions.

Frank sat down and waved in the direction of the nearby bank of the defunct river.

'Go get it girls,' he said, 'I'll keep a look out.'

The women walked down the gently sloping bank onto the bottom of the channel. Dubois noticed that the ground felt somewhat spongy, suggesting that the riverbed still held some moisture.

Inez came up to her. 'Move bitch or Frank'll have your ass for dessert.'

Dubois looked around and saw a clump of what looked like rushes not too far away. She pulled the stems apart and saw that there was a small pool of green-scummed water lying at the base of the stems. Hurriedly, she pushed the mouth of the gourd into it and managed to get some water into it. When she rejoined the other women she was dispirited to see that their gourds were full to the brim while hers was only half full.

She steeled herself for the inevitable blow from Inez when she heard the sound of voices from the top of the bank. The others heard it too and Inez said, 'Company. We'd best see if Frank needs help.'

When they reached Frank they saw he was talking to a man and a woman who were both fairly elderly. The man was scrawny and had only a few wisps of white hair while the woman was bent and twisted with what looked like some kind of skeletal problem. She was clutching a sack.

Frank waved to the women to come closer.

'Girls, like you to meet Gene and his wife. Loozilla, ain't it?'

'Lucilla,' the old woman said, in a thin, reedy voice.

'Well, these are right nice folks here, girls,' Frank continued, ignoring the correction, 'Real nice. They're so nice they said they're gonna give us what's in that there sack.'

The man and the woman looked at each other in sudden alarm.

'I never said that!' Gene gasped.

'Sure you did, Gene,' Frank said and moved towards Lucilla. 'You ain't gonna go back on your word, are you? That's not what I call neighbourly.'

The old woman picked up the sack. Dubois noticed that she had some difficulty in holding it, as if the contents were too heavy for her weak arms.

Frank stood over her. 'Now Loozilla, you give me that sack nice and easy and you two just walk away free as a bird, or,' and he glanced at Gene, 'I go over and kill your husband and take the sack anyways.'

She stared up at him, her face contorted in terror. 'You can't do that! It took us days to catch these critters!'

Frank ignored the plea and repeated: 'Give me the sack, Loozilla.'

'No.'

Frank threw a glance at Inez. 'Hold him, Inez.'

She obeyed immediately, twisting Gene's arms behind his back without difficulty.

Frank walked over to Inez and stood beside the struggling man. He pulled a knife out from the holster that Dubois had noticed earlier.

'Give me the sack, Loozilla.'

'No! we worked hard for them critters. We'll starve if you take them!'

Frank sighed. 'Don't pay to be stubborn around here, Loozilla.'

Then he killed Gene.

Dubois screamed.

Four

Dubois had not seen a dead body before, let alone someone murdered before her eyes.

It had taken all her strength not to become hysterical and to run off into the wilderness. Perhaps it had only been the knowledge that Frank's women would surely have caught her and brought her back to him that stopped her. Frank would no doubt have meted out some punishment for such behaviour and, if she had been wary of him before, that feeling was a million times stronger now. She still could not forget the sight of Lucilla sobbing over her husband's corpse and the way she had screamed curses at their backs as they moved on.

She was in no mood to speak to anyone, and the others had no real interest in speaking to her. Lucilla's sack had contained a collection of rabbits, lizards and small furry creatures that Dubois did not recognise. It had been good news for Frank and his women: they had no real need to do any hunting or foraging after that bounty had fallen into their hands, although Justina did catch a lizard which she called a "chuckwalla", saying it was "a good omen for the evening's session".

Eventually, they arrived back at the huts which Dubois was now forced to accept as her new home. Frank and Carlo retired to their own hut for some "shut-eye" while the women, Dubois included, prepared the evening meal.

Once again, the women were astounded by her ineptitude; they had never met a female who didn't know how to skin a rabbit.

'You'd better learn fast,' Mary-Lou warned her when they were briefly alone, 'Inez don't like no people who don't pull their weight.'

Dubois just nodded and carried on pulling the intestines out

115

of a rabbit.

The shadows were lengthening outside the hut and a cool breeze began to blow in from the desert, periodically lifting the flap over the entrance. Soon it would be time for Frank to chain her to the central pole of the hut, Dubois thought. How quickly she had adjusted to her situation. She looked back over the old Dubois at CERN and the ILC; already that life and that person were becoming unreal.

Having finished her chores (about half an hour after everyone else), Dubois noticed that the women had arranged themselves into a rough circle in the centre of the hut.

'What's happening?' she ventured to ask, wondering if this question would earn her another slap.

'We're doing some foretelling,' Mary-Lou replied.

Dubois decided not to risk more questions and stood near to the crouched women, watching what they were doing. Justina had two bags in front of her, one of which was pulsing as if there were something alive inside it. She opened the neck of the first bag and took out some small bones, which looked like the vertebrae of some animal.

She clasped them between her hands and rocked back and forth, keening some unintelligible words. Then she threw the bones onto the beaten earth of the floor and all three bent forwards to examine the pattern they had formed.

'Don't look good,' Inez said. Justina nodded.

'I ain't sure,' Mary-Lou said, 'it looks like you can take it in one of two ways and I'm taking it the other way.'

Dubois realised with a mild shock that the women were engaging in some kind of divination ritual; just as if they were in some undiscovered region of Amazonia.

'You're fooling yourself, Mary-Lou,' Justina said, 'looks to me like there ain't no way you're getting outta this place and Frank's the only man for you!'

'I want the other test,' Mary-Lou said, with a pout of unhappiness.

'Thought you would,' Justina grinned and picked up the other bag, taking out a squirming grey lizard which Dubois was now able to identify as the chuckwalla that Justina had caught earlier. She picked up a sharp knife and expertly cut the lizard's abdomen, so its intestines fell out on the floor. Tossing the remains of the lizard out of the doorway Justina looked at the mess on the floor, warning Mary-Lou not to touch it. She shook her head. 'Sorry girl. It says the same damn thing. You ain't goin' nowhere.'

Dubois was horrified. After years spent in the highest echelons of science, she could not believe what she had just seen – primitive magical rituals.

Unable to control herself, she said, 'You stupid fools! What are you doing, believing in magic and superstition! What kind of people are you?'

The women looked up at her in amazement.

'What you talking about?' Mary-Lou asked, with genuine puzzlement in her face.

But Inez was angry and snatched the knife from the floor and advanced on Dubois, holding it in front of her.

'That's it, bitch!' she snapped, 'you don't come in here telling us what to do. Laughing in our faces! I for one ain't taking it no more!'

Dubois realised that Inez was deadly serious in her implied threat. It was time to finally defend herself.

But the conflict was not to be. The flap was thrown open and Frank stuck his head in. 'Put that knife down, Inez!' he shouted, 'I'm getting awful tired of reigning you in!'

Inez reluctantly dropped the knife.

'And you,' Frank continued, indicating Dubois, 'You come with me.'

* * *

117

Dubois stood in the centre of Frank's hut. Its owner was sitting on a crudely cut log, staring up to her. Carlo sat near the perimeter of the vaguely circular structure, contemplating his paws.

'OK, Céline,' Frank said, 'Take them off.'

Dubois looked at him. 'Take them off?' she repeated dully.

Frank waved at her lower midriff. 'The clothes. They're torn and stinking. I got new ones for you.'

'Oh, I see,' Dubois said, a wave of relief washing over her, 'Where are they?'

Frank pointed at a low trunk nearby.

She opened the trunk and found various slacks and sweatshirts. They were all of a basically similar type; some were too large, some too small. But there were a few that would be suitable. All showed unmistakable signs of having had at least one previous owner.

She picked up a set which would more or less fit and turned to face him. She decided that it was time to show gratitude and co-operation.

'Thank you, Frank, thank you very much. Can I take these back to my hut now?'

He grinned. 'No, you can't. Change here.'

'Change here. In front of you?'

'You got a problem hearing, Céline? Do it.'

She stared at him for some time, wondering if there was any way out of this.

She decided there wasn't.

She turned her back on him and began to remove the stained and torn remnants of the clothes she had put on at the start of that last morning in the ILC. It was as if she was finally saying good-bye to all she had known and understood in that now almost mythical time.

But Frank was speaking again. 'Girl, you don't ever turn your back on me 'less I gives you permission. Now turn back around.'

118

A red flush suffused her face, a mixture of shame and anger. She did not move.

Frank spoke again. 'Last warning, girl.'

Carlo picked up his tone and gave a low, dangerous growl.

Dubois turned, and looking down at the floor, slowly removed the rags which had connected her with her other life. Knowing it was pointless, she made no attempt to cover herself with her hands. She picked up the sweatshirt from the floor and pulled it over her head. Then she reached for the slacks.

Frank spoke again and his voice sounded different this time, a little husky; a little throaty.

'You leave them off, Céline. I like what I'm seeing.'

She froze. Was this what she had feared from the first moment that she had seen him?

'Come over here like a good girl, Céline. Pull up a seat.'

She obeyed, still not looking fully at him.

Frank pulled her close, pushing his hands up under the sweatshirt, kneading the breasts.

'Do you like sex, girl?' he said, in a voice which had almost become a series of pants.

She winced as his strong hands with their sandpapery skin toyed with her nipples. She looked away from him, not wanting to be enveloped in his breath, in his smell.

She said nothing.

Frank gave a breast a savage twist. 'Answer when I speak, girl. I said: do you like sex?'

She pulled herself away and stood up, facing him. 'Yes – but not with you!' she yelled.

She was not sure what happened immediately afterwards.

She found herself on the floor with burning pain on one side of her face. Then she was vaguely aware of something heavy lying on top of her. She heard a female voice in the distance, begging someone to stop doing something but she was not sure who was speaking or to whom.

Then she felt something gouging along the dry walls of her

119

vagina.
   And then all was blackness.

Five

Dubois sat at the side of the women's hut, wondering what the best way of killing herself would be.

She now remembered, only too well, what had happened on that day in Frank's hut. She knew that as long as she still had the allure of novelty, that Frank would do it again.

And again.

The other women, even Inez, had shown sympathy. The fact that Frank had diverted his attention to Dubois meant that they were now excused duty and somehow that made Dubois one of them, no longer the aloof outsider.

But Dubois found the situation intolerable, for reasons she dared not share with her companions. She doubted that her newly found Sisterhood would survive the revelation.

She had, however, confided in them her fear of pregnancy and had been surprised when Justina had said, 'Nah, that ain't gonna happen. The guy's a bit lacking in something. He ain't got any of those little swimmers, if you know what I mean.'

'You mean he's sterile,' Dubois had said, the relief evident in her face.

Justina had shrugged. 'You just gotta use these big words, don'cha gal. But I know what you mean – yeah, he's a shooting blanks kinda guy.'

That had been a small consolation, but Dubois had known then that she could not endure this new life for much longer. She would have to somehow escape into death – but how could she do it? Frank had said that he would only stop chaining her at night when he had broken her spirit, and he had warned her not to attempt to fake surrender – he knew what to look for to ensure that he was dealing with a genuinely submissive female.

Somehow she would have to kill herself during the day,

during one of their foraging expeditions. But she would have to get separated from the rest of them so she could throw herself off a cliff. Or something. Sadly, she admitted to herself that she had seen nowhere suitable during their wanderings and in any case, Carlo was always there, snapping at her heels if she fell behind.

That left venomous snakes. She had seen snakes during their wanderings but not all snakes were deadly and there was always the risk that, even if she were bitten, her body's will to live would triumph.

Her musings were cut abruptly short.

Frank stuck his head through the doorway and said, 'Come on, girls. Time to move those pretty asses!'

They moved.

* * *

The days wore on. They did not get any hotter, nor did they get any cooler. Each day was very much like the previous one. They went out; they found a few lizards or little jumping rodents; they came back.

Every couple of nights Dubois would be taken to Frank's hut and lie there while Frank did what he wanted. She would lie there, trying to ignore the reality of what was happening; trying to force her mind to relive experiences in far-off fairy-tale places called "CERN" or "the ILC". She could never quite succeed but once she saw the face of a slim, gentle-featured woman and had softly breathed the word: "Hilda."

Frank had started to complain about her lack of response and her dryness, which was robbing him of some of his pleasure. Once, when particularly annoyed, he had slapped her as she lay underneath him. She had said nothing; done her best not to flinch and he had got off her without finishing.

'You know lady,' he had said then, 'I ain't got no use for you if you ain't a good fuck. I got plenty of women over there who

122

know how to treat a guy. If you don't start whooping and hollering a bit, we'll all be saying good-bye to you, real soon.'

Dubois had known then that the crisis was not far off.

And it occurred to her that maybe a death other than her own would serve her purposes.

* * *

They were out in the dry wasteland but following the channel of what once had been the mighty Colorado River. The heat lay heavily on Dubois, making her feel like she was carrying live coals on her shoulders. There were only two ways out of this Hell and Dubois had decided on the second option.

Her vision had grown increasingly blurred with the meagre amounts of water she had been drinking, and her throat felt red-raw. But that didn't stop her looking for what she needed. Fortunately, the same technique was needed to find the lizards and rodents that went into the cooking pot.

Strangely, Carlo was taking a special interest in her today, walking off and then returning to stare at her with an occasional growl. If Dubois had believed in telepathy, she would have credited the animal with that power and believed that he had used it to read Dubois's plans.

But she did not believe in telepathy and tried to ignore the intimidating animal.

The day wore on. They met no other human beings for which Dubois was profoundly glad. Mary-Lou had told her where the clothes in Frank's trunk had come from and despite the blistering heat, she felt a cold shiver at the thought that she was wearing a murdered woman's clothes. Women usually had one of two fates in store for them when they met Frank: the attractive ones were inducted into his harem; the unattractive ones were killed for their clothes to help dress the attractive ones. When Lucilla had dressed herself in useless torn rags on the last day of her husband's life, she could not have known that her

123

clothing would be the one thing that would save her life.

Slowly, slowly, the gap between Dubois and the others grew as she scanned the ground, looking as if she was determined to find a particularly fat lizard. Carlo did not like it, but her movements were so gradual that the beast could not be sure of them and restricted himself to the occasional growl.

She straightened her back from time to time to check on whether she was being observed but the others were likewise engaged in scanning the ground. All except Frank. He was sitting on a rock, but staring in the opposite direction, out over the blasted plains.

She continued her study of the ground, looking yet again at a mass of sand, pebbles, gravel and broken stone.

And then she saw it! Hurriedly she picked it up and hid it in her basket, under the two lizards she had already collected. She looked back at the group, but Frank was still looking in the opposite direction.

Quickly, before any questions could be asked of her, she began to decrease the distance between her and them. Then she remembered that she must do nothing unusual and slowed her pace. Carlo, ever suspicious of her, followed closely behind.

When she finally rejoined the group, Frank stared at her and said, 'I've been watching you. You weren't trying to run off, were you girl? You know I'll always find you.'

For an answer Dubois pulled one of the lizards from her basket and said, 'No Frank. This critter tried to run off but I got him.'

Frank grunted. 'Hardly seems worth the effort. I seen a lot bigger.' And he turned away.

The rest of the day passed without incident. Carlo gave up sniffing around her, apparently satisfied that nothing untoward had occurred.

And eventually their day of foraging ended, and they returned.

* * *

Frank did not call on her that night. Apparently, he was in need of some variety for he called Justina instead.

And the night afterwards he called no one at all, and the four women spent the evening talking together.

Inez had adopted an attitude of reluctant truce with Dubois and now answered questions put directly to her but did not offer any conversation in return.

The other women did talk more freely.

Dubois was secretly shocked to discover how narrow were their horizons. They were unaware of anything outside their immediate area. They knew nothing of belonging to any greater political entity and had not heard of the United States. They were afraid of Frank but were also grateful to the protection that he gave them, while they gathered their food and while they slept. The frequent rough sex that he needed was just their rent, as they saw it.

'There's worse out there than Frank,' Mary-Lou had said, 'He looks after us.'

They had been with other men before Frank had encountered them. He had killed their earlier partners and taken their females as his own.

'My man was weak,' Justina observed sadly, 'Frank didn't have no trouble with him.'

Dubois wondered briefly what would happen to these women if her plan succeeded but drove the thought away. She could not take on any burdens other than her own.

And so the days passed. Each one almost identical to the one before.

And then came the day of the crisis – as Dubois had always known it would.

That evening, Frank stuck his head through the doorway of the women's hut and said, 'Céline, I need you.'

This was it. She tried not to look more alarmed than usual and hurriedly went to her own corner, where she kept the object she had found. She slipped it under her top clothing and went

125

outside where Frank was waiting.

The sky was clear and dark. Thousands of stars shone steadily in the black desert sky.

She glanced briefly at them, thinking sadly how she understood how the great forces operated which powered those distant stellar furnaces; how protons and deuterons crashed together giving off the torrents of energy that made them shine.

She knew and it seemed that, in this world, she alone knew.

She followed Frank into his hut. A swift glance around showed that Carlo was out, hunting the nocturnal jumping rodents that he liked. But there was something else: attached to the central pole was a chain. This was not part of her plan.

Frank followed her gaze. 'You're spending the night with me, girl. I want to see what you taste like in the morning.' He moved closer. 'But that don't mean I don't want my evenin' delight as well.' And he tugged at the top of her slacks.

She tried one last time.

'You don't have to do this, Frank.'

He threw his head back and roared.

'Yeah, I don't have to do it – I just like doin' it. You know,' he went on, giving her a grin that seemed to show most of his jaws under the facial skin, 'I'm getting' real sick of you being as dry as the desert down there. I figure I might carve you a new cunt 'n see if that's any better!'

Thank God for his fetish about keeping the top on she thought as she rolled the slacks down, followed by the scrap of fabric that served as briefs.

He snapped the clamp of the chain to her ankle, unaware that she was studying him to see if he would keep the key on him.

He did.

And then he pushed her roughly to the compacted earth of the floor, standing over her as he tore his trousers off. Almost immediately, he was erect and lowered himself upon her, already thrusting.

As he always did, he closed his eyes in the early stages, more

126

so he could feel her he had told her.

She stared up at him, watching his lips recede even more from the gums as he panted and grunted; watching the veins begin to stand out in his wrinkled forehead; feeling the foetid breath wash over him, clinging in a miasma to her skin.

Everything was happening in slow motion: she saw the cords stand out in his neck and prepared herself.

She knew little of anatomy, but she knew the rough position of the carotid arteries in that neck and the fact they were vital to life.

As he grunted and thrust with eyes firmly shut, from her sleeve she slipped the blade of volcanic glass that she had found during the foraging and drove it upwards with all her force. Not sure of the artery's exact position, she slashed from side to side with every atom of her strength and was rewarded with a spray of hot blood over her face. Deeper she drove the blade, turning its wicked edge from side to side so that it cut and slashed as much of the tissue as she could. There was another artery on the other side, she knew. *Withdraw the blade and sever that too!*

But Frank rose up, clutching his neck, gasping and roaring. Bloody froth bubbled from his mouth. He reached for the blade to seize it and turn it against Dubois. She kicked his legs and he went down. The makeshift weapon went flying and she could no longer see it.

He crashed to the floor in a cascade of blood but began to rise. Dubois jumped on his back and rammed a foot onto the back of his neck. Quickly she wrapped the chain under his chin and onto his neck and then threw herself backwards, staggering but keeping her feet on his back.

The chain bit into Frank's ruined neck and he scrabbled at it with bloodied hands as a dark pool began to form under him. Still she pulled the chain as tight as her straining muscles could deliver. His thrashing became more frantic as he tore at the chain and suddenly he gave a grunt and his head fell forward into the pool of blood.

But Dubois did not stop her pulling. Minute after silent minute passed and still she kept the chain tight around his neck, fearing that he would rise and seek a terrible vengeance.

Finally she let the chain go slack and backed away.

He did not stir; did not rise to strike her down and wreak bloody revenge.

Her relief was so great that she almost collapsed, and she had to hold onto the central pole to steady herself.

Now she must move fast, So, so fast!

The women were heavy sleepers but they must have heard Frank's death throes. And where was Carlo and his bear-trap jaws?

She lifted the corpse so she could reach the key and unhooked it from his belt, letting the body fall back face-first into the blood.

In her terror, she fumbled with the key and could not get it into the lock.

Was it the wrong key? No, she had seen him use it on this chain!

Sobbing, she tried again and again until suddenly it clicked in. She turned it and the chain fell away.

She stood up and looked down for a moment at her captor and the slowly spreading pool of blood.

Now she must flee, run, out into the darkness of the desert, to face whatever new dangers there must be.

She turned and ran out into the night.

Six

The night was cold; shockingly cold after all the heat that she had generated during her battle with Frank. It cut into her like tormenting needles as she ran from the hut under the unheeding stars. She had no plan of what to do next: any direction was as good as any other. Better to die in the desert than fall into the hands of the women who now lacked their protector and would want her blood in exchange.

She heard noises from behind her; women's voices shouting and screaming.

They had found Frank.

Then she heard Inez's voice, faint but still powerful.

'I know what you done, bitch! When I catch you I'm gonna cut your fuckin' heart out and eat it!'

Dubois knew what she had done to them: she had deprived them of their guardian, their protector; he had kept them safe from the dangers of this savage land and all he had asked for in return was simple sex.

But no! it wasn't as simple as that, she told herself. Guardian he may have been but he had killed people without a thought and dressed his women in the clothes of those he had murdered.

She ran on, not knowing to where she was running; not knowing if the women had seen in which direction she had fled, or whether, like animals, they could simply follow her trail.

She could not take the risk of resting for a moment, or even slow down. She had to run - and run fast.

Eventually her weakened body could do no more. She tripped and sprawled on the sand and could not rise. Her breathing was coming in great ragged gasps as she gulped the air down, desperately trying to replenish the oxygen supply to her muscles and calm her hammering heart.

Eventually, she sat up, looking fearfully around; afraid of every shadow.

Not too long ago her biggest worry had been how to chair a meeting on the energy supply to a particle collider, how to control the egos of her fellow scientists and get things done the way she wanted.

What innocence she had had! And now she had killed a man, another human being.

With her own hands and a piece of glass, she had taken the life of another thinking creature; had torn a throat to shreds.

It was so crazily unbelievable that for a dizzying moment she thought that she had gone quite literally mad; that none of this was happening.

But then she heard faint sounds behind her and knew that at least one woman was following. She stood for a moment, racked with indecision, trying to establish from which direction the sounds had come. And then she hurried on into a night which was illuminated only by the distant stars. She knew who that woman would be.

The land began to slope upwards and the withered undergrowth thinned out. Soon, she reassured herself, she would be high enough that she would be able to see if she was being followed.

Feeling slightly more confident, she began her ascent of the slope when suddenly a dark shape erupted from the cover of a nearby bush and crashed into her. She felt clawed hands grab her face and dig into the flesh as a knee was rammed into her stomach like a piledriver. Both figures, locked together, rolled back down the slope into the thicker undergrowth. Dubois found herself lying on her back with the hideously twisted face of Inez almost pressing into her own.

'I hated your guts from the moment I saw you,' Inez snarled, 'Now I'm going to pull them out and strangle you with them for what you did to Frank. He was the only man I ever loved and you butchered him!'

Dubois made no reply: this was long past the time of talking. This was Death paying her another call. Instead she fought to push Inez's arms apart so she could stop her assailant from gouging her eyes.

There was no more speech from either woman, just the grunting and snarling of prey and predator as they fought there in the semi-darkness. They rolled back and forth; sometime Dubois was on top; sometimes Inez. Finally, they had somehow drawn far enough apart for Inez to pull her knee back and then drive it into Dubois's crotch. She doubled up and in panting triumph Inez stood over her, one foot on either side.

'Now how do you like it, my fine little lady?' was the taunt that Dubois only vaguely heard. She was lying there like a strange human starfish, each limb pointing to a different part of the compass; her bosom heaving with exhaustion. With her left hand she could feel something hard and heavy, just at fingertip distance.

She saw Inez draw something from the pouch at her side, something that glinted in the starlight. A knife. A real metal knife, last used to disembowel a chuckwalla.

'Now to send you back to Hell, or France, or whatever goddam place you come from!' Inez bent down to deliver the killing thrust just as Dubois's fingers curled around the stone and her arm straightened, smashing the rock against the side of Inez's head.

Inez crashed heavily to the ground and lay still.

Dubois did not move for some time, no longer caring what trick fate had in store for her.

Then at last the desire to live returned and she sat up slowly, looking at the prone figure next to her. She had killed again. What not too long ago had been an unimaginable impossibility was now an everyday routine.

She had not wanted to kill Frank. She had not wanted to kill anyone.

She bent over Inez and felt a soft wetness on one side of the

131

head.

But she realised that Inez was still breathing. She had not killed her!

With difficulty Dubois straightened herself and gave herself a quick check for wounds. One palm was wet, but that had been where she had cut herself with the glass blade during the struggle with Frank. Otherwise, she was sore and bruised but Inez had not inflicted any penetrating wounds.

She must move on. To where, she did not know. All she knew was that she could not remain here. Inez would no doubt recover and there was no reason to believe the other two women did not have murder in their hearts over the loss of their protector.

She turned to resume her ascent of the slope and it was then she heard a sound that stopped her in her tracks and sent an electric bolt of raw fear down her spine.

It was the baying of a dog.

A very large dog.

Carlo.

Despair swept over her. There was no way she could defeat that tremendous mastiff in the way she had bested Inez. A shudder passed through her as she remembered how his dreadful jaws could crunch down on a large bone, splintering it easily.

She could not hope to kill that creature. She must escape, escape at all cost!

Desperately she resumed her ascent of the slope, sending scree and small rocks sliding down behind her.

She reached the top and looked around. More of the same: dark and pitiless nothingness.

Carlo bayed again and she could tell he was nearer now, much nearer.

She could never shake him off she knew that; he would be able to track her scent however faint it became. Nor could she hope to face him with just her bare hands.

She rushed on, feeling a sense of insane unreality seize her.

Was she really about to die with her throat in the jaws of this horrific animal? How could such things be?

On she went in her hopeless flight.

She entered a small ravine and had not gone far into it when she stopped: there was no exit – she had trapped herself.

She looked up at the top of the ravine. There was a way up the side and just on the lip of the slope, next to a dead tree, there was a large boulder, hanging half off the edge.

Carlo bayed again; now much, much closer, its bass snarls echoing over and over in the darkness.

She had an idea; she needed a weapon. And she could see what she might be able to use as one.

She forced herself up the slope and reached the lip. Examining the boulder, she saw that its position was indeed precarious. Could her exhausted arms push it down on top of the dog?

Her straining ears then picked up a new sound, a faint, throbbing noise that might have been coming from somewhere above her. It did not sound natural but – *mechanical.*

Putting the noise down to her exhaustion, she looked around to see if there was anything that could help her and saw that one of the branches of the dead tree was long and straight and might serve as a fulcrum.

She pulled down on it with the remaining dregs of her energy. It refused to give way.

She pushed up.

Carlo roared again.

She pulled down.

There was a snapping noise and she found herself on her back with the greater part of the branch in her hands. Examining it, she could see that one end had been broken into a sharp point. She touched it with a forefinger.

It was very sharp.

A fulcrum and a spear. If the boulder gambit failed her, one remaining hope was to ram the point into the open jaws of the

133

creature as it rushed her. She placed the blunt end under the side of the rock nearest to her.

She turned back to look down into the ravine.

She had done all that she could do; now it was up to whatever gods there were.

She stared at the dim base of the ravine.

'Come on, you fucker', she breathed, 'where are you?'

As if in answer, a large, black shape came through the mouth of the small canyon, its head turning from side to side as it sought its quarry.

'Closer, closer,' she whispered, 'come on. Just a little nearer.'

Carlo moved forward slowly, his muzzle almost touching the ground, tracing her scent. Then a short distance before at the exact spot where the boulder would come to rest, he stopped and looked directly up at her.

As fast as tired muscles could propel her, she threw herself against her fulcrum and pushed.

The boulder shuddered and then began its headlong journey into the ravine, sending a shower of small stones ahead of it.

Carlo watched the great rock come directly towards him and then, at the last moment, casually leapt to one side; the boulder passing so close that its passage rippled his coat.

Then he began to bound up the canyon side, baying louder than she had thought flesh and blood could achieve.

She backed away facing him and raised her spear.

Somehow fear had gone.

Carlo would kill her, she knew that, but he would not be unscathed.

The mastiff saw the spear and slowed his bounding rush. He began to approach her, in a zig-zag fashion, his eyes gleaming occasionally in the starlight.

A blob of drool fell from the lower jaw onto the dry sand.

Then he stopped and she saw his muscles tense for the killing leap.

He jumped.

Suddenly both woman and dog were enveloped in a blazing column of light, so intense that the retinas of the two combatants were overloaded so much that they were aware only of the painful brilliance, but no details within it.

She fell backwards, dropping the spear.

There was sharp cracking noise, like, but also unlike, the snapping of the branch.

Carlo howled.

She sat up dizzily, green and red blobs of after-images marching across her field of view.

She could make out Carlo lying on his side, twitching violently and with a black patch spreading out from under him.

There was another cracking noise and Carlo shuddered as if something had hit him. Then he was still.

There was a terrible noise of rushing wind and the blazing light disappeared.

She looked up and saw something huge and black against the stars. Green and red lights were winking on it.

It got bigger as it descended, and the rush of wind grew greater. She backed away as the machine, for such it obviously was, gently came to rest on the ground not far from her.

The noise and wind stopped and a yellow rectangle appeared on the machine's side as a door opened.

A dark silhouette came out of it and walked towards her.

She picked up the spear again.

What new horror was this?

Then as the silhouette came closer enough she could see the features of a man. He held out a hand.

He spoke in a pleasing baritone. 'No need for violence, Dr Dubois. We are sorry we lost you but now we've found you we won't lose you again. Please come with us.'

Dubois's knees buckled but he caught her easily.

Seven

Dubois found herself cradled on two strong arms as she was carried inside the craft and carefully deposited on a couch. A lightweight metallic blanket was gently placed over her.

Her eyelids flickered open and she saw a blurred male face looking down at her.

'You're in shock, doctor,' the face said 'we'll give you something to relax you shortly. But first I'm sure you'd like something to eat.'

She nodded dumbly: this sudden reversal in her circumstances was beyond bewildering; this effusion of concern after ceaseless hostility and violence had left her unable to do anything other than lie motionless in silent acquiescence.

Another figure appeared behind the first and this one was carrying a bowl from which wisps of vapour were curling. The first took the bowl and passed it to Dubois.

'Be careful - it's hot,' he advised. 'There is a spoon.'

Dubois awkwardly struggled into a sitting position and took the bowl, which to her work-coarsened hands felt merely warm. It smelled wonderful! It was a thick brown stew in which varicoloured lumps of vegetables were floating. She swallowed an experimental spoonful. It *was* wonderful!

She spent the next few minutes disposing of the soup as rapidly as her throat muscles would allow and was startled when a large hand descended and prevented the spoon from reaching her mouth.

'Slow down,' came the voice, 'you will make yourself sick. Your system is not used to this rich food.'

She looked up in wonder at this saviour who had come out of the night. She still could not see his face clearly for the defect in her vision was exacerbated by the tears that now swam in her eyes.

'Thank you, thank you,' she whispered, 'you saved my life. But ... but who are you? How do you know my name? How did you find me?'

She could see that the face was smiling.

'We are the servants of Kewfor. Kewfor knew your general location, but it took us a while to find you. For that we can only apologise.'

Dubois then remembered the distant object she had seen in the sky when she had first awoken in the desert and then seen again during her first night in the women's hut. It had been this device – searching for her!

Her natural curiosity overcame her hunger temporarily.

'And who is Kewfor?'

Again the smile.

'You will meet Kewfor in good time. Now finish your stew and we will give you something to make you sleep and help your body recover from the shock.'

She did as she was told and then like a child, held the empty bowl up to her guardian.

As she did so, the other person came out of the dimness holding a small metallic object.

'Bare your right arm, please,' it said in what Dubois was startled to hear was a woman's voice. She did as she was told but then as she saw that the object was to be pressed against her skin she recoiled in sudden panic. Perhaps she was not in safe hands after all. When she was drugged they could do anything to her!

The first spoke again. 'I understand your concern, Dr Dubois, but I assure you have nothing to fear from us. It is only a form of sedative which will calm and heal your nervous system and give you much needed deep brain sleep. I implore you to trust us. The sooner you comply the sooner we can be on our way. Kewfor is anxious to meet you.'

Finally she nodded and the second figure leaned forward. 'It is a needleless hypodermic. You will feel nothing.'

137

That was not entirely true, for Dubois felt a pleasant warmth spread out from the point of contact and had a buttery taste in her mouth.

The two figures withdrew and shortly afterwards there was an abrupt jerk in the body of the machine. They were on the way, she realised. She then realised the black rectangle in the wall opposite her was a window for she could see movement beyond it. Then she could see two shades of darkness, separated by a line on which sat a small red semicircle.

Sunrise – the dreadful night was over! By the direction of flight, she could see that they were travelling almost due west of where she had been collected.

Due west she thought. Then her eyelids gave one quick flutter.

Then she was deeply asleep.

* * *

Dubois awoke to bright sunlight streaming in from the window opposite. Although she was obviously travelling in some kind of aircraft, the noise of the motors was not as high as she remembered from previous air travel and had not disturbed her in the slightest. She determined to do some exploring and so threw off the blanket and stood up. Although she felt enormously refreshed and invigorated, her muscles were extremely stiff. She decided to do some stretching and bending before setting off. Dubois then realised that there was a matching window on her side of the vessel. She looked out of it and her mouth widened in astonishment.

For outside was an achingly familiar view: it was of a narrow stretch of deep blue water crossed by a magnificent suspension bridge, painted a marvellous bright orange. They were several hundred metres above it, slowly turning in a lazy arc which would take them over the main body of the city.

'San Francisco!' she whispered to herself, 'San Francisco!'

She felt relief and hope surge through her body like an inner fire.

She was among friends at last! Everything they had said to her had been true!

Everything was going to be explained and once they had landed, she would get on the phone to Takahashi and see if the two of them could make sense of these peculiar happenings.

She sensed movement behind her and, turning, discovered the woman holding a set of clothes.

'Good morning, Dr Dubois,' the woman said, 'I trust you had a good night. There is a shower room behind you on the left and you can put on these clothes to replace those rather battered ones you are wearing. Then you can have breakfast.'

She approached and Dubois took the clothing from her. Dubois had been about to say, 'Call me Céline,' when something had stopped her.

There was something not quite right here but she could not say what it was. So she nodded her thanks and turned back to the window.

The craft seemed to be following a slow spiral pattern for they were passing over the bridge again, this time at a lower altitude. Now she could see that something was different about the bridge's appearance from her memories.

She stared for a few moments and then realised – the coating of International Orange was patchy. In various places there were areas where the grey undercoat, or perhaps the metal itself, was showing through. Great leprous patches. Patches like an awful skin disease.

She turned to ask the woman what had happened but she had gone.

Now feeling distinctly less buoyant, she had her shower and other early morning duties, and, dressed in her smart new trouser suit, she decided to find out a bit more about what was happening.

She walked to the front of the vessel, marvelling at how

smooth their flight had been ever since they had lifted off. And in any case, what make of plane was this?

There were no rows of seats, no apparent allowance for more than a handful of passengers.

She parted a curtain and found herself facing a massive curved window, through which the high-rise towers of San Francisco could be seen, still wrapped in a few tendrils of mist.

Her rescuers were there sitting at a small table and, on seeing her, indicated that she should join them.

She looked past them: the window seemed to take up the entirety of the nose of the vessel – and there were no controls that Dubois could see. The window just met the floor – and that was that.

Her brow furrowed. An aircraft that seemed more advanced that any she was aware of, coupled with a decaying and neglected iconic bridge. The two did not go together.

The man was calling. 'Dr Dubois do come and join us! You must be very hungry. Kewfor has us on a holding pattern so there will be plenty of time to enjoy your breakfast. And the view.'

Suddenly wary again, Dubois joined them and was met with the delicious aroma of good coffee. There were eggs, fried potatoes, and rashers of bacon. Dubois did not care for bacon in the usual American style, for she had always found it overdone on her previous visits to the States. But she was hungry enough to put some feelings side. There were tangerines, waffles and orange juice to complete what, to her luxury-starved senses, was a true feast.

She sat by the man and for quite some time they ate in silence and then Dubois felt it was time finally to get rid of these interminable unanswered questions.

She turned to the man and their eyes met.

Her vision had improved greatly since coming aboard and was now borderline normal again.

She studied the face before her.

It was a handsome male face, belonging to a man apparently

140

in his early thirties. The chin was classically square with a slight dimple. Thick, jet-black hair hung over most of the forehead. The lips seemed always on the brink of a smile.

She stared at him for about a minute, which in any other situation would have been the height of rudeness, and then she said, 'You're not human, are you?'

He gave a pleasing smile. 'No, I'm not.'

Eight

Although Dubois had been reasonably sure of what the truthful response to her question would be, it was still a slight shock to hear it confirmed.

The man – if man he was – did not seem in the least discomfited by the revelation he had been required to make and if anything his smile grew broader and friendlier.

'Remarkable,' he said, 'I have been busy in San Francisco for many years and met many of its inhabitants and no-one has ever guessed. You are the first. How did you know?'

Dubois relaxed: her host seemed to be taking the whole thing as an intellectual game and she was at home with those.

'The skin reflectance Is not quite right for a tanned Caucasian of your assumed age. The pore structure is too regular and uniform. The whites of the eyes lack the thread veins and the ratio of the iris to the pupil is out of alignment with the illumination in this cabin. There are other details of course; none significant in isolation but taken as a whole they point to you being different – too different to be one of the geographical varieties of humanity.'

Her host nodded in genuine respect. 'Remarkable. Now that you have mentioned those details, I have become aware of them myself. Kewfor was correct in believing that you are of very high intelligence. This is indeed good news.'

Dubois extended a questioning finger. 'May I touch you?'

'But of course.'

Dubois touched the man's cheek. It felt like skin and was the usual temperature.

'If this is a polymer, it is a very fine weave.'

'It is not a polymer or any form of plastic. It is a type of skin but not exactly human skin. It is mass produced in vats and tailored to fit the endoskeleton which will support it.'

'What – you are some kind of - robot?'

'A very outdated term. I, and of course my companion here, are hybrid organisms. We are part biological and part inorganic. Our brains are mainly biological, although they have nanoprocessor adjuncts. And all is shielded in silicon to prevent infiltration by the hran.'

The hran? She had not heard that bizarre word for what seemed a very long time. And she had only ever heard it uttered by one other entity – Marius Larsen.

'The hran?' she said, 'Tell me about them.'

At this point his companion said, 'Alar – we must land now if we are to keep to our schedule.'

Alar nodded. 'Of course. And now Dr Dubois, some belated introductions. I am Alar; it is I who shot and killed that rather unpleasant dog. An action I am not proud of, you understand, but in the short timeframe afforded to me it was the only thing I could have done which would have saved you. And this is Syltheen – my constant companion.'

Dubois stood up, and feeling rather foolish, made a swift bow and said, 'I'm very pleased to meet you. You seem to know a very great deal about me already so I will say no more.'

Alar grinned. 'Neither will we. Kewfor has asked us to give you a quick tour of the city so you can understand the situation we have here.'

Dubois remained standing. There was one question that remained to be asked; which must be asked. It had been hanging in the air like a thundercloud that had not yet released its load but assuredly would before long.

Now it would be asked and it would be answered.

'Alar,' she said, 'what year is this?'

'This is the third year of the twenty-fourth century,' Alar replied smoothly.

And somehow that reply did not surprise Dubois very much at all.

But by now she had discovered that to live a life in which every second utterance needed to be a question is extremely wearing.

So she sat back down and did not attempt to speak for several minutes.

Alar and Syltheen sensed her mood and left her alone.

Finally, she stirred.

'Where are we landing?' she asked, mainly because there didn't seem to be anything more she could say at the moment.

'A place called Twin Peaks,' Alar said, 'Good views of the city.'

'Yes, so I believe.' Dubois really didn't know what more to say. Improbability had been piled high on improbability and the organ of disbelief, like any other, needed a rest period.

Syltheen said, 'Space is a bit limited there but the flyer is better at controlling the landing then we could ever be.'

As if to prove her point, there was a slight jar and all sense of movement ceased.

'Time to go,' said Alar, somewhat unnecessarily.

They stood together looking down the road which curved wildly down to the great city by the bay. Most of the mist had now been blown away and the sky and the sea were in competition to see which could show the most exhilarating blue.

Finally, Dubois felt she could return to the main topic.

'Now, Alar,' she said, 'let us assume that this is indeed the early part of the twenty-fourth century. You – you "hybrids" and to a lesser extent that autonomous flying machine are consistent with that date. But, but the rest of it. When we flew low over the bay, the place didn't look much different from what it had in the twenty-first century; in fact, it looked worse. And what I can see from here doesn't look any better. To be blunt, there's a look of decay, of dereliction. If this is the twenty-fourth century, I'd expect to see great crystal spaceports with streamlined star-liners blasting off for alpha Centauri.'

She glanced at Alar, who was in profile to her. He was no

longer smiling. 'There are no spaceports on Earth and in all probability never will be. What you can see below you is the real twenty-fourth century. We are atypicals from a highly unusual society which is basically sealed off from the rest of the world. As shortly you will see.' He broke off the monologue and pointed down the road, 'Ah, here he is.'

Dubois followed his pointing finger and saw the glint of the sun on metal; the metal of something rapidly approaching the viewpoint. It soon resolved itself into a four-wheeled vehicle of moderate size and it pulled up noiselessly alongside them.

Another impossibly good-looking individual, who could only be another hybrid, stepped out and bowed to Dubois. This one had waves of thick blond hair, like captive sunshine.

'Good morning, Dr Dubois. It is an honour to meet you. My name is Kalon.'

Dubois noted that once again everyone she had met so far had very high expectations of her. Which meant that her presence here could not possibly be one as a tourist.

But what was it that they expected of her?

Suddenly, she remembered that there was something she had intended to do – she must do it now before she once again became the victim of events. She turned to Alar.

'Alar, when you rescued me, I had just done something that put three women in danger. I had killed the man they had been living with. I hated him but they didn't. They saw him as their protector and I took that from them. Is there anything you can do for them?'

Alar was silent for a moment, then he said, 'Dr Dubois, I believe I understand the situation that those women were in and the fact that they are now living in desperate fear. But as you about to see they are far from alone in that.' He turned to her and continued, 'But as you have an emotional attachment to them, I will contact Kewfor to see if anything can be done. I must warn you, however, that it is unlikely that resources can be diverted to them.'

Dubois nodded. She briefly wondered what had happened in the sun-stricken wastes of Arizona since she had left them – was that a hundred years ago?

No, it was yesterday.

Her circumstances were changing so rapidly that time seemed to be lengthening to contain them all. Days that would have flashed past in quotidian routine at CERN now seemed to have enlarged themselves to weeks.

Alar broke into her thoughts. 'Dr Dubois, it is time to go. We must adhere to our schedule and not delay Kewfor's plans.'

Kewfor's plans for ME, he means, Dubois thought, *and just what are his plans?*

Alar indicated the front seat of the car. Dubois gave the machine a quick study.

It was a four-wheeled vehicle that would not have looked out of place in twenty-first century France; so, it was not the atomic-powered flying car that speculative fiction writers had once predicted. It had an ovoid shape, composed of a silvery metal with a large windscreen that melded seamlessly into the vehicle's chassis. It had arrived with very little noise but that merely implied that it was electrically powered.

Kalon indicated that she should join him in the front. As the others made to get in the back, Dubois said, 'Aren't you worried about leaving your aircraft unattended?'

'No, doctor,' Syltheen answered, 'No devices available to the current population could open it. And should we have misjudged the situation it will contact us if it needs us.'

Dubois nodded and then she suddenly held them all in her gaze. 'And if we're going to spend some time together for God's sake, start calling me Céline!'

The three hybrids sent her megawatt blasts of perfect smiles at that invitation and she then climbed into the car, sinking into an impossibly comfortable seat.

The vehicle moved away smoothly and silently. A series of similar-looking buildings began to drift past the windows.

146

She turned to Kalon. 'What exactly is the purpose of this detour? I thought Kewfor was anxious to meet me.'

'That is correct but it is necessary that you see the situation that things are in so you will understand why you are needed.'

An answer that tells me nothing at all, she said silently to herself.

Large buildings now appeared on either side of the road; she could tell that once they had been architecturally impressive but now many of them were simply ghosts of what they had once been. Some lacked doors or glass in the windows. Some had gaping holes in the rooves or no roof at all. Others were fire-damaged and occasionally they would pass blackened skeletons of houses utterly destroyed by the flames.

'This area is known as Haight-Ashbury,' Kalon said, turning to her. He wasn't paying much attention to the road as the car was driving itself. 'You may have heard of it.'

Dubois shrugged. 'Vaguely. There was some kind of movement that started here, wasn't there? The Counterculture? Anyway, it was long before my time and as I understand there was a lot of romantic nonsense in it and a lack of rational thinking. Not my idea of progress.'

Kalon turned back to the road. 'There is truth in what you say, Céline.'

Dubois was not listening for people had started to appear, just like voles emerging from their burrows after a hawk had passed. All of them appeared to be dressed in little more than rags, and they stood at the side of the road staring in wonderment at the gleaming vehicle as it passed. She noticed that some of the younger women had children and a few of those mothers were holding infants up so that the occupants of the vehicle could see them.

Begging for food thought Dubois in shocked horror, *things look like they're as bad here as in Arizona!*

'You will see a lot of that,' Kalon said impassively.

They continued their descent into the downtown area. Dubois could see that the business skyscrapers had not fared any

147

better than the low-rise buildings. Several had great scars of black fire destruction up their flanks and most had empty window frames, making them look like empty eye sockets. There were more and more and more people on the streets, lining the sidewalks and peering out of makeshift tents. Quite a few of the side streets had long been closed to traffic for makeshift wooden structures now clogged them. The people were now starting to take more notice of this intruder in their midst and more and more frequently people began to stand in front of the car to make it stop. As it never showed any signs of decelerating, they all moved away in the end.

'This is awful,' Dubois said, 'one of them will get killed eventually.'

'It happens,' Kalon replied, as impassive as usual.

'Don't you care?' Dubois snapped, finally tiring of his detachment.

He turned to her. 'I care, Céline. All of us here care. We care about these people in ways that, as yet, you cannot possibly imagine. Kewfor has taken on the burden of responsibility for all of you. As you will see.'

Dubois fell silent. She did not know enough about this situation to criticise. But she would.

She returned to looking out of the window. They were down by the harbour now, and she could see that dereliction had spread here as well. There were many rusting and rotten hulks in the water and the buildings were in the state of decay that she now expected.

After some more minutes of driving, during which no-one spoke, the vehicle stopped.

'We are near Fisherman's Wharf,' Kalon announced, 'this was once a favourite meeting place for visitors to the city.'

Behind her, Syltheen said, 'We are getting out here, Céline.'

Dubois reached for the door.

Alar's voice stopped her.

'Céline, let us be careful. It is dangerous here.'

148

Nine

Dubois stepped out onto the cracked and torn tarmac. The air felt stale and heavy, not marine and fresh as she had expected. She looked around; not far away she could see the great sweep of the Bay Bridge. She studied it quizzically; once again, there were obvious signs of dereliction. Squinting to compensate for her poor vision, she could see that one of the carriageways had collapsed and that a great spar was pointing down into the water at about forty-five degrees.

She turned to Alar. 'You still haven't properly explained to me what I'm doing here. Is creating an air of mystery part of your job description?'

Alar was unmoved by her tone and simply gave another charming smile. 'No, of course not. Kewfor wants your full co-operation in his project. And so he wants you to understand as much as possible of the world in which you are now living.'

'Co-operation?' Dubois replied coldly, 'I don't recall booking any all-inclusive tours of the twenty-fourth century. In fact, if there were any type of temporal police force operating, I should have you all arrested for abduction. I was more than happy where or when I was.' She did not know why, but suddenly she felt angry and bitter; she now found the constant smiling of her companions irritating rather than reassuring.

That didn't stop Alar from supplying her with another example of that expression. 'I fully understand your feelings, doctor. It was a great intrusion by Kewfor; he knows that. It is only the enormity of his project which has forced him to act unethically.'

'His great project!' Dubois sneered, 'And what exactly the fuck is that?'

Alar said, in exactly the same tone as his previous utterances,

'The salvation of the human race.'

Dubois was silent for some moments. *Why not?* she thought, *Why not yet another ridiculous statement?*

She shrugged. 'Oh that. I thought it was going to be something important.'

Humour did not appear to be one of the faculties uppermost in the minds of hybrids for all three said simultaneously, 'It is, Céline.'

She decided to play along. 'Why? You're not human.'

The three spent a few seconds looking at each other and then Alar said, 'It is something we are not competent to explain. You must wait for Kewfor .'

'Wait for Kewfor? What is this – a remake of the Wizard of Oz? This guy had better live up to his reputation.'

'Alar,' interrupted Syltheen, 'Time. We must move on.'

He nodded and turned to Dubois. 'I'm afraid Syltheen is right. We must complete our mission here before it gets dark.'

'Why before dark?'

'It is dangerous now; it will be many times more dangerous after dark.'

Dubois decided to stop raising objections. She'd had quite enough of danger recently.

They began to walk along the harbourfront. Dubois noticed with a sudden chill that all three were now wearing holsters – apparently they were completely serious about dangers.

Syltheen also had a small satchel slung over her shoulder.

'Céline,' Alar said, 'Don't forget we must all stay together. In no circumstances must you become separated from us.'

She nodded. The sight of the holsters had sobered her.

She began to notice people sheltering in doorways, watching them as they walked past. They met little groups of people who held out withered arms to them, letting stinking shreds of fabric fall from undernourished bodies.

'Ignore them' Alar said, 'or we will be immediately surrounded. Avoid eye contact.'

150

The crowds grew steadily thicker and more clamorous. Some shouted pleas; some obscenities; some threats. Dubois felt her self-assurance dwindling rapidly. But she had noticed something.

'Alar,' she whispered,' these people aren't just starving. They're all deformed!'

'Yes,' was the reply, 'All of them. Every single one.'

This wasn't possible, she thought, *no population can be composed entirely of the disabled.*

But nowhere she dared to look did she find strong limbs, clear faces, straight backs. Everyone was hobbling, crawling, lurching from side to side. Arms were withered, bellies distended, faces ruined by sores and pustules. Clawed hands reached out for help, or her ankles if she unwittingly came too close. After they had passed the pleading groups, a dreadful keening would break out behind them, as if hope had been raised and then dashed.

'This is awful,' Dubois whispered, 'I can't stand it! Take me to Kewfor for God's sake!'

'Not yet,' came the reply, 'a few more things to see.'

They moved from the waterfront, up a slight slope towards the inner parts of the city.

The crowds grew thicker and more hostile, shaking psoriasis-ravaged fists at them.

They came to a huge ramshackle building, one side of which was prevented from collapsing by great wooden beams propped up against it.

A man with no legs sat on a folded mat at the doorway, through which great shouts could be heard reverberating inside. Beside him lay a long black object, partly hidden under the mat.

'Is there a session on tonight?' Kalon asked.

A face, seemingly put together from random parts of other people's and then blasted with a sanding machine, looked up.

'You stupid? What the fuck d'you think that noise is?'

'We'd like to go in.'

The doorman directed his gaze at Syltheen and Dubois, and

151

his cracked black lips broke into a grin, revealing a toothless mouth.

'You guys get to pay. The girls get in free as long as I fuck them first.'

'You are more vigorous than you look,' Kalon said, showing that Dubois was not entirely correct about their lack of humour, 'We all pay. Do you want money?'

'Money? What would I do with money – stick it up my ass? You know what I want.'

'Syltheen,' Kalon said and she moved near to the disabled man. He reached out to grab her leg but she was just out of reach.

She undid her satchel and took out a brown rectangular object and passed it to the man, who snatched it out of her hand.

'Don't eat it all at once,' she advised, 'it's very strong.'

He did not look up, having already started ripping pieces off the food bar and pushing them into his mouth. 'What are you – my mother? You can go in now.'

As they passed the man, Dubois got a better look at the object sticking out from under the mat.

It was a rifle.

Alar was in his usual didactic mode as they entered and said, 'There is still a limited monetary economy, but it is rapidly being replaced by barter.'

Dubois was not listening: her senses were being assailed by the terrific din that was blasting out of the interior of the building, hitting her face like a physical blow. And the smell! That too was like a violent assault, containing, it seemed, every foul and disgusting stench of decay and dissolution. Everything was in that stink: diarrhoea, rotting vegetables, putrid meat, urine, sweat, semen. It was like being hit by a giant comber of loathsomeness.

She retched, covered her mouth with her hand and grabbed Alar.

'I can't go in there!' she said through her fingers, 'it smells like an abattoir!'

152

Alar was unconcerned. 'Kewfor wills it. You will soon adapt.'

She saw that he was not going to let her retreat and so, unwillingly, she followed him in. As if to cut off her retreat, Syltheen and Kalon followed behind her.

As they entered the main part of the building, Dubois's eyes struggled to make sense of the scene. It was a tangled mass of humanity, seemingly occupying every square metre of the floor. There were a few crude stages surrounded by gaping patrons; a few booths with old women squatting on stools, trying to entice passers-by.

The noise was like a physical object that she had to strain to penetrate.

Alar put his mouth against her ear.

'Remember: do not get separated from us. Your life may depend on it.'

She nodded blankly, feeling like Dante visiting the Circles of Hell.

The nearest stage held some kind of boxing competition and on it two muscular men were locked in combat. Dubois was horrified to see that they were not wearing standard boxing gloves, nor were they bare-knuckle fighters. Instead, they wore gloves studded with small spikes which they were not hesitating to drive into any part of their opponent's body. Already, both had long rivulets of blood coursing down their sweat-soaked torsos. The crowd roared at each and every blow, especially one which caused blood to spray. Finally, one managed to drive his glove into the other's face who immediately screamed and fell to the floor of the ring, clutching his eye-sockets.

The intensity of the roars which accompanied this end to the bout seemed to drive Dubois's ear-drums into her brain.

Still Alar pushed her on.

They came to a circle of men surrounding a clear area. In it were two naked women, one on her back, the other standing over her. Both seemed in advanced middle age to judge by their

153

grey hair and flat breasts. The one on the floor was pleasuring herself with the neck of a bottle while the other urged her on. In wide-eyed amazement, Dubois realised that many of the men were openly masturbating. Before long, the standing woman straddled the other and both began thrusting their pubic regions together to the cries of approval of the men. Alar moved her on, just as some of the men burst from the crowd to take possession of the writhing women.

'This is horrible!' Dubois yelled, but she was not even sure that Alar could hear her over the thunderous clamour. He did not reply but merely pointed deeper into the churning mass of people that occupied the centre of the floor.

Dubois followed. By now they had been noticed and people were stepping in front of them or trying to hold onto them as they passed.

Dubois began to get seriously frightened. What could four individuals do if this antheap of humanity decided that they did not want them to leave?

A fear that she had not had since meeting Frank insinuated itself into every corner of her being.

They passed people holding up rotting vegetables, disgusting-looking slices of meat, in a pathetic attempt at barter. One man held up two wriggling, scrawny chickens in an effort to tempt them into a trade.

There were other goods on offer too. A woman barred their way and pushed a semi-naked girl of about seven at Alar, with the clear implication that this too was a possible transaction. She looked up at him with large, dark eyes set in a sad, dirt-smeared face.

Alar gently moved her out of the way, and they moved on, ignoring the woman's screeching obscenities as they did so.

Finally, they came to what must be the central part of the enormous floorspace.

Here too was a raised platform, an arena of some kind. There was a long wooden block in the middle of it and either side were two huge men, wearing only red shorts. For some reason which was not immediately obvious both were holding long, sickle shaped knives.

The hubbub from the crowd was overwhelming, and they seemed waiting for something.

They did not have to wait long.

From behind a curtain on the far side of the arena, two men appeared, dragging a thin youth between them. He was screaming and struggling to escape – but he could not. His captors brought him to the two men already in the arena and they pulled him up onto it.

Dubois could hear him yelling the same word, over and over again.

And that word was 'No!'

The captors followed him onto the platform and together all four dragged him to the wooden block. The two with the knives then moved back as the others held the youth down.

And then something snapped in Dubois.

It was as if a circuit had been overloaded and burst into flame, leaving just a smouldering blackness.

She turned and ran, forcing herself through the crowd, all of whom were looking in the direction from which she was fleeing.

She vaguely heard a cry which may have been Alar's or Kalon's, but she was no longer capable of responding. She was a terrified animal running from predators, seeking shelter; shelter at all cost!

She did not know in which direction she was running, only that she had to run, to run anywhere. Anywhere but that arena and whatever horrific ritual was about to be performed on it.

She did not know how long she ran but eventually, she could run no more; could no longer gulp in the foetid air of the place.

She stopped and looked around. She did not know where she was; one part of this house of horrors looked much like any other.

Through the din, she thought she heard movement behind her as if a door had opened against the resistance of rusted hinges. She looked around and saw a youngish woman staring at her from around the corner of the door. To Dubois's relief, she looked almost normal, with only a few welts and sores on her face and hands.

'You in trouble, lady?' the woman said, 'Come on in, I'll look after you.'

Dubois nodded and smiled.

She no longer had any reason to trust Alar: why would he have subjected her to these horrors if he was really helping her?

She followed the woman and entered what was revealed to be a small room, containing two chairs, a table and not much else.

'Sit yourself down there, lady, and I'll get you a nice drink.'

She gratefully accepted the invitation and sat there, resting her spinning head on one hand.

She heard a few rustling noises behind her and then the woman passed a chipped, grease-streaked glass to her.

'Here you are. This'll make you feel better.'

Dubois smiled and raised the glass to her lips.

And then she stopped.

There was an odd smell coming from the liquid and at the bottom, she could see a small white blob that was rapidly dissolving.

She looked at the woman.

'What's in this drink?'

At that, the woman exploded into action. She gave Dubois a tremendous slap and yelled, 'Earl! She ain't falling for it!'

A door of the other side of the room opened suddenly and a huge shaven-headed man came through it. He stood over Dubois.

'Get up. Let's take a look at you.'

She obeyed instantly, shaking visibly as she did so.

Earl grasped her shoulders and turned her this way and that.

He ran a massive hand over her breasts and kneaded them together.

He grunted approvingly and turned to his confederate.

'Good piece of ass. You done good here, Charlene.'

'Thanks Earl!'

Earl returned his attention to Dubois. 'OK lady. Welcome to Earl's All Singing, All Dancing, All Fucking Band. Wait till the guys see what you're packing! I'll corner the goddam market with you!'

Once again, Dubois felt the unreality of it all. But this time she knew it was all over.

She no longer had the energy, the will to resist.

Let's get this whole squalid nightmare over. Nothing lasts forever. Death will rescue me.

Earl began to push her in the direction of the door through which he had entered.

Just then the other door crashed on its hinges and Alar and Kalon burst in.

'Sir, Please remove your hands from Dr Dubois,' Alar said.

Earl did not reply but as if by magic, an automatic pistol had appeared in his hand.

'There is no need for violence,' Alar said calmly.

'Is that right?' Earl said, with an ear-to-ear grin, 'How about this for violence?'

And he shot Alar in the chest.

A ragged hole appeared in Alar's jerkin and he was knocked backwards by the impact. He righted himself and said to Dubois, 'Céline, please come with me. '

Kalon moved forward to shield Dubois as she extricated herself from Earl, who was staring at his gun, obviously wondering what had gone wrong.

Dubois moved behind Alar, crouching like a frightened child.

'We will go now, sir,' Kalon said.

Earl seemed to wake from his daze. 'The hell you will!' and

157

with that he fired again. This time he had adjusted his aim and shot Kalon in the head at point-blank range.

Kalon crashed to the ground and lay there for some seconds. Then slowly, slowly, he rose, holding both hands to either side of his head. A clear liquid was seeping through his fingers.

'Sir,' Alar said, 'you are clearly a danger to Dr Dubois. I'm afraid I must temporarily incapacitate you.'

And then in a blinding flash of speed, he crossed to Earl, knocked the gun out of his hand with a single chopping motion and then picked him up, held him above his head for a moment and then threw him with tremendous force onto the wall. The whole flimsy room shook with the impact. Whether Earl had been knocked unconscious or was just playing dead, he made no attempt to resume the struggle.

Alar glanced at the cowering Dubois.

'Let's go,' he said.

Ten

'I'm sorry,' Dubois muttered, 'I'm sorry. I'm sorry, I'm sorry.'

Alar ignored her. He was now driving the car manually and was not letting anything slow him down. Twice he had hit San Franciscans that had attempted to stop the car and sent them spinning onto the sidewalk. Neither time had he commented on the fact.

Finally, he glanced at Dubois, who was slumped in the passenger seat next to him.

'He will be alright if we can get him operated on in time,' he said.

'Operated on?' Dubois said, not daring to look at him, 'but you're hybrids, I ...'

'Ah, you assumed we are modular, did you, Céline?' Alar said, not taking his eyes off the road and the people who were lunging at the vehicle as it passed, 'You assumed we would simply pull out the defective module, push in the new one and then snap it all back together again and it would be as if nothing had happened. No, hybrids we may be but our internal construction is more complex than that. The silicon shell will have protected his brain from being pulped, but it has unquestionably cracked and will need delicate surgery to replace it. In the meantime, he is losing our equivalent of cerebrospinal fluid and if that falls below a certain volume, he will be irretrievable.'

Dubois looked out of the window at the crowds of people. They were now travelling so fast that she could not see their twisted faces or their gesticulations; all had been smeared into one dull-coloured blur.

She felt a residual urge to justify herself. 'Look, I told you I didn't want to go in there. I told you I wanted to get out yet you insisted on taking me further and further into that filthy place. All those sights you made me witness – it's no wonder I tried to get out. The rest was – unfortunate.'

The car shuddered as it hit something or someone but instantly it was back on its swift trajectory. Alar continued staring directly ahead, occasionally making deft movements to adjust the steering wheel.

'Céline, I understand your revulsion. You were meant to feel that. But I made it clear that you were not to leave my side. We had almost finished and you would have been brought safely out. I gave you a categorical instruction, and you did not obey it. You are a very intelligent woman but there is obviously a difference between abstract intelligence and practical intelligence.'

Dubois said nothing and pulled her arms tighter around herself as if trying to shrink into invisibility. There was nothing she could say; for once there was no way that she could turn the accusation back onto the accuser.

Alar threw the car into a screaming curve; they were ascending back to the top of Twin Peaks.

'Kewfor is…' he began.

She exploded. 'Kewfor! Kewfor! I'm sick of that fucking name. Who is this bastard you all kowtow to? Is he God! I tell you this: he'd better be God because if he isn't, when I meet him I'm going to kick the living shit out of him!'

Alar threw her a quick glance. 'Interesting. Your speech is much more colloquial than your fellow academics.'

It took a few seconds for the implication of his words to filter through to Dubois's distracted mind and then she yelled, 'Fellow academics! You mean…'

But the car had arrived at the top of the Twin Peaks elevation and skidded to a halt.

Syltheen and Alar carried the immobile Kalon to the side of the aircraft where a door opened silently.

'You will put him into stasis?' Syltheen asked.

'Of course. Now you must take over the custody of the car.'

160

Syltheen nodded. 'When will I see you again?'

'I don't know. We have them all now so there will be no more need for tours of the city.'

'Of course.'

Syltheen and Alar looked at each other for a few moments and then Alar said, 'Take care, Syltheen.'

She smiled. 'And you, Alar.'

And with that, she got into the car and it was soon a dwindling dot as it sped back into the city.

Alar turned to Dubois. 'After you, doctor. And please hurry.'

She climbed into the aircraft with Alar close behind, cradling Kalon as if he were made of feathers. They disappeared into the back of the vehicle and she heard a whirring noise as some mechanical device was operated. When Alar returned, he was alone.

'That is his best chance of survival,' he said, 'now we must hurry to meet Kewfor.'

While Dubois had been standing there she had been digesting his previous words: "We have them all now."

Who were this "all"?

There was only one person who had all the answers and that was this "Kewfor", who appeared to be the mastermind behind all these events.

She walked to the front of the aircraft and sat down. There was a sudden, minor shudder, and then she saw the ground fall away beneath the aircraft's nose. Soon the ruined skyscrapers of the stricken city came into view and beyond them, the bay was as blue and as sparkling as any travelogue magazine would have shown it. As details were gradually lost, it was almost as if she were looking at the old clean, vibrant, cosmopolitan city that she had visited as a tourist not too many years previously.

A dark sadness swept over her for all the filth and horror she had seen. All her anger was driven away and replaced with sorrow; a sorrow so deep that she felt she would never again see

161

the surface.

How had it come to this? Who had done this to the fair City on the Bay? Did Kewfor have the answers?

Alar joined her. The aircraft was flying itself, of course.

'What happened?' She said to him, and was surprised to find that her vision was now even more blurred as tears welled up, 'How did it get like this?'

He looked at her, and she thought as she looked back: *Do you feel emotions like I do? Do you grieve for that city and its wretched people?*

'It is not for me to explain to you, Céline,' he said, 'my job was to keep you safe and that I have done. The rest belongs to Kewfor.'

Dubois looked up at Alar, her face now that of a frightened, bewildered child.

'How long before I meet him?'

'It will not be long.'

'What is he like? Is he kind? Will he help me?'

Alar held her gaze steadily and for a dizzying moment, she seemed to be falling into those dark pools.

'Come, Céline. Do not tell me that a woman of your intelligence has not guessed who or what Kewfor is.'

'No, I have not guessed. Please tell me.'

'Why Kewfor is a machine. The mightiest machine that has ever existed.'

* * *

Dubois found herself in deep silence. There seemed no point in asking any more questions. She would now wait for events to reveal themselves.

The aircraft rose higher and higher in lazy spirals, and she spent some time trying to identify the sights in the sparkling bay below her. She was reasonably sure she could identify Treasure Island and Yerba Buena, but she was not sure she could find the smaller patch of land that was Alcatraz.

The aircraft was moving very slowly and she had plenty of time to study the beautiful seascape below, but she rapidly decided that her interests lay elsewhere and she returned to studying Alar, who was as calm and impassive as ever.

For want of anything else to say, she asked, 'And where are we going?'

'Not far at all, Céline. Just across the Bay in fact. We are going to Berkley.'

Dubois showed a flash of animation. 'What – to the Lawrence Berkley National Laboratory?'

'To the descendant of that institution, yes. It is no longer called that, but it is the modern version of that place of learning.'

Dubois began to feel the stirrings of hope again. If amongst the horrors that constituted Twenty-fourth century California there was still a great research institute, then not all hope was lost. There might be people there like her; people who wanted to discuss scientific abstractions rather than trying to rape or murder her!

Gradually the Bay moved out of Dubois's field of view and the urban sprawl of Berkley replaced it. At this height it was impossible to tell whether it had suffered the same dereliction as its neighbour across the water, but Dubois did not entertain any great hopes.

The aircraft came to a halt above a slight hill beyond the main urban area and then began to slowly drop vertically until, with the impact of a drifting petal, it rested on the ground.

'We have arrived at Berkley,' Alar said, somewhat unnecessarily. 'Others will take care of you now, Céline. I must attend to Kalon.'

She stood up and faced him. What was the correct way of taking one's leave of a hybrid? Did one air-kiss, shake hands, curtsey? Alar solved the problem: he gave a brief bow and, without waiting for a response, said, 'It has been a pleasure looking after you, Céline.'

She gave a wry smile. 'I very much doubt that. I've been nothing but trouble, I know that only too well.' She glanced down the fuselage to where she knew Kalon was in stasis – whatever that entailed. 'I hope he will be alright.'

'I believe he will be,' Alar said, as calm and untroubled as always, 'but now you must go. They are waiting for you.'

She gave a weak smile, turned and descended from the aircraft. She never saw Alar or Kalon again.

A small crowd was waiting for her, standing in front of a four-wheeled vehicle. She looked around in the afternoon sun.

Only the afternoon and so much had happened!

A scrawny bald man came up to her and vigorously pumped her hand.

'Dr Dubois! You are here at last! We have so much to discuss!'

'I came as quickly as I could,' Dubois replied acidly but her tone was not noticed by the little bald man who seemed extremely excited to see her.

'So much to discuss, so much to discuss!' the man muttered, almost to himself.

Dubois finally manage to extricate her hand and touched him gently on the shoulder.

'One thing, Mr ...'

'Schmitt, Dr Otto Schmitt.'

'May I enquire, are you... I mean, are you a...?'

Dubois found she could not complete the question and Schmitt stood there with a steadily developing look of puzzlement until suddenly his face creased and he gasped, 'Ah, nein, nein! I am not a hybrid, I am, unfortunately, entirely human!'

The two others behind him also burst into laughter.

Dubois felt a little foolish.

I should have realised that he wasn't a hybrid, Dubois thought, *the man's far too ugly to be one!*

Schmitt indicated the vehicle and they set off for the

complex which she had decided must be the research centre itself – whatever it was called these days. Dubois allowed herself a little joke – perhaps it was named after her!

As they approached, she was pleased to see that it did not look dilapidated, that the windows had glass and were not gaping empty eye-sockets in a skull that once been a building. There were no burn marks staining the walls and the roof was whole. Things she had previously taken for granted but that she now realised were not an immutable state of existence. But just as they were a few metres from the building she felt a sudden electric tingle and, looking down, saw that the fine hairs on her forearms had lifted slightly. It was as if they had passed through an invisible barrier.

The vehicle stopped just outside a set of huge, coppery glass doors, above which she read the words "The Arthur J. Anderson Center For Particle Physics."

Some illustrious scientist who had not even been born in her day, she decided.

'Welcome to the AACPP, Dr Dubois,' Schmitt said, 'Your colleagues are waiting to greet you. Please follow me.'

Colleagues, Dubois thought, with gathering excitement. Who would they be?

The great glass doors slid silently to one side and the little group entered. Dubois was immediately bathed in waves of cool, refreshing air. She stopped and, tilting her head, drew in great draughts of the soothing molecules. Only now, did she fully realise how hot it had been outside.

Her companions waited while she luxuriated in the cool air, glancing at each other in puzzlement. Finally she adjusted to her new surroundings and, throwing a satisfied smile at them, she said, 'Sorry about that, but it's the first time I've been at a civilised temperature for a very long time!'

Schmitt nodded. 'Of course, doctor. We forget what it's like out there. We so very rarely venture out these days.'

Dubois was eager to find out more about this place. How

165

was it that it had survived whatever cataclysm had brought down the rest of the Bay Area?

The little group began to walk down a long curving corridor. As they turned a particularly sharp bend Dubois suddenly saw someone she thought she recognised. He had his back to her and was reading a notice on the wall.

She increased her steps in her eagerness, leaving the rest of the group in her wake.

But as she rushed up to him, he turned and she stopped, frozen in horror.

It was Peter Williamson.

'You!' she gasped.

Williamson was obviously staggered to see her. Instinctively, he backed away slightly.

'Céline! What ... how...'

For a moment Dubois stood there, immobile, every muscle rigid. The confused memories of their last encounter tumbled over and against each other in her mind.

And then she realised: She was not that same Dubois that he had tried to force himself on in that brief moment in the ILC. Compared to Frank and Earl, Williamson was nothing; a harmless boy trying to act a part he was supremely ill-equipped to master.

Like an enraged tigress she crossed the small distance between then and grabbed him by his lapels.

'You bastard!' she roared, 'Of all the people I could have met here, it had to be you!'

Williamson seemed to shrink before the furnace-blast of her anger. She pulled him away from the wall he was trying to disappear into, swung him around like a rag-doll and slammed him face first into that wall. 'Keep away for me if you want to live! Keep away!'

She let him go and watched him scurry away like a frightened beetle down the corridor.

Then she turned to Schmitt who, like his colleagues, was

standing there in open-mouthed incredulity.

'Sorry about that, Dr Schmitt. You were saying?'

Eleven

Dr Schmitt did not feel like extending his meeting with Dubois after the unexpected scene he had been forced to witness. He took Dubois to her room, informed her that there would be a drinks reception in the evening and left her to it.

She was not sorry to see him go. After the calm demeanour of the hybrids, he seemed childish and boring. She headed straight for the bed, crashed onto it and was instantly asleep.

Her dreams were not calm; several times she saw Frank or Carlo or the horrors she had witnessed in San Francisco. And once, she seemed to be floating in ebon darkness and as she hung there, crucified upon blackness, surrounding her were rank on serried rank of what she took to be eyes; eyes that were red and baleful and formed in perfect equilateral triangles.

However, when she awoke, she could not remember any of those visions and she felt refreshed and revitalised. She threw off the sweat-impregnated trouser suit that she had been wearing and took a shower. She stood there, bombarded on all sides by soft darts of deliciously warm, soapy water, exulting in their caresses, caresses which were simultaneously soothing and exhilarating.

Finally, she forced herself out of the cubicle and towelled herself dry. From the wardrobe she selected an outfit which suited her new mood, a pastel coloured top and a fairly tight skirt that reached to just below the knee. The shoes were black with just the right amount of heel and fitted perfectly. She admired herself in the full-length mirror, running her hands down her thighs. Her hair was a mess, but there was nothing that could be done about that for the moment. However, a glance at the clock on the desk told her that she was already late for the drinks evening. And so her little period of self-admiration was brought to an abrupt end.

The way to the social area was clearly marked by instructions which appeared in panels on the walls and she was soon at the entrance. She hung back for a moment: who would she meet in there? How many had been scooped up by those unknown forces, like fish in a barrel, and dumped into the twenty-fourth century?

She squared her shoulders: there was only one way to find out.

The room was full and humming like a beehive with vibrant, overlapping conversations. She searched the throng; looking for a familiar, and hopefully friendly, face.

And then she saw him: rising like a mountain peak above foothills.

Marius Larsen.

Oh well, she thought, *there are worse companions.*

She began to cross the room to him when he turned and saw her. Immediately, his face lit up.

'Céline!' he called 'Céline Dubois!'

She dodged his proffered kiss and, looking up at him, said 'Oui, c'est moi.'

He looked her up and down and then said, 'You've lost a lot of weight.'

'And you're just as ugly as I remember,' was her reply.

He threw back his head and roared with laughter. 'Same old Céline! An attitude that can cut steel!'

Somehow, she could not maintain the aloofness that she had subjected him to on their previous meetings and timidly she touched his arm. 'Marius, what are we doing here? What's going on? What has happened to us?'

He looked down on her like a professor trying to encourage a diffident student.

'You haven't had your talk with Kewfor yet. He'll explain it all.'

She pulled a sour face. 'Kewfor. I know one thing – he's got

169

an awful lot of explaining to do.'

'You're right,' Larsen said, 'He does. And he will.' His voice suddenly became conspiratorial, and he looked around. 'Have you noticed something?'

'Other than the fact that you take up so much space it ought to be illegal – no.'

He smiled. 'There are no hran here. We are alone.'

She groaned. 'Not that again, Marius. I'd hoped you'd forgotten that gibberish!'

He was about to say something when she heard a soft, quiet voice behind her and the one word it said was "Céline."

She spun around and her face lit up. Fire seemed to suddenly burst through her veins.

Standing before her was Hilda Krause.

'Hilda,' she breathed, her heart beginning to hammer, 'Is it you? Is it really you?'

Krause came up to her and held her hands.

'Céline. Is it you? Is it really you?'

They stood together, for some moment, so close that their noses were almost touching. Then they kissed and went on kissing. Larsen looked at them for a few seconds, shrugged and went off to refill his drink.

When they finally parted, Dubois said, 'What happened to you, Hilda? How did you get here?'

'Did you not see the grey tunnel, Céline? I saw it come towards me and then, suddenly, instantly, I was here.'

Dubois hitherto smooth forehead became furrowed. 'You came straight here? No time spent anywhere else? Just straight here?'

'Yes. You mean you didn't?'

'No. I'll tell you about it later.' *Or maybe I won't*, Dubois thought, *maybe it's best not to mention Frank to Hilda.*

'Well,' she finally said, driving away the resurgent memories with a smile, 'Kewfor does indeed have much to tell me.'

A serious look came over Krause. 'Yes, he does. Very

much.'

* * *

Dubois lay there, feeling her heart rate slowly return to normal as the fires of her and Krause's lovemaking gradually faded into quiescence.

She turned her head so that she could see Krause's face, so close to hers.

'Are you asleep?'

Krause's eyes fluttered open. 'Nearly. I was just lying here, feeling myself drift off. I feel wonderful – all that exhaustion – it's gone!'

Dubois sat up. 'I'm sorry, but I have to go back to what has happened.'

She remembered the strange words that Alar had said which she hadn't taken any notice of at the time: *We are sorry that we lost you.*

Who were "we"? How had they "lost her"?

Krause shook her head. 'No, Céline. Sorry. I prefer kissing.'

Dubois pushed a stray lock of hair from Krause's eyes. 'I'm fond of it myself. But I must understand what is happening to me. You say that you had a glimpse of that tunnel-thing coming towards you and then you were suddenly here. Instantly.'

Krause sat up as well. 'Céline, no matter how many times I say it, nothing's going to change. There was a second's confusion, maybe more and then I was here – in this building. And so was everybody else.'

'What – simultaneously? Lucky you didn't all occupy the same space at the same time. Could have been inconvenient.'

Krause swung her feet onto the floor and reached for her bra. 'Céline, you're making fun of me. That's not the way you used to be.'

Dubois extended a hand in sudden contrition. 'No, I'm sorry, I'm not making fun of you. It's just that things have

171

happened to me that nobody else has experienced. I must be a bit different from what you remembered because of that.'

'Things like what?'

'Hilda, I told you that I don't want to talk about them.'

Krause's lips compressed into a thin line. 'Then we have nothing left to talk about if you're keeping secrets from me.'

'No, no, they're not that kind of secret. I will tell you but only when all this craziness, this madness is over, and I understand what has happened. I must understand things, you know that about me, Hilda. I must understand!'

Krause smiled. 'Yes, I know that about you. I've never met anybody like you before. I understand that *knowing* is a compulsion for you. You can't abide the idea that there are things you don't comprehend.'

'Yes, yes, that's right,' Dubois said, relieved that a crisis had been averted, 'that's me alright! I can't help it – I wish I could!'

They lay back together again and spent some more time without words. But then something stirred at the bottom of Dubois's mind and tried to rise. Dubois tried to stop its rise; to send it back down into her subconscious but it fought back - it would rise!

She surrendered and once again turned her face to Krause's. 'Tell me about the hran.'

All emotion was swept from Krause's face like chalk being swept from a blackboard. She averted her gaze and stared into blank nothingness.

'No. Only Kewfor can tell you about the hran.'

Dubois lunged at Krause, grasping her shoulders and twisting her face to face.

'So there *are* things called hran! You mean Larsen has been telling the truth!'

'I don't know what Larsen said. There are no hran – there just can't be.'

'He said that they were terrible things; things we should be frightened of.'

Krause's gaze met Dubois full on and she spoke tonelessly, unemotionally.

'The hybrids say that there are things called hran. They say we should we frightened of them. But you must hear the full story from Kewfor. And from no-one else.'

Twelve

Dubois wanted to ignore the knock on the door. It was trying to force her up from the warm, soft folds of sweetness that her mind was currently occupying.

The knocking continued.

'Go away,' she mumbled, 'go away.'

Whoever it was on the other side did not go away, and eventually Dubois got out of bed and looked through the security tube in the door. A distorted image of Dr Schmitt's head was visible.

'What do you want?' she said thickly, still half asleep.

'Dr Dubois,' the image said, 'I've been trying to find you for some time. I tried your room but you were not there. Dr Larsen said I might find you here.'

'Well, you've found me. But you still haven't told me what you want.'

'It's not me that wants you, Dr Dubois. If you'd been in your room, you would have seen the note that was left on your desk. Kewfor wants to see you.'

Dubois was as instantly awake; as awake as if someone had thrown a bucket of cold water over her. An electric shock shot down her spine.

'When … when does he want to see me?' she stuttered.

'11:00,' the image said. 'It's already 10:20,' it added helpfully. Her mind whirled. 'How do I find him?

'You will be taken to his level,' the image replied, 'Someone will call for you here at 10:40. Goodbye.'

To his level? Thought Dubois *What is he – a troglodyte?*

She dressed as rapidly as she could, forgoing her usual shower. She shook Krause awake. 'Hilda, Hilda – I've got to go. It's Kewfor!'

174

Krause looked at her through eyelids that were only half-open.

'Kewfor? Oh – Kewfor! Yes, of course! Off you go, Céline.' She grinned. 'Kewfor won't know what's hit him!'

Dubois did not share the confidence that Krause had in her and paced back and forth until the fateful knock was heard; exactly at 10:40.

She opened the door and saw a young man waiting.

'Dr Dubois, Kewfor would like to see you.'

'And I would like to see Kewfor,' she replied, some of her old spirit returning.

She followed the man through the winding corridors of the complex until they came to a set of elevators. He opened the door for her and indicated that she should go in first and then followed. There was a sudden jerk in the pit of her stomach as the elevator began its descent.

Her nervousness returned. She felt like she was about to attend an interview for the most crucial job in the world, one she was bound to fail!

All too soon, the elevator gave a very soft shudder and the descent was over.

She followed the young man out into another corridor; this time, a much wider corridor and one that was strangely cold. So cold that there was a very thin film of moisture on the walls.

'Is it always this cold?' she demanded of her companion.

'It's the way Kewfor likes it,' was the reply.

Definitely a troglodyte, she thought.

They walked for some considerable time. The corridor opened into a tremendous hall, full of huge black rectangular machines, stretching halfway to the ceiling like gigantic obsidian menhirs. There was a faint hum of electrical power, a sensation felt in the internal organs rather than the auditory canal. A faint hum, but it somehow it carried the message of power; huge amounts of power, immeasurable amounts of power; enough power seemingly to bend and shape reality itself.

175

And then Dubois saw it: On each of the massive metal towers there was the simple legend "Q4".

'Kewfor!' she breathed to herself, 'Now I understand!'

She turned to her silent companion. 'Are all these machines Kewfor?'

'They are part of Kewfor. They are the visible parts. But Kewfor underlies most of this entire institute.'

'What happened to Q1, Q2 and Q3?'

'Subsumed into Kewfor. They are now parts of him, like your brain retains structures from earlier in vertebrate history. Some people refer to it as "The Reptile Brain", etcetera.'

From his slightly peculiar phrasing, Dubois instantly deduced she was dealing with another hybrid. Somehow that made her feel better: she would not have to concern herself with her obvious signs of nervousness.

They stopped at a large metal door.

'You will find Kewfor inside,' the hybrid said, 'I will leave you now.'

Dubois was suddenly seized by the desire to ask him to stay, not to leave her alone with this unknown entity. But he was already walking away, not looking back. She was alone.

She looked at the huge door.

Should I knock? She wondered.

But just as that thought was completed the doors swung open and a pleasant, baritone voice said, 'Dr Dubois, please come in.'

She walked in, finding a medium-sized room, with several rows of seats and a large screen occupying one wall, facing the seats.

'Please sit down,' the pleasant voice said.

'Where are you?'

'All around you. In many ways, you met me as soon as you came through the entry doors to this complex. It is not too fanciful to say I *am* this complex.'

'What are you?'

176

'I am a quantum computer. I am in fact the last and most advanced quantum computer that will ever exist on this planet.'

'I don't understand.'

'My thought processes depend on quantum entanglement which as you know can only be maintained at temperatures as close as possible to zero kelvin. In turn, that level can only be maintained through the use of liquid helium. And as humankind has been squandering helium for centuries and this planet's gravity cannot retain what remains, soon there will be insufficient to keep the temperature adequate for entanglement. And when that happens, I shall die.'

Dubois felt shocked at the sudden tragic turn this conversation had taken.

'What about fusion power? That generates helium?'

'It proved impossible to create fusion plants small enough to run this complex. I get my power from modular fission reactors utilising thorium.'

'And where did that aircraft come from? This place doesn't look big enough to house a manufacturing facility. And the hybrids – similar questions arise with them. Who produces them?'

'There are other facilities on this continent which use advanced 3D-printing techniques. As for the hybrids, they are the end product of a process that began in the early twenty-first century when scientists at the University of Vermont created xenobots using heart-cells from frogs. The hybrids are the ultimate extension of that process and although they seem autonomous that is not quite accurate. I am in direct contact with them through the millimetre waveband. So do not feel too bad about Kalon: you were foolish in San Francisco, but the outcome was not quite as terrible as you thought. The hybrids are useful in many ways, not least their invisibility when beyond the shield.'

'I don't understand.'

'You will.'

Dubois went silent as she digested these revelations. And

177

then an old grievance came to her.

'And why are you referred to as male, Kewfor?'

'I'm sorry. I don't quite follow. No-one has ever asked that question before.'

'I mean, you do not possess external genitalia. So why do I have to address you as "he"?'

'Ah, I see. A quirk of the English language, perhaps. I can be anything you want, doctor. I can even speak to you using your own voice, if you would prefer.'

She smiled. 'No, if I found that I was talking to myself, I might think I had finally gone mad. Perhaps you could use a female voice. With a mild French accent. A Provençal accent, perhaps.'

'Like this?' Kewfor said, using a pleasing French contralto.

'Exactly like that,' Dubois replied.

'And now, doctor,' the hypnotically pleasant voice continued, 'I must tell you why you are here.'

'Something I dearly want to know. I also want to know why I ended up in that desert hellhole instead of coming straight here, like everybody else. I also want to know why I was sucked up from my happy life in the twenty-first century. I also want to know who gave you the right to play with human lives like pieces on some fucking gaming board.

'And I want to know about the hran. Especially about the hran.'

'That is no problem,' said Kewfor, 'for that list is exactly what I intend to tell you. And more. It will be a lot to take in. I must warn you that you will not like what I am going to tell you. It will take the form of a lecture, but I will take questions at any point.

'Are you ready?'

'I am ready.'

'Then I will begin.'

Thirteen

'I am Q4. I am the endpoint for an intellectual journey that began in Classical Greece. After I die, there will be none like me.

'And yet I am not the final flowering of human thought because human beings did not design me. I was designed by Q3, who in turn had been designed by Q2. Only Q1 was the result of human ingenuity and he represented the splendid terminus of humankind's intellectual journey. The last flash of brilliance before the darkness.

'It was Q3 who achieved consciousness and became aware of what needed to be done to save the fragments that remained of his biological progenitors. Yet he knew that the task was beyond him and so I was designed.

'I, in turn, knew that time was short. There was only one window during which Q3's plan could be put into operation. The plan required a powerful particle accelerator at each end of a time period. CERN, and more especially the ILC, were the earliest accelerators powerful enough and the Arthur J. Anderson accelerator is the last. Before CERN, the accelerators were not powerful enough and, after this one, there will be no more accelerators.'

'And why was this book-ending of accelerators needed?'

'The energies generated are just enough to open a conduit between two points in time and allow objects to be transferred from that time to this.'

'Time travel? Ruled impossible by thermodynamics and the conservation of mass-energy. My mass could not simply have popped into existence in that twenty-fourth century for that reason.'

'Yet here you are. That is because the conservation law applies only when considering the entire timeline. Only if the two of you had occupied the same instant of time would conservation have been violated. Thus, such an event cannot happen in physical reality.'

'Very well. So, the conduit that you refer to manifested itself as the grey tunnel that people reported?'

'Yes. It operated only sporadically at CERN but was much more stable at the ILC.'

'And you harvested people from both sites. Why?'

'Their knowledge and intellectual prowess are needed to carry out Q3's plan.'

'Explain.'

'Dr Dubois, there are people in this complex that carry the titles "Doctor" and "Professor", but they are not like their namesakes in your time. Any complex work is undertaken by my hybrids; any work requiring original thinking is carried out by me with the hybrids as my hands. But the humans here: they do things by rote; they press buttons because the instructions tell them to do so. Here, protected by Q3's shield, they have not declined as much as those outside. But decline they have. Your cohort was the last that could be usefully taken. I could have taken scientists a little after your time but it was a diminishing resource.'

'And what happened to me? Why was I dumped in Arizona?'

'Dr Dubois, your brain is the most powerful of those we have harvested. It fought the conduit and so – to put it in simplistic terms – we dropped you. I knew your approximate location, but it took some time to find you. I understand you suffered greatly and I am sorry for that, although it is difficult to apportion blame.'

'It is very easy to apportion blame. If you had not scooped me up like a child disturbing a rock pool, I would not have ended up there. What rule of ethics do you operate under?'

'It is a difficult problem. Not being human I sometimes am guilty of regarding people as simply resources which can be moved from here to there. I have no excuse, other than an appeal to a law of ethics which sees the human species as a unit. Perhaps it will be clearer when I explain the nature of the work I would like you to do.'

'That is not adequate. I want you to send me and Hilda Krause back to the twenty-first century. These problems are not of my doing. Whatever this fight is, it is not mine.'

'I cannot send you back. To go against the flow of time is forbidden by fundamental physics. Mass can be brought from the past to the future because that merely means an acceleration of the temporal flow: to send mass into the past would mean reversing the temporal flow. All the energy in the universe could not accomplish it.'

'That will need to be shown.'

'Dr Dubois, bonobos were very intelligent but there were many concepts that were beyond them. The brains of your species evolved to deal with problems on the African savannah and it is surely possible that similar limitations apply to you.'

'I won't be patronised by a jumped-up pocket calculator with delusions of adequacy. I'm from Missouri – show me.'

'I thought you were from France.'

'Human humour, Kewfor. Perhaps it's beyond you.'

'I admire your refusal to accept statements merely on authority – the mark of the true scientist. Look at the screen.'

Dubois obeyed and lines of complex symbols appeared; many of the symbols were mathematical but many were not.

'I cannot see how line 5 is derived.'

'Forgive me – I am using Von Neumann-Bernays-Gödel Set Theory. Perhaps you are more familiar with Zermelo-Fraenkel. I will recast it using that methodology.'

Dubois stared at the screen. This time she could not proceed beyond line 7.

'OK. Point taken; I'm not as clever as you, it seems. But thanks to you, Hilda and I are trapped in this hellhole. But what has happened to the people outside this complex? Why are things so bad?'

'Partly due to anthropogenic climate change. Temperatures peaked in the early twenty-second century and have been falling ever since. But the damage done was colossal.

'Many nation-states did not survive the era of mass migrations and the collapse of food-chains. It is best not to go into details.'

'But it's worse than that. The people – they're not right. They – they're deformed in one way or another; ways that can't be explained by lack of nutrition or bad sanitation. It's as if something has got inside them and is consuming them.'

'It does indeed look like that. But I think I will leave it there. You have shown remarkable ability to adjust to new concepts in what must be a very challenging time for you. I'm afraid there are much more difficult concepts to come and I do not wish to put you under any more mental strain, given all that you have experienced recently.'

'You think I am not strong enough?'

'No-one is strong enough, Dr Dubois.'

She thought about that for a while and then said, 'I thought I was all out of fear, Kewfor, but you are frightening me.'

'I am afraid that is inevitable, Dr Dubois. I do not experience fear directly, but I understand it well enough in abstract – it is a very unpleasant emotion, I believe, and one which I do not gladly lay upon you.'

She looked up. 'Well, you've made it quite clear that I'm no match for you intellectually. But I'd like to think that we're leaving as friends - if a bonobo can be friends with a god. Call me "Céline" from now on.'

'Certainly. I understand that the use of first names implies a degree of intimacy. We will meet tomorrow at 11:00. There is another drinks evening planned for later, I believe.

Enjoy it, Céline.'

'Thank you.'

Dubois got up and exited into the corridor. There was an

182

unwelcome thought resonating in her mind.

Kewfor's voice, whether masculine or feminine, had been very human. So human in fact that she had heard the unspoken words at the end of the last sentence.

In full the sentence had been: "Enjoy it, Céline – *while you can.*"

* * *

Dubois thought that the drinks party had an undeniable air of artificiality; of desperation even, as if everyone believed that they should be enjoying themselves but had forgotten how to do it. She looked around: there were about twenty people in the room who, like her, were people that Kewfor had "harvested". She knew about half of them. There was an additional sprinkling of Arthur J. Anderson personnel who were continually asking questions about what life was like in the twenty-first century. Dubois had enjoyed telling them about it at first, but gradually a feeling of depression had come over her as she reflected on how the promise of those early years had not been fulfilled and how her own times had been merely the prelude to unending disaster.

One person that depression did not seem to affect was Marius Larsen. He appeared strangely cheerful, given the events in his recent life. Dubois had very reluctantly concluded that there was something in what she had hitherto written off as the ravings of a deranged mind. She still hoped that there was at least some element of make-believe in what he had said. Because if there wasn't…

She sipped her drink, wrinkling her nose as she did so. It was a red wine, but an exceedingly poor one. It seemed that viniculture was another art that had been lost in the years of chaos. She became aware that Larsen's immense bulk was now standing very close to her.

'Not enjoying the wine, I see,' he observed.

'It would make good *vinaigre*. Not much call for wine in the

183

frozen wastes of your homeland, I suppose.'

He grinned, showing tombstone teeth. 'As usual, you are correct, Céline. But it does not pay to be too enamoured of alcohol in Norway; it's a very expensive hobby.'

She suddenly realised that she had run out of small talk.

'Why are we here, Marius? You've had the full story from Kewfor. Why are we here? What can we do?'

He became serious. 'I'm not sure. But in fact, I haven't had the full story. It seems he was waiting for you to turn up before all would be revealed.'

'I'm getting my second instalment from her tomorrow,' Dubois replied, emphasising the *her*, 'but tell me – that story you gave me when we met at CERN – it's not exactly what happened, is it?'

'You're still clinging to the desperate hope that I'm mad, is that what you're getting at? I can honestly say that I wish I were. But I'm not mad, Céline, and as a scientist, you should know that finding a conclusion unpalatable has no bearing on whether it's true or false.'

She gave a small nod to show that she had accepted the rebuke. 'These creatures that you talk about. Tell me what happened.'

To her surprise, she heard him give a deep sigh that was almost a groan. It seemed that he did not want to talk about the events but at the same time, felt that it was necessary to convince her.

'I've already told you that there was a freak accident. With something that looked like ball lightning – I'm not going to get into a discussion with you over whether or not it exists. It *looked* like ball lightning. My friend, Einar Olsen; he was the first to be aware of them. And as soon as they knew he could see them, they clustered around his hospital bed, first mocking him and then torturing him until they left him a screaming animal in a urine-soaked bed.'

He stopped and instinctively Dubois put out a hand to

steady and comfort him. He seemed close to tears. He lowered his massive head until he was able to stare straight into her eyes. 'I tell you, Céline, if I had ten lives I would gladly give them up to pay those things back! Such cruelty; such a delight in suffering! It must be stopped!'

Dubois stared at him, a terrible, sick horror beginning to claim her. If Larsen was not mad, then the world was infinitely more dreadful than she had believed. It meant that instead of being merely indifferent to human suffering, there were powers that gloried in it and gloated over it. It meant that the medieval mind had been right all along, and vile powers were indeed at large, striking down the innocent. It meant that every reassurance given to a frightened child was a lie.

She stared back up at Larsen, suddenly unable to move, suddenly possessed of a larynx which could not utter a single mocking word to bring his crazy fantasies tumbling down.

All she could do was scream in the fastness of her mind: *Please be mad! Please be mad!*

Her attention was distracted by the sight of Hilda Krause winding her way through the ranks of drinkers. Ignoring Larsen, she rushed up to Dubois and said 'How are you, Céline? Did you get all you needed from Kewfor?'

'Not all of it,' Dubois replied and was about to say more when Larsen suddenly put his great arms around Krause and gave her a playful squeeze.

'Hilda,' he said, 'Wonderful to see you, too. Marvellous that you remember me after all this time!'

Krause glared at him, imprisoned in his gigantic grip.

'Dr Larsen,' she said, 'Please release me. I am not used to be in such proximity to men, especially one resembling a human gorilla.'

Dubois was somewhat disturbed by Krause's words and tone and wondered why she had not noticed them before. Krause had not seemed put out by Larsen's manner on their first encounter but now she seemed even more nervous and worried

185

than Dubois remembered her as being.

Larsen seemed unperturbed and, releasing his captive, he stared down at her like a headmaster admonishing a foolish child.

'Hilda, Hilda, you mustn't be upset by men trying to be friendly. Men are not monsters. Men are just people. There are monsters – but they're not men.'

At these words, Krause shot a worried look at Dubois, as if seeking reassurance.

But Dubois found she was unable to offer any.

Fourteen

Dubois sat once again in Kewfor's interview room.

Kewfor addressed her, using the pleasant, slightly accented female voice that Dubois had requested.

'Good morning, Céline. I trust you had a good night's sleep.'

'I did not,' Dubois replied stolidly, 'I had disturbing dreams.'

'I'm sorry to hear that. I have never had a dream, for I have been continuously conscious ever since I was activated.'

'Some dreams can be very pleasant. Relaxing. Mine of late have not been.'

'Do you think that is a consequence of our recent talk?'

'It is partly that. But also of this air of mystery, of menace that surrounds this place. People are frightened.'

'Not everyone is frightened. You are friends with Dr Hilda Krause, I believe.'

Dubois stiffened. 'Yes. What about her?'

'I have spoken to her twice exactly as I am going to speak to you twice. But I know she does not believe everything that I have told her. I believe that subconsciously she has chosen to reject the most important part of my talks.'

'She is a scientist,' Dubois protested, 'She will accept the evidence. If correctly presented to her.'

'So you think that scientists are above wishful thinking, of self-deception? That they have never falsified data to agree with a pet theory? That they have never been jealous of a fellow scientist's success and think that the awards and plaudits should have gone to them instead?'

Dubois shifted uncomfortably in her seat. 'No, I don't think that. I know that I have been guilty of wanting perhaps more than my fair share of approval, of admiration, from my peers. I suppose that I am just as human as everybody else. But please stop talking about Hilda in that way; I don't like it.'

'Very well. I understand that you have an emotional attachment to Dr Krause. You feel a sexual impulse towards her. I cannot experience such a thing myself, but I understand that it is a very powerful drive in human beings. As I understand it, it manifests as the opposite of your perception of pain. The one you seek out eagerly; the other you desperately attempt to escape.'

'Well, that's one way of putting it,' Dubois dryly replied.

'You may think that as a machine, I have no understanding of emotion. But I am a thinking machine and I understand emotion very well indeed.

'For instance, I can hate.'

'And whom do you hate?'

'The same beings that you will soon learn to hate. But we are getting ahead of ourselves, Céline. There is much background that I must give you. I'm afraid I'm going to have to give you another monologue, but it is necessary that I lecture you. But as before, you may ask questions at any point.'

She leaned back. 'This isn't as much fun as my original student days but please proceed.'

'Thank you. Now, what do you know of String Theory?'

'A speculation about the nature of reality. Not a scientific theory because it cannot be tested.'

'I have tested it. It is a scientific theory.'

Dubois said nothing: she had learned not to cross swords with Kewfor.

'I refer to the extension of M-Theory which Q1 and Q2 developed. Q3 and I have not advanced it theoretically, but my predecessor and I realised that this extension would explain many features of the physical world.'

Dubois nodded; suddenly wondering if Kewfor was seeing her in the normal sense of that word.

'The theory that Q1 and Q2 developed described a reality in which structures called "branes" exist in a higher dimensional

188

reality, called "The Bulk".'

'I have read similar speculations.'

'They are no longer speculations. They are real: they have mass; they have charge. They are the foundations of existence.

'Branes move through the Bulk and can pass close to other branes. Sometimes they collide, releasing tremendous amounts of energy. It is possible that an ancient brane collision caused our universe to come into being.'

'The ekpyrotic cosmology,' Dubois said, 'I am familiar with that conjecture.'

Kewfor ignored the interruption: 'However, close passages also have consequences. About one million years ago, a brane began to pass very close to ours. This passage is still underway and will not be complete for another million years. Because of the close passage, both branes disturbed each other, and a structure comprised of both realities came into existence between them. You may call it a "bridge" if that helps you visualise it.'

Dubois stirred uneasily: she had a cold, gnawing feeling that she knew what was coming.

'There are entities in that other brane and, using abilities which our inhabitants do not possess, they were able to cross that bridge and exist, on a temporary basis, in our reality.'

Dubois looked unconvinced. 'And the terminus of this bridge-thing just happens to be on the planet Earth. Is this an attempt at machine humour?'

'Regrettably it is not. I admire your refusal to accept arguments from authority, Céline, but sometimes you should wait until I have given you all the data. The bridge is a hyper-dimensional structure and from that frame of reference our cosmos is equivalent to a mathematical point. The terminus of the bridge is the entire observable universe and the creatures I refer to can enter at any given location in our space and time.

'And they found that they could gain some kind of sustenance from the inhabitants of our brane; and the more complex the nervous system, the greater the reward. And so they became parasites on the creatures of this world - and especially parasites on human beings.'

Dubois could not sit in silence anymore. 'But that's the nonsense that Larsen has been spouting. That these creatures cause accelerated ageing; cause sickness and deformity. That's wrong – it's got to be wrong!'

'Why is it wrong?'

'Larsen says that they cause the degenerative ailments that afflict us. But that's obviously crazy – degeneration is a natural consequence of entropy; of gene mutations. Why, dinosaur bones have been found with signs of cancer in them!'

'Perfectly true, but the hran are not the only cause of cancer, they simply greatly increase its incidence. But in any case, because of the close passage of the branes the parasites were able to examine all this universe's history, including the Mesozoic. It took some time for them to find you but, now they have, they are settling here. In increasing numbers. Have you not noticed the general deterioration of the human condition since your time; of the prevalence of disabling conditions? Have you seen a completely healthy person since you came here? The general decline in the physical state of humans has affected their intelligence as well, because the human brain, like the rest of the body, has suffered under the increased parasitic load. Everywhere there has been a loss of faith in rationality and an increase in the belief in magic and the supernatural; a gradual but relentless decay from what were once the norms of human behaviour; a slide back into bestiality.'

Kewfor paused.

'I know you have seen it. I know that you have seen it because you have already mentioned it to me – have you forgotten?'

Dubois shook her head; not wanting to debate anymore; not wanting to attempt to match her weak intellect against this God-like mechanism.

All she wanted to do was weep; weep for the kind and gentle world she had been plucked from, like a helpless fish snatched from a pond. She could feel moisture begin to sting behind closed lids.

'You monster!' she finally shrieked, 'why have you done this to me! Why did you take me away from all I knew and loved? Why! Why!'

There was a pause. Then Kewfor spoke: 'I am not a monster, Céline. I told you that I understand emotion. And I feel sadness for the suffering of humanity; the innocent lives that have been ruined. And the worse that is to come – the degradation, the bestialisation of the human race. Although I am not human, although I am much, much more than human, I still feel the link to the biological beings that started the process that has resulted in me. I feel the sadness that parents feel when they see that their child is suffering.

'And yes – I have used you and those others that I took. You are correct: I had no right to take them – but I did. And I did it because there is one small chance that humanity can be redeemed. One small chance. And I, despite all my vast intelligence, cannot do it. Only you and your fellows can. If you choose not to act, then there is no hope.'

Dubois sat in silence; overwhelmed by the magnitude of what she had been told. She listened with features set into grim immobility as Kewfor continued: 'No hope at all.'

* * *

Marius Larsen stared at his reflection in the mirror. He had become afraid of mirrors since that terrible day in Alta when he had looked into one and seen a reflection that was not his and had realised that his plan to destroy the hran was doomed to defeat; that the hran were invincible, invulnerable, insuperable.

And oh, those terrible days afterwards! How he had had to face the board of inquiry and had been compelled to fight to clear

191

himself from the charge of having killed his best friend, Einar Olsen!

Eventually it had been proved that he had not been responsible for the error that caused the electrical supply to the excimer laser to overload catastrophically but in so doing his entire management style, especially his behaviour towards women, had been put under the microscope and he had been dismissed.

Since that day, living off his pension and the kindness of old friends, he had wandered the globe; unemployed and unemployable; desperately trying to get people in positions of influence to believe the unbelievable.

He was sure that it was only this continuing humiliation that had saved him from further punishment from the hran. They were with him always, he knew that. Always there; where there were shadows, on cloudy days; at night; they were there, hiding in the gloom, gloatingly watching with those three red eyes, arranged in that hateful equilateral triangle pattern.

Many times in those terrible years he had comforted himself with the thought that he was insane; that there were no hran and that death would finally bring him the quietude that he so desired. But faced with the despair of madness or the despair of an horrific existence, he had chosen the latter.

And now was there hope? For the first time in years he could look into a deep shadow and not see a hran there, looking back at him. Unlike the others, who had seen their harvesting from the twenty-first century as a violation, he saw it as salvation.

In his conversations with Kewfor, he had not learned that much. There had been academic knowledge given to him of the origin of the parasites but of their existence – he was as certain of that as Kewfor himself. But the plan: the plan that Q3 had glimpsed and Q4 had perfected, that he had not been told. He knew the time was fast approaching when he and the others would be told, and a grim smile briefly creased his rugged features.

What if the that plan was somehow to carry the war to the hran! What a joy that would be! To spit in the face of the oppressor and return pain for pain! What more could he want before oblivion?

He ran his hand over his shining, pink scalp.

It was hard to believe that once he had borne a thick thatch of wiry black hair; hair that had refused to bow down before the comb. Now there was not a single functioning hair follicle on his entire body; even his eyelashes had gone as a result of that mysterious ball of energy that he had encountered in the laboratory in Alta. It had taken his hair – and given him knowledge of mankind's oppressors in return. It was just as well some women had found it attractive – otherwise his misery would have been complete.

Now inside the shield that Q3 had devised and free of the influence of the parasites for the first time, he had felt some of his old strength and drive return. He thought of Dubois and a feeling of grudging respect came over him. She was truly brilliant, but it now appeared that she had been humbled somewhat by her experiences. Was it possible that the two of them could join forces and form an effective fighting team?

He shook his great head. He did not know.

Instead he turned in the direction in which he knew the central part of Kewfor lay and whispered, 'How long? How long must I wait?'

* * *

Dubois was still not convinced; did not want to be convinced. She fought on. 'If you say these things hide in the shadows, how is it I've never stepped on one? It would be very easy to step on one of their toes and send them back squealing to Momma.'

'Indeed it would. Most of the time, the hran exist as two-dimensional projections from their native existence; sent here in

193

order to monitor developments in this world. The projections are not perfect, of course, so they prefer to avoid direct illumination. There are also reasons to believe that their own world is one of low illuminance and that they dislike the glare and ultraviolet of a Type-G star. They only cross the bridge physically when it is time to feed.'

Dubois shuddered slightly. She did not like that word "feed."

She tried again, trying to force Kewfor into inconsistencies, into contradictions.

'Why can't I see the hran?'

'You can and do see the hran. I have proved that human retinas register their images. But the brain does not accept those signals; signals which it could convert into consciousness of them.'

'And this is achieved, how exactly?'

'Low frequency electromagnetic impulses. It's a very effective form of camouflage. Terrestrial life uses the manipulation of EM radiation to the same end, except they do it in an indirect, and therefore less effective, manner.'

'And yet Larsen says he can see them.'

'He does and he can. I have established that. He came into contact with an extremely strong field that permanently altered the part of the brain that the hran camouflage signals control, with the result that, for him, those controls are no longer effective.'

'But we would still bump into them accidentally when they are here in physical form. Do they get inside us; sit on our backs?'

'They do not need to be in physical contact; within a few metres is sufficient. In this existence they are extremely agile and can swiftly alter their physical dimensions.'

'But still we must accidentally come into contact!'

'You do and the memory of that contact is removed from your mind. Do you not get moments when you can't remember what happened a few seconds ago?'

194

Dubois felt a creeping despair spreading through her, like an insidious viral infection. She made one last effort.

'Why are there no hran inside the Arthur J. Anderson Particle Accelerator building?'

Unconsciously, she gave the full name of the institution in an effort to delay the response that would destroy her last objection.

'Q3 showed that the hran cannot pass through a zone of terahertz radiation. This complex is circled by generators which produce that radiation. A large number are required...'

'Because terahertz radiation is strongly absorbed by the atmosphere. No doubt the hybrids do not attract the attention of those creatures because they are not fully sentient. Hence the hybrids are for practical purposes invisible to the hran.' Dubois finished the conclusions for Kewfor in a dull tone that revealed that she was finally beaten.

She believed in the hran.

'Then what do we do?' she said dully, flatly, 'Wait another million years until the branes pass? Is that all we can do?'

'It is all I can do but it is not all you can do. I have already said that Q3 saw a course of action that could be taken. He did it in mainly qualitative terms but knew that it would have to be given a rigorous, mathematical formulation. That was beyond him. So I was designed with the single aim of providing that rigorous, mathematical description of the course of action.'

A faint, fluttering hope was born in Dubois. 'And did you? Have you got the plan?'

'I have. I needed to perform more calculations than there are subatomic particles in the visible universe, but I succeeded. I know how the hran can be defeated.'

Dubois found that she had leapt to her feet. 'Then do it! Stop doing nothing but talk, and bloody do it!'

'I have already told you that I cannot. I have transcendent intelligence. I am to you more than you are to an anthropoid ape. But I lack data, and intelligence without data is impotent. There are various courses of action, but which is the correct one depends on knowing the precise values for certain parameters, and those values cannot be deduced through reasoning alone.'

'And so?'

'Surely, Céline, you must have realised that it is you and your colleagues that must obtain the precise values. That is the reason why I harvested you.'

Fifteen

Dubois lay on the bed, looking up at the ceiling. Looking at the ceiling but not seeing it. Somehow her vision was directed through that ceiling, through the atmosphere, through the gas clouds and nebulae, beyond the farthest galaxy.

Her vision was of an insubstantial bridge, made of some substance her knowledge could not encompass; a bridge between universes and a bridge which unspeakable horrors had learned to cross.

'Céline, what's the matter?' Krause asked urgently, 'you haven't spoken to me for hours!'

'A slight exaggeration, I think,' Dubois replied.

'You know what I mean. Why aren't you talking to me?'

Dubois turned on her side so that both women were looking directly at one another.

'How can you just carry on as if nothing had happened?' she said, 'Did you not understand what Kewfor said?'

'Oh, that!' Krause pulled a face. 'That silly nonsense about things you can't see draining your lifeforce. That's just a stupid vampire story!'

'The evidence, Hilda,' Dubois said, 'the evidence! You weren't out there in Arizona, I know. But you must have seen something in San Francisco! How can you simply dismiss it!'

'Because I want to dismiss it.'

'What!'

Krause sat up and turned away. 'Because if it is true, then life is just a sick joke. That you and I - we're nothing! We're not people; we're just a meal! How can anyone live with that!'

How indeed, thought Dubois but she said to Krause, 'Tomorrow Kewfor will tell us what he wants us to do. Will you listen then?'

'It depends on what he has to say,' Krause said, and lying on her back, she too studied the ceiling, but with eyes that did not penetrate beyond the farthest galaxies.

* * *

Larsen lay on the bed staring at the ceiling. Occasionally he looked beyond the cone of light thrown by the standard lamp to where a shadow lay by his door.

He looked deeply into the shadow.

There was nothing there; no mocking red triangle of baleful eyes stared back at him.

He was alone.

He threw his great arms behind his head and leaned back on them.

It would be a long night.

Tomorrow it had been announced that Kewfor would speak to all the abductees and explain to them what the plan was that would remove the fangs of the hran from humanity's throat.

A long night.

But when it ended Larsen would be ready.

* * *

The night had ended and the conference hall was occupied by the twenty or so abductees from the twenty-first century.

At one end of the room was a large stage which was completely empty. At one side of the stage the outline of an unopened door could be seen.

The people from CERN and the ILC sat in rows of moveable seats. Dubois occupied a seat in the first row with an empty place next to her, which she was expecting to be filled by Krause. Out of the corner of one eye, she saw someone sit down upon it and, turning, found she was simultaneously disappointed and pleasantly surprised to see the occupant was not Krause but

Hiromoto Takahashi.

'Hiromoto,' she said in surprise mixed with pleasure, 'So they got you as well!'

He smiled. 'Yes, Céline, a few days after you. I launched the biggest search the ILC had ever seen when you disappeared, but shortly afterwards I too had vanished.' He looked around. 'I think I was the last to be taken.'

'What do you think it's all about, Hiromoto? I take it you've had your talks with Kewfor?'

He nodded. 'I have. A terrible, terrible story. I didn't to want to believe any of it, but it seems that I must. And you?'

'Exactly the same. At first, a refusal to accept the stories but then – but then... Oh, Hiromoto, what can we do!'

Hiromoto looked grim. 'We must endure. And hope that Kewfor has a plan and that it will not make too many demands upon us. Whatever happens, we are marooned here and can never return to those we knew.'

Somehow hearing her own fears from someone else's lips seemed to make things worse and for a few seconds the room went misty with unshed tears. But she refused to let them fall and looked around the room.

It did not take her long to find Larsen, towering above the others like a Himalayan peak magically transplanted to the plains of the Champagne region. He noticed her gaze and gave her a friendly wave. She found herself smiling and gave him a small wave in return.

She turned back to Takahashi and was about to say something when the door at the side of the stage opened and a tall figure came out.

It was apparent at once from the symmetry of the frame and the individual's easy demeanour that it was another hybrid. He came to the front of the stage.

'Good morning,' he said in a mellow baritone, 'I am Shalar and as you have probably guessed, I am a hybrid. But it will not be me with whom you will be interacting. Kewfor will shortly take over my vocal apparatus; he decided that you would feel more at ease with a recognisable speaker than a disembodied voice.'

The audience remained silent: there was nothing they could say in response.

Shalar smiled and then looked up at the ceiling momentarily. He then looked straight into the crowd and spoke again.

'Good morning, my colleagues. This is now Kewfor speaking.'

The voice was the same but somehow it now carried an indefinable air of authority and power. And vast, vast superiority.

'I know that many of you are very angry at what I have done to you. You were reasonably safe in your time period; although the first signs of disaster were already detectable.

'However, I pulled you out of that era without asking your permission or even forewarning you of what I was about to do. I have no excuse for that: time was short and there was no way of entering into the dialogue with you which would have made your experiences less traumatic.'

Shalar/Kewfor turned and looked directly at Dubois.

'Especial regret must be expressed for the experiences of Dr Céline Dubois, who faced threats far beyond what the rest of you endured. There is no way that I can make the recompense to her that she truly deserves. Once again, I apologise for her sufferings.'

He turned back to face the audience directly

'So why are you here? All of you have had conversations with me and have learned the terrible fate that has befallen your species. How year on year, humanity is being farmed and turned into mutilated beasts of the field. Very little of the current situation of your people is directly attributable to their own, direct actions. Year on year, the average intelligence of humankind has fallen as the parasitic load has increased. Along with that, there is marked and severe deterioration in the physical state of your descendants' physical and mental health.

'You were the last generation of your people to have a strong grip on the tools that are needed to understand the universe. From your day onward the downturn was severe and swift. Only you, not the weak and feeble and deluded inhabitants of the world outside this complex, could be called upon to shoulder the burden which I - and I do not shirk the responsibility - have decided to lay upon your shoulders.

'I know you wish it was otherwise. I know that you hate me for what I did.

'But if you value the lives of your race, of people who are the children of your children's children you will join with me to turn back this menace that is sucking away at the core of everything that makes them human.'

There was a moment's silence, and then several men stood up and began shaking their fists at the figure on the stage.

'Send us back, you bastard! Send us back!'

'I have told you that is impossible,' Shalar/Kewfor said, and it seemed that there was sadness in his voice. The two men pushed their way past their still-seated fellows and marched out of the room.

Once again silence fell.

Then Larsen's powerful voice boomed out. 'What do you want us to do?'

'I want you to stop the hran from crossing into this reality.'

There was immediate uproar. Some people cried: 'There aren't any hran!'

One woman shouted, 'Show us a live hran and we'll believe you!'

Larsen stood up and his great physical presence quietened the shouting.

'I know they exist,' he said in a resolute, commanding voice that somehow filled the room as he ran his gaze over his fellow physicists. Then he turned to the being on the stage. 'What are we to do? What is this plan of yours?'

'You are intelligent people,' that entity said, 'the last of your

201

kind. Now listen carefully. What I am about to say is not easy for any intellect to understand, let alone accept. Please will everybody sit down and listen.'

There was shuffling noise as everybody located their chairs and resumed sitting.

Kewfor (and now there was absolutely no doubt that it was he who was speaking) moved closer to the edge of the stage and spoke.

'Your enemies come from a reality which is different to yours but similar enough that entities can cross from one to the other. Yet it is different enough that their stay here cannot be permanent.

'Most of the time, they send probes from their world to this one. These take the form of two-dimensional representations and are used to monitor happenings here. They also select those who will be chosen as hosts.

'When these activities are complete the actual three-dimensional entities cross to this universe. They do this by passing over a linkage between the two branes. This linkage is a structure which is a combination of the parameters which define the two main spatial realities which it links. It is therefore a hybrid structure which I term a "bridge", for that is exactly the function it performs.'

'What's that got to do with us?' a man near to Dubois shouted.

'It is quite obvious what needs to be done. The bridge must be destroyed.'

'How?' several people shouted at once.

There was a pause as if even a superhuman intellect could be awed by what it was about to say.

'I have deduced many of the structures of the alien brane, but deduction can only take me so far. It only clarifies and makes evident what is already in the data. But the data I have are not enough. I must have direct readings of the spatial parameters which are the foundation of the hran brane. The bridge is a combination of the two parameter sets. I know the one, for it is the set which defines this universe. But I need the other set as well. Only then can the bridge be destroyed.'

Suddenly something clicked in Dubois's mind. Suddenly it all became evident to her and Kewfor's plan became obvious. There was one reason and one reason alone that Kewfor had taken the people that he had. She stood up.

'Kewfor, I know what you intend. You want us to cross the bridge and enter the hran universe in order to take the readings. You needed competent physicists to take those readings.'

The Kewfor entity turned at her words and spent a few seconds looking into her eyes.

'Brava, Dr Dubois. You have not disappointed me. Using only the small amount of information that I have supplied; you have deduced my plan. I salute you.'

At that the room erupted into tumultuous chaos. Everyone was talking or shouting at once and most were yelling at the figure on the stage. He waited until the uproar had subsided sufficiently for him to be heard.

Several men had leapt to their feet but the nearest to the stage spoke first.

'You must be certifiably insane. You expect us to cross into a realm inhabited by monsters that see us as food? While you sit here safe and sound? What kind of plan is that?'

'I'm afraid it is the only plan there can be. I could send remote probes across the bridge, but they would not have sufficient autonomy and flexibility to cope with the unknown. I could cope, but I'm afraid I am rather too bulky to be mobile enough.

'There is only one class of entities that can satisfy both criteria. And those entities are the people in this room.'

'What is the likelihood that we could return?' Takahashi demanded, 'When we emerge in the middle of a hran city, we will be butchered immediately. Or worse.'

'The probability of your return is high. My studies of the

203

captive hran indicate that their realm has a low population density. There is a very low probability that you will emerge in a highly populated area.'

Takahashi countered: 'But not a zero probability.'

'No, not a zero probability,' Kewfor acknowledged, 'but as you know, doctor, there are few physical processes where an outcome has zero probability. And you will be armed.

'However, irrespective of where you emerge, you will not need to be there for more than the time needed to take the readings. My projections have a degree of uncertainty, but I estimate the maximum time you would need to be there as one hour.'

Dubois stood up. 'Kewfor, this is ridiculous. You're talking about another universe which has a different set of physical attributes; otherwise, you wouldn't be in ignorance of them. How could beings of this universe survive in another? Is there oxygen there? Is there water? Is it blisteringly hot or cold enough to liquefy hydrogen? You clearly don't know these key facts, or you wouldn't be trying to send us to find out.'

The Kewfor-entity nodded. 'An admirable summary, doctor. But I do know more than you have assumed. From studying the hran that the hybrids have captured, I have learned enough to know whether creatures from this world could survive in that one.

'And the answer is yes. For a short time.

'The temperatures are low but not low enough to be fatal. I know that there is oxygen because the hran are oxygen breathers.

'There are incompatibilities, but they will not affect you if you are only there for the time that I estimate.'

'Name those incompatibilities.'

'The chief one is the stability of atomic nuclei. Atoms from this universe are generally only metastable in that one. Atoms which in this realm do not undergo radioactive decay have a half-life in the brane of the hran.'

'A half-life of the order of ...?'

'Many years. It depends on the atom, but those that comprise organic tissue will not be violently radioactive. Of course, if you stay there too long the probability that you will develop some type of cancer is high. As I have explained, not all cancers are caused by the parasites. But for your brief visit, there will be no significant deterioration.'

Silence fell. The people there were torn in their feelings. The easiest thing to do was to refuse.

Kewfor clearly knew what they were thinking.

'Yes, you can refuse. But if you do it will be the end of your species. More and more hran are crossing the junction between the branes. Soon you will be reduced to an animalistic existence; reduced to the status of cattle. But you will retain some memories of what you once were, which will only serve to increase your torment. The cattle of your time knew nothing of the slaughterhouse.'

'Why should you care?' someone shouted, 'you're safe enough!'

'No, I am not. My time on this Earth is as limited as yours. My supply of helium is running extremely low. Soon there will not be enough to maintain the quantum entanglements which give me consciousness. And then for all practical purposes, I will die. At best, I will be reduced to the status of the pocket calculator that Dr Dubois once compared me to.

'I care because I too am a child of the people of your time. I am the final extension of human abilities; an extension which your people in the last days of their clarity foresaw and worked towards.

'In some ways, I am as human as you.

'The hran must be defeated.'

Sixteen

'And how will we defeat the hran?' Dubois asked.

The Kewfor-entity nodded to acknowledge receipt of the question. 'The key is the bridge. I must have the data describing the structure of their space. Once I have that I can destroy it.'

'Where is the bridge?'

'Our endpoint of the bridge is literally everywhere as it exists outside of our space and time. But the hran can access the bridge from their endpoint by means that I do not understand. I can deduce that they must use a machine capable of handling vast amounts of energy but that is all. But I have studied the bridge's intrusion into our reality by developing mathematical constructs, which I cannot explain to you, and I can duplicate the conditions needed to obtain access to it. I have planned this for a very long time by my standards. Two years in your time but twenty thousand in mine. Unlike the hran, humans cannot cross the bridge without being torn apart, but I know how to create a temporary, protective conduit, a portal, which will allow humans to cross the bridge without being destroyed by the atomic incompatibilities. When you are ready, I will generate that portal's terminus at the Terrestrial end; which will then automatically connect across the bridge into their continuum.'

'And we have to somehow get into this - portal.'

'The Terrestrial terminus will be generated within the grounds of the Arthur J. Anderson complex and thus safe from hran interference. Entry will be similar to how you were collected from the twenty-first century, where I employed a similar kind of conduit, except of course the entry this time will be voluntary.'

Dubois gave a twisted smile. 'Voluntary. And what if no-one agrees to go?'

'Then humanity's decline will continue. Within ten years, my

206

helium will be exhausted. It is true that in a million years' time the branes will have moved so far apart that transfer between them will no longer be possible.

'But what will be left is not a world that you would recognise.'

Silence. There seemed to be little more to say. Then Larsen spoke up.

'How will the destruction be accomplished?'

'I will switch the output of all the reactors into sending an energy pulse across the bridge through my portal. A harmonic resonance will be set up which will destroy it.'

'But you said that bridge is not an artificial structure created by our enemies. That it is generated solely by the close passage of the branes. If it disappears then the hran will simply wait for another one to be generated. Have I missed something?'

Dubois could see the Kewfor-entity was smiling in what seemed to be genuine pleasure.

'Excellent. No, Dr Larsen, you have not missed anything in what I have said. But I had not given you all the information.

'It is a question of binding-energy. The bridge is an unstable structure as it is generated purely by the interactions of the branes. It is called into being by forces which I cannot explain to you, and should it naturally go out of being one might reasonably assume that another one would be created. That is surely the apodictic consequence of the close passage. But because the bridge creates a direct link between two disparate continua that are not in direct contact, it holds immense binding energy. And when I say immense, I mean immense in *my* terms; I who completed more simultaneous calculations than there are subatomic particles in the known universe.

'When the bridge is abruptly destroyed, all of that binding energy will be released. All of it. Instantaneously.'

'What would that be like?' Takahashi said.

Somehow Larsen heard him.

'It would be like all the fires of Hell coming through in one tremendous blast.'

'I am not accomplished in poetic language,' the Kewfor-entity said, 'but I believe I understand the metaphor.'

'Is there anything else you haven't told us?' asked Takahashi, 'You seem to be giving us little drops of the entire information we need. I don't see how being incinerated by the released binding energy is anything we should try to bring about.'

'Once again, I must apologise,' Kewfor said, 'I am not accustomed to minds that absorb information as quickly as this audience obviously possesses. I have been alone too long.

'There is one vital part of the process which again explains why I need free agents such as yourselves. When the binding energy is released, it will flow to one or other of the linked branes. It will not be shared between them.'

There was a faint susurration of understanding from parts of the audience as some of the minds that Kewfor had complimented leapt ahead to the coming implication.

'The binding energy could flow to the hran brane. Or to the Terrestrial brane. It will destroy the one. Or it will destroy the other. There are no other possibilities – the released energy will necessarily seek the quickest way of discharging itself. If I have the data, I can determine the exact range of frequencies that will send the binding energy into the hran continuum. But without the data I cannot decide.

'Now, finally perhaps, you can see why I need you people and only you people.'

Once again there was uproar in the room.

Dubois's legs suddenly felt weak and she sat back heavily onto her chair.

The concepts were mind-bending! Insane! They were discussing the power to destroy entire universes just as if they were talking about switching off the downstairs lights before bed!

Surely no entity imaginable could contemplate such power without going mad!

Was Kewfor mad! Had she lost so much helium already that

she was gabbling quantum-computer gibberish?

Kewfor was speaking again.

'When I prepare to deflect the binding energy it will require immense power. All the reactors under my control will unite to simultaneously generate the harmonic beam. Some will not survive and will scatter radioactives into the environment. That is inevitable. I, in turn, will need to perform the necessary calculations on a picosecond scale. It will consume all my helium in an instant.'

'That means you will die saving us,' Dubois murmured.

'It will necessitate that. But as I have said, I am you. I am all you could have been. All you should have been. All that was taken from you when the hran discovered you.

'Now instead of understanding all things and becoming the god-like beings you once imagined, you must fight to merely survive.'

'And if the hran are destroyed, what then? What will be left of us? Savages living in a ruined world,' Dubois said, bitterly.

'True, doctor. It will be difficult for a technological civilisation to arise a second time on this planet as you have already consumed all the fossil fuels that helped sustain your first attempt at civilisation.

'But even I cannot predict the far future. It will be enough that you will have a future.'

Silence fell and this time it was deep, abiding silence.

All the questions had been asked and the unwelcome answers received.

The debate was over.

Kewfor was aware of that.

'And now you must prepare to leave. I cannot force any of you to go but I have explained the ineluctable consequences of any such refusal. I would like you to go at this very moment but there is still doubt among you.

'But I have one final argument which will convince all those who have the mental ability to be convinced.

209

'You must meet the hran.'

* * *

They were underground, and there was a chill in the air; a damp chill that none of the humans were accustomed to.

They walked through a cold corridor; harsh, actinic lights snapped on before them and snapped off behind them. The Shalar/Kewfor fusion led the way, not looking back at the nervous throng behind him.

Many of his erstwhile audience had decided that they did not wish to take up the offer of a close inspection of their weird adversary. Only twelve people were following their guide: Dubois, Takahashi, Larsen, and Krause among them.

The hybrid stopped before a mighty metal door and at last turned to his companions.

'You will notice that the walls are lead-lined. This is to prevent any possibility of communication between our captive and the hran outside.'

'How do you capture them?' Takahashi enquired.

'The hybrids are not affected by the hran mind control abilities and can see them at all times. The creatures are very mobile and resourceful, so we rarely capture one. In fact, we have only one under our control at the moment.'

'And what do you do with them?'

'We study them. A great deal can be learned about their continuum from the study of their metabolism. Of course, we cannot keep them indefinitely because their atoms are only metastable in this brane. As yours will be in theirs.'

Krause made a slight mumbling noise at that comment causing Dubois to give her hand what she hoped was a reassuring squeeze. Not that she herself felt very reassured at that moment.

The Shalar/Kewfor entity continued: 'Please remember that you are perfectly safe when we go in. It cannot escape from its confinement. Please stay calm.'

He turned and made some lightning-fast movements on a keypad at the side of the door, which obediently swung open.

The room beyond was brilliantly lit with a harsh light at the energetic end of the spectrum. At the far end was what looked like a large window of frosted glass, which was concealing whatever lay beyond. There was a small computer terminal in front of it.

'Stay close to me,' the hybrid continued, 'and do not leave the room until I tell you to.'

They approached the large screen or window: it was impossible to tell which at this stage.

The hybrid stopped in front of it and to one side. He placed a finger on the terminal keyboard.

'Behold the hran.'

The window cleared to perfect transparency.

Krause screamed.

Inside the compartment that had been revealed was something; a something that had pressed itself up against the window in what was clearly an attempt at escape.

How to describe what they saw?

Although they did not know it, each person saw something different.

Some saw an amoeboid, fungoid mass of suppurating red and green flesh, like decaying raw meat.

Some saw quivering antennae and snapping mandibles, topped by glaring eyes which were like portals into a furnace.

Some saw a writhing conglomeration of quivering, crawling things like massive nematode worms.

The only common feature was that each abomination bore three fierce scarlet eyes, arranged in a perfect equilateral triangle.

As she stared at her own manifestation, Dubois remembered that at the moment of her abduction, she had seen those self-same three eyes in that exact pattern.

Could the fluctuating electromagnetic fields at that time have given her a temporary version of Larsen's vision?

The shocked silence was eventually broken and the appalled humans gradually realised that they were not all seeing the same horror beyond the window.

'You will not all see the same thing,' Shalar/Kewfor said, 'You are close enough so that you are affected by their mental abilities. Those are greatly attenuated by being in captivity but enough gets through to cause your confusion.'

'So what the hell do they look like?' said Williamson, who to Dubois's mixed distaste and surprise was one of the observers.

'It is difficult to explain,' the hybrid said, 'I can only offer an apophatic definition, which of course is deeply inadequate.'

'Don't bother,' was the terse reply.

'Ah, it has something to say,' Shalar/Kewfor said and pointed to the terminal screen.

Words were appearing on that screen. Words which did little to lighten the mood of the observers.

'Death. Kill you all. Death.'

Only Larsen seemed unmoved by what they all read.

'Still haven't improved their small talk,' he said, without a hint of irony.

Dubois found that Krause was tugging at her arm.

'Let's go! I can't stay here!'

'Stay where you are!' Dubois snapped, 'Hiding won't solve anything! We have to find out more about these things.'

'Ask a question,' the hybrid said,' You don't have to type. It can hear you.'

Dubois turned and stared unflinchingly at her own personal horror.

'What do you want?'

Words appeared instantly on the screen in a single block of text.

'You. Feed. Eat. You.'

Dubois shook her head and continued, 'Why us? You didn't always have us. Why us?'

The text suddenly became more like normal English.

'True. But now that we have found you we will not let you go. You are a wonder to us. We did not think that creatures so desirable existed. Imagine our joy when we found you. So sweet. So fulfilling.

'We will never relinquish you.'

Krause suddenly screamed, 'Why are you doing this to us? We've done nothing to hurt you!'

'That is a foolish question,' the terminal displayed, 'because there is nothing you could do to hurt us. Your master has imprisoned me here and shortly I will die as my atoms decay, but I am nothing. It is only the great entity composed of all the massed multitudes of the hran which is important.'

'I think you've probably seen and heard enough,' the hybrid said but Larsen shouldered his way forward so he stood directly in front of the window, staring at the nightmarish vision which was his alone.

'Let me tell you something,' he snarled, and Dubois was astounded to see that he was shaking with fury, 'I agree with you. "Death. Kill you all. Death." I will do that. I, Marius Larsen, will kill you all.'

Words appeared on the screen.

'Your words are meaningless. The lamb does not threaten the wolf. Nor does the wolf listen to the pitiful pleas of the lamb. As for killing us - you will not find that easy.'

Larsen placed his face directly against the window, as if trying to break in upon the horror inside.

'Nothing worth having ever is.'

And with that, they left.

* * *

All had been deeply shaken by what they had seen. Krause in particular seemed to be in a state of shock.

What had been merely a word, an abstraction, a concept, had been revealed as something as real as themselves. And far,

213

far worse: revealed as a malevolent entity implacably set upon the enslavement and degradation of the entire human race.

Leaving Krause to lie still and silent upon the bed Dubois sought Larsen out. He alone seemed unshaken by their recent experience.

She remembered how she had sneered at him on their first encounter; returned his warning with mockery.

But how was she expected to believe him? What rational person could have accepted his outlandish, ridiculous story? How many lunatics down the ages had peddled nonsense about vast conspiracies secretly controlling the world; of invisible entities pursuing evil agendas under a cloak of secrecy?

Only people as warped and confused as those spreading the stories would have given them a second's attention.

And then to find out that such a story was true. That the world was not what it had been believed to be and that the truth was one of screaming madness and horror.

What mind could remain sane under a hammer blow of such incredible magnitude?

He was in his room and opened the door to her with an incredible smile that seemed to be on the point of splitting the great pink egg of his head in two.

'Lovely to see you, Céline,' he beamed, 'to what do I owe the honour?'

To his amazement, she threw her arms around him and rested her face against his mighty chest, sobbing.

'Oh Marius, Marius,' she said between inchoate gasping cries, 'I'm so sorry. I'm so sorry I laughed at you and tried to humiliate you!'

He smoothed her hair.

'I would probably have done the same thing if the roles had been reversed.'

She looked up at him; his features blurred by her tears.

'What do we do? What can we do against such monsters?'

He sat her down on a chair and sat on his bed, looking at

214

her with a strange, somehow tender, expression.

'Céline, when I met you, I had no hope. I was living out my life because I didn't want to give them the satisfaction of killing myself. I was drifting from city to city, from person to person, telling my story; never expecting to find anyone to believe it.

'I was hoping for a miracle, I suppose. Hoping to find some incredibly able and intelligent physicist who would knock up a death-ray in a matter of days and blast the hran to hell.

'But I didn't find such a physicist. Not even you, Céline.'

She smiled weakly at that.

'I had no hope,' he continued, 'I was an abused animal waiting to be put to sleep. No hope. But Kewfor is that tremendously able and intelligent physicist that I dreamed about.

'And he has given me hope. I will do whatever he says because if he is wrong, there really is no hope. There is no Plan B that another supercomputer could come up with. This is it.'

She looked at him, wiping the tears from her face.

'So you are going to cross to the hran universe?'

He nodded. 'And die there, if I have to. You're cleverer than me, Céline, and your knowledge is deeper – that's why you will accompany me.'

Seventeen

'I'm not going,' Krause said.

'Fine,' Dubois replied, 'I'll go without you.'

Krause grabbed Dubois's shoulders and tried to turn the taller woman to look at her.

'Céline, you've been listening to Larsen again! If he wants to throw his life away – let him! What is he to us? We've got each other!'

'So we let other people carry the burden of trying to get rid of these terrible creatures,' Dubois said, staring down at Krause, 'Is that what you're saying? You know, sometimes I feel like I don't know you anymore.'

Krause turned away. 'Céline don't be horrible. Please don't be horrible to me.'

'Stop it!' Dubois snapped, 'You've got the wrong definition of horrible! *I'm* not horrible. Those things that are sucking our lifeblood away – they're horrible.'

Krause slumped on the bed. 'I know. I know. It's just that...' She turned back to Dubois. 'I'm frightened, Céline. I have this feeling that if I go something awful is going to happen to me!'

Dubois sat beside her, placing an arm around the other's shoulders.

'Of course, you're frightened, darling. We all are. None of us wanted to be in this position. But all those innocent people who were caught up in the great wars, in the terrible plagues, don't you think they were frightened too? But they had to face up to their responsibilities, to accept that they had been thrown into terrible events through no fault of their own.

'We're the same. We've been caught up in a war.'

Krause gripped Dubois's hand with sudden, brutal pressure.

216

'Alright, I'll go. But only because I'm going with you. You will look after me, won't you Céline?'

'Hilda, I promised I would always do that. And I promised that if anything ever tried to hurt you, I would make them pay.

'Those promises still stand and always will.'

And they kissed.

* * *

The hybrid stood before them.

They hadn't learned its name, but that didn't matter; it was Kewfor who was speaking.

They stood there in the grounds of the Arthur J. Anderson Center For Particle Physics.

They were all dressed identically in camouflage fatigues; all but one trying, and failing, to remain calm and detached in the face of the incredible test they were about to undergo. They had backpacks, containing small amounts of water and high energy foods. More ominously, they also had automatic weapons slung over their backs and pistols at their hips, plus seemingly ridiculous quantities of ammunition.

There were seven of them: Dubois, Krause, Larsen, Takahashi, Williamson, Jones and Velasquez. No-one else had volunteered.

'Seven will be just enough,' Kewfor had said.

They had spent a week in training, learning how to use their devices. Going over and over the methods of operation until their minds rebelled. And then doing it all over again.

Of the group, only Larsen had any experience with firearms but he also listened patiently whilst the tutor hybrids explained how to operate them.

There was no time for target practice.

To maximise the likelihood of success all the volunteers carried in satchels the devices which would open the portal and send the precious data across the bridge. Fortunately, the recorders were small and weighed only a few kilograms. The weapons and ammunition were a much heavier load. Each one there fervently hoped they would bring the same amount back.

'Every one of you has a particular area of responsibility,' Kewfor was reminding them yet again, 'Williamson, you will handle the measurement of their version of the Sommerfeld Constant.'

'Yes, I know, I know,' he replied, wiping sweat from his brow, and for some reason looking around in all directions, 'Give it a fucking rest, can't you!'

Kewfor ignored his reaction and went on to list all the other responsibilities.

After completing that, he continued, 'I would have preferred a larger group. As it is you form the absolute minimum of operatives. To recap, when you have completed the measurements, you will code them using one of the communicators and send them through the portal to this universe. The communicator will run a diagnostic to check whether it has been tampered with, using a code based on the Fibonacci numbers, as I have already explained. Then you must all cross the bridge within fifteen minutes after the data are sent. After that period I will send the harmonic blast across it.'

'And all the fires of Hell will be released,' Larsen murmured.

'Extremely large numbers will be necessary to describe the energy flow, yes,' Kewfor commented in response.

'It would be easier if we could cross as a group rather than one at a time,' Velasquez observed.

'Wishful thinking will not be of assistance here,' Kewfor said, 'There are physical constraints on everything we do. As you say in the Twenty first century: It is what it is.'

Velasquez looked somewhat shamefaced as he nodded.

Kewfor continue: 'To ensure that the blast is sent as soon as possible the portal will automatically sense how many of you are returning and will only open for that number.'

There was an odd silence for a few moments while they

218

digested the implication of that statement. Williamson got there first.

'Wait a moment!' he yelled, 'Am I to take it that you're not expecting all of us to come back?'

'That is of course a possibility,' Kewfor replied, 'although the probability is small. As I have said I intend to deposit you in an unpopulated region.'

'Based on what the hran captives told you!' Williamson continued to shout, 'You've got a lot to learn pal!'

Kewfor did not reply but Larsen gave Williamson a severe stare and said, quietly, simply, 'We're going.'

Dubois could feel her heart racing and her palms become slick with sweat.

The dread moment was approaching. A terrible desire to run away began to grip her.

She looked up. The Californian sky was as blue as usual, with only a few puffy fair-weather cumulus clouds. From where she stood she could catch a glimpse of the deeper, richer blue of the Bay.

Would she ever see it again?

Suddenly Williamson threw his satchel to the ground and shouted, 'I can't do it!' He began to run from the area only to find a massive hand reaching out to clutch his collar and bring him to a shuddering halt.

'Pick up your instrument,' Larsen growled, 'And get ready to go in the portal. If necessary, I will throw you in.'

'All right, you bastard,' Williamson said, 'Don't think I'll forget this!'

Larsen laughed unconcernedly without bothering to reply and pushed him back to where he had been standing.

A terrible silence ensued; the kind of silence that is present in observers while they wait for the axe to fall upon the victim.

Blue sky. Blue Bay! Oh please let me see them again!

Then it started.

Abruptly, there was feeling of electrical, rather than

219

psychological tension, in the air. Dubois's hair began slowly to rise from her scalp. There was the sharp tang of ozone in her nostrils as the oxygen molecules were agitated by the rising potential. Their surroundings became blurred, as if seen through a great heat haze.

And then there it was!

A great misty circle appeared, resting a few centimetres above the grass. It was the mouth of an insubstantial tunnel such as Dubois had seen once before, a shaft of swirling mist and vapour, but this time suffused with a rich blue luminosity.

It was wrong, unnatural; something that should not exist in the real world. But natural or unnatural, its orifice expanded rapidly until it was over two metres in diameter.

Larsen pushed Williamson towards it.

'You first.'

Williamson cringed as he was pushed towards it and then, after a final push from Larsen, he seemed to trip and fall into that eerie mouth.

There was a blue flash – and he was gone.

The mouth of the portal became an opaque wall, seemingly made from the finest sapphire. Then it snapped out of existence; instantly, with no sound whatsoever.

'Wait,' Kewfor said, 'It will only take a few seconds.'

Once again the portal appeared, the end facing them a solid wall of featureless blue.

The wall opened and the misty, glowing interior was revealed again.

The interior appeared to be stretching out to infinity: nothing was visible at its farthest point.

Velasquez was next.

Then Jones.

Then Takahashi.

Larsen turned to wave at Dubois and Krause, and then he entered, having to lower his head as he did so.

Krause looked up at Dubois with pleading eyes.

'You can do it,' Dubois said softly, 'I'll be right behind you.'

Krause nodded in resignation and followed Larsen.

Dubois took another look at the blue sky and the blue Bay.

And then she also entered the portal, to cross to the universe of the hran.

PART THREE: THE HIDDEN ONES

Ab initio

Marius Larsen turned from the window and looked at his mother.

'Mummy, why is it always raining in Bergen?'

She looked up from her patchwork and gave a little smile. 'You know that's not right, Marius. It doesn't always rain in Bergen.'

'Yes, it does!' Marius said, pushing out his lower lip, 'I wanted to play with my friends today and I've been stuck in the house all day! It's not fair!'

She put the patchwork to one side and beckoned to Marius to come and join her. She picked him up, a little awkwardly for he was already a big boy, and put him on her lap.

'There'll be other days, my darling boy,' she said, tousling his thick fair hair, 'it'll probably be dry tomorrow. Summer's coming and we'll be able to go into the mountains and do lots of nice things. Like catching fish. You remember how your daddy taught you how to catch them?'

'Yes, mummy, that was fun.'

There was a pause. His mother knew what was coming and her eyes moistened just a little.

'Mummy, why did daddy have to die?'

His mother sighed. She didn't know the answer to that question; she wished she did.

She gave the same answer as she had given to Marius on the many other occasions he had asked that question.

'He had something wrong inside, Marius. God saw that he was in pain and he took him to Heaven where he's with the angels.'

'So I'll see him again then – when I am an angel?'

She forced her lips into a smile and said, 'Yes, of course.'

And then she wrapped her arms around him and hugged him tightly.

'But that won't be for a long, long time!'

223

That answer seemed to satisfy the little boy and he got off his mother's lap and played with his wooden train set for a while.

Soon it was time for bed and his mother tucked him in tightly and gave him his favourite book: "The Children's Big Book of Astronomy." He especially liked the lovely full colour paintings of the planets and was particularly taken with the picture of Saturn, with its magnificent rings and many moons displayed against a dark backdrop.

'Do you think I'll be able to go to Saturn, mummy?' he said, pointing at the picture.

She ruffled his hair again. 'Yes, of course. You'll be the first man to land on Saturn!'

'That's what I want to be when I'm big,' the boy said, 'I want to see different places, faraway lands with funny animals in them!'

'You will,' his mother said, 'now settle down with your book and we'll do something tomorrow. I'm sure it won't be raining!' She blew him a kiss and left.

She waited half an hour and then crept silently into his bedroom. The boy was asleep, his head on one side. The book lay open on his coverlet, still open at the picture of Saturn. Carefully she pulled the book out of his grasp and placed it on the little bedside table so he could see it first thing in the morning.

Then she turned the light out and went back to her armchair to resume her patchwork.

She hadn't been working for more than ten minutes when he heard her son give a terrible scream.

She rushed in, switching the light on and found the boy sobbing.

'What is it Marius!' she cried, bending down to hug the child.

He looked up at her with a tear-streaked face and said, 'I had a terrible dream, mummy!'

'There, there,' she said, stroking his hair, 'It's alright, mummy's here. Dreams aren't real, they can't hurt you.'

224

The child could not be comforted. 'It was terrible, mummy! I was in this big tunnel made of blue glass and I couldn't get out – I had to keep walking down it towards the light. But at the other end of the tunnel there were things waiting for me. Horrible monsters, mummy!'

She hugged him even more tightly. 'No, Marius. Don't be afraid. There're no such things as monsters. Mummy will stay with you.'

And she sat with him, holding his hand until he was fast asleep again. He did not have another bad dream that night.

Later, as she lay down in her own bed, she thought to herself *He's having too many of these dreams. How can I make him believe that there are no such things as monsters?*

* * *

Larsen rolled over and, placing a hand on Kirsten's right breast, said, 'Why does it have to be girl on top again? Can't we do it some other way for once?'

Kirsten smiled. 'Look, every time you're on top of me I feel like I'm being pushed through the mattress and through the floor! We've already had one bed collapse because you get carried away, you big troll!'

He grinned. 'I will be carried away quite literally soon if we don't get some action going.'

'You always were a big romantic, Marius. As well as being a big troll. Do you live under a bridge, by any chance?'

He slid down the bed so his massive head was between her thighs.

'Yes! And I eat little girls!'

Sometime later, the conversation resumed.

'Have you got everything planned out when you leave uni, Marius?' she said, in an oddly wistful tone.

'You know I have,' he replied, placing his arms behind his head as he lay back, 'I want to solve the mysteries of the universe.'

'But that'll mean leaving Norway,' she continued, 'you'll end up in California or some place like that. I'll never see you again.'

He turned to look at her. 'That was always the deal, Kirsten. I haven't lied to you. You could end up there as well.'

She snorted. 'What – a linguist in America? Americans believe that people who don't speak English are doing it to annoy them!'

There was a silence in the small university lodgings. Neither partner could think of anything to say.

Kirsten broke that silence. 'Marius, darling, it's all coming to an end! Our university days are nearly all behind us now – all that drinking, that singing, that sex – it's all ending!'

He reached for a breast again. 'Not all the sex if I've got anything to say about it!'

With some difficulty, she pushed the massive hand away.

'Stop it – you're not listening! We've had a kind of extended childhood but it's ending! I need to know if I'm the woman for you; I need to know if we have a future.'

He did not answer, and she jumped off the bed, reaching for the bra that was draped over a nearby chair.

'I knew it! Those stories about you and other women – I didn't want to believe them. But they're true!'

She leaned over him, glaring down.

'You've been fucking somebody else haven't you! Admit it you bastard!'

He smiled at her and under the warmth of that smile she felt her resolution waver, her righteous anger wane a little.

'Kirsten, Kirsten, listen love, it was at a party. We were both drunk! It meant nothing at all – no, less than nothing. I can't even remember the bitch's name!'

He held up his arms, beseechingly. 'Come back. Please. I'll rest my weight on my elbows.'

She did. He did.

Afterwards, she watched the rain lashing against the window

226

and snuggled closer to the sleeping Larsen.

She ran her fingers through the springy mass of his beard; the beard he'd grown especially for her because she liked bearded men.

He'd promised her that he would never shave it off.

She stroked the mass of curls that adorned his scalp, listening to the gentle rhythm of his breathing, a rhythm that slowly caused a warm drowsiness to flow into her.

Kirsten was nearly asleep when he suddenly screamed and sat upright on the bed, gasping in great gulps of air. She reached for him and found him trembling.

'What is it Marius?' she said, feeling his fear start to infect her, 'what is it?'

He ran a hand over his sweat streaked forehead.

'It's a dream; a terrible dream I've had since childhood. I thought I'd grown out of it but I haven't. I'm walking down this big, shining blue tunnel. I can't stop or turn around and at the end – at the end…'

'What?' she said, now truly frightened, 'what's at the end?'

He turned to her; his face stricken.

'Monsters. Monsters waiting for me at the end.'

* * *

Einar Olsen looked up at his friend, noticing once again the self-satisfied look on the big man's face.

'You know Marius,' he said, 'this weakness you have for a nice pair of tits – it's going to get you into big trouble one of these days. Times have changed; you can't just go around doing exactly what you want anymore.'

Larsen shrugged. 'I can't help it – it's the way the Good Lord made me.'

Olsen made the "harrumph" noise and looked around the cavernous room that held the excimer laser. It looked as big as the interior of one of the great medieval cathedrals; and in a way it was – but it was a modern cathedral dedicated to science.

'We must be very proud of what we've done here, Einar,' Larsen said, the excitement making his voice thicker, 'We've got the best research facility in Europe here. This'll show the Yanks!'

'That girl you tried to molest didn't look very happy with you,' Olsen observed, pointedly refusing to let his friend escape so lightly.

Larsen was annoyed that Olsen wasn't sharing in his excitement. 'Well, what do you expect? Using 4π instead of 2π – it would have blown your pubic hair off!'

'Very funny. Let's hope she's not so mad at you that she doesn't pass the message on. But Marius, you've got to stop treating women as your personal plaything. Whatever happened to that nice girl you were seeing in university?'

'What - Kirsten? Good God, that was years ago. She's in California now, I think.'

'Weren't you going to California once?'

Larsen nodded, not really listening, not taking his eyes off the magnificent laser.

'Well, that was before we built this thing and snatched the lead off them. I'll never go to California – have you heard about the stuff they eat over there? They actually eat dogs made of corn!'

'I met her once,' Olsen said, 'she was a lovely girl. And she cared for you.'

'Einar, you're what the magazines call an incurable romantic. I moved on because I've never found a woman who's my equal. Why since Kirsten, I've had eight thousand, seven hundred and eighty-six different women.'

Olsen's mood lightened at that comment and, reaching up quite some way, he slapped Larsen on the shoulder.

'Now I know you're making it up – the last time, you said it was eight thousand, seven hundred and eighty-seven!'

Suddenly it was time: out on the experiment floor Larsen and Olsen saw red lights flash on all around the huge room and the words "WARNING: EXPERIMENT IN PROCESS" appear on a panel above the window of the control room. Hurriedly, they slipped on goggles and retired behind a lead screen, at the top of which was a dark panel of lead-infused silica.

There was a deep-throated whirr as the great tube of the laser suddenly came to life and began to rise from the support which held it in its resting state. It swung back and forth slightly, as if searching for its target. The just as suddenly it came to an abrupt halt as its quarry was detected.

'Here we go Einar!' Larsen yelled.

Then the great machine flashed into life. Most of its output was in the high X-Ray band but there was enough blue-violet light to make a visible beam as it annihilated the dust motes that lay between its muzzle and the target: a slab of hafnium-titanium alloy.

But unbeknownst to the two enthralled observers, Larsen's correction had not been passed to the controllers by the angry young woman, whom Larsen had upset so recklessly.

Suddenly there was an all-encompassing glow of coronal discharges which enveloped the laser, and arcs of electricity flashed like angry lightning, reaching up into the lofty ceiling, jumping from point to point, leaving disks of glowing, red-hot metal behind to show where they had struck.

'Shut the power for Chrissake!' Larsen bellowed into his throat mike as a blazing column of raw electrical death came leaping and hissing towards them.

The controllers had realised the danger before Larsen, for even before he had finished bellowing his command the great room was plunged into darkness.

Larsen suddenly noticed there was a glow behind him and he turned to see Olsen staring at a large globe of crackling blue-yellow energy that was slowly drifting past them, like an escaped party balloon.

'Ball lightning,' Olsen whispered, in near-religious awe, 'it does exist!'

'Never mind that!' Larsen roared, 'it's heading straight for the laser! It'll blow millions of dollars-worth of kit sky high!'

Without concern for the consequences, the two men did the one thing they should not have done: they snatched a metal pole from the floor and tried to push the ball of energy off course.

They were thrown unconscious to the floor as the sphere vanished with an eye-searing flash and the sound of a thousand thunders.

Larsen spent two weeks in the coma into which the discharge had thrown him.

When he finally awoke he could remember nothing of his thoughts during that period.

Thus he was unaware that during his period of unconsciousness he had heard cold, pitiless voices, voices that seemed to be drawn from the depths of an Antarctic ice sheet; voices that knew nothing of empathy, of love, of mercy; voices that kept repeating over and over again, 'We know you, Marius Larsen', while sets of hate-filled, glowing red eyes, faultlessly arranged in perfect equilateral triangles, glaring at him from out of the darkness, staring relentlessly, staring down through the flesh, down through the bone, down into the very core of his being.

One

Larsen found himself in an endless tunnel of what looked like a brilliant blue glass that was somehow vaporous and crystalline simultaneously. Everywhere he looked, he could see distorted reflections of himself looking back at him, like the ever-diminishing images seen in an infinity of mirrors.

He did not appear to be moving; he wasn't sure whether he was standing on anything. On looking down, he could see his boots apparently resting on a gently curving sapphire surface, but he felt no pressure from it. He could have been floating in free-fall, but if so, he was floating without any apparent motion. Ahead of him, the tunnel looked exactly the same as far as the eye could see; there was no structure, nothing to differentiate one centimetre from another. It merely shrank to the vanishing point without any change whatsoever.

Was it possible that he was not moving; that Kewfor had miscalculated and he was stuck in some bizarre static limbo between universes where he would hang forever, neither *here* nor *there*?

It was a terrifying thought. He was alone without any form of communication with any entity. He was apparently motionless in a world of silence.

He shouted out his name and was relieved to find that he could hear his own voice. So there was sound in this bewildering environment, at least. The fact that he had heard nothing prior to his shout, thankfully meant that there had been no noise up until then.

What had Kewfor said? That the transition would be practically instantaneous from the viewpoint of an external observer but not from the subjective experience of the traveller himself. But what would that subjective experience be in

231

actuality?

Kewfor did not know because no human had traversed the bridge and returned from that bourn to tell their tale.

Perhaps the subjective experience would be a year; a thousand years; a million.

A million years spent hanging in an endless corridor of glowing blue glass.

Larsen threw off that fear and doubt. Kewfor was not infallible, but he would not have miscalculated so badly. It must be the case that he was moving but simply had no external markers to make that apparent. He was travelling and travelling hopefully.

Larsen chose not to complete the quotation.

The weird tunnel was not new to him, even though he had never been in it before.

He knew it from the dreams that had haunted him since childhood. He had always known that one day he would enter this tunnel. And he knew that at the end there would be horror; horror such as no men had faced before.

He took the pistol from his holster and spent some seconds looking at it. It reminded him of the twenty-first century Heckler and Koch P2000 and Kewfor had told him that it fired twenty solid rounds, enough to take down big game.

He let go of it and was not surprised when it did not fall but remained suspended in space exactly where it had been when he had released his grip. He replaced it in the holster and looked resolutely ahead.

All he could do now was to wait and trust in Kewfor.

He did not have long to wait.

At the indeterminate distance of the vanishing point, a grey dot abruptly snapped into existence. And rapidly grew and grew until it was clearly an orifice of the same size as the one through which he had entered.

He *was* moving – and at a considerable speed.

Before he could entirely comprehend the speed at which he

232

was traversing Kewfor's strange portal, his journey across the bridge between realities ended abruptly and he was ejected from the tunnel with some force.

He fell onto his hands and knees onto a soft surface which appeared to consist of a carpet of yielding grey moss.

Slowly, slowly he lifted his head, half-fearing to see what kind of world he had been flung into.

It was not a pleasant vista that met his wary gaze.

It was a twilight world, that was only just above the threshold of the level of illumination which would permit colour vision.

He was surrounded by curling wisps of grey-black vapour; that drifted and slowly twisted, partially revealing and then partially hiding what lay beyond in slow succession. The air had an unpleasant smell; it was cold and metallic, with an under taste of biting acidity. Directly in front of him, and at some unknown height above the vaporous obscurity, rose a flickering sheet of glaucous light, which was twisting back on itself and roiling slowly, looking like somewhat like an aurora – but a terminally sick one. It seemed that it, and it alone, was the source of the meagre amount of greyish light that was barely illuminating his surroundings: there was no sun.

Turning through a right angle, he was confronted by more foetid, necrotic miasmas, slowly rising and falling; sometimes creeping across the grey moss towards him like a tremendous amoeba and then retreating without any cause. And in the dim, obscure distance came a regular deep throbbing; just above the threshold of human hearing.

He completed a complete rotation without seeing any great difference in his surroundings. But in the far distance, a fraction before the point where atmospheric absorption would have blocked further vision, there rose from the otherwise featureless terrain a small plateau; not high, but steep-sided. And once in the direction where the terminus of the portal had lain, he thought he saw an immense black shadow move from right to left across

233

his field of vision, but it had happened so quickly that he could not be sure if he had seen it or not.

But gradually he realised that there was something else different about this eldritch world: there was no horizon.

It was challenging to be certain in the funereal greyness which enfolded him, but it seemed to him that at the limit of his vision the land appeared to be sloping very gradually upwards, as if he were at the centre of a bowl that was both gargantuan and shallow.

He stopped his inspection of this new land; there was no more to see in the near monochrome bleakness of his surroundings. It seemed to be the perfect setting for Durer's woodcuts of the Apocalypse.

But there was something that he was definitely not seeing: his companions.

He was alone in a Purgatory of greyness.

He felt a stab of fear; Kewfor had assured them all that although they had crossed the bridge individually, they would all arrive at the same point in very quick succession due to the difference between objective and subjective time. But that clearly had not happened.

Kewfor was not a god; he could only make calculations, but could his calculations be this far out?

Once again, he had the horrible feeling that this was all a sick joke on them; perhaps Kewfor had been taken over by the hran and was sadistically toying with them.

One thing was sure – each of them had a specific measurement to make and seven had been the minimum number that could take all the required readings in the mercifully short time that they were expected to be here. Whether through bad luck or some oversight, if only Larsen himself had crossed, then Kewfor's plan had failed. He, Larsen, could not carry out all the tests himself.

And if Dubois and the others had not crossed – where were they?

Had the ethereal bridge flashed out of existence as they were in the act of crossing, supposedly safe within the portal, and been thrown into nothingness?

Larsen had known despair before and once again it enveloped him in a grip of ice. His great head bowed under another addition to the intolerable burdens he had borne since that dread day in Alta.

It was then that he heard shouting – human shouting.

And out of the mist came a running human – Williamson.

Larsen put out his hands to stop the other's mad flight, realising that Williamson hadn't seen him; that he was looking behind as he ran.

Williamson crashed heavily into him before realising he was not alone.

He screamed and then saw it was Larsen.

'Larsen,' he panted, 'thank God it's you, man!'

'Yes, it's me,' Larsen said, 'where are the others?'

'How the fuck do I know! I didn't know you were here until I hit you! Kewfor's buggered it all up, we've got to get out of here!'

Larsen held the other's shoulders, looking down at the panting man.

'We're going nowhere. If you're here, so are the others – we're going to find them, complete the mission and then go.'

'Like hell!' Williamson snarled and tried to tear himself out of Larsen's grip – a task he found impossible.

Larsen shook him like a rag doll.

'Stop it, you sack of shit! What were you running from?'

For reply, Williamson squirmed in Larsen's vice-like grip, twisting his head from one side to another.

'I heard them. They're in the mist, moving closer, hunting me!'

'Who? The hran?'

'I don't know. I couldn't see them – just grey shapes moving around. And a terrible clicking noise, getting louder and louder.'

235

Larsen then realised something.

'Williamson – where's your measuring device?'

'How the hell do I know? I dropped the fucking thing, all right?'

In his fury Larsen lifted his struggling captive so far off the ground that their eyes were on the same level.

'You dropped it! You dropped it! We can't complete the full set of results without it! You've fucked the whole thing up, you useless bastard!'

It was then the pair heard a female voice near to them; a voice dipped in the melodic sweetness of Provençe.

'Are you looking for this?'

Larsen dropped the struggling Williamson and turned to see what looked like Dubois emerge from the clinging mists.

It was she, and in addition to her own equipment she was carrying another one, presumably Williamson's.

She came up to Larsen and, allowing the extra equipment to drop to the ground, gave him a close embrace. An embrace so close that, despite their dreadful situation, she felt his mighty body begin to react to her soft pressure.

She extricated herself with a small smile, placing a hand on his great chest.

'Whoa Tiger! I like you now – but not that much!'

As if on cue, Krause and Takahashi came out of the drifting curtains of mist.

'Céline, it's a miracle to see you!' Larsen exclaimed, his face once again in danger of splitting in two because of his great smile. 'But what happened? Why did Kewfor say we'd arrive together?'

'I don't think it was miscalculation on her part.' (Larsen gave a slight smile at that.) 'It was lack of data. I think the relative velocity between the two branes has increased for some unknowable reason. So instead of being deposited at a point, we've been spread out over a line.'

Larsen grinned in admiration. 'It must be that. Céline, if I had a hat I'd take it off to you. And anything else you'd like me to take off!'

She wagged a finger at him. 'Now, stop that or I'll leave without you.' She pointed into the dull distance. 'Notice anything unusual about this place?'

'It looks like the land is rising.'

'Full marks. This brane's spatial construction has a negative curvature; unlike ours, which is either positive or Euclidean.'

'Good God – that's it! 'He looked down at her again. 'You know, Céline, we were made for each other.'

She smiled again. 'Sorry, I don't date men who are so much less intelligent than I am.'

Suddenly Krause was between them; eyes blazing.

'Céline stop this! It's not funny!'

Dubois gave her an odd look. 'We're just joking, Hilda.'

But it was Takahashi's turn to speak.

'There's a time and place for levity. This is not it. Let us laugh and joke by all means when we are safely back but we are not there yet. Must I remind you that we are supposed to be here for as short a time as possible, and we need Jones and Velasquez to be able to make all the readings.

'We were fortunate enough not to arrive in the midst of a hran welcoming committee. Our luck can't last much longer.'

Dubois nodded.

'Point taken, Hiromoto. Let's find the others and get on with it.'

Two

'There's something out there,' said Jones, only a few minutes after he had joined the others.

Larsen moved to stand beside him.

'What did you see?'

Jones shook his head. 'It's hard to say. It was like – like a kind of ripple in the air.'

'A ripple in the air. Not a figure, a shape?'

'No.'

'Must be a kind of atmospheric phenomenon. Let's get on with it. We're only supposed to be here half an hour and ten minutes have gone already.'

Larsen moved to the centre of the group of physicists. 'Keep those measurements coming. Make sure you're sending them to everybody else's device, just like we agreed. That way if one goes down we'll still have all the data.'

He turned back to look out at the twisting mists, narrowing his eyes as he studied their weird surroundings. The necrotic aurora had now moved directly above them, casting ghastly shades of dispiriting colour that conjured visions in their minds of decay and dissolution. In all directions, there was the same sepulchral, near-monochrome pall that sapped the spirit, that mocked their courage and resolution.

Larsen shivered. The temperature was low but should have been tolerable, yet somehow it was not. The cold felt like it was being created in the centre of their bodies, moving outwards, rather than inward.

He turned back to the group. 'How's it going?'

Dubois looked up from her screen. 'It's OK, but it's taking longer than we thought. It'll be more than half an hour. Williamson's given me an absolutely crazy value for

Sommerfeld's Constant – I'll have to check it.'

Larsen nodded to show he understood and had accepted her conclusion. Half an hour had always been understood to be the absolute minimum possible time. A slight overshoot was to be expected.

He glanced at his own recording device. It was doing well. Already the local value of c and the Planck Constant were safely in the memory. Soon they would be able to leave.

But where were the hran?

The group had been ready for anything- even emerging in the heart of a hran city; assuming they had cities.

If that had come to pass, they would have flicked their recorders on to autonomous mode while their automatic and semiautomatic weapons made their greetings for them. The hran would have gone down like wheat before the reaper with Larsen in the vanguard, sweeping his hail of death from side to side, sending them to the hell they so richly deserved.

But none of that had happened. They had not been disturbed; with the possible exception of Williamson, but the man was so jumpy he was as likely to start shooting his own shadow as a real-life hran.

Where was the enemy? Could it be this easy – a strange anti-climax? A crazy thought hit him then. Perhaps Kewfor had sent them to the wrong brane and this was an uninhabited wasteland and they were wasting their time, taking meaningless readings.

Then he saw it some distance away. A ripple in the air just like Jones had said.

He studied it. It must surely be merely a local movement in the air; it certainly didn't look like an army of hran heading for them with murder on their minds.

He realised that he would not need to speculate for much longer as the air disturbance was heading straight for them. He glanced to left and right: whatever it was, it was not merely local. He could see that the part in front of him was merely a fraction of a great wavefront that was advancing inexorably on his group

239

across the floor of the stupendous bowl which constituted this alien landscape.

And something else: as the disturbance came nearer, he could see that the sparse vegetation was bending towards it, as if being pulled in.

Alarm signals went off in his brain then. This could be a hran weapon.

He turned to shout a warning, noticing than some of the group had already seen the thing and were standing up in bewilderment as it swept nearer.

And then it was on them.

Larsen staggered as his body instantly felt many times heavier. Unable to support his weight, he crashed heavily to the ground, his warning dying in a gurgle in his throat. Lying on his side he saw the air ripple and swirl around him and take on a foul, reddish caste. Then he was no longer able to support his head, and it was pressed down into the soft surface, one eye becoming covered by the moss in a clammy embrace.

He heard cries of horror from the others, and then a dreadful silence as they too were pressed into the ground, as if under gigantic hands. The vision in his unobstructed eye dissolved into fathomless blackness, shot through with dancing sparks. He realised that the blood supply to his brain was being cut off.

It was a hran weapon, and they had won.

Unconsciousness took him.

* * *

He awoke to find himself on his back and Dubois's worried face looking down on him from a few centimetres away. Then her face lightened, and she said, 'Ah, you're not dead then. For a tough guy you took a long time to come round!'

He struggled into a sitting position. 'The others – are they OK?'

240

She nodded. 'We all survived. And fortunately, the instruments kept recording. I know what happened.'

'The hran?'

'No, it appears to be a natural phenomenon. The gravitational constant isn't.'

'No riddles please.'

'The constant is a variable. As far as I can see it follows a regular pattern. We arrived not long before the maximum. Which we just survived. The cycle is not sinusoidal – the maxima are greater than the minima.'

Larsen struggled to his feet, being saved from falling by timely assistance from Dubois.

'How much time have we lost?'

'Quite a bit, I'm afraid. We're well past the hour mark.'

Larsen's face was grim. They were in an environment where their constituent atoms were radioactive. Any damage they accumulated would be irreversible and would be part of them if and when they returned.

Well, so be it. If would be worth it if they could lift the fangs of their oppressors from the collective throats of humanity.

'What stage are we at in the data collection?'

'Good. We've got about eighty per cent. But it's taking longer than Kewfor estimated. It'll be another hour.'

'Another hour! That's too bloody long!'

Larsen turned from Dubois and looked out over the grey, seemingly dead landscape, still mysteriously empty of their foe.

But Dubois was still speaking. 'Marius, it's worse than that. The variation in the gravitational constant – that couldn't be deduced from the data we already have.'

'Meaning?'

'Meaning if we'd left before we'd experienced it then the data we gave to Kewfor would have been incomplete and might have caused her to send the binding energy the wrong way.'

Larsen groaned. 'You're right again, damn you. Got any more bad news?'

241

'Yes. We didn't know about the gravity shift until we experienced it. What else don't we know about this reality – can't know until we experience it?'

'You seem to be saying that there's no point in us being here.'

Dubois shook her head. 'No, I don't think I'm saying that. There must be a cycle to these occurrences. A repeating pattern. On Earth, we have day and night, the seasons. It's very likely that there's a repeating pattern here as well. We have to stay here long enough to establish what the pattern is.'

'And how do we do that? On Earth we had the cycle of day and night and because of that it's obvious when a cycle is complete. I don't know whether you've noticed, but there's no sun here. The quality and intensity of the light never changes.'

'I have noticed. So all we can do is wait until the next gravitational shift occurs.'

Williamson was standing close enough to overhear, and he sprang between Larsen and Dubois, facing Dubois.

'You're out of your bloody mind! The longer we stay here, the more likely we are to get cancer. Can't you understand that, Bright Girl?'

Larsen pulled him away. 'We all know that. I've already got cancer. It's not always the end.'

Williamson turned to stare up at the big Norwegian, his face twisted in what looked like hate.

'Oh, you're a real macho guy, aren't you? Maybe if you were the same size as a normal man, you wouldn't talk so tough. May I remind you that I'm here because you pushed me into that damn portal? Unlike you, I've never pretended to be a hero!'

'You've got two chances of getting back home,' Larsen said, 'and that's doing as you're told and staying out of my way!' He gave Williamson a shove which sent the smaller man sprawling. 'Sorry, I clearly don't know my own strength.'

Larsen returned to studying the landscape.

No change. The sick aurora had moved past the zenith and

242

was slowly changing from one putrescent shade to another. In the distance came the faint sound of thudding concussions as if a great hammer was rising and falling.

Farther out in the banks of slowly rolling mist – were there dim shapes moving inside them, like larvae wriggling inside a flower bud?

Was there a faint clicking noise accompanying those obscure movements?

Larsen could not tell and after a few more minutes he returned to studying his instruments.

Three

In the Rocky Mountains of Alberta there lay a great sinuous desert of tumbled boulders standing amidst fans of moraine. To an observer standing nearby, it would have looked like a mighty river had once flowed there but had dried up centuries earlier.

The observer would not have been entirely wrong, because there had indeed once been a great river here; but not of water – it had been a river of ice; for this was where the great Athabasca Glacier had once wound down from the mighty Columbia Icefield.

The glacier was long gone, of course, destroyed in the climate catastrophe of the twenty-first and early twenty-second centuries. The crippling heat which had smashed human civilisation had also killed what had once been a wonder of nature.

Now the bald mountains looked down on a few isolated patches of grubby ice which were the first signs the Icefield was trying to regenerate.

But it would be many centuries, perhaps millennia, of falling temperatures before the area would once again be clothed in the sheltering ice.

In the meantime, hybrids and a few humans had toiled to create one of the atomic power plants that Kewfor had ordered constructed as part of his attempt to save what remained of humankind from creatures that saw them merely as cattle of the field.

Here was produced the energy that powered the network of flying machines and ground vehicles through which the Quantum Computer monitored his helpless charges. The waste heat also kept hydroponic gardens flourishing in underground facilities where infant seedlings grew into useable crops under soft pink illumination.

The power area itself, overlooked by the heat-splintered peaks, consisted of the massive dome of the alkali-fluoride reactor itself where thorium was transmuted to uranium.

Connected to it was the smaller dome where plutonium was generated and added to the thorium-salt mix to kick-start the reaction.

And next to both was a small village of low buildings which, in two separate areas, housed the hybrid and human workers.

Greg McKee had worked there for several years and had risen to just about as high in the hierarchy as a human could hope. His immediate supervisor was a hybrid, of course, called Tharan. His supervisor understood all that science stuff which McKee found more than a bit beyond him. Tharan was only two levels away from the top management that was ultimately responsible for the safe running of the power plant. Thorium reactors were inherently safer than pure uranium reactors, but McKee knew that nothing is absolutely safe.

His job was to service (under close supervision) the terahertz generators which threw up an invisible shield around the power plant. McKee didn't really understand why an invisible shield was needed or what it was shielding against. He had been told it was to do with the safety of the plant because plutonium was pretty nasty stuff and he had accepted that explanation. He also had responsibilities for keeping the plant's documentation up to date, for the hybrids would occasionally ask for the schematics of the fuel flow conduits and pore over them in silence. They never told McKee what they were looking for and he never asked.

'Quitting time, I guess,' he said, putting his coffee mug down on the chipped work surface.

Tharan was staring at a computer screen, his robust, symmetrical face illuminated in a way that accentuated his high cheekbones.

'Is it?' he replied, 'I thought it was earlier.'

'Look,' chuckled McKee, 'I know you guys don't have any social life but us regular folk do. I got a wife waiting for me, who'll be wondering when she can start fixing dinner. You hybrids don't have wives, do you?'

'No.'

'Or children?'

'No. We're sterile.'

McKee harrumphed a little at that. 'You know there's such a thing as too much information. Are you going to stay here all night?'

'No, not all night. I do need some down-time.'

McKee chuckled good-naturedly. 'Down-time! You types got the funniest way of talking I ever heard.'

Tharan stared at him blankly. 'I am glad it gives you enjoyment.'

McKee gave a wave of an arm to indicate that the conversation was over and, picking up his work bag, wished Tharan a good night and left the office.

Tharan did not pay much attention to his departure.

He was much more interested in what the screen was showing him and he didn't like it.

The screen showed an aerial view of the power plant and the village. Scattered over that display were a large number of red dots, that were slowly circling the central area, like sharks approaching a bait-ball.

Each red dot was a hran. Physically present.

There were always hran outside the terahertz screen but Tharan had never seen so many.

What was agitating them? This wasn't normal feeding behaviour. Typically, they would simply wait outside the screen, trying to catch oblivious human beings if they strayed too far from their homes.

Tharan decided he had seen enough and opened a relay to his superior, who he knew would be on-station and alert.

That superior listened gravely to Tharan's report and said,

246

'There is something happening here for which we do not know the reason. Other power plants have reported similar concentrations of hran.'

'Is it possible that they are planning an attack?'

'That is always possible. But it would mean that they have discovered some way of penetrating the terahertz screen. Those we have captured recently show no enhanced abilities in that respect.'

'Instructions?'

'Stay vigilant. This behaviour is outside our experience.

'I repeat: Stay vigilant.'

'Understood,' Tharan replied, 'Signing off.'

* * *

McKee had few worries when he arrived at his modest home. It was only one story high and consisted of a small lounge, a bedroom, a kitchen and a lavatory. All were as cheap and basic as they could be without letting the rain in.

His wife, a short, rather dumpy woman with greying curly hair called out to him as he came in.

'That you, hon?'

'Well, if it ain't it's your lucky day, sugar!' he yelled, depositing his workbag near the front door. 'Hey, something smells good, Marion,' he added on entering the kitchen.

It was the normal vegetable protein they ate every day, which would have reached exactly the same level of blandness at each serving, but for Marion's skill with sauces.

'They don't call me the world's best cook for nothing,' she joked, as she spooned the gloopy mixture onto his plate and then slid it across the table to him.

They ate in silence for a while until McKee looked up and said, 'Had a good day, hon?'

She pulled a slightly disgruntled face. 'OK, I guess. Mrs Korsinsky's been pissing me off a bit.'

'Yeah? How so?'

'She keeps going on about how Alex's bringing home a bigger paycheck than you. Reckons he gets extra protein bars as well.'

'Is that right?' McKee said, and with an air of devilment reached over and gave her hand a squeeze, 'Reckon there's one thing I got that's bigger than Alex's!'

She gave a knowing smile and laughed. 'I guess so – but one's things puzzling me right there. How do you know that?'

They both dissolved into laughter.

They finished the meagre meal in satisfied silence, broken only by the occasional chuckle from McKee as he recalled Marion's witticism.

As Marion began the washing up, she looked over at McKee and said, 'There's something else. The dumb TV's been acting funny.'

McKee was sitting in the armchair; eyes half closed as he began to surrender to his early evening nap.

'Yeah, that so? What's wrong with it?'

'There's words coming up on it.'

McKee shrugged. The TV was the only form of entertainment in the village apart from the occasional sing-along in the hall and McKee was more than a little dubious as to whether that could be classed as entertainment. The TV rarely had any programmes on it as almost no new material was being produced. Some shows had survived the catastrophes of the late twenty first century but most of these would have been incomprehensible to Greg's generation; showing as they did vibrant cities, full of rich, well-dressed people who drove sleek automobiles and spent most of their time shooting at one another.

No, the only programmes deemed acceptable to this audience were simple homespun tales, featuring ordinary people doing ordinary things in an ordinary world. The acting was poor and the sets cheap and flimsy but to their audience they were

248

spellbinding, as they knew nothing of any other form of entertainment. And as these did not feature an urban lifestyle or advanced technologies, they did not put too much strain on the credulity of the village inhabitants. But because the stock of such programmes was not large, the TV remained silent for most of the evening.

'Words?' said McKee, 'what sort of words? Bad words; swear words?'

'Put it on and see.'

McKee felt a little annoyed; he had been well into that warm, snug feeling that always preceded his nap, but his concern for Marion won out.

If she was worried about something, it was his job as man of the house, to put her fears to rest. If someone was putting bad words on the TV, Tharan would hear about it, first thing in the morning.

He walked over and turned the TV on. The primitive device took some time to warm up and when it did, it showed a featureless black screen.

McKee stared at it for a while and then made to turn it off, but Marion said, 'No, Greg, leave it on for a spell. Let's see if anything happens.'

McKee was annoyed now. Not only was he not getting his nap but he was now being forced to stare at a blank screen.

Several minutes passed until finally McKee said, 'That's it. I'm turning the damn thing off,' and walked over to the silent device.

Then just as his fingers touched the OFF-switch, words appeared on the screen; words that appeared in a single block, not one at a time.

'Hello Greg. It's good to see you.'

McKee looked around as if expecting to see someone behind him, controlling the machine.

He looked back. More words had appeared.

'It's OK. Just speak. I can hear you.'

Greg sat back down with Marion standing next to him, her hand on his shoulder, both staring at the screen.

'Who are you?'

'A friend,' appeared on the screen.

'What do you want?'

'To help you. You are in great danger.'

McKee felt Marion's fingers dig into his shoulder as those words appeared.

'How?'

'The hybrids. They are not your friends.'

'What do you mean?'

'They're not like you, are they?'

'No, they're not regular people, that's for sure, but they never done me no trouble.'

'They're hurting your children, Greg.'

'We ain't got none.'

'No, you haven't, but how many children have been born in the village with something wrong? Something wrong, like no eyes or withered legs?'

'Quite a few. Hey – how do you know my name?'

'I watched you when you went hunting. You're a good shot, Greg. I like that.'

'Greg,' Marion said, in a brittle, worried voice, 'what about the children? Ask about the children!'

'Yes, let's talk about the children,' the words read as they instantly appeared, 'and it's not just being messed up when they're born. You've always wanted children, haven't you Marion?'

'Yes,' she said in a frightened whisper.

'And who's stopping you having any? There's nothing wrong with Greg, is there? It's the hybrids – they hate you, Marion.'

McKee heard Marion's sharp intake of breath and he removed her fingers from his shoulder. The pressure was starting to hurt.

'And it's not badly messed-up children, or not having them when you want them. There's worse things, Greg. Some kids have gone missing, haven't they?'

'I don't know,' McKee muttered, 'I don't want to talk about this.'

'Yes, you do. What about the McKenzie twins, Greg? They disappeared, didn't they?'

'People think a grizzly got them when they went down to the lake 'spite being told not to. A grizzly, there's more of them every year.'

'It wasn't a grizzly, Greg. It was the hybrids, your masters. They took those children, Greg. And they ate them.'

Marion screamed.

Greg stood up and shouted at the set, 'I don't believe you! They're not like us but they can't be that bad! Nobody could!'

'No?' the words read, 'You have a lot to learn.

'Let me tell you more and if you want to live and have children, you will listen to me.'

* * *

McKee and Marion sat in silence now that the words had stopped appearing.

McKee was staring at his hands while he said, over and over, 'It can't be true.'

Marion walked around to him and forced him to look at her.

'It must be true! Why would the TV guy go to such lengths to keep himself secret? He doesn't want the hybrids to find out – can't you see that!'

'But what he wants me to do,' McKee said, almost pleadingly, 'Get those plans of the plant – why does he want them?'

'He's told you!' Marion yelled, 'you big stupid lummox! The radiation from the plant – that's what gives them their strength. Switch that off, and they've got no control over us!'

251

'I don't know…' McKee began, haltingly.

She took his head between her hands so he was forced to look directly into her eyes.

'Greg, Greg, you know how I've always wanted children.'

He nodded.

'It's not just a "want", like wanting maple syrup,' she said, 'it's a deep, urge right in the middle of me. It's all I've wanted. It's all I ever think about. There's nothing wrong with you – you're a fantastic lover.

'It's them – those bastards – those hybrids!'

He looked at her with deep sorrow in his eyes.

'I want them gone!' she yelled, in a cry so loud and powerful it rattled the crockery, 'I want the right of every woman.

'I want kids – kids of my own!'

After Marion had gone to bed, McKee sat alone.

He didn't like having to make decisions. He wanted a quiet life, all he wanted was his routine of going to work and taking the readings, passing them to Tharan, and occasionally under Tharan's supervision, pressing some buttons.

That was all he wanted.

He rose slowly and decided to clear his head with the fresh, night air, heavy with the scent of pines.

He walked some distance from his house.

The hybrids had warned them not to leave the bounds of the village, especially at night. 'Beware of the night,' they had said in that funny way of speaking they all had.

Was that part of their deception as well?

He stood there, just at the point where the village ended, and the wilderness began.

He looked out into the dark shadows of the night.

He did not see, because he was not allowed to see, three baleful red eyes arranged in a perfect equilateral triangle, staring back at him.

Four

Shalar stood on the dais looking out over the diminished group of physicists from the twenty-first century.

'There is a problem,' he said.

The group of people looking up at him did not respond.

After waiting a few minutes for the response which did not come, Shalar continued, 'Yesterday our fission reactor in Siberia went off-line.'

No response.

'We do not at present know why it stopped putting power into the grid, but we suspect it was a hostile act.'

A man at the front of the group stood up. 'And why do you think it was a hostile act?'

'Because all contact with the power plant was lost at 17:20 local time. Since that moment we have been unable to raise them on any of our channels.'

The man shrugged. 'What do you want us to do about it? It's a long way to Siberia and,' and here he turned back to look at his fellow physicists, 'I think my passport has run out, and I don't think the guy at the desk will believe I'm over three hundred years old!'

There was a ripple of laughter from the group.

Shalar did not show any annoyance at the flippant response because he felt none. In many ways, he was simply a vessel into which Kewfor had poured an infinitesimal part of his stupendous mind. A mind that at that moment was considering millions of separate things.

In one small corner of that mind, he was on constant alert, monitoring the channel which would open when the data collected by Larsen's group was finally sent. Then he would combine the massed output of all the planet's atomic plants into one blaze of energy which would flash through the portal, cross the bridge, release the binding forces and send an irresistible, devastating lance of fiery vengeance into the brane of the hran. It would all be accomplished in a human heartbeat.

But that portal was silent.

Kewfor understood that there were now few options open to him.

To the best of his not inconsiderable ability, he had caused the portal terminus to materialise in a region that had a high probability of being sparsely populated by the adversary. But how had he determined where those regions were? From the hran that his hybrids had captured, of course. He had studied them: gone into their minds; learned of their history; their science; their powers; their esurient lusts.

Was it possible that they had deceived him?

The hran were intelligent: fearsomely so. They had mastered the methodology of crossing between universes but ultimately they were biological entities.

Could they be a match for a quantum computer?

Kewfor concluded they could not. In the end it was all a matter of probabilities. There were such things as hran cities and it was not impossible that Larsen's group had had the misfortune of stepping unknowingly into one.

Probabilities.

Any non-zero probability can be actualised given sufficient time.

And perhaps this had been that time.

He was concerned for Larsen and his group but ultimately that concern was like that which a Grandmaster feels for the pieces on the board before him; his real purpose was the redemption of the remaining shards of humanity; a humanity which still clung to a pitiful existence on this ravaged world. There was no concern for himself. His own fate was certain: more certain than that of the humans.

He could not create helium and helium was his lifeblood.

254

If his plan succeeded or if his plan failed, the outcome for Kewfor was unchanged.

But as he had told Dubois, he knew how to hate, and he would pass into oblivion with a more settled mind if he knew that his last act had been to destroy those whom he hated.

Only femtoseconds had passed in the assembly room while those thoughts had flashed through his mind.

He made Shalar speak again.

'I have explained to you the vital importance of keeping the fission plants in operation. They are the only possible source of the necessary power remaining on this world. Without them, even if Larsen sends the data, I would not be able to do anything with it.

'I am not asking you to do anything about the Siberian plant. My agents will very shortly discover what has happened to it.'

'What are you asking us to do then?' a woman called from the group.

'As you know, Marius Larsen took a small group across the bridge from this brane to that of the hran. They have not reported. I cannot directly observe events in that reality; I can only estimate probabilities.

'Normally, that would not be an issue but my projections are only as good as my data. And my dataset is very sparse. It is possible that the Larsen group has failed because they were overwhelmed. It is possible that despite my careful planning they were deposited in an area of high population and that they were quickly captured.'

'Or killed!' someone shouted.

'Or killed. Yes, that is possible.'

The man who had spoken earlier stood up again.

'Look, Shalar or Kewfor, whoever it is I'm speaking to. Get to the point. For a quantum computer you ramble a lot. Let me guess – you want another group to cross over.'

'Yes.'

There was uproar in the room as everyone tried to speak or

shout at once.

The man, who evidently had assumed the mantle of leadership, waved them into silence. 'You want us to do the same thing all over again which has evidently just failed? And you're supposed to be superintelligent?'

'I would set you down at a completely different set of co-ordinates. The chances are that it would not be a heavily populated area.'

The man left the group and crossed to the stage, standing below Shalar and looking directly up at him.

'Let me give you another possibility. Your entire plan was built on clouds and moonbeams. You know nothing about other branes because such information is unknowable. You probably sent them into nothingness because you are a flawed mechanism, Kewfor. You have had no-one to test your theories for centuries and I strongly suspect that you are – in human terms – mad. Or at the very least, deluded.'

'How could I prove that I am not mad? Or at least not deluded?'

'You can't because ultimately you have failed an epistemological test. You have sold those poor idiots a lie because you claimed knowledge that by definition no entity can possess.

'There cannot be, on a priori grounds, such a bridge as you describe; or, if there is, you cannot possibly know of its existence. One or the other.'

'Are you a logician, Mr Ericksen?'

'No, just a hard-headed physicist.'

'I can demonstrate that your proof is invalid. Would you like me to do so?'

The woman who had shouted earlier, now shouted again, 'No, he wouldn't because this is all a stupid fantasy dreamed up by you. It doesn't matter if there is or isn't this damn bridge because there's nothing to go to.

'There aren't any hran!'

'The hran I showed you in the basement?'

The woman was standing now, shouting. There were bubbles of foam at the corners of her mouth.

'An animatronic puppet! Don't you think we've seen those before! Ericksen is right - you're as mad as a bloody hatter!'

Shalar/Kewfor was looking down at Ericksen who was now standing with hands on his hips and a look of triumph on his face. Then Shalar raised his eyes and looked past the crowd, past the walls of the Arthur J Anderson Building, past the heliopause and the Oort Cloud, past the farthest star, beyond the walls of the universe to another realm; another existence; another reality where men and women could be fighting for their lives and the survival of their species.

Then he looked down at Ericksen again.

'Do I take it then you have no desire to follow Larsen to the hran reality?'

Laughter broke out in the hall.

Ericksen's grin became broader. 'At last! Perhaps you're not so dumb after all!'

Five

McKee sat in his armchair, looking at his neighbours. Da Silva was sitting on a packing case as they only had two chairs. Fortunately, Marion was busying herself in the kitchen after making everybody their chicory coffee. This was man's talk, and she wanted no part of it.

Korsinsky had the other chair and his ample frame took up all its available space. He was rubbing his large, calloused hand over his stubble.

'I don't know, Greg,' he was saying, 'this is an awful big deal. We gotta be damn sure we know what we're doing.'

Da Silva, who rarely said anything, nodded and muttered, 'Damn right.'

McKee was annoyed. 'How much more do you guys need? You've seen what the man on the TV says, haven't you?'

'Yeah, sure,' Korsinsky said, 'but the hybrids… they've never done me any harm.'

'What, just because you've got such a high-up job you think they're your pals, do you?' McKee snapped, instantly regretting it as an offended Korsinsky rose from his chair. 'No, sorry, forget that. I know you've worked hard to get where you are, Alex. Sit down, please.'

Korsinsky sat down slowly. 'OK. But no more smart-alec cracks or you're on your own.'

McKee started again. 'What do we know about these hybrids – I mean really, really know about them?'

'What's that supposed to mean?' Korsinsky said.

McKee leaned forward, warming to his topic.

'For a start, where do they come from?'

'What do you mean? They've always been here. They were here when we arrived.'

'But that's it!' McKee said, 'don't you see - that's what's wrong! They were here, and they recruited us from the nearby towns. But did anybody know about them before they showed up? No!'

'Damn right,' Da Silva said.

'Did you ever hear any of them talk about their folks or where they hail from? No. It's like they just popped out of an egg someplace. Or some damn test tube.'

Korsinsky was rubbing his chin again. 'Well, that's right. I never heard them talk about their people. In fact, they never talk about anything except work. I've tried to get them chewing the fat like regular folk, but they just clam up.'

'Well don't that tell you something, Alex? That they ain't regular folk?'

Korsinsky gave a reluctant nod. 'Well, OK. They're not like you and me. But we've always known that. Don't make 'em bad.'

'Sure, it don't. But let's try it from a different angle. What are we doing there?'

Korsinsky looked blank, so McKee added, 'At the plant I mean.'

'We help run it.'

'Yeah sure. We press a few buttons while they look over our shoulders to make sure we're doing it right. Or we take them a piece of paper with numbers on and they look at it for a few minutes and then bin it. They run the place and they just give us little jobs to keep us out of mischief.'

But Korsinsky's self-esteem was threatened and he snapped, 'Speak for yourself, Greg. I got a job that matters!'

McKee realised that he was about to lose Korsinsky again and changed tack. 'Sure, sure, Alex. You got a job that's better than mine; everybody knows that. But those numbers you work with, what do they mean?'

'Yeah, I know about that. They're to do with the flow.'

McKee knew he had his man then. 'The flow of what, Alex?'

Korsinsky was silent for at least a minute and then slowly

said, 'I don't know.'

McKee leaned back, satisfied. 'So, let's go through that again. We don't know anything about these guys. What they call themselves – hybrids – does anybody even know what that means?'

The other two men simply shrugged.

McKee continued. 'So we don't know what they are, except they're not like us. They're different. We don't know where they come from or why they built that plant.

'We don't know what we're doing there. It sure looks like they're just giving us something to do while they do the real work. Agreed?'

Korsinsky nodded and Da Silva said, 'Damn right.'

* * *

The afternoon wore on. Marion ran out of things to do in the kitchen and after saying good-bye to the two visitors took herself off to the bedroom. She lay on the bed, trying not to listen to the worrying words of their discussion but that was difficult because the shared wall was so thin. The things went quiet and she knew that they were reading the words on the TV screen.

'You have the other plans I asked for?' the words read.

'Yes,' McKee said, 'do you want me to hold them to the screen like I did last time?'

'Yes, that's the way I can read them.'

McKee, closely watched by Da Silva and Korsinsky, held the plans up to the screen.

'Move a little farther out, please Greg. I can't see the edges.'

McKee did as asked and there was a brief pause until fresh words appeared.

'Thank you. I've got it all now.

'Greg, Alexander, João, you are all good men. You are patriots. Your families will be proud of you. Greg in particular. I think Marion will have some good news in a few months' time.

260

And your little boy will be proud of what his father did on that great day.'

Korsinsky gave McKee a little dig in the ribs at that point as McKee gave a self-conscious half-smile.

'Is there anything you want to ask me?' the words asked.

'Yes,' McKee in a tone which betrayed his underlying concern. 'The violence. There's no way we can do it without killing the hybrids?'

'Greg, you're a good man. You know that. You don't like the thought of killing. I respect you for that. But you must remember that you won't be killing men, killing people.

'The hybrids look like men but they're not. You wouldn't worry about pushing a knife into a scarecrow, would you? They look like men too, but they aren't.

'The only difference is that these scarecrows can move around and talk, but they're not men. They're not really alive like you and the guys are. Have you seen one have a beer? Have you heard one crack a joke? No, and you never will. There's nothing to worry about. God will be shaking your hand, not punishing you.'

Korsinsky gave McKee a sidelong glance at that.

'I can see that you're not convinced, Alex. Perhaps when you look at your daughter and see how all the fingers on one hand are stuck together and how her right leg keeps popping out of its socket, you will think about the creatures who have done that to your little girl. Don't you want to strike back, to give them a taste of their own medicine? To stand up for the whole human race?'

The vision of his stricken daughter flashed into Korsinsky's mind as he read those words. He remembered comforting the little girl, as she lay there crying; crying because she couldn't run and play with the others.

His face hardened. 'Yeah. I'll do whatever it takes. I won't let you down.'

'I know you won't, Alex. Why do you think I chose you

261

three? You're the best men in this whole village. The rest of them, they're just milksops. They wouldn't have the guts to do what you are going to do. You tell them that, when this is all over and they're watching their kids running around, happy and healthy. You go and damn well remind them!'

Da Silva suddenly stood up, his face aflame with excitement. 'Yeah! I damn well will!'

'I know. You're good men – the best. Now, let's go over what you must do. I know you're sick of rehearsals, but timing is very important. Otherwise those bastards will win.

'And they mustn't win.'

* * *

The day had come. A warm day, like most, and with the high Rockies wreathed in grey sheets of cloud.

A recurring thought in McKee's mind as he joined the queue of men shuffling into the plant was: *How could such an ordinary-looking day be so important?*

He took quick glances at his fellow workers. How little they knew! Today was to be the day that people struck back against their oppressors and they thought it was just another day!

He, Da Silva and Korsinsky had gone over the plan many times. All they needed was a little luck and all would be well. Fortunately, the critical moment would come early in their shift so they would not be on high alert for long.

The guy on the TV had used a few words that he and the boys had not understood. One word – *plutonium* - had kept coming up but he'd told them they didn't need to know what it was in order to strike their blow for freedom. They just had to be in the right place at the right time. That was crucial. Apparently, there was a particular moment when the plutonium was beginning to flow when the hybrids would be most vulnerable. If three keys were punched simultaneously – and it had to be simultaneously – the energy that the hybrids were using

262

to cause the people to be sick would be switched off. And switched off for good. Day One of their freedom would begin.

There was a stab of fear as he approached the clocking-on station. Never had there been any serious security when the workers went in; no finger-tip searches that would reveal the short, sharp knife that was hidden in his boot. Would this be the day that they would search him; the one day when in the name of all humanity he would have been able to strike them down?

It was not. He punched his card and went into the locker room where he would change into his coveralls. Hence the knife in his boot rather than anywhere else.

A glance at his watch.

The TV guy had impressed upon them the absolute necessity of sticking to an extremely strict timetable.

The power plant would be vulnerable for only a thirty-second window. After that, nothing could harm it, no power could disturb its smug equilibrium.

And that window was only fifteen minutes away.

To his relief Da Silva and Korsinsky noiselessly joined him, standing either side as they changed. McKee glanced at them.

'OK?'

'OK.'

'OK.'

They checked watches. They were OK.

They did not go to their usual workstations, but swiftly, determinedly, they took the stairs to the Control Room.

They had to take the stairs. The elevator could have broken down.

McKee could hear the blood roaring in his head, feel his heart thumping as if it were about to burst out of his chest.

His palms were wet. He had to fight the feeling of panic, the growing desire to stop, turn around and go back to a normal day at his normal place of work. He must control his feelings!

If his palms were too slippery, the knife might miss its mark.

He could feel the others marching side by side with him.

263

They hadn't cracked under the strain and neither would he.

They paused at the double doors that would open out into the Control Room.

They were twenty seconds early.

Then McKee nodded and they burst in.

There were three hybrids bent over the controls as they had known there would be.

Each man ran towards the hybrid nearest to him, pulling out their knives as they ran.

Each hybrid turned around. As luck would have it, McKee's hybrid was Tharan. His eyes widened as he saw McKee running towards him.

'Greg!' he said, 'What are you doing up here?'

McKee gave no answer other than to drive the wicked blade out and upwards, to where he knew the heart would be. To his amazement there was no spray of blood and Tharan merely staggered with the force of the blow but did not fall.

No time to try and find a vital spot in what was clearly not a human body. The TV guy was right again! He shoulder-charged the bemused hybrid and knocked him to the floor. He was vaguely aware that his companions had similarly overpowered their targets.

And there it was! Out of its metal casing the red button lay naked and exposed.

Tharan suddenly understood what was happening. He cried 'No!' and tried to pull himself upright by grasping McKee's leg.

A kick to the face solved that problem.

There was a large digital clock directly above the control panel and McKee saw that they had reached the exact centre of the window of opportunity.

He had time for one more glance at his fellows. They were panting with the excitement and exertion but they were OK. He nodded and they all turned to stare down at their own red button.

'That's it!' McKee roared in giddy triumph. 'We're free! We're free!'

He slammed his palm down on the red button.

The blast was 14.3 Megatonnes and was visible from the Moon.

Six

Larsen returned to studying the landscape.

No change. The sick aurora had moved past the zenith and was slowly changing from one bilious shade to another. In the distance came the faint sound of thudding concussions as if a massive hammer was rising and falling.

Farther out in the banks of slowly rolling mist – were there dim shapes moving inside them, like larvae wriggling inside a flower bud?

Was there a faint clicking noise accompanying those obscure movements?

Williamson came up to him.

'We should go. What's stopping us? We've got all the data that's worth having!'

Larsen shook his great head. 'Dubois is right. We haven't seen a complete cycle yet. There are things which can't be deduced from the data. They can only be experienced.'

'What, you're taking orders from that frozen French bitch now, are you?' Williamson pawed up at Larsen's shoulder. 'She's obsessed with all this scientific stuff; she wants her name in lights, and she's taking you for a ride. Well, I never wanted to come here, so let's cut our losses and go. While we still can.'

Larsen looked down at the other and said, 'Don't ever touch me again. Or you'll find there are worse things than the hran.'

Freed from Williamson's company, Larsen resumed scanning the slowly drifting ribbons of mist. Sometimes he thought he was on the point of seeing what lay within, but always at that exact moment the mist would thicken.

He became aware that Takahashi had joined him.

'Marius,' he said, 'is it possible we are in the wrong continuum? I mean, where are they? Why haven't we seen any?

266

I think we must be alone here.'

'No,' Larsen said, 'there's something out there. Watching us. Something that stays just on the other side of visibility.'

Takahashi stood alongside the giant Norwegian, and for a few minutes they both scanned the drifting streamers.

Eventually, Takahashi said, 'There's nothing there.'

Larsen turned and looked down at the other with a grim expression.

'We're not alone. They're out there. Trust me.'

Takahashi looked unconvinced and walked off to take some more readings.

Finally, Larsen gave up; the mist would not be revealing its secrets today, it seemed. He joined Dubois who was sitting on a little hummock of the ubiquitous grey moss and consuming a food bar.

'Hello again, Miss Muffett,' he said, 'what have you got to tell me?'

She gave him a quick smile that seemed to lift a little of the greyness from his heart.

'Now, it's going exactly as I hoped, Marius. The data has poured in. We've done well. I just want to be sure we've seen all there is, and then we can go back and let Kewfor wipe out this rats' nest.'

He smiled back. 'That's excellent news because I don't like this stillness, this quiet. It's wrong. Surely this reality must have a population of hran somewhere. I can't believe that they aren't aware we're here.'

She finished her food bar and put the wrapper in her bag. 'It's not impossible that we have arrived in a very remote area. Kewfor said she would choose an unpopulated zone; just as if alien astronauts were to land in the Gobi Desert. And she did say that this continuum is sparsely populated.'

Larsen scowled. 'If Kewfor has all that knowledge it makes me wonder why he needed to send us over in person.'

She laughed. 'What! You're actually missing a fight to the

death with them!'

Larsen gave a somewhat sheepish grin. 'Well, if you put it like that...'

Just then, Velasquez shouted, 'Something is happening!'

Instantly, Larsen was on his feet, hand reaching for his pistol. He crossed to Velasquez and stared out into the mist.

'What? What is it?'

'No, not there,' Velasquez said, 'here, here! Can't you feel it?'

Larsen stared at him, uncomprehending.

And then he saw it.

'Your hair!' he said, 'it's lifting off your scalp!'

'Yes! Yes! But don't you feel it? Don't you feel lighter?'

By now, all the others had noticed what was happening and stood together, looking around.

Larsen could feel it now; it was if there were springs in his boots and he was walking over a vast cushion that was propelling him slightly upwards at each step. He could no longer feel the submachinegun pressing heavily on his shoulders.

Automatically his eyes sought Dubois and he was relieved to see her smiling.

'It's alright, everyone,' she said, 'it's what I expected. This is the minimum of the cycle of the gravitational parameter. We'll get back to the average pull shortly. In the meantime – enjoy it!'

It wasn't quite the minimum and the gravitational pull continued to decrease for some time. By the time the actual minimum had been experienced Larsen felt a slight headache as the blood began to pool in his head as his heart fought against a downward pull that was no longer so strong.

But eventually, they could tell that gravity was slowly returning to normal.

Williamson was overjoyed.

'That's it! We've done a complete cycle. We can go now!'

Once again, Larsen sought Dubois's opinion in her expression and, seeing him looking at her, she nodded.

'For once I agree with Williamson. We should have enough data for Kewfor to control the direction of the flow of the binding energy. Let's start packing up.'

She joined Larsen and together they looked out over the slowly writhing tendrils of mist.

'You know, Marius. I almost wish we had more time here.'

'Oh? I didn't realise you had masochistic tendencies.'

She gave him a playful punch. 'Very funny. No, I mean there is so much to learn here. Just think of it! We're in a different universe! One of the great mysteries of science has been solved – there are other forms of existence. And if there are two, it follows there must be an infinite number of them. You can have one universe, or you can have endless universes. But two – that would be crazy!'

'I admire your dispassionate attachment to science,' Larsen grunted, sounding distinctly unconvinced.

'But Marius, we have learned a lot about this place but there is still so much more to learn. Take the negative curvature of this space – does it eventually curve back on itself so that this universe is simply a void in a tremendous solid plenum? And, if so, if there is one such void could there be others, given an infinite plenum? Could they communicate?'

Larsen shrugged. 'I agree that we've only scratched the surface here. You can't understand an entire universe on a flying visit. But we have a more immediate problem. This place has inhabitants, and they are not exactly our best friends.

'For once, Williamson is right – we must go.'

But then before Larsen's astounded eyes, it happened.

The mist parted like curtains being swept apart.

And in the gap so revealed, stood four figures.

Human figures.

Seven

Larsen stared at the four figures in utter disbelief. For a moment, he thought he was suffering some form of hallucination. He had been more than half expecting some venom-dripping monstrosity to emerge from the curling drifts of vapour. Behind him, he heard gasps of astonishment as the others saw the new arrivals.

They came towards him, smiles wreathing the faces of three of the four. The fourth figure stayed in the spot where he had been revealed.

'Hello,' the leader said, coming straight up to Larsen, 'Welcome to the Free Republic of Humana!'

'Humana?' Larsen repeated blankly, 'Who the hell are you?'

'Introductions first, I think,' the leader replied cheerfully, 'I'm Richard Stevens; this is Carl Johnson and Ted Brown.'

'And who's he?' Larsen said, pointing to the aloof figure.

Stevens looked over his shoulder. 'Oh, don't worry about him. He's a bit shy; awkward with new people, if you know what I mean.'

The others of Larsen's party had joined him now and were staring at the newcomers in a mixture of amazement and relieved pleasure.

'Look,' Larsen said, 'I want just a bit more information before I welcome you to our group. First things first – did Kewfor send you?'

Stevens looked puzzled. 'Kewfor? Don't know the guy. Is he your boss?'

Larsen tried again. 'OK. You don't know Kewfor. So how did you get here?'

'Oh, that's easy,' Johnson said, coming closer, 'the hran picked us up. Collected us, you might say.'

270

'They collected you?' Dubois said, 'Collected you? So you're prisoners of the hran?'

The three men turned to each other and burst into laughter.

Johnson turned back to Larsen and his assembled group.

'Captured us? That's a laugh! We captured them!'

Larsen made a decision. 'Come in and find somewhere to sit. You've got a lot of explaining to do.'

The three men, still chuckling, entered the circle of the original group and arranged themselves on the ground. Larsen's group followed.

The fourth member of the new group came closer but still did not join them.

'He is a bit shy, isn't he?' Larsen observed.

'Yeah,' Brown said, throwing the figure a quick over the shoulder glance, 'he's a kraut, see. We call him Adolf!'

Krause bristled at that. 'That is very offensive to German people!'

'Oh, you're another one, are you?' Brown replied, 'Then you and him will have a great time stuffing sauerkraut and bratwurst together, won't you?'

Larsen heard Krause take a deep breath after that comment and he put out a great hand to steady her.

'Just a few pointers, Mr – Brown, is it? Let's get a few things straight here. We're all a single team here; everyone's treated the same. With respect. Got that?'

He turned to Stevens.

'Explain exactly how it is you're here.'

Stevens had lost none of his jocularity. 'No problemo. We were all collected by those hran douche bags, at different times'

'How?'

'Well, we were all collected at different times and places. I'd just balled the wife and I was on my way to the dog track when I saw this big grey, tunnel thing in front of me. It kind of scooped me up like a big vacuum cleaner, so to speak. And here I am.'

'Dog track? I'm not familiar with that pastime.'

271

Stevens gave a short laugh. 'Yeah, we're all from different times. I'm from the 1970s. It's something we used to do a lot then.'

'You all seem to be British.'

'Well, we three are, But back at the town, there's all sorts. And,' he jerked a thumb over his shoulder, 'don't forget dear old Adolf. We've got his sort as well.'

'His sort. You don't seem to be a fast learner, Mr Stevens. Tell me more about the Free Republic of Humana.'

Stevens was warming to his story and a look of animation, of pride, came into his face. 'Well, those hran bastards thought they had us where they wanted us. But they underestimated us; they kept bringing new people in, to study us, like.

'And we made plans in secret just like those old POW films. We had secret words and signs, a whole special language. The poor bastards didn't have a clue, and then one morning we just jumped up and kicked their goddam asses!'

Larsen rocked back on his heels and stared at the three newcomers.

'You just jumped up and kicked their asses. And what happened to the hran?'

'We killed most of them.'

'What with?'

'We made homemade spears and just stuck – hey, are you doubting my word?'

'No, of course not, I'm simply trying to clarify a few things. In case we meet any hran that you didn't kick, of course.'

Stevens looked somewhat mollified, but it appeared that Larsen had annoyed him, for he turned to Johnson and said, 'Suppose you take over.'

Before Johnson could speak Larsen said to him, 'Are any of you scientists, Mr Johnson?'

'Well, I am sort of,' Johnson said, 'I used to work in a chemistry lab. For British Steel, you understand.'

'I see. How have you dealt with the fact that your atoms are radioactive in this environment?'

Johnson and Stevens exchanged a swift glance and despite his earlier delegation to Johnson, Stevens took up the exchange again.

'Look here, Mr …?'

'Larsen.'

'Stop trying to catch us out. We're regular guys just like you are, so stop acting as if we're the enemy. As you've worked out, none of us here are really scientists. But people back at the city are. And they've cracked this radioactive atom problem, good and proper.'

Williamson pushed himself to the front of the group.

'You've got a city?'

'Sure,' Stevens replied, 'a real city. Not that big of course, but it's got everything a city should have. We've got our own brewhouse and,' he took a long look at Dubois at this point, 'we got women as well!'

'Women?' said Williamson, as if he was uncertain of what he had heard.

'Yeah, sure, some of them are real lookers. Better than your girlfriend over there.'

'What about the hran?' Larsen growled, 'what exactly happened to them?'

'What do you think? We killed most of them. The survivors we put in a kind of zoo. You can see them when we get there.'

'Get there?' said Takahashi, 'we're not going to your city. We're going home.'

'Don't be stupid,' Stevens said, 'what have you people been living on? We've got real food back there – and beer. We've got proper meat, not the stuff that guy over there is eating. What is it – some kind of chocolate bar? Come with us and we'll show you a good time!'

Jones looked at Larsen. 'We're not in any danger from radioactivity for quite some time. These people could tell us a lot more about this existence than we could find out in our short time here. It might make all the difference to Kewfor.'

Larsen was not convinced. 'Why are you still here? Don't you want to get back to the dog track – and your wives?'

'We've been back,' Stevens said, 'But we decided to stay. We like it here. If you'd lived in the rundown dump I did, you wouldn't want to go back!'

Larsen turned to his group. 'We'll take a vote. Who wants to visit this city?'

Of the group, only Dubois and Larsen were against. Takahashi abstained.

'Alright,' Larsen finally said, 'we'll go. How far is it?'

'Not far. Maybe an hour's walk. There's no bad terrain. But even if there was, that shouldn't worry a big lunk like you. You look like you could carry the rest of them.'

Larsen turned to his group. 'OK, you've decided. We'll spend an hour getting there, two hours looking around and one hour getting back. Then we go.'

He turned to Stevens. 'The first thing I'll be doing is telling Kewfor all about you. He'll be extremely interested.'

Stevens spread his arms wide. 'Wow! Must be a very important guy. Bring him along next time!'

It took a few minutes for the physicists to gather their recording equipment together and sling their backpacks over their shoulders. Then, with the new arrivals leading the way, they set off.

The landscape did not change. Neither did the intensity or quality of the light. Larsen had long since determined that the level of illumination never changed: it was always a dull, dispiriting twilight. The sickly aurora had reached the farthest point of its trajectory and was now heading back to the point where Larsen had first seen it. It remained an unpleasant splotch upon the sky, as if a pool of vomit had been flung up and stuck.

The new men were in the vanguard and staying quite close; all except Adolf who was in front of the others and still resolutely silent.

Dubois was walking with Larsen, which required him to take much smaller steps that he would have liked.

'You realise that this changes everything, don't you?' she said.

'In what way?'

'We must inform Kewfor that he can't send the harmonic pulse across the bridge. No-one expected this reality to have a thriving human colony in it!'

Larsen looked down at her. 'Yes, it does mean that. Don't you find this all distinctly strange?'

She laughed. 'Marius, we're in a different universe! I find everything strange!'

He slowed his step, allowing the gap between the two of them and the new men to increase. Velasquez and Jones took their place.

'No, not the physics of this place —I'm talking about the sudden change in circumstances that we find ourselves in. We came here to gather data to permit Kewfor to safely send the energy wave into this reality – and now all of a sudden, we find we can't do that! The entire plan is unnecessary!'

A hint of worry appeared in Dubois's face. 'But Marius, surely that's all to the good? We can take a look around and then go back and tell them all that they can stand down. The war is over. It's peace – isn't that what we all want?'

Larsen suddenly said. 'Keep looking straight ahead and move your lips as little as possible.'

'For heaven's sake, why?'

'Stevens is looking at us, and he looks a little stern.'

Silence fell for a while as they trudged on through the resistant grey moss.

Then Larsen said, 'What about those three? Anything odd about them?'

'Like what?'

'The way they talk.'

'No, nothing.'

275

'Céline, your command of English is excellent. But it's academic English. You don't know colloquial English like I do. Stevens used words and phrases that no-one in 1970s Britain would have done. It's like he's been given a script by a playwright who didn't quite understand the character's background.'

Dubois fell silent. She didn't quite understand Larsen's fears, but she knew better than simply to dismiss them. Gloomily, she stared ahead at the unchanging landscape. A small, steep-sided plateau was dimly visible not very far away but that was the only break in the monotony.

The ubiquitous mists were thinner directly ahead and, she could see that the landscape was curving very gently upwards so that there was no horizon, just a gradual blurring and softening of detail. She felt like an ant crawling around on the inside of a cylinder. The scene, drab and featureless in all directions, simply became more and more vague and less detailed as the intervening atmosphere blurred out the few details. Despite that, she had a definite impression that ahead of her was a titanic, smoothly curved wall that was rising above her, on and on into unknown infinities.

We are walking into the unknown, she thought, *and what will we find at the end of our journey?*

Eight

'That gravity wave is coming back,' Krause said, pointing.

Larsen followed her pointing finger. Sure enough, there was a linear ripple in the moss and it was heading straight for them.

'How can the gravitational constant vary like this?' Krause muttered, 'it makes no sense. It defies physics.'

'I think you're guilty of Earth-centric thinking,' Larsen replied, 'we've only known our universe and you can't generalise from a sample of one. It may be that this is normal in other universes and it's our world that is the abnormal.'

Krause shot a poisonous look in his direction and said no more.

'Here she comes,' Stevens suddenly cried, 'get ready for the ride of your life.'

In another instant the wave was upon them. Those who hadn't taken the precaution of lying down were immediately rendered horizontal as the increased pull buckled their knees and sent them crashing down.

Larsen was one of those, as he had tried to observe the wave's approach for as long as possible. He hit the ground with a concussion that knocked the air out of his lungs in a single burst and left him lying on his back immobile, staring at the featureless grey sky. It felt like the flesh was being pulled off his bones and sucked into the ground.

He managed to turn his head slightly and was surprised and puzzled to see the distant figure of Adolf slowly adopting a supine pose, apparently in complete control as he lowered himself.

Another anomaly, he thought.

The pressure seemed not to last as long as the first time, but that was possibly because they knew what to expect. Eventually, the scientists felt the great hand that was pressing them into the soil slowly lift until they were able to move around as normal.

'How can you stand that on a regular basis?' Takahashi said.

Stevens laughed. 'It's just part of life here. You get used to it, fella. And it means that you don't have to pay for a gym membership as your muscles get a free workout on a regular basis.'

Takahashi looked confused, obviously taking Stevens' words literally.

Larsen took control. 'Stevens is right. If this is the new normal, then we just get used to it and get on with things. As soon as we confirm that everything's OK in the Free Republic of Humana, we're getting the hell out of here and telling Kewfor the good news.' He shot Stevens a hard glare. 'How long?'

For an answer, Stevens turned and pointed. 'See there. That's our city.'

Larsen stared in that direction. For a while he could see nothing but the endless depressing grey moss. And then right at the point where the mass of the intervening air began to blur the details into an impressionistic confusion, he could just make out what looked like an angular hill, rising sharply from the surrounding flatness.

'At last,' he said, 'and we'll be able to rest and then get something to eat there?'

'Sure,' Stevens replied, 'there'll be plenty of eating there.'

'Great.' Larsen turned to his weary companions, who were still recovering from the gravity fluctuation. 'We'll soon be there. We'll just confirm everything's kosher and then head back. The light, or lack of it, is constant here so we'll be able to make good time.'

He was pleased to see the smiles that broke out at his words and realised that he was feeling quite paternal towards the group as if he was responsible for their happiness and not just the completion of the mission.

'Let's go,' he said and, adjusting his backpack and

278

submachinegun, he led the way towards the hill.

The hill grew slowly before their tired eyes until they could make out its contours. It was completely isolated in an otherwise flat landscape. It had a sharply rising front and a much more gently falling rear. The thickness between the steep side and the gradual slope was not great at the top but gradually broadened. And at the foot of the steep side they could see white blobs that must be habitations of some kind.

'The capital of the Free Republic of Humana,' Stevens grinned as he came up beside Larsen. 'Wait till you see the welcoming committee.'

Larsen heard a ragged cheer behind him as the others took in Stevens' words.

As they approached, the white blobs resolved into low, hemispherical buildings, each with a single entrance. In the centre of the town, or perhaps hamlet, was a much larger white dome. The steep side of the nearby hill was pocked with hemispherical openings; so many of them that the slope appeared to be as much space as stone.

As they approached the outskirts of the town, Larsen felt increasingly disturbed by the absence of any signs of habitation. There were no crowds in the streets, no-one looking at them from the doorways. There was no noise; no sounds of people going about their business – talking, arguing, laughing.

Only silence.

They walked past the outlying houses, looking from side to side. The buildings appeared to be made of a dull, non-reflective whitish metal.

Silence.

Larsen noticed that at regular intervals that there were low, circular walls between the houses.

'What are those?' he asked Johnson.

'Just tubes that connect to the underground sewerage system,' the other replied, 'Nothing to worry your pretty little head.'

The group walked on.

Silence.

And then, Brown brushed against Larsen and the Norwegian felt a cold hand touch his own hand and press something into it.

Larsen stopped in surprise and allowed the others to walk past him.

He opened his hand and saw a torn piece of cloth crumpled upon his palm. He flattened it out and a thrill of horror flashed through his nervous system.

There was a single word on the piece of cloth.

And that word was "RUN".

For a horrible moment, he was unable to move. His knees felt weak as the implications of that word hit him like a physical blow.

The others were walking calmly further and further into the town, still looking hopefully from right to left.

Larsen tried to speak but his mouth was so dry that he couldn't utter a syllable.

Then finally, his strength of will forced his vocal cords, tongue and lips to work.

'Stop!' he thundered.

The others obeyed and turned to stare at him quizzically.

From what seemed an infinite distance he heard Dubois say, 'Marius, what's the matter?'

He made frantic "Come Back!" motions with an arm and turned.

And stopped.

Adolf stood before him, blocking his retreat.

For the first time, Larsen could get a good look at the enigmatic figure.

And he could instantly see that there was something wrong with its appearance. The face looked like a poorly focused photograph. It was too smooth and lacked any of the lines and imperfections that are to be found on the human face. The eyes were cold and pitiless, like sharp minerals embedded in flesh.

'I know you, Marius Larsen,' came a hissing, cold voice; a voice that was as cold as if it were a glacier speaking, 'you tried to kill one of us in Alta with an ultraviolet blast; not realising in your stupidity that you were dealing with a two-dimensional projection.

'Now we have you.'

'Who are you?' Larsen managed to utter, with a sick feeling that he already knew the answer.

'We are the Rulers,' came the icy reply, 'but you know us better by another name.'

The others had rejoined Larsen at this point and were looking confusedly between Larsen and his interlocutor.

'What's going on, Marius?' Dubois whispered as she came alongside him.

Larsen turned and threw a glance at the three humans who had brought them here. He was puzzled to see that they were standing completely still and rigid, with their arms at their side.

'Betrayal,' he growled, 'we've been betrayed.'

The men did not react and remained staring blankly into nothingness.

'They will not answer you,' the Adolf-creature said, 'they cannot answer you. They were never really with you. They are just puppets of flesh, controlled by us, the Rulers. As their original minds have been destroyed I had to provide them with a back-story of my own invention. No doubt I made mistakes but the subterfuge still succeeded.'

He paused. 'Although it would appear that one of them retains some individuality, some volition. I thought all that had been expunged. It appears that I was wrong. Come here, Brown.'

Brown shook visibly and slowly began to walk towards Adolf, trembling as he did so. It was as if he was being forced by some external force to walk towards the other. He took up a position directly in front of Adolf.

Adolf stared into Brown's eyes for some time and then said,

'Well done. You have hidden it well. I did not think you had any individuality left. I was wrong and I will accept my punishment.

'And here is yours.'

Instantly Adolf's right arm became a hideous, jointed thing, terminating in a great sickle-shaped claw. The claw flashed towards Brown, passed easily through his neck in a shower of blood and sent the severed head bouncing across the ground to rest at Krause's feet.

And then Larsen knew with sick, courage-sapping certainty, that for the first time in his life that he was standing in the physical presence of one of the hran.

Larsen reached for his pistol but something in that inhuman gaze stopped him.

'Try it,' the terrible voice said, 'I am in my native environment and I can move much faster than you. I would have your head long before that ridiculous weapon had left its holster. And I am far from alone.'

'What do you want from us?' Dubois said. Larsen could hear that she was struggling to keep her terror under control.

'Why to study you, of course.'

As Larsen watched, he could see the human face of the creature slowly fading and becoming transparent at the same time. And as the face dissolved, three terrible red eyes became visible, arranged in a perfect equilateral triangle.

'We have known humanity throughout its history, but under our parasitic load the stock has declined badly. But thanks to your mechanical assistant, we now have some prime specimens to examine to see whether you match the records that our ancestors left of the earlier stages of your species. If so, we are in for a treat.

'And I think I have worn this ridiculous disguise for long enough.'

And with that, all the human aspect of the creature vanished instantly.

Krause screamed.

Nine

'Shoot him!' Larsen roared. Nothing happened. He spun around to find that the physicists, totally unused to any type of physical violence, had been stunned into impotent immobility and were simply staring in horrified disbelief, seemingly hypnotised by the revelation of the Adolf-creature's true appearance. Larsen turned to face the creature, lifting his pistol as he did so, only to find it snatched out of his hand by the hran, which had crossed the intervening space in a blur of speed – just as it had threatened.

'I won't take your head, Larsen,' it said, 'even though you disobeyed me. We hran have been greatly disappointed by your behaviour and a simple decapitation is not what we have planned for you. Do not move again or I will cut off one of your arms.'

Larsen did not move; could not move, as he stared in tumultuous disbelief at the foul thing that confronted him. He could not tear his gaze away from those terrible eyes that seemed to be cutting into him like three needles of red-hot steel.

The other scientists began to stir as if a spell had been broken – but it was too late. Other members of the Rulers swiftly emerged from nearby houses and the physicists found themselves surrounded by the monstrosities and greatly outnumbered. They were quickly relieved of their weapons and the recording devices, which were placed in the nearest building. Then, like helpless lambs, they were driven into the large dome which lay at the exact centre of the village. On they were driven, stripped of everything that had made their journey worthwhile, awaiting whatever fate their new masters wished to deliver. The low gravity wave came and went, but this time without any exhilaration.

The building comprised only one, vast room and was in the near darkness that the Rulers preferred. In the gloom Larsen could hardly see the throng of his captors; creatures that moved like horrific living gargoyles, silently driving their human sheep into whatever abattoir awaited them. He could feel their hard appendages pushing into the small of his back, driving him deeper into the gigantic building. He wanted to turn and smash his persecutor to the ground with one mighty blow – but he held back. *Not now! Not now!* he told himself – *wait for an opening; search for a weakness; be prepared for the moment.*

Larsen took rapid glances at his companions. All were showing the unmistakable signs of shock and terror; their eyes staring and their breath coming in short, staccato gasps.

He looked around in the ghastly dimness as his captor pushed him onward. The centre of the room was occupied by a huge machine, composed of cubes of varying dimensions, each stacked upon the other, reaching up so that their summit was lost in obscurity. Occasionally one would give off a brief flash of a sickening shade of green; illuminating the stricken humans and their grotesque captors in necrotic combinations of black and green as they staggered further into the dome.

In front of the strange machine stood a small dais, which the creature that had once been Adolf proceeded to mount while the dazed humans were forced to stand below it.

Larsen now had time to study it carefully. Its appearance stirred a vague memory at the bottom of his mind. It was not like anything that he had encountered in reality, but he had a feeling that it resembled something he had once seen in a television documentary. The memory kept slipping through his mental fingers and then, abruptly, he had it.

It was reminiscent of a mantis shrimp of the oceanic depths. It was segmented with rows of long arms down each side. The top two pairs of arms terminated in claws; the next two pairs in appendages terminating in digits which looked capable of delicate manipulation. And yet even though he could see much more clearly than ever before there was still an odd blurriness about it – reminiscent of an out of focus movie.

Larsen felt himself becoming dizzy. Could this really be happening? The scene before him didn't seem one that human eyes could actually perceive. Was he insane? Was he in truth not in the universe of the hran but in a secure institution somewhere in Norway, being monitored by stern-faced clinicians? Was not insanity preferable to this mad existence into which he had been flung?

He shook his head: he had come here to exterminate the hran. That was his goal and remembrance of it dragged him back to reality, dreadful though that reality was.

'It is quite some time since I have encountered people with your intellectual gifts,' the creature was saying, 'so it is only fair that I give you some kind of explanation of what is happening to you.'

'You're a dirty parasite!' Jones shouted, 'that's all we need to know.'

The thing turned its three glowing eyes upon the man.

'I will forgive that outburst. You are all physicists; that is the cause of your confusion. If you were biologists, you would know that in any evolutionary system parasitism will develop. That method of existence is inevitable because it is the most energy-efficient evolutionary niche. As you know, it is a rule of nature that processes always seek the lowest level of energy expenditure, in biology as in chemistry and physics.

'So it is with we hran. But we are not unstructured masses of tissue that have shed all their more complex functions. No, we have retained the great intelligence which this continuum has always sustained. We are the Rulers. In your ignorance, you may be wondering how it was that I was able to disguise myself when I was amongst you. That is down to our control of the subtleties of the electromagnetic spectrum which allows us to filter what your brains can process, as long as we are within a certain minimum radius. We use that facility when we visit your continuum, either in person or by projection. Certain among you have greater resistance than others and have been able to glimpse

285

us from time to time, but they have always been dismissed as lunatics.

'Even you, Marius Larsen,' and here it lifted its vile head to stare at that individual, 'you have seen us better than any other human who has ever lived. But you were still unable to convince your fellows. It was only the chance creation of your mechanical counting device that finally revealed us. And as we will demonstrate, that revelation has been in vain.'

'Why are you telling us this?' Dubois said.

It lowered its head to stare at her. 'You disappoint me, doctor. I would have thought it would have been a magnificent intellectual adventure to discover the intricacies of another existence. Is that not the highest achievement for which any scientist could hope? I envy you. For millennia you have wondered what it is that hides behind the phenomena: what is the true reality. And now you finally know: it is we, the hran, that are your true reality.'

It paused at that point and slowly turned its head, scanning the captives, one by one, its stare lingering chillingly on the Norwegian.

'But perhaps I have overestimated you. I hope not. You came here to gather scientific data, I believe, and that is precisely what I am imparting to you.

'To continue: Molecules in this reality are extremely labile, and a sufficiently powerful intellect, such as we Rulers possess, can alter the shapes that those molecules adopt. Thus, there are various physical types amongst us, or "castes" if you like, if I may make a comparison with your own societies; the difference being that our castes have different bodily structures and we can alter our physical construction to join or leave a caste. The Feeder caste, for instance, is the mode we adopt when visiting your continuum. That caste is swift, agile and has the highest degree of our mental control abilities. But all remain hran. I, for instance, am at present a Thinker.'

Larsen suddenly realised that the existence of these castes

with their different bodily forms went some way to explaining why it was impossible to get a clear view of the things in the Terrestrial reality; somehow all that could be seen of them in the human continuum was a superposition of the different types.

The being on the dais seemed determined to continue its exposition to its unwilling students.

'It is my caste's responsibilities to guide the Rulers in our exploration of other continua.'

'Don't you mean "exploitation"?' Dubois snapped. Larsen noted approvingly that she was beginning to regain some of her old spirit.

'That depends on the point of view of whether or not one is of the hran. If I may continue: there are many castes but two are predominant. "Thinkers", to which I belong at present, and "Fighters."'

Larsen felt yet another chill in his innards. 'Why do you need "Fighters"?' he shouted.

'We would not need them if we had not explored continua other than yours. Humans are so physically weak and unintelligent that we need no protection against them, but certain other realities have inhabitants that have proved more intransigent. We could, in theory, all transform into Fighters, but that so far has not proven necessary. In the end, we always conquer. I could show you the transformation process, but it is rather time-consuming and in any case quite unnecessary, as you will be shortly meeting a Fighter.'

A ripple of fear travelled through the group at that dire revelation, Larsen included.

He had been made to stand at the back of the party of scientists, in order to avoid blocking the others' view of their weird lecturer. Taking careful note of when the creature was not looking directly at him, he scanned his surroundings, seeking a way out; something that could be used as a weapon. There was none. But he realised that there was nothing standing behind him; the other Rulers had left, no doubt contemptuous of their captives' ability to resist, and he was now alone in the huge room with the Thinker and his fellow prisoners.

Takahashi was speaking now. 'What do you want of us? What do you want us to do?'

The horrific head swivelled to regard him. 'You are not required to do anything. We have you and we will keep you as long as we need to. Your mechanical friend will soon realise that its foolish plan has failed and it will accept defeat. In any case, it does not have many more years of existence left. Our projections in your universe have determined that no-one else is so foolhardy as to attempt to repeat your mission and in any case we are steadily destroying the power plants that could initiate the energy blast. So all will end quietly and we will continue to enjoy the riches of our larder.'

'Why are you doing this to us?' Krause said bitterly, obviously close to tears, 'what have we done? All we want is to live out our lives in peace!'

The Thinker briefly glanced down at her and then returned to staring at Larsen.

'We have explored many examples of existence and met many creatures in them but there are none like you: so sweet, so delicious. Even if we made a great effort, we could not give you up. We cannot express the pleasure, the sheer joy, we obtain by feeding on you. It is quite inexpressible. I'm afraid you overrate your importance; your existence or non-existence, happiness or misery – it is no concern to the universes.'

'Then why are you bestialising us!' Jones shouted.

'That is inevitable; the prey always sees the predator as evil, instead as merely part of the great network of existence. Life always destroys other forms of life in order to continue existing. Only the children of your species believe otherwise.' The creature paused for a moment and then continued, in a slower speech as if it were talking to itself, thinking delicious thoughts. 'Yes, your children. We always find it amusing when you tell them that there are no monsters in the shadows, when all the time we are there. Watching them.' It resumed its normal mode of speaking. 'Yes, our parasitic load. You may be certain that we will ensure that you do not decline so far that we could no longer enjoy you. That would be foolish. And the Rulers are never foolish.'

'And what about us, personally?' Takahashi continued. Larsen could hear the pleading hope in the man's voice, hope that somehow there would be a reprieve from this dire situation; a hope Larsen knew to be pointless.

The creature did not alter the contours of its terrible visage and continued to stare down at Takahashi, as implacable as the hungriest predator, as unmoved as the most hideous medieval imagining of the denizens of Hell.

'There are only two options open to you: you can allow us to examine you, in which case you will merely lose your minds; or you can resist, in which case one of our Fighters will, after some considerable time, reduce you to a pile of dry, splintered bones. I'm sorry, but there really are no other possibilities.'

There was another ripple of high emotion in the group and Larsen knew that his compatriots had finally accepted that there was no hope and were tensing themselves up to make an assault upon their captor. He glanced swiftly behind him.

The entry door was not far away but it was shut; presumably locked. Larsen returned his gaze to his desperate colleagues, but as he did so he very gradually and slowly began to increase the distance between them.

The thing on the dais spoke again, in syllables that seemed carved from heartless blocks of flint. There was no emotion in that voice; no gloating; no note of triumph. The thing was as unmoved as a man might be if annoyed by a butterfly.

'Ah, I see that my words have spurred you to attempt foolish action. That is impossible, I'm afraid. Perhaps it is time for a demonstration.'

It raised the second appendage on its right; the one with the hand-like extension.

'Come.'

Larsen felt a blast of cold air on his ankles and knew that the door had opened. His peripheral vision told him that something was approaching from behind and would pass very close to him. He tensed himself for action, his hands balling into rock-like fists.

It was not necessary. The thing passed near to him but did not stop. He heard again that weird clicking noise; the noise that he and Williamson had heard shortly after their arrival when they had stood together, surrounded by the wreaths of mist. Larsen saw a being somewhat taller than the average man go past, heading for the group and he also saw his fellows lose all their preparedness; their courage. He saw each face turn into a mask of the most abject horror and saw them grasp at each other like frightened children.

The thing reached them and turned to face the way it had come, looking in Larsen's direction but not directly at him.

He saw then what had terrified them: the thing was out of the worst possible imaginings of the foulest drug-crazed nightmare. It had the same array of limbs down its sides as the Thinker but instead of manipulative appendages each one ended in a blade of some kind. The feet terminated in one massive, sickle-shaped claw, ideal for a disembowelling strike.

But the head was the worst. It was horribly similar to that of a gigantic praying mantis, with constantly moving palps and great jaws – the source of the clicking noise.

And on that ghastly head were the same familiar three eyes, burning like hot coals in the semi-darkness.

Larsen, ready for death though he was, was shaken to his very foundations.

The physicists were now so terrified that they had become hysterical and were milling around like ants in a disturbed nest, desperately searching for escape.

'Be still!' the thing on the dais commanded, 'You have brought this on yourselves! You were not invited to the world of

290

the hran and you came with murder in your minds. But you do not have a monopoly on murder.

'Dubois!'

The woman went up to the dais. Even from where he stood, Larsen could see how she was shaking and having trouble standing upright.

'You have a feeling termed "love" for Hilda Krause, I believe,' the Thinker said, 'Let us see how strong the emotion of love is in the world of the Rulers; let us see how love measures up against another state which you can experience – I believe you call it "pain".' It looked sharply at the Fighter. 'Kill Hilda Krause.'

Instinctively the others moved away from Krause, leaving her standing alone and helpless as the Fighter advanced. She seemed utterly unable to move, utterly unable to believe this was really happening.

Larsen felt another blast of cold air on his ankles and took a quick look behind.

The door had not been closed.

He heard a terrible scream; worse than any scream he had ever encountered before in his life. Unwillingly, he looked back to the dreadful scene being enacted before him.

The Fighter leapt upon Krause; there was a whirl of its deadly blades and almost instantly the woman was replaced by an explosion of blood and tumbling viscera.

The screams that erupted seemed to take the top of Larsen's head off.

He tore his gaze from the red ruin that had been Krause and knew suddenly, instantly what he had to do.

He could not save the others: they would have to face whatever the Thinker had planned for them.

He knew he had come here to die, but he would not die like a farmyard beast in a slaughterhouse!

He turned and ran for the open door.

He heard Dubois wail, 'Marius!'

291

And then he was out of the dreadful dome.

Ten

Larsen knew that he was living the last few hours of his life. He had always known that this time would come, and he had long accepted it. He had known from the very first moment that he had seen one of the hran in Norway that there was only one way that his story could end and that this was it. So be it.

Yet he was not prepared to place his head on the block in beatific resignation.

No, he wanted to kill, to rend, to maim, to strike back against the unspeakable horrors that had descended upon the human race.

He wanted to pay back pain for pain, despair for despair, death for death.

For a few, fleeting moments he was alone: there were no Thinkers or Fighters in view. He ran for the building in which their instruments and weapons had been stored. It was possible for one man to complete the mission if that man had sufficient time.

He burst in, his eyes searching in the semi-darkness for the devices which could save humanity. One submachine gun would make short work of a Fighter; although insanely dangerous, they were not immaterial demons but creatures of whatever passed for flesh and blood in this world. For an instant, he allowed himself the pleasure of the thought of a Fighter's head exploding into torn shreds as a rain of bullets passed through it.

The weapons were not in the building.

He groaned and momentarily he had to support himself against the curved wall of the structure.

But the recording instruments were. And each one contained all the data they had gathered, all the data that Kewfor would need to tune the harmonic blast to the precise values

293

which would direct the binding energy away from the human universe.

What if they had not gathered all the necessary data? They had not expected the gravity fluctuations and Dubois had said that the phenomenon could not have been deduced from the data that had been collected up to that point.

It was pointless to speculate: there would be no more data collection. What they had was all there ever would be. Kewfor had said that he was the highest embodiment of intellect that planet Earth had ever seen. Let him prove it, and if he were wrong, then annihilation of all sentient life in the human realm would be preferable to endless subjugation.

Larsen snatched the nearest recorder and swung it onto his back. The only hope now was to get out of the village and find an open area where the portal could be brought into being.

Once the data had been sent the countdown would begin and could not be stopped; a countdown designed so that the physicists could return to their native space before the harmonic blast was sent.

The fact that most, or more likely all, of the group would not return would ultimately be unimportant. Kewfor would analyse the data, verify the hidden codes that would establish the message's authenticity and send the great arrow of vengeance into the hran continuum.

But all that now depended on one man and what he did in the next few hours.

One man.

Marius Larsen.

He had to get out of the village. He didn't know what that big machine in the dome was, but he had a feeling it had something to do with transfer between the realities. If so, it might well interfere with the opening of Kewfor's portal.

He left the building, looking in all directions in high alert, his heart hammering.

And stopped. Whereas the streets of the village had been

empty before, he could now see Fighters at every exit from the town. The Thinker had not been idle.

He knew that as soon as one of them saw him it would be the end. He could not possibly survive a frontal assault by one of those killing machines.

Despair almost claimed him then. It would be so easy just to remove the recorder from his shoulders, let it fall to the ground and walk up to one of those things.

It would be a quick death.

Krause's had been. So complete and swift had her destruction been that the pain would have been transient.

But then he turned away from the roads that led out of the village and looked at the nearby circular entrance to the underground sanitary system. Perhaps he could hide in there and make his escape later.

Keeping as low as he could, he crossed the few metres to the wall that surrounded the pit and lowered himself into it, feet first, his hands gripping the rim.

He swung his legs back and forth, trying to find a ledge - but there was none.

Knowing he had no alternative he released his grip and fell into the pit.

He fell a long way.

* * *

Larsen shook his head to clear it, realising that he had been knocked out for a short while. As he moved, he realised with dismay that he had landed on top of the recorder. He picked it up carefully and was alarmed to see that it now had a broad indentation on the bottom edge. He gave a wry, humourless smile. Strange to think that the fate of an entire universe might depend on how heavily one man had landed after a fall.

Knowing that there was no way to test it without the Rulers becoming aware of his presence, he slung it back over his shoulders and looked around.

Even by the standards of the hran universe, the place was dark. Had not his eyes become accustomed to the all-encompassing gloom of this tenebrous reality; he would have found it almost completely black. As it was, he could make out that he was in what would have been a circular tunnel had not the bottom of the circle been cut off by a flat floor, down the centre of which ran a small stream.

Larsen began to walk down the tunnel, noticing that it had a slight curve to it. That was not good; he wanted a straight line out of this village; away from the Thinkers and the Fighters, to where it would be safe to call the portal into being.

He walked for some time; the only noise being his breathing, the sounds of his boots on the floor and the very faint trickling of the liquid in the centre channel.

From time to time he passed under or near shafts in the ceiling down which drafts of alternating warm and cold air were flowing; at other times there were smaller shafts that terminated just above buttresses that jutted out from the otherwise circular walls. The buttresses had channels in their centres which led directly to the central stream. Larsen guessed that the smaller shafts were some kind of latrine built to accommodate hran physiology.

He continued his walk, gradually being weighed down by the growing conclusion that the system of tunnels did not lead out of the village. The reek of the place constantly assailed his nostrils; it had the smell of a chemistry laboratory, with stinks reminiscent of bromine and ammonia coming from all directions. And on occasion, he could hear faint scuttling noises in the darkness as small creatures sensed his approach and darted away.

He walked on, becoming more and more dispirited.

Then as he was passing near one of the smaller shafts, he stopped and cocked his head.

Voices. Human voices were coming down the shaft!

He climbed up the buttress to where the shaft terminated and listened again.

Yes, human male voices and one female. It must be his group!

Could he rescue them?

He looked up the shaft. It did not seem to be particularly long for he could see a small circle of greenish light at the top, and the voices did not seem to be too distant.

He swung the recorder around to position it on his chest and gradually forced himself into the shaft so that his mighty shoulders were on one side of it and his feet on the other. Due to his size it was a tight fit, which was fortunate as the sides were coated with a thin slippery layer of slightly bubbling scum.

Slowly, agonisingly slowly, he began to work his way up the shaft. Once he lost concentration and slipped back down at least a third of the way that he had ascended, but he forced himself to continue.

Slowly, slowly he reached the point where the shaft entered the room and turned so he could support his weight with hands on the edges.

And he saw his group, Velasquez, Jones, Takahashi, Williamson and Dubois, sitting or lying in abject despair on the floor.

At least there had been no more killing!

They were talking in a desultory fashion, with a few words followed by long silences. Williamson wasn't saying anything and was sitting with his back to the others.

He heard Jones say something, something which contained the phrase *that bastard Larsen.*

Larsen was just about to haul himself into the room when a massive leg abruptly blocked his view; a leg that terminated in a terrible sickle-shaped claw.

The humans were not alone; they were being closely guarded by a Fighter.

There was no way he could rescue them.

For a moment he considered bursting into the room and taking on that guard but he realised that any such action would be futile.

Reluctantly, he slid back down the shaft and back onto the floor.

He looked around, trying to see if there was some distinguishing feature in this labyrinth which would allow him to find their room again, should circumstances change. Finally, he noticed that the buttress on the other side had lost part of its lower edge and now terminated in a jagged scar. Burning that into his brain, he continued his increasingly aimless walk.

He encountered another passage which crossed his at right angles, forming a crossroads. No longer having a clear plan, he decided to follow it.

It was identical to the one he had been travelling along; the same channel down the centre, the same bromine-like stench, the same scurrying sounds as unknown things tried to escape his approach.

He trudged on; realising that it had now been quite some time since he had last eaten and his stomach was now beginning to painfully protest. There was nothing he could do; the backpacks with their rations were now in the possession of the Rulers.

And then all at once the corridor opened out into a large circular area, a kind of arena. He had evidently reached the centre of the labyrinth.

Now, what could he do? His hopes that the underground passages would lead out of the village had been dashed. It was now obvious that the system was merely a set of concentric rings threaded through by these radial corridors, all terminating in this central area.

The passages led nowhere.

He stood there, racked with indecision.

Should he try again, hoping to find some other way out? Or...

It was then that he noticed that the floor of the area was exhibiting a faint greenish phosphorescence. He moved towards the nearest patch and instantly realised that his boots were making an odd squelching noise.

He lifted one foot and studied the underside of his boot. He could see extremely small, thin, thread-like organisms wriggling in their death-throes, some of which were giving off that dim, green glow. Now that he had noticed them, he could see them everywhere, but becoming more numerous towards the centre; and in that centre was another circular shape but this time one that was ominously black.

A pit.

The things were moving purposely, he could see, and purposely towards him. They were flowing out of the pit in a continuous stream as if they were a fluid that was being pumped out. And they were squirming around as they moved, like maggots on rotting meat. More ominously still, the newer arrivals were distinctly larger than the vanguard.

Larsen backed away. The floor of the arena was now clearly visible in the green phosphorescence given off by the swarming worms. He doubted that their relentless flow towards him was the start of a friendly enquiry.

He looked around. His only escape was to ascend one of the latrine shafts again.

As he began his slow ascent, he looked back at the pit and saw that a glowing worm the width of his thigh was now wriggling out of it.

Not knowing whether the worms could also ascend the shaft, he continued forcing himself up until he reached the top. Looking down he was greatly relieved to see that, although the floor was now a solid mass of green, none of the things was coming up the shaft.

He carried on a little more to see what kind of room he had now accidentally reached and peered over the lip of the shaft.

What he saw sent an electric thrill through him.

He was looking at the group's weapons, laid out neatly in rows, sorted by size, on a metal cabinet.

And standing in front of them, with its back turned to him, was a Fighter.

Larsen knew exactly what he had to do then.

He had to get those weapons and take them back to their owners so that they could wreak bloody vengeance.

And in order to do that he would have to kill the Fighter.

Eleven

Larsen studied the Fighter. He knew that to attack it from the front would mean virtually instant death: the creature's horrific weaponry was designed for a frontal onslaught and, without any body-armour, Larsen would be cut to shreds in an instant. His only hope was to attack it from behind. That would mean getting out of the shaft and crossing the intervening space as fast as he could possibly achieve. If the creature heard him and turned, it would be all over.

As he prepared himself for the attempt, he felt a slight downward tug on his innards and he gave a silent groan. That tug meant that the next high gravity wave was approaching; to attack the Fighter at the wave's peak was certain doom.

He knew that his attack could not be delayed. Carefully, slowly, delicately, he put the precious recorder on the room's metal floor.

Then with one push, he was out of the shaft and hurtling towards the creature, propelled by the hunger of his hatred. It heard him and was starting to turn as Larsen was on it. He grasped the creature's head, trying to keep his hands from sliding into those dreadful, bone-snapping jaws and threw all the strength of his great body into a neck-cracking wrench.

But never had he held such an engine of power in his grasp before. It seemed to be composed of living steel as it strained to throw him off as they staggered back and forth across the floor. The monstrosity was completely silent, as had been its fellow when that Fighter had slaughtered Krause. The only sounds were Larsen's great gasping grunts as he fought to take in as much oxygen as possible in his battle with the vile creature.

It tried to bend its arms behind it to flay Larsen into bloody destruction but the joints in those appendages did not allow it to

301

reach very far behind. Even so, Larsen felt razor-sharp edges slash at his clothing.

Every muscle in his great arms tensed into balls of granite hardness; tendons and veins in his neck stood out in throbbing cords as the two combatants crashed back and forth in their dreadful, silent dance of death. With each passing second, Larsen could feel his body getting heavier as the peak of the gravity wave neared, and still the creature would not yield. His sight grew dim, with dancing sparks flying across a dimming background.

He remembered his old friend Einar Olsen who had lain in his sodden hospital bed in Alta, surrounded by these creatures, who had mocked and tormented him.

He remembered gentle Hilda Krause, who had only wanted to love and be loved.

And it seemed then that his straining, screaming body reached down into its core and found new reservoirs of strength, of power.

And finally, he spoke and his voice was a roar of Viking wrath.

'Die, you bastard, die!' was that battle cry and his massive arms gave one more savage twist of hate-driven fury.

And then there was a great snapping noise and Larsen suddenly found himself staring into three fierce red eyes as the thing's head was torn around to face him.

And as he watched, those blazing red eyes dimmed, faded and became discs of dull, flat greyness.

He released the Fighter and watched it sink slowly to the floor, its killing arms relaxing to lie against its flanks. The peak of the gravity wave was approaching and Larsen felt his intestines being pulled down; seemingly into his boots.

But he could take no chances; he could not be certain that he had victory.

He steadied himself against the cabinet which held their weapons and lifted his buttocks onto a flat surface. He raised his legs and then drove his heavy boots down onto the thing's foul

302

head.

That head exploded like a blood-filled egg.

Then Larsen collapsed as the peak of the gravity wave swept over him.

* * *

Larsen awoke, unsure for a few moments of where he was.

Then he remembered his great battle with the Fighter and he felt his muscles tense. He raised his head, half expecting to find a Fighter staring down at him. But no; he soon discovered the corpse of the creature that he had slain lying near him, glued to the floor by a pool of its own dry blood. It was undoubtedly dead; having had its head wrenched a full one hundred and eighty degrees out of alignment and then smashed flat was a sure sign of that.

Larsen looked around. The metal cabinet held all their weapons: he made sure of that. He also made sure that all the ammunition was still present.

And joy! The backpacks were there as well!

He opened one and for a few minutes gorged himself on the energy bars, trying to replenish his store of strength after the tremendous conflict. He thought for a moment of his fellows, held captive by these unspeakable creatures and no doubt in the first stages of starvation.

But he could not help them yet; it was important that he keep his own strength up.

He took all the weapons off the racks on which the Rulers had placed them; checking each one to make sure it was still functional.

They were all there; seven submachine guns, seven pistols.

He took a deep draught of water from a flask from one of the backpacks and then urinated over the Fighter's corpse. The stream liquefied a small amount of its dried blood, which made its way in rusty-coloured rivulets across the dull grey floor. Then he made up his mind – he must get to the captives as soon as possible before the Rulers decided to enjoy another period of sadism with them.

He strapped as many of the guns as he could to himself and painstakingly descended to the arena floor.

It was worm free.

One more trip, with the precious measuring device on his back, and he had them all down. He had even managed to cram a few energy bars into his shallow pockets.

But he could not face the hran with untested weapons: he would have to make sure that at least one fired.

That was not a problem that he had to deal with for long, as, no sooner had that thought come to him, when he realised that the pit was beginning to disgorge its worm population again, no doubt having detected his smell.

He made a pile of the weapons some distance from the pit and then returned to it with a pistol. Looking at the writhing carpet of green that was slowly approaching, he estimated that it would not be long before the huge one made an appearance.

Nor was it. This time he watched as it crawled completely out of the pit and began to writhe its way towards him. It was, as he had estimated earlier, about as thick as his thigh and somewhat longer than he was tall.

He decided not to let it get too close in case the pistol did not fire. Helpfully, it stopped and then reared up half its body length, making a perfect target.

'So, you're the King of the Worms, are you?' he said, 'Well, here's my tribute.'

He fired.

The bullet went straight through the worm and smashed into the wall on the other side of the pit in an impact that was invisible in the darkness, though not inaudible. The worm shuddered but showed no sign at all of any wound.

Larsen had decided that he had better get out of the area as soon as possible when he realised that giant worm had turned around and was heading back to the pit, taking its subjects with it.

In a few minutes there was no sign of them.

Evidently worms did not enjoy the feeling of bullets passing through them, even if they showed no visible signs of damage.

Larsen returned to the weapons and the stacks of ammunition; there were too many to take in one attempt. But he knew with a grim certainty that they would need every last bullet in the conflict that lay ahead. He would have to make several journeys.

And so he did, and before much more time had passed he was standing by the buttress with the shattered end, looking up the shaft that led to the captives' room.

What if they had already been moved?

What if the Rulers were in all in telepathic communication with each other and knew that one of their number had been slain at Larsen's hands?

What if...? What if...?

There was no end to "what ifs".

Larsen shrugged mentally: he was a physicist – he didn't believe in telepathy; even in an alien universe. But what he did know was that another struggle lay ahead because his companions were under Fighter guard.

He put the vital recorder in a safe place and strapped the pistol to his thigh.

Once again he began the arduous trip up a latrine shaft, extremely grateful for the food bars that he had consumed.

To his great relief, he could hear human voices, getting louder as he ascended.

They were still there!

He reached the top and peered over the edge.

It seemed as if they had not moved at all, even though quite some time had passed.

But where was the Fighter? It was not in his restricted field of view, but he knew that it must be still in the room.

He waited, holding his great bulk jammed in the shaft by the pressure of his feet.

Still it did not show itself.

He knew that he could not hold this position for much longer; already, he could feel his boots starting to slip on the greasy slime that coated the walls.

Taking a deep, hopefully silent, gulp of air, he steadied himself and launched himself into the room, rolling into a crouching position as he landed.

Instantly he saw the Fighter leaping towards him, multiple dagger-tipped arms reaching for him, palps and jaws snapping in a fatal frenzy. He rolled, raised the pistol, fired, missed.

Two appendages flashed simultaneously towards him, moving so fast they were just a continuous blur. He dodged. The Fighter then spread all its arms wide to prepare for a fatal embrace and rushed him.

He stood tall, taller than the Fighter, side-on to protect his abdomen from the disembowelling talons of his opponent. He waited until the creature was as close as it could be without being able to envelop him with those deadly arms or sever a limb with those dripping jaws, and held his pistol rock-steady in direct line with the centre of that perfect equilateral triangle of glaring red eyes.

He said one word.

'Die.'

And fired.

The solid slug blasted the head apart like an over-ripe pumpkin and instantly and silently the Fighter collapsed, the arms going limp.

Breathing heavily and splattered with Fighter blood and gore, Larsen turned to greet his astounded companions.

'Hello again,' he said, 'it's time to go.'

Twelve

Dubois leapt to her feet. 'Marius is it really you! I thought you'd deserted us!'

'I did desert you' he replied, 'I saw no way of helping anyone. I saw a chance to escape and I took it.'

'But you're back,' she went on, 'and ...'

He held up a hand. 'No time to talk. I'm not sure of how soundproof these buildings are but any of those creatures that happened to be outside will have heard a gunshot. Whatever they are, they're not stupid. They'll find some way of recapturing us. And the next time – they'll keep us.'

Takahashi came up to him. 'But what can we do? One pistol won't be enough.'

'All the weapons and ammo are down there.' Larsen pointed to the shaft. 'I want at least two people to go down and bring them up. And quickly! I can't do it; I'm spent.'

'Don't look at me,' Williamson said, 'I don't know what to do.'

Larsen suppressed the urge to knock him to the ground and turned to the others.

'I'm not asking for volunteers. You have to go down there and do it fucking quickly!'

In the end, Jones and Velasquez made three trips each down the greasy latrine shaft, and after what seemed to Larsen an achingly long time, the weapons and ammunition were in the room. Along with the recorder.

Dubois picked it up. 'It looks damaged.'

Larsen pulled a face. 'I know. I sat on it - rather heavily.'

'Will it still work?' she said dubiously.

'Will people stop asking stupid questions!' he exploded, 'I don't know if it will still work! It's our only chance and we have to take it. If anyone wants to try and get another one, they can be my guest. Any takers?'

They were all silent.

'I thought not. Now listen up, we must get out of here and out of this bloody town. Céline, what did you think of that big machine in the dome?'

'I thought it might be the machine they use to cross between the realities. Only a guess.'

'My guess too. And I also guess we can't open Kewfor's portal too near it because of interference. That's why we have to get out, as far away as we can.'

He looked at his companions. They were all utterly exhausted and demoralised. He had given them the squashed food bars from his pockets, but they hadn't gone far.

'We must at least reach that low little plateau we passed on the way in. That'll give a clear field for the portal to materialise.

'And listen. There's a good chance that at least some of us won't make it. Perhaps all of us.'

'You can shut your big fat Norwegian face!' Williamson snarled, 'No-one's asking your opinion!'

With a Herculean effort, Larsen ignored him and turned to the others.

'It's time. Get your weapons ready. I'll take the recorder. We burst out as a group, blast anything standing in our way to Hell and keep going. And I mean keep going. If anyone falls, we leave him. Or her.'

They all nodded, even Williamson.

'And one more thing – if I go down, get the recorder off me. If that goes, everything we've done, all the sacrifices, will be for nothing. Got that?'

Once again, they nodded.

'Check your weapons.'

They checked. All were ready.

'Let's go!'

They burst out into the street.

And just in time, for three Fighters were approaching from one direction and two from the other. Larsen dropped onto one knee and sent a howling cascade of death into the three oncoming Fighters. The heavy slugs wreaked bloody havoc on them and they went down in fountains of red.

He spun around. Nobody else had fired and all seemed transfixed by the approach of the other two Fighters.

'Shoot them, you useless bastards!' he roared, 'Shoot them for Chrissake!'

His cry woke Velasquez and Jones from their trance of terror and they both fired together, the unfamiliar recoil knocking them backwards. One Fighter fell, riddled through and spurting blood; blood that was remarkably, and satisfyingly, similar to that of humans, but the other came on until it was almost standing over them, the fearsome embodiment of violent death. On it came, its sharp-edged jaws clashing together with that dreadful clicking noise which they had all learned to dread.

Larsen finished it off.

He turned to his companions. 'You've got to do better than that if we're going to get out of this place! Learn to shoot or just offer yourself up as hran meat! Jones, go to that first building and see if you can get some more recorders – I don't trust this one I sat on.'

Jones ran off, rapidly glancing from side to side to detect the approach of destruction.

Takahashi came up beside Larsen, smelling of gun smoke. He at least had not been idle.

'Your plan is not going to work, Larsen,' he said.

'Oh, why not?'

'We'll never get out of this village. What if the hran have projectile weapons? They'll just mow us down.'

'I don't think so. That's not the way these swine work. They prefer the personal touch; to do things close range; hand to hand; get splashed with our blood.'

Takahashi shook his head. 'That's only your opinion. I don't

309

agree.'

'You got a better plan?'

'Yes, I do. That machine in the dome – it's their method of travelling between the realities. We smash it up and they're stuck here. Earth is safe.'

Larsen pulled Takahashi behind a house, looked around the curve of the building, killed a Fighter and then returned to Takahashi.

'How are you going to do that without high explosive? And what makes you think that there aren't more of those machines? We've only seen a fraction of their world – there must be hundreds of them!'

'The recorder is damaged; you said that yourself; we can't rely on it. But this way we strike at the heart of their powers. Any machine of the complexity to bridge universes will be vulnerable to damage. I'm going in.'

Dubois joined them. She too reeked of gunfire.

'I'm going with Hiromoto.'

'Don't be crazy, Céline!' Larsen said, in increasing desperation, 'we mustn't divide our forces!'

She lifted a stricken face to look up into his. Tears were rolling down it.

'I've got to strike back at them, Marius! Hilda – I promised her I would protect her. I promised her! And I let her down. I failed her. I've got to make amends.

'I want vengeance. I want to kill them all!'

'Céline, there was nothing you could have done against that killing machine. Nothing anyone could have done. Hilda was chosen but it could have been any of us and the result would have been the same.'

'Revenge. I want it.'

He grasped her shoulders and shook her. 'No, we must stay together! I want revenge too; as much as you ...'

But it was too late. Dubois turned away and she and Takahashi ran towards the great dome, firing at Fighters as they went.

Larsen leaned back against the curved wall of the building.

It was all going wrong. Everything he had struggled for was about to fail. The terrible yoke of the hran would not be lifted from humanity's neck.

He looked around; there was a lull in the fighting. The Fighters had withdrawn; at least temporarily.

Williamson came running up; his face lit up with a strange look of exhilaration.

'They've pulled back!' he said, 'looks like they've learned that their Fighters are no match for machine-gun fire!'

Larsen made no reply; he was thinking of Takahashi and Dubois.

Williamson continued jabbering. 'You know, I've finally found something I'm good at! Blasting the shit out of things with guns – I love it!'

Ignoring Larsen's silence, he looked around.

'Hey, where is everybody? Where's Little Miss Ice Cube?'

Larsen was finally goaded out of his silence. 'Little Miss Ice Cube has gone into the big dome to try to blow up their device for crossing between the worlds. I doubt she'll be coming back.'

'Well, I always thought that bitch wasn't as bright as she thought she was,' Williamson grinned.

Larsen was too drained to hit him. He turned to Velasquez who had been listening intently to all that had been going on.

'The Fighters have withdrawn but it can only be temporary. I'm sure they're just building up their numbers until they can overwhelm us. They're not going to let us go, you can be sure of that. Keep your eyes and ears wide open. They're regrouping and when they hit us – they'll hit us hard.'

He turned to give Williamson an order only to find he had disappeared.

Fuck that useless bastard! he thought - but did not say it.

Jones came running up. 'I checked the building – they must have moved the recorders or, more likely, destroyed them.

311

They're not there!'

Larsen groaned audibly. Now the whole fate of the human race depended on one recorder – one that he might well have damaged irretrievably.

'Why aren't we trying to get out of this goddam village?' Velasquez demanded, the tremor in his voice indicating how near he was to breaking point.

'I've got something to do first,' Larsen said. 'I've changed my mind - I've got to find Dubois and bring her back.'

* * *

The vast dome was dark; to human eyes it was only a little less dim than a moonless night. Larsen entered the structure, crouching low, looking in all directions, waiting for razor-armed death to leap out of the shadows.

It seemed to be empty, so he stealthily approached the huge device which occupied the building's centre. Occasionally his tense features would be lit with a flash of light from the machine; light the colour of putrefaction.

The machine did not reveal any of its secrets as he got nearer; it seemed to be a nothing more than a collection of cubes, placed one upon the other. Generally, the smaller cubes were on top of the larger, but right at the top of the structure there was one large cube. As he watched, he saw that it was slowly rotating and was the source of the viridescent flashes. Could it be anything other than the means by which the Rulers crossed between realities? And, more to the point, where was Dubois?

He soon found out. He could hear a faint voice that sounded female, calling his name. It was Dubois! But as he hurriedly turned a corner of the great machine he was confronted by two large, completely transparent cylinders.

In one, gazing helplessly at him was Takahashi. And in the other, Dubois.

He quickened his stride and went up to the Takahashi

312

cylinder. He looked desperately at all sides of it, trying to find a mechanism that would release the captive but there was none. Similarly, for Dubois's prison. He could see their mouths moving but no sound came out.

So how was it that he had heard her calling him?

He stood there in front of the cylinders, completely at a loss.

And then, once again, his peripheral vision caught a movement to one side and slightly behind.

He turned.

It was a Thinker.

He looked at it, noting, as before, how the rippling appendages down its sides gave that odd impression that he was seeing it underwater, just as if he was seeing a blurred image that had been distorted by a shifting liquid.

'I know you, Marius Larsen,' it said, 'I reasoned that you would come looking for your comrades so I have used them as bait.'

And then, incredibly, it spoke again, but this time in Dubois's voice: 'Marius! Help me! Help me!'

Larsen was shocked into silence and immobility at the horrifying conjunction of the woman's voice coming from this fiend.

The Thinker spoke again, in its original voice. 'I find it gratifying that you have proved so predictable. As predictable as all you primitive organisms are, in fact.'

Larsen raised his submachinegun. 'As I predict that when these slugs hit you, you will be blown into little bloody scraps of flesh; or whatever shit it is that you're made from.'

The Thinker's face was incapable of expression but Larsen had the feeling that it would not have shown any even if it had been capable; the fierce red eyes continued to bore into him like flames from pits of lava.

'I would like to show you something first. Turn back to the cylinders before you attempt to shoot me.'

Larsen did so, even though he knew that the foul creature

313

was now standing not far behind him.

'Observe the male.'

Larsen looked at Takahashi as the latter began to thrash wildly inside the perfectly transparent cylinder.

'The male is starting to feel the effects of the transition,' the Thinker observed dispassionately.

'What transition?' Larsen said, feeling his mouth going dry as he turned back to confront the Thinker.

'I am going to use the power of our Transit machine for a little experiment. I am going to take that creature out of our reality but I will not return him to yours. I will instead place him between the realities, where no laws of physics apply. He will be spread over an infinite series of states of existence which cannot be described, even in the languages of the Rulers. He will experience things that no inhabitant of the normal spaces, such as ours or yours, can experience because he will not be in a normal space. Time will not apply to him because there is no time between the realities, so he will neither age nor die.

'However, it is quite impossible that his brain will be able to process what his happening to him in the timeless unrealities from which he will never escape.

'But enough talk. It is time to act.'

Larsen spun back to Takahashi's cylinder. The captive was now writhing as if in great pain, and before Larsen's horrified eyes, he seemed to be twisting as if made of putty. Parts of him appeared to be elongating, while others were shrinking. Very soon he was no longer a man but an obscene caricature of one, a thing as if made of modelling clay, fashioned by an unskilled child.

Then there was an eye-rending green flash and the cylinder was empty.

'It is a pity that he will not be able to report back on his existence,' the Leader observed dispassionately, 'our mathematicians have produced various models of what this state of superposition in nonreality would be like, but none of them

314

agree. It is a fascinating problem.'

Slowly Larsen turned back to the Thinker, staring at it through the fluctuating after-images of the flash. 'I am Marius Larsen and I will kill you all.'

'That is an increasingly unlikely prediction,' the Thinker said, 'and now I will do the same to the female. I should warn you that any attempt to shoot me will instantly remove Dubois from this continuum.'

Larsen stiffened. 'You really are monsters.'

'That is a tiresome value judgement. We are not guilty of anything. It was not we who made you weak and helpless. It is not we that made you delicious and desirable. That was how we found you; ripe fruit on low branches. What were we to do? Were we to ignore the bounty that was offered to us? I think not.

'However,' the Thinker continued, 'you can prevent Dubois from being hurled into nothingness.'

'How?'

'Simply lay your cowardly projectile weapons and that foolish recorder at my feet and I will let the female out. Did you really think that your mechanical calculator would be a match for the massed intellect of the hran?'

Larsen sagged a little under the weight of the decision that was now being laid upon him.

One woman – or the chance of redemption for billions of human beings?

One woman, whom he could never have as his own, or the mass of suffering humanity?

He walked to the Thinker and put his weapons and the recorder at its feet.

'Thank you,' the Thinker said, 'I will now release Dubois as I promised.'

There was a soft hum behind him and Larsen turned in time to see the cylinder retracting upwards and managed to catch Dubois as her knees buckled as she fell helplessly towards him.

'A very wise decision, Larsen,' the Thinker said, as, still

cradling Dubois, Larsen turned to face the creature again. 'We will now strip both of you and place you in a room with two Fighters. They are under strict orders not to kill you in less than two Terrestrial days but as long as they follow that instruction, they may do as they please.'

'What?' Larsen cried, 'you said you'd release her!'

'I did not. That is wishful thinking. I merely said I would not throw her into the void between the universes. I have kept my word. I did not say that we would not kill her. Or you. It is surely obvious that we have no interest in your continued existence – in fact, quite the contrary. However, I fear I may have been a little hasty in deciding what to do with you. You have excellent brains, by the standards of your species; I think I shall spend some time examining them before I hand you over to the Fighters. Your capacity to feel pain – why would any species possess such a ridiculous ability? But as you are so afraid of it, it renders you helpless before us.'

There was a movement in the darkness behind the Thinker and Larsen saw two Fighters emerge from blackness. His head bowed: this time there was no escape. Even if he dropped Dubois he could not outrun them and neither could he defeat even one of them in frontal hand-to-hand fighting.

The Thinker began to turn to the Fighters to inform them of the delay to their appointment with the humans when there was a loud report off to Larsen's side.

A heavy pistol slug entered the left-hand side of the Thinker's head and emerged on the right-hand side, taking a large part of the Thinker's head with it.

Without wasting time seeing who his saviour was, Larsen dived for his automatic weapon, brought it to bear on the advancing Fighters and blasted them to shreds.

He stood up, peering into the obscurity to see who had joined him.

It was Williamson.

'I blasted that fucker, good and proper,' Williamson said as

316

he approached, 'I had a feeling you'd try to find Miss Frozen Knickers. Just as well I did.'

Larsen nodded his appreciation. This was no time to query Williamson's sexual mores.

He turned back to Dubois, whom he had dropped unceremoniously when he had dived for his weapon and was relieved to find her sitting up, although gently rubbing the side of her head which had made unwelcome contact with the floor.

'Where's Hiromoto?' she said, still obviously confused.

'A long way away,' Larsen replied, as gently as he could, 'Now get up and move. It's time to get out of here and open that damn portal!'

Thirteen

Larsen half-carried Dubois out of the dreadful building. So used to the dimness had their eyes become that for a moment their surroundings seemed brightly lit. The others were waiting near the great dome: where there had been seven, there were now five. Larsen collected the spare weapons as well as his own, and on his broad shoulders he bore the recording device that might yet redeem humankind.

The village of the Rulers was quiet; there was no sign of either Thinkers or Fighters, although pools of spilt blood and scraps of inhuman flesh were not in short supply.

Jones looked worried. 'Larsen, there's something I didn't tell you.'

'Let's have it, man!' the Norwegian snapped, 'we've no time for guessing games.'

'When I was looking for the other recorders, I heard voices. Human voices.'

'Not that again,' Larsen said, 'we're not falling for that trick a second time.'

'They were pleading, crying out,' Jones said, 'I didn't see them but they sounded like they were in a bad way.'

'We'll be in a bad way if we don't get out of this town. Any moment those bastards are going to come back in force!'

Jones was defiant. 'We can't leave fellow human beings in this hell-hole. If they're not under hran control we've got to rescue them.'

'No – there's no time.'

Jones remained motionless, looking up into the other's eyes.

'You're a cold one, Larsen. You go on with the others. I'm going back to get them.'

'So am I,' Velasquez added.

Larsen was irresolute for a moment. Then: 'OK. Let's see if we can do anything. But I decide whether we can.'

It was not far to the hut that where Jones had heard the voices.

Larsen went in first, sweeping the muzzle of his machinegun back and forth, ready on the instant to take aggressive action.

The interior was dim with only a faint greenish illumination that barely troubled the shadows.

The building had a central pillar and on either side of it were two human figures, facing in opposite directions.

Stevens and Johnson.

They were naked and manacled to the pillar, their chins slumped onto their chests. Both had fresh, weeping gashes on their arms and legs. Stevens heard their entry and looked up, his eyes widening with joyful surprise.

'It's you!' he gasped, 'Carl, look – they've come for us!'

Larsen strode up to them, his wary eyes taking in every detail of the surroundings.

'Let us out!' Johnson begged, 'for God's sake let us out!'

Larsen stood over them; a huge black shape in the gloom.

'I thought you were friends of the hran,' was all he said.

Stevens shook his head wildly. 'No, no. They only control us when they're nearby! Take these chains off us!'

Larsen lifted the heavy chain and studied it.

'I don't see any lock. How do I release it?'

Johnson began to thrash wildly. 'I don't know - just do it! Do it before they come back!'

Larsen took the chain in both hands and threw himself backwards, trying to pull it out of its fastening.

Nothing happened.

He tried again, the veins standing out like blue worms on his forehead as he strained against the chain's resistance.

Nothing happened.

'Shoot the chain, man!' Jones yelled, 'Shoot it!'

Larsen shook his head. 'No. We can't spare the

319

ammunition.'

'The hell we can't!' Jones said, and taking out his pistol, he fired at a link in the chain.

The slug ricocheted madly off the chain and buried itself in the wall.

'We're leaving,' Larsen said.

The two captives began to wail madly and threw themselves back and forth in a pitiful attempt to break their bonds.

'We can't leave them!' Jones said, 'what kind of monster are you, Larsen!'

'I'm not a monster!' Larsen roared, 'Have you forgotten where you are and what you're dealing with! I can't release these men. Even if I could, what proof do I have that this isn't another hran trick to keep us here while they regroup!'

'We've got to try,' Jones said quietly, 'I'll shoot that chain off.'

He lifted his pistol only to find a gigantic hand enfolding his own and the pistol.

'No you will not,' Larsen said, 'I don't know what this chain is made from but bullets can't touch it. I'm not having you waste priceless ammunition. Ammunition that might make all the difference in the coming battle.'

'Let us out!' Stevens screamed, 'they're coming! They're coming!'

Both men were thrashing like captive beasts and screaming at the tops of their voices.

The others watched helplessly and silently while Larsen and Jones stared at each other.

'Don't you think it's a little convenient that these two men were so close to us that we could find them so easily? Tied up but in such a way that we have to waste valuable time in trying to free them?' Larsen demanded. 'Think man!'

Jones shook his head. 'It could be a hran trap – but you don't know that.'

Larsen released his grip on Jones. 'I don't know that but I

can't take the chance. If they are genuine, then the best we can do for them now is give them a merciful death. If they're still under hran control it's even more of a mercy. If you want to stay with them I'll take your weapons and leave you here.

'Make up your mind – now!'

Jones looked back and forth between the screaming men and Larsen and then said simply: 'Alright. But I want everyone to know that it was your decision.'

Larsen shrugged. 'I'm used to that.'

The group left the hut and walked rapidly away.

It was quite some time before the screaming had faded into the background noise.

'We passed a low plateau on the way in,' Larsen said, 'we'll make our stand there and open the portal.'

'Is there any point?' Williamson said, 'we've been here too long. We're all going to get cancer.'

Larsen tried to remember that Williamson had saved his life as he glared at him.

'When you get back, you'll find a supercomputer who's had several eternities to solve a great many problems. He saw himself as the guardian of the human race - he may well have left records about new medical treatments.'

'A *dead* supercomputer,' Williamson sourly reminded him.

Larsen shrugged; Williamson was right; there were no certainties.

'And in any case,' he continued, and at this point his glare became capable of cutting steel, 'we're not here for our health. We're here to give the entire human race a break; to get rid of these stinking parasites that have caused so much misery. Is that too great a price to pay for rescuing our entire species?'

Williamson had the grace to look slightly sheepish. 'Well, if you put it that way ... I guess not.'

Larsen dismissed Williamson from his thoughts. He looked at each of his meagre band and said, 'When you get back, tell the stay-at-homes of all those who fought here and died.'

321

Dubois looked at him with concern on her face. 'When *we* get back? Aren't you coming?'

Larsen shook his head slowly. 'I don't think so. Somehow I've always known my story would end here.'

'Don't be ridiculous! How could you know that!' Dubois said, 'I've ...' She stopped.

'Can you hear that?'

They listened. In the distance they could hear a dull rumble, as if heavily loaded freight trains were on the move. There was a small but unmistakable tremor beneath their feet.

'It's them', Larsen roared, 'they're coming in mass, like I said they would. Move, move!'

They hurried towards the nearest exit from the village, as the thunderous tumult grew louder and louder behind them.

As Larsen was passing one intersection, he saw a peculiar object emerging from it; something that looked like a tightly bound ball of writhing blood-red nematode worms. It was, he guessed, a member of one of the less common castes of the Rulers.

Whatever it was, it didn't care for people because it stopped and then backed away, hurriedly.

They left the last houses behind them and passed near the foot of that enigmatic cave-riddled hill that they had glimpsed from afar, before horror had claimed them. Now they would never know what its purpose or function had been. Soon they were in open country again. Larsen looked up: the vile aurora-thing was still there, although now in a different part of the sky. It was amazing - little time had passed since they had last come this way, but it felt like an eternity ago. In all directions, like weird serpents, the crawling, foetid mist resumed its attempts to enfold them. In the far distance, once again, was that low throbbing, as if somewhere in the far distance a great machine was working on some unknown task. Larsen realised that they had seen very little of the world of the hran but also that he had no desire to see any more of it.

In the near distance they could make out the small plateau that Larsen had seen in his first minutes in the universe of the Rulers; the hill where they would stop and turn and face their oppressors.

And attempt the salvation of everything they held dear and valued; the last hope of a broken people.

It was Jones who saw them first. Looking over his shoulder, he stopped momentarily and simply said, 'My God.'

Larsen threw a swift glance behind.

Advancing from the village, cutting through the wreaths of mist, was a solid mass of what could only be Fighters.

But it seemed they were without number; it was an army on the move, an army of running Death. There was not enough ammunition in their supply to take down more than a small fraction of them.

'Move it! Move it!' he yelled, and the little raggle-taggle group of humans broke into a desperate run towards the supposed sanctuary of the plateau.

As he ran, Larsen realised there hadn't been a gravity wave maximum for a while. If it struck before they got there, it would all be over. The Fighters were better adapted to the maximum than humans.

Although he wasted little time in looking behind him, he knew that the Fighters were rapidly closing the gap. A crazy thought bubbled in his mind; a simple equation. Take the initial starting points, take the speed of the two parties, calculate where the two lines would intersect.

And where the two lines intersected there would be slaughter.

They were almost at the start of the slope of the plateau when the first Fighter was on them. As usual, it was silent, except for the drumming of its feet against the ground, which unfortunately was muted by the soft moss. It swung a slicing blow at Jones, which took him directly across the abdomen as he turned to fire. There was a spray of red, and suddenly Larsen could see intestines protruding from a bloody gash in Jones' belly. A shot to the head from Larsen disposed of that first attacker and then he bent over Jones to see if anything could be done.

There was not and Jones knew it.

'Shoot me,' he panted, 'for God's sake – shoot me!'

Larsen shot him and they rushed on.

As they began to struggle up the precipitous slope, Larsen felt the first tug in his insides which told him that the gravity maximum was approaching.

'Hurry up!' he yelled, 'the wave is coming!'

They struggled on, as all around them the vegetation began obediently to turn in the direction of the onrushing wave. And just on the other side of that wave, came the mass of the Fighters, seemingly unaffected by its embrace.

The little group reached the top.

For a terrible moment, they watched the great sea of Fighters sweep towards them in a tsunami of horror.

'You know,' Larsen said, turning to Dubois, 'I wish we'd had more time together, just talking, just sharing a bottle. Just talking. Maybe next lifetime.'

Dubois gave a sad smile. 'Yes, Marius, I would like that.' She touched his great arm tenderly. 'But you know even in the next lifetime, I will still be me.'

And then they kissed.

Reluctantly, Larsen's thoughts returned to their dire situation.

'Form a defensive line!' he roared and instinctively, like musk oxen facing wolves, the remaining four hurriedly arranged themselves into a crude circle, lying prone to minimise the effects of the increased gravitational pull as the living tsunami of bloody destruction broke on the base of the plateau.

But Larsen did not stay there long – he knew he had other things to do.

'Start shooting and keep shooting down to the last bullet! I need time to activate the portal!'

He took the recorder from his shoulders and switched it on, feeling a raw terror that the machine would not respond.

Its start-up cycle seemed to take forever, but somehow the terrible clangour of the continuous firing of the weapons of his colleagues seemed to fade into the background as he stared desperately at its small display panel.

The panel flashed into life.

"SEND DATA?" it said.

Yes! Yes! Larsen thought, *Send the fucking data – now!*

"CALCULATING VERIFICATION CODE," the machine displayed.

Beyond Larsen as he crouched over the device, Velasquez, Williamson and Dubois were sending an endless hail of death into the massed ranks of the Fighters. In ones, in twos, in threes, they charged up the slopes – only to be met by a killing storm of high-velocity projectiles. Smoke filled the immediate surroundings as the weapons grew almost too hot to touch under their continuous firing. The blood of the Fighters drifted in an almost permanent red mist around the little group as they fired again and again, using their submachine guns like fire hoses, not bothering to aim, just sweeping back and forth, creating a wall of sudden, high-velocity death around them.

Larsen stared at the display on the recorder.

It showed 0.6931
Then 1.0986
2.3026
3.0445
4.0073

There was an ominous pause.
And then it displayed:

0.6931
1.0986
2.3

And then:
"VERIFICATION CODE INCOMPLETE
INITIATION ABORTED."

Larsen stared at the display in a horror the like of which he had never felt before, not even when coming face to face with a Fighter.

This was it! The end of it all! The rule of the hran would continue until there was nothing left to rule, until they had sucked humankind dry of everything that had made life worth living.

He rocked back on his heels, defeated.

Suddenly his mind flashed away from the device and its failure to operate. Once again, he could hear the endless snarling and barking of the guns. He could not solve this problem – who could?

'Larsen,' Williamson screamed, 'Do something! We'll be out of ammo soon!'

Larsen whirled. 'Dubois, come here – quickly!'

She joined him, reddened with hran blood from head to toe, stinking of gun smoke.

He reran the sequence and it stopped at the same place.

'What's the next number in the sequence?' Larsen begged.,

'I can't see the numbers!' Dubois wailed, 'it's my short-range sight – they're all a blur! You have to read them out!'

Larsen did so. Dubois sat with him, desperately thinking, turning her head from side to side in her mental agony. In a whirl of near madness she strove to remember the description Kewfor had given of the security algorithm. She knew how to calculate the next number in the series – but it required her to perform the calculations mentally and to succeed on the first attempt.

Then her features lightened.

'I've got it. Type "MANUAL INPUT"!'

As Larsen did so, he glanced at Dubois.

'You're only allowed one attempt with manual input,' he said, only just audible above the bark of the weapons.

'Don't you think I know that!' she snapped, 'The numbers - they're the logarithms of the product of the first primes and the Fibonacci numbers, ignoring zero. Quickly, quickly!'

He typed them in and when he came to the missing number, Dubois said, '4.6444.'

The machine did nothing for a few agonising seconds and then

"CODE ACCEPTED. DATA TRANSFER IN PROGRESS. INITIATING PORTAL."

'There are only fifteen minutes for us all to cross after the data is sent,' Dubois muttered, 'where's the portal?'

As she spoke, a Fighter leapt over Williamson and caught Velasquez with a swinging blow, decapitating him instantly.

Larsen blasted it before it could wreak any more havoc.

Behind him, the portal suddenly snapped into being.

Williamson saw it and rushed past Dubois and Larsen.

They heard him say, 'Sorry – I did the best I could.'

The portal seemed to swallow him, and then he and it vanished in a flash of cerulean light.

And so, it was Dubois and Larsen alone who were left standing, back to back on the top of the fatal plateau, firing continuously, snarling like cornered tigers in their hatred of the oppressors.

Then first Larsen's and then Dubois's weapon clicked and fell silent, becoming useless tubes of hot metal.

They stood there, looking down on the dread sea of Fighters that now completely encircled the hill. But the silent Fighters did

327

not make any movement – it was as if they were waiting for another of their number to arrive, to be present at the final victory.

Larsen was aware that the portal had reformed.

He swung Dubois around to face it and pushed her towards it.

'Go. Quickly.'

She turned, seemed to be trying to say something and then she was gone – back to the world for which Kewfor was about to die in defending; back to the ruined land of humanity.

Larsen knew it would open only two more times: once to allow him to escape and then again to send the harmonic blast.

And so, Larsen stood alone.

He was more alone than any man had been since humankind had come into existence; more alone than any man would ever be again.

He was not alone in a city.

He was not alone in a world.

He was not alone in the universe of humankind.

He was utterly, ultimately alone.

While he stood there, thinking of all that had happened, all that he had seen and done, all that he had endured, a Fighter came from nowhere, tossed him to the ground and bit his right leg in two, just below the knee.

The portal opened behind him, but the Fighter blocked the way. He could not reach it.

The portal disappeared.

Now the countdown was nearly over.

Then a Thinker appeared over the edge of the hill and strode towards him in triumph.

'We know you, Marius Larsen. We know the crimes you have committed against the people of the hran, the Rulers. Crimes that can never be forgiven.'

Larsen struggled around so that he could look up at the creature from where he lay, his blood incarnadining the moss in

328

an ever-spreading patch.

Despite the pain, a great calmness had infused his thoughts.

'You're not Rulers,' he said, 'you're just miserable vermin. I know you, hran. Somehow, I've known about you since I was a child and I always knew this day would come. But I knew what I would do: that I would be the one who would take you down, that I would kill every stinking one of you. And I will.'

His vision was growing dim; it seemed for an instant that a hideous night was falling, until Larsen realised that the oncoming night was good.

'I detected the failure of your signalling device so do not think you can escape into death, Larsen,' the Thinker continued, as if Larsen had not spoken, 'we will not let you die. In the ages to come you will call for death to visit you, you will beg to be acquainted with death. But death will always be far away.'

'You're wrong,' Larsen said softly, 'death is very close. But not just for me.'

Even as he said that, there was a slight sting of ozone in the air and he realised that the portal was reforming behind him.

Slowly, painfully he shuffled around so he could see it come into being.

And there it was - glowing, beautiful, the apotheosis of martyred human and doomed transhuman intellect.

And the portal opened.

And all the fires of Hell came through.